PRESS **START** TO PLAY

Edited by Daniel H. Wilson and John Joseph Adams

Daniel H. Wilson is a *New York Times* bestselling author and coeditor of the *Press Start to Play* anthology. He earned a PhD in robotics from Carnegie Mellon University in Pittsburgh, where he also received master's degrees in robotics and in machine learning. He has published more than a dozen scientific papers, holds four patents, and has written eight books. Wilson has written for *Popular Science*, *Wired*, and *Discover*, as well as online venues such as MSNBC.com, *Gizmodo*, *Lightspeed*, and Tor.com. In 2008, Wilson hosted *The Works*, a television series on the History Channel that uncovered the science behind everyday stuff. His books include *How to Survive a Robot Uprising*, *A Boy and His Bot*, *Amped*, and *Robopocalypse* (the film adaptation of which is stated to be directed by Steven Spielberg). He lives and writes in Portland, Oregon. Find him on Twitter @danielwilsonPDX.

www.danielhwilson.com

John Joseph Adams is the series editor of *Best American Science Fiction & Fantasy*, published by Houghton Mifflin Harcourt. He is also the editor of many other bestselling anthologies, such as *The Mad Scientist's Guide to World Domination*, *Armored*, *Brave New Worlds*, *Wastelands*, and *The Living Dead*. Recent and forthcoming projects include *Loosed Upon the World*, *Robot Uprisings*, *Dead Man's Hand*, *Operation Arcana*, *Wastelands 2*, and The Apocalypse Triptych, which consists of *The End Is Nigh*, *The End Is Now*, and *The End Has Come*. Called "the reigning king of the anthology world" by Barnes & Noble, Adams is a winner of the Hugo Award (for which he has been nominated eight times) and is a six-time World Fantasy Award finalist. Adams is also the editor and publisher of the digital magazines *Lightspeed* and *Nightmare* and is a producer for Wired.com's *The Geek's Guide to the Galaxy* podcast. Find him on Twitter @johnjosephadams.

www.johnjosephadams.com

OTHER BOOKS BY DANIEL H. WILSON

ALSO EDITED BY JOHN JOSEPH ADAMS

PRESS **START**
TO **PLAY**

PRESS **START**

TO **PLAY**

Edited by

Daniel H. Wilson
and **John Joseph Adams**

VINTAGE BOOKS

A DIVISION OF PENGUIN RANDOM HOUSE LLC

NEW YORK

A VINTAGE ORIGINAL, AUGUST 2015

The Library of Congress Cataloging-in-Publication Data
Press start to play / edited by Daniel H. Wilson and John Joseph Adams.
pages cm
1. Video games—Fiction.   2. Video gamers—Fiction.   3. Virtual reality—
Fiction.   4. Science fiction, American.   I. Wilson, Daniel H. (Daniel
Howard), 1978– editor.   II. Adams, John Joseph, 1976– editor.
PS374.V54P74 2015   813'.010839—dc23   2015008526

Vintage Books Trade Paperback ISBN: 978-1-101-87330-4
eBook ISBN: 978-1-101-87331-1

Adams author photograph © Will Clark
Wilson author photograph © Ryan J. Anfuso
Book design by Joy O'Meara

www.vintagebooks.com

Printed in the United States of America
10 9 8 7 6 5 4 3 2 1

CONTENTS

FOREWORD

Since their invention about half a century ago, video games have come to play a vital role in modern human civilization. I think this is because we modern humans were never designed to live like we do now—sitting in traffic, working in offices, shopping in stores. We are, by design, hunter-gatherers. Millions of years of evolution have wired our brains with an inherent need to hunt, gather, explore, solve puzzles, form teams, and conquer challenge after challenge in order to survive as we claw our way to the top of the food chain. For most people, day-to-day life no longer requires many of those experiences or challenges, and so those primal, instinctive needs inside us have no natural outlet. To keep our minds and bodies healthy, we have to simulate those old ways in the midst of our modern, technological lives, where everything on the planet has already been hunted and gathered. Thankfully, the technology that created this problem also gave rise to its solution—a way for us modern city dwellers to exorcise our inner evolutionary demons: video games.

Playing video games has been a daily stress outlet for

me since the age of five, when I received my Atari 2600 for Christmas. It seems like I spent the next few years of my childhood spot-welded to that Darth Vader–black heavy-sixer game console. Despite the crude, blocky graphics and *primitive* sound effects, it felt like having a virtual reality simulator in my living room. I could simulate battling space invaders or flying a jet or slaying a dragon inside the digital reality created by those old-school games. And this new interactive storytelling medium allowed me to be the *hero* of the story, *instead of just a passive participant*, and to influence the narrative's outcome.

It was the dawn of a new era. I didn't realize it back then, of course—probably because I was just a kid wearing Spider-Man Underoos. But the experience of growing up part of the very first generation of gamers would change the whole course of my life and set me on the path to becoming a storyteller myself.

Since video games have now become a major facet of the human experience, to me it seems only fitting that they also become a more prominent feature in our culture's noninteractive fiction. My first two novels, *Ready Player One* and *Armada*, both explore humanity's evolving relationship with video games, and how it informs and alters our reality, as well as our perception of it.

I love telling stories about video games almost as much as I love playing them. That's why I'm honored to write the foreword for this anthology. I'm genuinely excited to see how each of the contributors approaches the same subject matter, and how each draws on their own adventures and experiences growing up on this new digital frontier to creative a narrative in a completely different medium.

I'm also anxious to find out if I'm the only one who missed their deadline because they spent way too much time doing "research" for their story . . .

MTFBWYA,
Ernest Cline
Austin, Texas
November 30, 2014

INTRODUCTION

John Joseph Adams

I'm an editor through and through; I eat, sleep, and breathe prose fiction and am a relentless consumer of narrative entertainment. But my earliest, most formative pop culture memories from my childhood are not from books.

They're from video games.

Video games have been such a formative force, in fact, that you could say I *owe my anthology-editing career* to them. My first anthology, *Wastelands: Stories of the Apocalypse*, was a reprint anthology of post-apocalyptic fiction, which I grew to love while playing the 1988 game *Wasteland* and then 1997's *Fallout*, both created by the brilliant Brian Fargo. Immersing myself in *Wasteland*'s apocalyptic setting for hours on end (not to mention the many hours copying floppy disks each time I wanted to start a new game) instilled in me a love for that particular subgenre that I've never been able to shake—despite having read many hundreds of books and short stories on the subject, and even having now done five different anthologies centered on the theme. (Or seven if you count zombie fiction as part of the same genre. Or eight if you also count my previous anthology with Daniel H. Wilson, *Robot Uprisings*.)

But *Wasteland* was hardly my first gaming love; I can remember playing video games as early as five or six years old—playing *Gorf* on my Commodore VIC-20, or *Space Invaders* on my Atari 2600, or *Zork* on my sister's TRS-80. When my mom got us an IBM with—get this—*a whole megabyte* of RAM, I played the hell out of *King's Quest* in glorious CGA color. And even later, on my trusty Commodore 64—which would become my primary gaming device for many years—I lost many months of my life to the magnificent *Ultima IV*. Because of its focus on virtues and how the choices you make have consequences, surely I'm not the only one to think that that game made me grow up to be a better person than I might have otherwise?

And then of course came the Nintendo Entertainment System, which revolutionized gaming—and my brain—with games like *Metroid*, *Final Fantasy*, and *The Legend of Zelda*. (One of the bitterest traumas of my youth was that I lost my copy of *Zelda II: The Adventure of Link* when my house was robbed. I was only three-quarters of the way through. Oh, the despair I felt at having to start all over!) That was soon followed by the Sega Genesis, whose allure actually got me to truly care about school for the first time in my life after I made a deal with my mom that I'd get one for Christmas if I got straight As one semester. (Spoiler alert: I did it! My one and only time to meet that goal in any of my precollege schooling.)

In my teens, I took a detour where I mostly played games on an Amiga computer, including *Carmageddon*, *Bard's Tale*, *Populous*, and two of my favorite games ever—Sid Meier's *Pirates!* and *Civilization*. During that "Amiga summer," a kid in my neighborhood was up on his roof with a .22 rifle shooting stuff for fun. He decided to shoot at the roof of my house, only he missed and shot at the *walls* of my house. Had I been sitting at the Amiga playing a game—as was pretty damn likely, as this was the middle of summer vacation—I very well could have been killed. Fortunately I was a teenager and slept till noon that day.

Since staying up late gaming the night before possibly saved me from being shot, it seemed only reasonable that I should devote the extra life (get it?) I'd been given to gaming even more. So I progressed to a PlayStation 1, then PS2, then to an Xbox 360 and PS3. Along the way I became a wizard at playing fake plastic guitar and can pick a *Skyrim* or *Fallout 3* lock like nobody's business; sometimes I'll pick locks for my wife, and she's astonished each time, as if I'm performing a magic trick. Just last year, video games caused me to do perhaps the geekiest thing I've ever done—and as someone who is essentially a professional geek, I don't say that lightly. I created a custom football team in *Madden* and named all of the players after characters from science fiction and fantasy. There's something so appropriate about watching a player named "the Nazgûl" relentlessly pursuing a quarterback.

That brings us more or less to the present. This has been by no means a comprehensive overview of my *life* as a gamer, but merely some highlights that stick out in my mind. Alas, at this point in my *life*, because I work from home and have only myself to keep me on task, I have to actually consciously *avoid* video games (though that doesn't always work). If I even start one, before I know it I'm sucked in and want to do nothing but play.

The truth is: *I love them too much.*

And I'm not alone.

Video games have become a multibillion-dollar-a-year industry that has outpaced movies and books combined. The humble, pixelated games of the '70s and '80s have evolved into the vivid, realistic, and immersive form of entertainment that now rivals all other forms of media for dominance in the consumer marketplace. For many, video games have become *the* cultural icons around which the entire entertainment industry revolves.

So if exploring video games has become one of the primary ways we create and experience narratives, I thought: Why not create some narratives that explore the way we create and experience video games?

In this book you will find twenty-six stories that re-create the feel of a video game in prose form, stories that play with the core concepts of video games, and stories about the creation or playing of video games themselves.

We asked a wide array of writers to participate, several of whom work in the video game industry—such as Marc Laidlaw (*Half-Life*), Austin Grossman (*Dishonored*), Micky Neilson (*World of Warcraft*), Rhianna Pratchett (*Tomb Raider*), and Chris Avellone (*Fallout: New Vegas*)—as well as new and notable writers of science fiction and fantasy, including original stories by Hiroshi Sakurazaka (*All You Need Is Kill*, basis for the film *Edge of Tomorrow*), Seanan McGuire (*Half-Off Ragnarok*), Charles Yu (*How to Live Safely in a Science Fictional Universe*), Robin Wasserman (*The Waking Dark*), Andy Weir (*The Martian*), and Hugh Howey (*Wool*), and reprints by T. C. Boyle (*World's End*), Catherynne M. Valente (*Deathless*), Ken Liu (*The Grace of Kings*), Cory Doctorow (*Little Brother*), and others.

Admittedly I can't really be impartial about any of my books, but, to quote GLaDOS: it's *hard to overstate my satisfaction* with how the anthology turned out. I might even go so far as to say *this was a triumph*. And if I had to *make a note here*, it would say *huge success*.

PRESS **START**
TO **PLAY**

GOD MODE

Daniel H. Wilson

Memories. Nauseous snatches of infinity trickling in, thumbing into my forehead, pinning me to this flower-smelling bed. My fractured thoughts are bursting away with the cannon-shot split of glaciers, broken towers that knife into a sea of amnesia.

In all of the forgetting, there is this one constant thing.

Her name is Sarah. I will always remember that.

She is holding my right hand with her left. Our fingers are interlaced, familiar. The two of us have held hands this way before. The memory of it is there, in our grasp.

Her hand in mine. This is all that matters to me now. Here in the aftermath of the great forgetting.

I'm twenty. Studying abroad at the University of Melbourne in Australia, learning how to make video games. Today I'm riding on a crowded tram, south to St. Kilda Beach.

Sarah.

Another American mixed in among dozens of Aussie college kids in board shorts and bikinis, all of us packed into the heaving car, bare shoulders kissing as the heat rolls off sticky black plastic floorboards. We are headed to the beach on Christmas holiday.

Her hair is brown streaked with blonde. Her lips are red. Teeth white.

The tram pulls to a stop. Double doors open accordion-style and a cool salty breeze floods in. I'm watching her when she faints. Her eyes roll up and she falls and I try to catch her. But my grip isn't strong enough. She's beautiful and lean and tan under a sheen of sweat. She slips through my grasp and instead of saving her, I leave four bright-red scratch marks across her shoulder blades.

Her sun-kissed hair swirls as her head hits the floor.

Sarah is only unconscious for a few seconds. Then her brown eyes are fluttering open and I'm holding her left hand with my right, pulling her up toward me, apologizing to her for the scratches and never for a moment realizing that our lives have now been grafted together, forever.

I remember. I think I can remember.

This is the day that the stars disappeared.

For the rest of the day, Sarah is woozy from the fall. Bright light hurts her eyes, so I'm pulling the plastic rolling shade down over her small dorm window. Outside, downtown Melbourne is babbling to itself. Her room is tiny, just four white-painted concrete walls cradling a college twin-size bed across from a sink. Drawers are built into the wall. We haven't stopped talking since I pulled her to her feet.

We sit together on sheets that smell like flowers. The sun falls.

Later, we lie whispering in the dark. My bare feet are pressed against the cool wall. Muffled sounds of the dormitory reverberate around us: laughter, slamming drawers, music, the slap of feet on tile floors.

Sarah and I are talking philosophy while the stars blink out one by one, billions of miles away. The rules of physics are splintering and the foundation of rational thinking is dissolving like a half-remembered dream.

Holding hands in bed, we talk.

I can remember now. If I try very hard.

Sarah studies English. I am in Melbourne to study how to build virtual worlds. She doesn't blame me for the scratches I left on her back when she fell. She says I was only trying to hold on. Her teeth are so white. The sharp angles of her face are tanned and an unlikely round dimple is tucked into the corner of her cheek.

A few nights later, she leaves scratches on my back.

We are both trying to hold on.

"What's beyond the mountains?" Sarah asks me.

I am building my video game world, hands sweaty on the controller. This is my honors project. I call it *Synthesis*. As I create this world, my point of view leaps across valleys and over mountains. I am gazing down on a fractally generated city and its myriad, faceless inhabitants.

"Nothing," I say.

"Nothing?" she asks. "There must be something."

"If it isn't rendered by the computer . . . it doesn't exist."

"So . . . if you can't see it, then it isn't there?"

"Right," I say.

"What if you look anyway?" she asks.

On the news, they can't stop talking about how the stars are gone.

There are quiet classes and subdued parties and always *Synthesis*. I lose track. We are reassured that the loss above us is some trick of the universe. Got to be. It's impossible for stars to all disappear from the sky at the same time. They're different distances away. The light takes different amounts of time to reach us. To disappear at once, they'd all have to have gone supernova at different moments, based on how far away from Earth they were.

Which is impossible.

Another day and I'm creating the world again. Sarah tells me I should get a hobby. Play a sport. I tell her that I'm saving my body for old age. If I don't use up my energy now, I say, then I'll have it ready for later. Some people burn the candle at both ends, but I blew mine out. I am saving the wax.

She laughs and laughs.

In *Synthesis*, I float through walls. Putting things together, you've got to see all the moving pieces. Sarah sits cross-legged next to me on her bed, wearing knee-length yoga pants and watching me work. She says she likes seeing how the textures roll across the landscape. A flat plane sprouts into a tangled wilderness. A gray cube shivers and grows a brick skin studded with glinting windows.

This is called "God Mode."

It's the act of creation, she says.

It's just a simulation, I say.

You can simulate a nuclear blast on a supercomputer and nobody gets blown up. You can simulate the birth of a universe, but that doesn't make you a god. The simulation is convincing, but it doesn't have the intrinsic quality of the real thing.

The real-realness just isn't there.

"Right?" I ask.

Sarah is quiet for a long time. I have hurt her feelings somehow.

She scoots in behind me on the bed, wrapping her long legs around my waist. Now she settles her elbows onto my shoulder blades. When she speaks I can feel her lips brushing my neck.

"If you can see it, then it's there," she says. "Even if it's only gray."

After the lights are out, Sarah and I walk up to the roof. Laying beach towels over the scabby asphalt and pebbles, we lie on our backs and peer up into a nothing sky. There are no clouds. No light coming down. Just the light of the city going up.

Like our city is at the bottom of a black ocean.

I turn my head and my cheek touches Sarah's. I can feel that her cheek is wet.

Sarah is crying silently to see it. This emptiness.

"It's okay," she says. "I'm just a little scared."

"The scientists can explain it," I say and I don't sound convinced.

We don't go back up to the roof again.

I do not want to see what's beyond the mountains.

They don't cancel classes right away.

The man on the news interviews scientists. They have theories to explain why the stars are gone. An invisible storm of electromagnetic energy reacting with the atmosphere to block the light. An envelope of gas engulfing the planet. A primordial cloud of matter has floated in from intersolar space and swallowed our solar system.

We cling to the explanations.

———

I'm from Oklahoma. Sarah is from Manhattan. I call home once a month. She calls her mom once a week. And then one day—no more calls.

There is a story about it in the last newspaper.

All the satellites have gone. The government advises people to stay calm and in their homes. Scientists are going to figure this out, they say. The headline is that Australia has lost contact with the other continents.

Classes are canceled after that.

Things are loud in the dormitories for a little while. The walls are so thin. Friends and couples argue. Doors bang open and closed. Bags are packed and dragged down hallways. Sarah and I sit on her bed and we whisper. She keeps the panic from surging up my throat. Her hand is in mine and we squeeze until our fingers are numb. After a little while, things are much quieter.

I bring all my leftover food and a trash bag full of clothes to Sarah's dorm and I throw it in the corner. We both agree that I should stay here from now on. My roommate was already gone when I went back to my room. He left a note saying that he had decided to head down to the coast to see if there was any news off the boats that dock there.

I don't remember ever seeing him again.

Sarah and I lie side by side in the dark. The black of no stars has been getting more gray lately. It has been hard to keep track of the time.

"Should we run?" I ask.

"Where would we go?" she asks. "Our families are on the

other side of the planet. We're stuck between the desert and an ocean."

The normal things. They used to be so simple. Now it is so hard to keep track.

"I don't feel hungry," I say.

"Me neither," she says.

"When did we eat last?"

"I don't know," she whispers, and I feel her fingers searching for my hand.

Did we run? Did Sarah and I take off across the continent, searching for an explanation?

I think . . .

I can't remember.

It always comes back to the dormitory.

The most familiar things . . . they always come back to me in the end.

We are lying in Sarah's bed, where the sheets smell like flowers, our fingers intertwined. I stand up and I cannot remember how long I have been sleeping. Or whether I was sleeping or just lying, looking at a white ceiling.

"Final stage," says a whisper.

"What?" I ask.

"Nothing," Sarah says, face muffled by her pillow. "I didn't say anything."

I peek out the small window. In the street, I see that a Royal Australian Naval Reserve guard is posted on the intersection. A young blond guy in tan camouflage, sweating under his helmet. The sun is only a golden hint in a gray sky. The soldier is watching the streets. He does not have a shadow.

"We're sleeping too much," I say to Sarah. "Let's go outside."

___

Sarah and I are walking down Swanston Street. Down the middle of the tram tracks, bright slices of metal curving through clean concrete. The electric wires are shivering overhead, twanging in a nonexistent breeze.

The sky is gray.

No more clouds.

"It's quiet," she says, and her words are flat, without an echo.

"Where did the people go?" I ask.

The soldier is gone.

"I don't know," she says. "I don't really remember anyone here very well, anyway."

I turn abruptly and walk down a side street.

The grayness has a way of growing thicker. Details fade. My vision collapses until I am seeing the world from the bottom of a well. I spin and reach for Sarah in a sudden panic.

Her fingers feel hard and real. She pulls me back, our fingertips connecting like antennae, hands curling together into their familiar embrace.

"Are we in a video game?" I ask. "Did I fall asleep?"

"No," she says. "You aren't in a video game. Come back."

In the distance, I see the silhouettes of the campus buildings. But they look strange.

Two-dimensional.

"Okay," I say.

We walk, our footsteps echoing flatly against the pavement. There is no detail to the cement anymore. No dark patches of long-chewed gum or pale scratches from skateboards. It's just . . . gray. Like everything.

"I feel like I've known you a long time, Sarah," I say.

"I know," she says, and we walk on.

"That's weird," she says, after a few moments.

"What?"

"The only thing left out here . . . is the way I walk to campus," she says. "Everything else is just gray."

An apocalypse should be loud. Gunshots and rioting, that kind of thing. Life screaming out to live. But this is quiet. Dark. The gray of forgotten details. The people are just gone. People I never knew. Never will know.

Standing at the dorm window, I watch as the round eye of the sun bursts and spreads into a light that comes from all directions and none. The cardboard city outside goes dull. Even flatter, somehow.

After that, the dark doesn't come again.

Sarah lies on her bed, asleep. She is so clear to me. Her colors are vibrant.

The radius of reality is shrinking, but Sarah is this one constant thing. The curve of her cheek on the pillow is so familiar. How strange that I am twenty. How strange that I have known her for so long in such a short amount of life.

I think we are the last ones living in Sarah's dormitory.

Sometimes I wander through the empty hallways, peek into the rooms.

Before, each room was different. But now they're all the same.

A twin bed across from a sink. A whining fluorescent light. Always on, flickering. Wooden drawers built into the wall and a gray square of glass.

"I don't know if the campus is really there anymore," I

say to Sarah, and panic is building in my throat. "It's just this room. It's just us."

Her hand closes onto mine.

My thoughts are lazy ripples through still water. The realization comes slow, like mist evaporating off a pond.

Sarah is the dreamer.

We lost the stars on the day she hit her head. The more she sleeps, the more we lose. The gray of her forgetting is eating the world. Now only her strongest memories are alive. The walk to class. This room.

Me.

I move closer to her sleeping body, press myself against her.

This morning—*morning, is there such a thing anymore?*—I walk to the front door of the dormitory and I look out and I see that the sky is missing. A postbox is on its side in the street, half-buried in the pavement. The red metal skin of it is juddering on and off. Between the blinks I can see mail inside.

Before I go back upstairs, I put my hand on the glass of the door and it doesn't feel cool. It doesn't feel warm, either. It doesn't feel like anything.

Sarah is curled on her bed. Shaking. She is shaking and moaning.

I hold her, feel her hair slithering over my arms.

The world outside is getting smaller.

Sarah shakes. The forgetting grows.

I don't remember waking up. I am floating in gray. My body is falling through the walls and it's so familiar.

———

I am holding Sarah in my arms and I can feel the cool sand of the beach under my hip. I am stroking her sea-smelling hair and murmuring into the soft dampness. "It will be okay," I'm saying. "You're the dreamer, Sarah."

"We can find each other in your dreams," I say to her.

And then the smell of her hair is gone, along with the feel of the sand. I open my eyes to look down at my body and I am tumbling, spinning in space because I have no eyes. There is no body. All of it has finally gone away.

Things unseen are not rendered.

And yet I am still here.

I am thinking. My thoughts are somewhere. Churning in the gray.

Sarah slipped through my fingers.

Was she my dream?

Am I the dreamer?

Even now, there is this one constant thing.

A pressure where my hand should be.

Fingers, laced into mine. Squeezing.

I can remember if I try very hard.

"Final stage," I hear the whisper.

Something beats at my eyes. A flutter of reality. A line of hard light appears and shatters my vision into a briar patch of eyelashes.

I am opening my eyes.

———

And I find myself lying in a flower-smelling bed under a clean white ceiling that is chopped into neat squares. There is a gray video screen hanging on the wall.

"Final stage," says that unfamiliar voice. "Neural calibration and transmission complete."

Sarah?

Eyes swiveling down, I see that my right hand is a leathery claw, laced with blue-black veins, knuckles twisted and humped.

A small moan comes from my dry, cracked throat.

I am old. I am ancient. *I am twenty how am I twenty?*

And my Sarah.

She is lying next to me on the bed—*it's a hospital bed, this isn't right, where is our dorm?* Her lips are peeled back into a sweet worried smile and I can see a hint of that beauty I remember in her youthful angular face—a dimple still lodged stubbornly in her sagging cheek.

We are . . . old. Melted like wax.

I was saving my wax. I blew out my candle. I was twenty.

Years have draped themselves over us. Did we fall asleep?

"I lost you," I say.

"No," she whispers. "We're together now. Always."

The screen on the wall flickers, shows me something painful.

Sarah and I are standing together on the screen.

Versions of us. In the computer.

We are holding hands and smiling.

It makes me cry to see us so young.

———

"Neural upload complete," says the voice in the gray. "Both computational entities are viable. It's a success, people."

I think the world is running away between my blinks. The screen and the ceiling and the walls are splitting off and falling into the great forgetting.

Only she is vibrant.

"Hosts are losing mental cohesion," says a gray whisper.

Sarah.

She is lying next to me on her back with tears tracing down her temple. Our fingers have found their old familiar places. Her face is so bright that it hurts my eyes. Her lips are red again. Her hair is a sun-kissed brown.

We are both trying so hard to hold on.

"Sarah?" I ask.

"I'm not scared anymore," she says, and her teeth are so white. "It will be okay. We'll find each other in our dreams."

Her hand in mine. It's all that matters.

In all of the forgetting, there is this one constant thing.

Her name is Sarah. I will always remember that.

═══════════════

Daniel H. Wilson is a *New York Times* bestselling author and coeditor of the *Press Start to Play* anthology. He earned a PhD in robotics from Carnegie Mellon University in Pittsburgh, where he also received master's degrees in robotics and in machine learning. He has published more than a dozen scientific papers, holds four patents, and has written eight books. Wilson has written for *Popular Science*, *Wired*, and *Discover*, as well as online venues such as MSNBC.com, *Gizmodo*, *Lightspeed*, and Tor.com. In 2008, Wilson hosted *The Works*, a television series on the History Channel that uncovered the science behind everyday stuff. His books include *How to Survive a Robot Uprising*, *A Boy and His Bot*, *Amped*, and *Robopocalypse* (the film adaptation of which is slated to be directed by Steven Spielberg). He lives and writes in Portland, Oregon. Find him on Twitter @danielwilsonPDX.

NPC

Charles Yu

Moon base six is visible in the distance, but you keep your eyes down. You keep them trained on the ground, in the patch in front of you. You have your sensor and your collection tool and you're going to find iridium. There. There's some iridium. Awesome. The tool hoovers it up. Cha-ching.

Moon base six over there. Close but far. Eyes down, like always, fixed on the iridium patch. You have your sensor, your collection thingy. Iridium is so rare. Really, really rare. You'd be lucky if you—oh wait. The sensor is saying you got some. Cha-ching.

You warm up your Lean Cuisine in the break room. Pasta primavera and a can of Sprite Zero. Oh shit, Carla's here. You try to hand-comb your hair a little. She smiles. Oh shit oh shit. She's having a Cup Noodles and a Dr Pepper. You move your iridium collection tool off the table on the off chance she wants to sit across from you. She says don't worry about it and your stomach drops a foot. And then she comes around the table and sits right next to you. Oh shit oh shit oh shit. You talk for seventeen whole minutes, the rest of your lunch break. As you're putting your bio-suit back on, you notice you are lightly sweating. It feels good.

Moon base six. What, maybe one fifty, two hundred yards away? You could get there in thirty seconds. Flat-out sprint. You could do it. You've seen fast, watched them do it. You know it can be done. You're not sure why, but you feel it—there's more to it than just this. You have big things ahead of you.

Cha-*chung*. Iridium. Big piece. It's been a good week.

Is Carla seeing anyone? You ask around a little. Mixed messages, but bottom line what you are hearing is that she's available. You have no chance. But. Hmm. You never know.

Moon base six. You do the work. The day goes fast. You keep your eyes down, but your head is in the stars. Iridium, schmiridium. Carla carla carla.

Plasma rains down on the surface of the planet, melting almost everything into molten death. In other words, it's Tuesday. This week, though, you're standing right here, in the crease. *Stay away from the crease. Far far away.* That's what they teach you in training. They never explain why, but you know better. Stuff happens in the crease. Weird stuff. You can always get iridium there. You hoover it all up, leave for a few minutes, come back, and there it is. So, no. You're not going to stay away from the crease. What do they think, you're an idiot?

Apparently, you are an idiot.

Because this Tuesday, when the plasma rains down, melting everything, molten death, blah blah blah, et cetera, you're standing in the crease when it happens. There is so much iridium coating your bio-suit, it's fusing into a protective layer, shielding you.

The whole of creation seems to be falling down from above, raining down on your head, and you're in your suit, feeling all warm and fuzzy inside. Tingly. You check your body parts, which seem intact. Fine. More than fine, in fact.

You seem to have been . . . changed.

Moon base six. Right there. Now there's a whole mess of activity. Preparations being made, fanfare, all kinds of official-looking window dressing going up. There is literally a red carpet being rolled out toward the landing dock. Rumor has it CENTCOM Council is coming to investigate the incident. The Incident. That's what they're calling it. That's not what you'd call it, though. You don't know what you'd call it yet.

There's that dude. He's right there. In the middle. Of everything. At all times. Did he just grab his junk? He just grabbed his junk.

Get back to your iridium mining, someone says. You look up and see a CENTCOM noncommissioned officer, about five feet above you, riding one of those hover pads. You wonder if he realizes how much of a tool he is, balancing on that thing. You wish you could just take your iridium-collection thingy and whack him right in the nuts.

You whack him. Not in the nuts. In the shin. Which is probably worse, because it sounds like it shatters on impact.

People lose their minds. They have no idea what to do with you.

They are taking you down to the base. Holy crap. You are in an actual jeep, actually riding toward the actual base. You cannot believe it. You look around, try to take it all in. You have no idea what has happened. One day you're an iridium-mining grunt, working for four and a quarter chits per year, on, like, a billion-year contract or something, and the next thing you know, you're zooming toward moon base six with electromagnetic restraints on and two plasma rifles trained at your head. You are smiling like an idiot.

The smiling probably pissed them off, them being the dudes on the other ends of those plasma rifles, because you wake up in an antigravity holding cage floating ten feet off the ground. You're floating around, bumping into the walls and ceiling of the cage. Your head is throbbing, probably because they clocked you in the skull with the butt of an RZT-195, but it was worth it. You're still smiling, although a little less obviously.

Hey, you say.

What?

One of the dudes turns to the other. They both look perplexed.

Did he just?

Yeah.

Huh.

Hey, you say again.

Stop talking. You aren't supposed to be talking.

Huh. Okay. Well, I am.

Again with the smashing of the skull. This time, your brain feels like it's broken. That last hit did something. Between the plasma storm and having your brain bashed, you don't feel quite yourself anymore.

You know better than to smile again. You're not in the cage anymore. Now you're being walked down a long corridor. This corridor is ridiculous, how long it is. Is it repeating? It seems like it's repeating. There are doors as far as the eye can see. Doors, doors, doors. You know better. You could easily kick a dude from behind, maybe sucker-punch the other one with both cuffed fists and then smash through one of these doors. They all probably lead *somewhere*. Technically. There are rooms on the other sides of those doors. Maybe a break room, two people sitting at a table, staring at each other. In silence. For eternity. Just blinking. Maybe one goes to the microwave to refill a coffee mug every few hours. You've been in those rooms. You know what it's like. You don't want to be in those rooms anymore. Ever. Again. These fools think you're a flight risk, so their fingers are on triggers. Little do they know, they're leading you right to exactly where you want to be. You have no idea where that is, only that it's at the other end of this corridor. A corridor is good. Interesting stuff happens in corridors. You've always wanted to be here. Right here. Somewhere. Wherever this is. Inside. On the map. Not out there in the infinite fields of iridium. They think they're guarding you, but really, they're escorting you. Right to your destiny.

This is him?

She says it so dismissively, you want to melt into a puddle on the table. You may be in love. You are definitely in lust. This is Oona Bantu, which is a ridiculous name for a very serious person. Bio-suit helmet off, long red hair pulled back into a tight ponytail. Stripes on her sleeve make her seem like someone important. This is good.

What's your name?

Name?

Yeah. You have a name, don't you?

Uh, one of the dudes tries to break in.

Shut up, Sergeant. I was talking to him, she says, indicating you with a pointed, sexy finger. Everything is so sexy about her.

I don't, I don't.

You don't what? You don't know your own name?

I don't have a name. Ma'am.

That's, uh, what I was trying to tell you, Commander.

Shut the hell up, Corporal.

Yes, ma'am.

Also, you should have told me.

Yes, ma'am.

Super Sexy Commander Lady turns her attention back to you.

So. An NPC, huh?

After all these years, it's a weird feeling to know the name. Of what you are. You've heard that term before, but without understanding the context or what it stands for (you still aren't sure—although your awareness, like a spreading gas, is starting to creep around the edges of the term and you feel that soon it may come to you, all at once). Now this CENTCOM officer from twenty thousand light-years away has come all this way. And for you. For you!

It works. You get a promotion, then a gun. They start sending you out on missions. You get stats, a profile, a backstory.

You get *hit points*. Just a few, at first. People know your name. Oona Bantu knows your name. Sometimes she flirts with you in the elevator. You level up, then you level up again. With every mission you can feel it more and more. You don't know how it happened. Actually, you do. You finally took control of your own actions. You're free. No more of that iridium-collection bullshit. No more Lean Cuisines in the break room. No more . . .

Carla.

Hmm.

Well, you can get Carla. Right? You're *you* now. If she liked you before, of course she's gonna like you know. You just need to know how to keep this going. So far, it's worked. Just do the worst possible thing you can think of doing. And then do something worse. Something you would never imagine anyone doing in any situation.

You go on missions. You level up. Up and up and up you go. Your armor looks great. You catch sight of yourself in the reflection of your pod craft and, you hate to say it, but you kinda look like a badass. How did this happen? You hover over the grunts in the iridium fields. Poor suckers. If only they could see what you see, the world from up here.

There are just a couple of things that bug you.

You used to be stuck down there, with those losers. And your life was the same every day. Wake up, brush teeth, put on the bio-suit. Get the thingy, use the thingy to collect iridium. At the end of the day, detach the basin, load it into the spectrometer. The number pops up, you get your chits for the day, and that's that. Every day the same. Every single crap day the same.

Now you're a player. You get to do what you want, when

you want. When you're not doing what you want, you get to chill out here, in this air-conditioned lounge with couches and free snacks and a cappuccino maker, waiting for the next mission. The music is a little repetitive, but the people are cool, if a little aloof. You're you now. That's something. It *means* something. It's just that—how do you say this—to keep this going, you can't help but feel as if your days aren't any more free than they were before. They might even be, and you can't believe you're saying this, less free. How is that possible? You don't know. But it is.

That's the first thing that bothers you. The second thing is Carla.

You don't know if she doesn't recognize you now that you're kind of a badass or what. Whatever it is, when you wave at her, from a pod craft or if you're doing a perimeter sweep of moon base six, she doesn't wave back. She sometimes gives a little smile, but you can't tell if it's because she still remembers your lunch chats or if maybe she's just smiling because a second grade lieutenant is waving at her. Plus, the smile she gives you is one of those sad smiles.

All of which is to sort of make it a little more understandable that when Oona Bantu comes to your quarters wearing just her under-skin armor, you don't turn her away. She comes to sit on your bunk, and things get a little kissy for a hot and sweaty five minutes, and you feel really terrible the whole time and confused but also you are *kissing Oona Bantu*, so you don't stop right away but then Carla's sad little smile face keeps inserting itself into your head and you break off the kissing and Oona can't believe it. She just laughs, gathers her underthings, and walks out of your room.

———

You don't know if it was that whole weirdness with Oona or what, but after that day in your quarters, you kind of hit a plateau in your career. The leveling up slows down. No more weapons upgrades. Your number doesn't come up as often, and those missions you do get seem smaller, more like diversions, just messing around. And the thing is, you don't even get to see Carla anymore. You got transferred to base nine, which is on the other side of the moon.

Mission selected. Gear up. Player chosen. Save save save. Complete the mission. Power down.

Mission selected. Gear up. Player chosen. Kill kill kill. Complete the mission. Power down.

Mission selected. Gear up. Player chosen. Blah blah blah. Complete the mission. Blah blah blah.

Mission selected. Gear up. Player chosen.
You look at the brief.
Moon base nine, collateral damage acceptable.
The ride over is only twenty minutes, but it feels like half a day. As you reach the base, the twin suns rise on the horizon. Oona's up front, barking orders—she's leading the mission— but all you can think of is Carla. You know she's in that base somewhere, in one of the five thousand rooms. If only you could guess which one.

Blam. Blam. Ska-doosh. Ska-doosh.
Your team rips through the east wing in a minute forty-

five, then up to the second floor and the third, clearing out the entire side of the building in four flat. Oona radios for your squad to secure the wing and await further instructions. A couple of the guys use vending machines as target practice. Wanger decides he's going to flush a grenade down the toilet. You tell him you'll stand guard in the hallway, but no one really seems to care as you wander down the corridor, peeking into rooms here and there. Nothing to see, nothing to see. A couple of randoms walking into corners here and there. You hear Wanger and Gutierrez messing around back there. Sounds like they're torturing a couple of NPCs for fun. For a minute you think of going down and saving them, because it's not cool and also an actionable offense punishable by court-martial, but mostly because, hell, you haven't forgotten where you came from. Hey, you say, and turn back to go knock some sense into those two idiots, but then from a door behind you, you hear a *soft* voice say, *Yes?* And you recognize the voice.

You poke your head into a generic break room, not meant for any kind of action, barely even rendered. A table, a few chairs, a fridge, and a microwave. And Carla, sitting there, staring straight ahead. She looks scared. You take off your helmet, try to hand-comb your hair a little, give her a second to process. When she recognizes you, her eyes *soften*, and she says:

I know you. Or, at least, I used to. Right?

Yeah.

Look at you. Wow. I mean. Wow.

You look great.

At this, she blushes. You want to hug her, or reach out and take her to safety, or marry her, or something, but you have an ionized plasma rifle in one hand and an RPG launcher in the other. In your ear-comm, Oona's voice blares out, all staticky and aggressive. Base is clear. Mission complete. Return to shuttle. Your feet don't move. You feel pulled, like you know you're supposed to go back. It's all wrong. First you were trapped, shuffling around like a mindless iridium-collecting zombie. But your thoughts were free. And then that plasma storm, and whatever came next. You could move your body, go where you wanted, but it was your mind that felt trapped, controlled by something else. This job, this life, whatever it is. And now, standing here, you have a choice. You want what you want and you can't help it. Oona's voice blurts again, all units accounted for except for one. Lieutenant, you headed back? You copy?

You take off the rest of your suit, throw it in a pile in the corner, blast it into nonexistence with your plasma rifle. You go into the freezer, pull out a Lean Cuisine, start it in the microwave. Wait right here, you say to Carla, and you take both weapons, go into another room, and leave them there for some other sucker to find. When you go back to the room, Carla is sitting, staring forward. She takes a second to recognize you again. Oh hey, she says. Hey, you say, and you sit down and wait for your lunch to defrost.

———————

Charles Yu is the author of *How to Live Safely in a Science Fictional Universe*, which was a *New York Times* Notable Book and named one of the best books of the year by *Time* magazine. He was a National Book Foundation 5 Under 35 honoree for his story collection *Third Class Superhero*, and was a finalist for the PEN Center USA's literary awards. His work has been published in *The New York Times* and *Playboy*, among other periodicals, as well as on *Slate*. His latest book, *Sorry Please Thank You*, was named one of the best science fiction/fantasy books of the year by the *San Francisco Chronicle*. Yu lives in Santa Monica, California, with his wife, Michelle, and their two children.

RESPAWN

Hiroshi Sakurazaka
(translated by Nathan Allan Collins)

In the beginning God created the screen.

And the screen was without form, and void; and all the pixels were dark.

And God said, "Let there be a dot," and there was a dot. The dot was light, and the screen was darkness.

And God said, "Let there be a paddle," and there was a paddle.

When the paddle struck the dot, a beep sounded. The dot ricocheted, and then bounced at the edge of the screen, returning, and the paddle struck it again. And God saw that it was good.

God took one of the paddle's ribs, and with it, He made another paddle. One paddle struck the dot, and the other returned it. There was evening, and there was morning. The paddles struck the dot without food or rest, and when they needed to urinate, they remained in place and used an empty plastic bottle. And God blessed them, and said to them, "Be fruitful, and multiply, and fill the Earth."

My nose only itches in critical moments.

I was working alone late at night in a beef bowl joint when it all happened. Situated away from the city's center, the place was like a feeding trough for humans to come shovel down their food in a matter of minutes. But even cows and horses—and chickens only able to stick out their heads from their cages—ate because they liked the taste, and people were no different. For me, the beef bowls I was permitted to eat during my shift were even more; they were my primary diet, my lifeline.

I had finished wiping a table, about to prepare it for the next customer, when he arrived. The robber.

The drowsiness lifted from my mind in an instant, but my very first thought was: This is gonna be a pain in the ass. Naturally, I was irritated that he was going to stroll out of here with the money I'd earned over hours of scooping out beef bowls. But annoyance came to me first, when I pictured all the extra work I'd have to do after he'd gone.

I'll give you the money in the register, I said to him in my mind, just hurry on out of here. Taking the money might be the end of this for you, but I don't have it so easy—I'll have to call the cops, report to the head office, do the paperwork, and all that. I'm paid by the hour, not by what I do, so don't add to my duties.

Having only one worker on shift in the middle of the night was an invitation for robberies. Due to changes in our parent company—said by some to be a momentary cause for public concern—a single part-timer, me, was left to tend the store. This practice was introduced as a product of cold financial calculation: even after accounting for losses due to the occasional robbery, the company made more profit by trimming shifts nationwide from two people down to one.

Beside the sliding glass doors of the entrance, a multi-colored strip of tape was marked 160 cm, 170 cm, 180 cm, and 190 cm. The sticker had been put there so that the entry-way's security camera could measure the height of anyone who passed through. These cameras took particularly crisp images; brazen robbers drawn in by desire for a little bit of scratch would eventually leave a clear capture of their like-nesses, and their careers would end with an arrest. Japanese police were good enough at that sort of thing.

In that case, I considered, we should put a button beside the door for robbers, so that when they pushed it, a machine would dispense a few ten-thousand-yen bills, take a picture of their face, then automatically report it to the police. Maybe then the criminals would form an orderly queue and await their turn in solemn silence. I could avoid the police inter-view, and the other customers could go on eating their beef bowls undisturbed. *Well, I guess it's cheaper to give a part-timer like me overtime instead.*

Kitchen knife in hand, the robber demanded my money, and I raised my arms high, indicating my lack of resistance as I slowly walked behind the counter to the register.

His eyes were like little marbles glaring at me through the visor of his motorcycle helmet. I suspected that he was devoid of any foresight or planning. For just a tiny amount of money and the short-lived freedom it would provide, he was com-mitting himself to spend a vast stretch of time in prison. Sure, he might believe he could get away with this, but otherwise, he would one day be thrown into jail and forced into labor. Why not just work now, instead? In a way, the robber and I, we were both doing our jobs, all for a little bit of money.

The robber brandished his knife, urging me to hurry. Light reflected from the metal and bounced around the little restaurant.

It's not my money anyway. So, sure, take it and get out of here.

But this must have been my unlucky day. Just as I had opened the register and was about to take out the money, another customer came in. This one covered the 190 cm mark of the sticker. He was a big man, the type who would order a jumbo beef bowl, extra beef. Steam rose from his bulging T-shirt. As he crossed the doorway, wiping sweat from his brow, he took one look at the scene and shouted, "You, what are you doing?"

I saw the tip of the robber's knife tremble. I went stiff, my hand clutching the money in the cash drawer. With what I'm sure was a fraught expression, I thought to the interloper, Hey, man, keep it cool. A beef bowl restaurant in the night has no need for your clumsy justice. This guy here is a necessary business expense. I'll give you your beef bowl afterward, so just pretend you didn't see anything and take your seat. Don't cause me any more trouble than I've already got.

But my hopes went unheard. The large man leaned forward in an aggressive stance. He was going to rush this way, his bulk as his weapon. The robber, on the other hand, was an older guy of average build; even accounting for the knife, the big man looked like he had the advantage.

The robber shouted something. It might have been words, but I couldn't tell. It was like the cry of a cornered cat. He waved the knife around as the big man began his charge, but even as he did so, the robber shrunk back. Even worse, he tried to hide behind my counter.

What the hell are you doing? I thought to the robber. Damn it. Keep away from me. I'm not your ally.

My body was frozen; my hand in the money tray. The robber turned around. A streak of light drew a line from right to left, left to right. I felt a warm impact run along my neck. A curtain of red fanned out before me, filling my vision.

A thing of beauty and art, the red curtain ill suited the dingy mass-produced decor of the beef bowl joint. With no flaws in the fabric, the folds, or the way light reflected from it, the curtain evoked velvet woven with care by an artisan's hand. Such a thing had no reason to be in a place like this; yet here it was, swaying in the air conditioner breeze.

For a while, I was mesmerized by the movement of the folds, but soon the strength left my knees, and my chin slammed on the register as I dropped. It didn't hurt. As coins rained down, I kissed the floor, which smelled like an old mop, and I finally realized that blood was spurting from my carotid artery.

Shit, this is going to be hard to clean up, I thought, and I died.

The next instant, I was standing in the restaurant, gripping a knife drenched in my black-red blood. "I" was lying behind the counter, looking as miserable and unattractive as I had always been in the mirror. The blood from "my" neck felt warm on my hands.

The deluge of blood had given a blotchy red-and-white pattern to the big man's T-shirt. He looked like a murderer as he stood in stunned shock.

Leaving behind the large dumbstruck man and my fallen self, I ran into the washroom. I checked the mirror that I had wiped clean at the beginning of my shift not long before. I was wearing a motorcycle helmet. I took it off. The slickness of the gore made the helmet hard to remove.

Reflected in the mirror was a man I didn't know, of average build and with eyes like marbles.

When I returned to the lobby, the dead man behind the counter was, as I had thought, me. No sign of the big man. He must have fled. What a jerk. My corpse was still. The thick smell of blood, ill suited to a beef bowl restaurant, filled the room.

Does this mean that I killed me?

I heard a police car siren in the distance.

My new stomach protested with a fierce hunger. Leaving "my" dead body where it was, I made myself a jumbo beef bowl and was eating it when the police arrested me.

They took me to interrogation, where I insisted that I was really me, and I didn't know anything about my killer. But the investigator wouldn't listen, his face taking a disapproving expression straight out of a religious painting from some bygone century. My background and record, as told to me, were of no relation to my own, and my parents who visited were strangers. I was grateful for the money they sent in for me, so even though they were the parents of my murderer, I decided to think of them as my mysterious benefactors.

I lost count of how many times I looked at myself in the mirror, but each time my face and my body unmistakably belonged to the man who knifed me. If I knew nothing else, I could be sure that the body I now inhabited had been the one that killed me. I underwent a psychiatric evaluation, but according to the result, I wasn't insane, but rather in perfect mental health. At this news, my public defender looked distressed, while the investigator seemed happy. I kept on insisting that my inner self had been put into this body, but my lawyer admonished me, saying, "You're only going to hurt the feelings of the bereaved family." My parents—that is, the parents of the me that was killed—were apparently seeking a harsh sentence. This was unfortunate for me, yet knowing that my parents felt that way brought me tears of happiness.

Ultimately, since I didn't show any signs of remorse, I was sentenced to thirty years of imprisonment with hard labor. I argued that it was unreasonable for me, who had been killed, to also receive the punishment for that killing, but doing so only lowered the judge's opinion of me.

I was taken to a prison somewhere in the north called Asahikawa, though the place must have been well heated, because it was considerably warmer there than the detention center in Tokyo's Katsushika Ward. Less favorable was my bed's location, closest to the toilet stall in a room of six, and that my mattress's sheets were already torn. In the detention center, being a murderer placed me at the top of the pecking order, but only murderers were in Asahikawa, and a mere single knifing was nothing special. I felt like a piglet wearing a fake mane locked in a cage of lions.

The first night, someone snuck up to me while I was asleep.

He slunk through the darkness, and without a word, he wrapped something ropelike around my neck and pulled tight. I tried to resist, but the strength left my body in a matter of seconds. Wait. I'm no criminal. I was sent here by mistake. What's the point of killing me? But my thoughts never made it into words. Instead, I slowly began to feel better. So, getting strangled really does make you feel good, I noted, and then I was staring down at my former self with new eyes, my former tongue lolling, body lying dead on the mattress. My former face looked like a hard-boiled egg, only black and red. Upon a closer look, I saw that the thing squeezed around my neck was a piece of torn bedsheet twisted into a rope.

What had been a vague hunch was now proven true: when my body died, my consciousness somehow survived. Where the consciousness of my new body went, I had no idea. I didn't know why it happened. Whatever. It's all bullshit.

My cellmates were all quietly asleep. Maybe none had noticed the midnight murder drama, or maybe some had and were only pretending to sleep. Then I realized something: I had been strangled by sheets torn from my own bedding. In other words: the murder had been premeditated. If that was the case, my killer had surely planned on leaving no evidence of his deed. There had to be some way to make my former self's death appear a suicide.

I surveyed the cell, and the half-open door to the toilet caught my eye. I dragged my former self over, tied one end of the sheet to the doorknob, and made it look like I had strangled myself.

The new me returned to my new me's bed.

When the guards made their rounds, they saw my suicide and made a fuss, but none of this had anything to do with the new me; to my surprise, the very next day was the last day of my sentence, and I was released.

As I set foot outside the prison gate, some hoodlum came to meet me. He was missing a front tooth and looked none too bright. He seemed to know me, but I didn't even know his name.

"Nice work," he said, cackling. "Sounds like ya pulled it off. The Aniki's happy too."

I was deflated. A gold watch glittered on my wrist; I couldn't believe the gaudy thing was mine. I was wearing a square-shouldered suit like the yakuza used to wear twenty years ago. I hadn't checked yet, but I was sure I had a dragon or something tattooed across my back. And whoever this gang was, they must have had some connection with my murder.

The punk insisted I get in his car, so I did. At a rest stop along the way, I pretended to use the bathroom and escaped. I didn't have anywhere to go, and these yakuza held the only clues to my new self, but I wasn't going to let this guy take me to the kind of people who would order a murder in a prison, no matter what reason they might have had.

I ran as hard as I could.

I was scared. I was scared of what was happening to me, and I was terrified of this body I was now using. If my former self had been marked for death, then the murder of my former-former self may have been planned as well. And if the government knew that someone like me existed, they would certainly work to keep me under control. And if they captured me? They would keep me alive and under wraps. And they would experiment. And experiment. And experiment. That's what I would do. I knew that's what I would do. It would be for the good of mankind. I would spare no concern for the rights of one individual.

Here a convenience store worker, there a uniformed delivery driver, a middle-aged man in a suit swinging his umbrella like a golf club—I saw everyone as a pursuer.

Luckily, my new self's decade-and-change-long stint in prison had earned me a stipend of two hundred thousand yen. I bought new clothes from a home-improvement store and discarded my old ones, and I sold the gaudy gold watch at a pawn shop. By taking a succession of local trains, I returned to the Tokyo where I was born.

For a little while, I lingered around my original self's parents' house. But I was no longer that me, nor even the me who had killed me; I was now a total stranger to my earliest self, with no connection to my parents. I had to run away when it looked like the old lady next door was going to report me. My current face was just too villainous.

For a while, I drifted from one business hotel to the next, but when my wallet started getting light, I applied for a part-time job at a beef bowl restaurant. I still remembered how to do the job, but they didn't hire me, whether due to my forbidding face or the tattoos, faintly visible through my shirt, that betrayed my yakuza past. In the end, I decided to make my home on the banks of the Arakawa River.

It was a place where the homeless gathered, a tiny village hidden behind the tall river reeds. The scattering of simple structures with their blue tarp roofs was visible from the train line that crossed the water, but from the side, the settlement was entirely unnoticeable. This was the best place for me now. I built myself a grand home with scavenged cardboard and blue tarp I'd bought at the hardware store.

In the weeds next door lived a white-haired old man called Lon. I didn't know if that was his family name, his given name, or a nickname. He claimed it meant "dragon."

Lon earned his living by collecting magazines from trash cans and selling them to used bookstores. When business was slow, he fished with a handmade pole. He told me the bluegills in the Arakawa tasted muddy, but when he added curry powder, he found that the fish were not inedible. He welcomed me with some one-cup sake and proclaimed that he would bestow me his magazine territory after he kicked the bucket. Every now and then I caught a sign of senility in him, but he was a very kindhearted man.

We often fished together, standing side by side, talking about this or that. Usually the topics were trivial, like tomorrow's weather, or a lady who shared her bento boxes on the days she didn't sell out, or a nasty old woman who sicced her dog on my new neighbor.

There were mornings, and there were evenings. I'm not sure whether I had told him what had happened to me or if Lon came up with the notion on his own—but at some point, my neighbor had begun to claim that he would come back to life as another person after he died. Maybe he'd gone full-on senile, or maybe he'd reworked his story to mirror mine. That he could respawn or something like that was of course impossible. I couldn't prove it, but I was certain.

And then I wondered if I had been coming back to life as myself. Maybe I had some mental illness that made me think I had died multiple times. That would make me a homeless ex-con who falsely believed he had been murdered at his part-time job in a beef bowl joint then taken to prison where he was murdered again. The slippery blood on my palm, the feeling of the rope on my neck, and the pleasure of ascension—maybe it was all some delusion conjured up by a diseased mind during my imprisonment.

In the end, I decided to buy into Lon's tall tales. It was my way of finding enjoyment in my life on the riverbank teeming with bugs.

"How long ago was it now, I wonder," Lon said, "that I heard there was a new kind of hot dog in L.A., so I went all the way there to try it. When I came back home, I started selling the same dogs. And they really sold."

According to him, he was actually an American. He looked entirely Japanese, and he never spoke English, but that was his story. He had laughed and said that becoming Japanese was handy, because a gentle smile could answer any question.

"That went well for a while," he continued, "until a rival hot dog cart opened up, and then it was all over. Deep in debt, I fled from my wife and children and drove to some uninhabited desert, then put a gun in my mouth and killed myself. And what happened next? I became a wealthy man who was getting himself drunk at the bar nearest where I was."

"You say nearest," I said, "but it had to be pretty far away."

"That's what's interesting about it." He licked his lips, his mouth a black cavern. "After that, I went to where I had died. The car I had driven supposedly the day before was covered in dust, and my body, practically mummified. I hadn't been revived immediately, but rather had been reborn as someone else many years later."

Lon was talkative today. It might have been due to the *happoshu*—the cans of almost-beer he'd bought at a discount store for thirty yen each.

Lon said that we shouldn't think of ourselves as being reborn, but as having a kind of mental illness or something, transmitted through death. In other words, "I" really was dying each time. Then, some bystander seeing "my" death would begin to wonder, Maybe I'm "me," and by doing so began taking my place. Only in retrospect would it seem that "my" consciousness continued on. When Lon came back to life in Arizona, he did so only because someone had discovered the mummy inside the car, and the memories of the bar and everything else were nothing more than fabrications after the fact.

As Lon explained it, people like to believe, "I think, and then I act," but the reality is that the speed of communication of the nervous system is not that fast. There's just not enough time for the brain to think in response to an event and then to act. The brain is nothing more than a circuit that recognizes the automatic actions of the body, then finds self-satisfaction in the belief, "I thought it, therefore I acted." Given that, it was entirely believable that a person, having acted as if he or she was someone else, could end up thinking, "I was the other person all along."

What Lon said had logic. I saw no other explanation for my condition, outside of the paranormal phenomenon of post-death possession, or the existence of another, higher-level me controlling each successive me down here. And neither of those were at all believable.

Lon said, "This me here is me, but I don't think I'm me. I have a transmissible mental illness that makes me think I'm not me. So can I really say that I'm alive? Meanwhile, the me who now believes this to be my body—he died a long time ago, and is being roasted in the fires of hell. The actions of the me here can do nothing for the me there. The me now is like the living dead, and without intervention, I'll continue like this for eternity. It's terrifying."

"Don't talk like that—you're spooking me."

"Well, there's still a few things I haven't tried. For one, what if I die when the closest person near me is another reincarnator? In that case, I think my illness wouldn't be transmitted. Maybe I'd be able to die in peace."

"Come on, old man. Do you really want to die?"

"Maybe," Lon said.

"Why?"

"I'm . . . weary."

Lon turned his gaze to the water. A chill breeze came downriver from far away in inland Saitama. Huddled down, the old man looked terribly small.

I didn't know if he was tired of our existences in death and rebirth repeated, or if he was referring to our present homeless lifestyle. Whether his tale of reincarnation was real or fake, our lives were without prospects. There was nothing here but bug bites, trash collecting, fishing, and the stink of grass and dirt and mud mingling together. Lon's life would soon be at its end, and I could understand his desire for a grander punctuation mark than worsening senility followed by a miserable death. But I had finally found someone I could open up to, and the thought of attending him to his death held no appeal for me.

"Listen, Lon—"

"It's okay," he said softly, facing the river. "Forget I said anything."

That was when I heard a familiar voice behind me.

"Finally, I found ya! I've been searchin' all over. I never would've thought you'd be in a place like this."

I turned to see that mouth with the missing tooth, opened wide, throwing me a brutish cackle.

My current self was apparently a man of few words. When Missing-Tooth took me to the yakuza office, I managed to escape suspicion by simply nodding and pretending that my memory was hazy. I gathered that I was the kind of guy most useful to a violent organization: one willing to get his hands dirty without a single complaint. No wonder they had searched for me with such dedication.

The man Missing-Tooth called Aniki was in his mid-forties. A real show-off, he wore a red shirt under a garishly patterned suit that practically screamed yakuza. Aniki and I were sworn brothers, and while his ascent in the ranks during my decade-and-change in prison had left a considerable gap in our respective ranks, he treated me—on, the surface, at least—as a brother.

After happily taking me out on a night of drinks followed by women at more than one *soapland*, Aniki didn't wait to ask me the favor. He phrased it as a request, but I sensed no room to refuse.

I was ordered to perform another killing. The murder I committed before becoming me in the prison—that is, the murder of me—had been requested by clients who were now deemed as untrustworthy. Even though they requested the killing, the clients' guilt seemed likely to drive them to confess to the police. Since we had already received payment in full, all that was left was to keep them from talking before they caused any trouble.

Then Aniki handed me a photograph—a surveillance shot, an elderly couple in profile, their expressions troubled. I recognized them immediately. My birth parents.

Now I understood. The assassin who killed my second self had been hired by my real parents. Having seen my thirty-year sentence as poor recompense for their son's death, they had risked the danger that came from associating with a violent organization so that they could bring about the ultimate act of vengeance. What they did was wrong, uncivilized, and was to be despised, but through that act I saw that as pitiful as I had been, I was still loved by my parents. The back of my nose—though it wasn't my nose—began to tingle.

This yakuza was telling me to kill that dear old couple. You bastard, I thought. You human garbage. Go to hell.

I wanted to go berserk on him then and there, but I stifled the impulse. This killing had to be stopped, whatever it took.

And the only one who could stop it was me. Pressed into a van outside the office with Missing-Tooth, I desperately tried to think of how I could prevent the killing.

The neon lights of the city passed by the tinted windows. It was nearing midnight. The pop music blaring from the stereo irritated me more than it should have.

I asked, "How should I do it?"

Missing-Tooth's answer was as concise as the directions on a cup of instant ramen. "Wait'll they're asleep. Pick the lock. Give 'em a good zap with the stun gun. Kill 'em with a hammer to the head. Wrap 'em up in a futon and haul 'em out. Don't forget to lock the door. Take 'em to the disposers. The end."

"What, no knife or sword?"

"The disposers yell at us when we get too much blood in the futon. These days, we mostly use disposable hammers from the hundred-yen store."

"That's too bad," I said.

"Well, we do keep a blade on hand, just in case. It's hidden under your seat so the cops don't find it."

Including me, four men occupied the van's dim interior. Myself and one other were in the back, and Missing-Tooth had taken the front passenger seat. These guys saw murder as something trivial. They were rotten to the core, and society would be no worse off without them. But did that make it all right for me to kill them? I felt like that would be a wrong. But while I was debating it, the van was heading for my parents' house. I began to recognize the view from the windows. My parents' executions were drawing nigh.

"What's wrong?" Missing-Tooth asked.

I made up my mind.

I reached under my seat and pulled out a knife with a

thirty-centimeter blade. Still hunched over, I swung my arm in a fluid motion, building momentum as I thrust the blade into the stomach of the man next to me.

He groaned an "Oof." I stabbed him twice. Three times. He died.

"Wh—what are ya doing?" Missing-Tooth said with disappointed dismay.

I didn't answer. The blood and gore was warm on my hand, but the sensation came as no surprise. This wasn't the first time I'd felt the blood of another spraying upon me. I renewed my grip on the knife and thrust it between the front seats, aiming for Missing-Tooth's neck.

He twisted away and pulled out a knife of his own. Despite the way he looked and talked, he was apparently the real deal. We grappled across the seat back, and his knife pierced between my ribs, penetrating my heart. My blade sliced open his carotid artery. In the end, it was a draw. My consciousness began to fade. I wondered, Did I save my parents? and in the next moment I was the man in the driver's seat.

Apparently, "I" truly was immortal. I died again and again, but "I" never died. All right, then. No time to ponder it now. I have something I need to do.

With three corpses along for the ride, I pulled a U-turn and drove back the way we came. Our starting point was still stored in the GPS. The music on the radio sounded more pleasing than maybe it should have. When the song reached its bridge, I realized it was still the same tune that had been playing before.

I arrived at the yakuza office, where a man was standing guard outside. I ran him over and drove headlong into the front door. The van struck the concrete car stop, and my body shattered the windshield, sailing through, hitting a wall. I died instantly.

I came back as an underling inside the office. Directly in front of me was the back of a garish suit. I'd seen it before: Aniki. All around me, the men were beginning to react to the intrusion.

I looked around and saw a katana decorating the wall. I grabbed it and thrust it through Aniki's back.

"What the fuck!" he shouted. "Are you fucking crazy?"

He wasn't dead. This one was persistent. He knocked me down with a single punch. The other men swarmed me and kicked me backward. Still clutching the katana, I swung the sword at their legs. Take that! Then one of them stabbed me. It hurt. Whatever. I don't care. This body's not done yet. I got back to my feet and stabbed and killed the man who had stabbed me. Bullets pummeled my back and the underling-me died.

In a stroke of fortune, I came back as the man with the gun. On my command, my new body put the weapon's sights on the heads of the moving targets and squeezed the trigger.

The gun was plastic, toylike, but the explosive flashes of its muzzle and the power of its bullets were the real thing. Until that point, I'd always thought that bullets came out like arrows. But inside this tiny room, firing a pistol for myself felt quite a bit different. When I squeezed the trigger, the recoil jolted up my arm to my shoulder. Almost simultaneously, an object flew out the other side of the gunsight. A small dot, the object seemed to move at the speed of light, and I couldn't follow it with my eyes. Inside this room, my targets had nowhere to escape.

Well, this is surprisingly easy, I thought. However my opponents moved about, all I had to do was have my sights on them the moment I squeezed the trigger. Trigger. Bang. Exploding head. One more down.

Another shooter had already fired six rounds at me without making a scratch. I wasn't sure if my body knew how to expertly handle the weapon through muscle memory or if the other shooter was too nervous to hit me—if he took a steady aim, he might have. Instead, his bullets flew off into nowhere, gouging at a wall, shattering an ashtray on a tabletop.

You'll never hit me like that. I was starting to feel bad for my opponent. If you didn't care about your body, as I don't about mine, you could take your time to aim, and *bang!* See, like I just hit you now. He died. I kept on firing, and with each shot, my enemies were fewer.

Soon, nothing moved.

From behind a sofa where he was hiding, Aniki shouted, "What do you want?"

To wipe you all out. Without a word, I held my gun at the ready and slowly advanced. The floor was slippery with blood. Smoke hung in the air. I wondered, Is this what gunpowder smells like?

By the time I reached his side, Aniki was near death. He clutched at his side, soaked bright red, and breathed weakly. I looked down at this man called Aniki.

"What is all this?" he said. I didn't reply. But he was the kind of man who could command a criminal organization, and he seemed to notice something about me. He peered into my eyes and asked, "You. Who the hell are you?"

"I don't know."

I didn't have any other answer for him. I pulled the trigger.

I had blown apart nine heads with twelve bullets. No one moved in the office now. I checked the magazine and saw two rounds remained. This was an incredible gun. Two bullets had been spent before I became me, meaning that the weapon had held nearly twenty.

I fired one more shot into Aniki's corpse. I didn't relish doing so, but I didn't want to risk being transferred to a half-dead man.

Surveying the now-quiet room, I was reminded of an arcade crane game. The bodies, scattered everywhere, looked like dolls. But what had opened their eyes so wide wasn't some artful appreciation for the painting on the ceiling drawn with their own blood. What had opened their eyes was the giant arm that had come from above to take them to some other place.

I set fires all around the room, and when the tongues of flame grew too large to be stopped, I put the gun to the top of my head, and *bang!*

The next moment, I was a man in a suit, recording the yakuza office with my cell phone.

"It's so scary," someone said.

A woman was clinging to my left arm. I didn't know her. Of course I didn't—I didn't even know my own face.

I had fulfilled my mission. The office would burn and leave no evidence. The yakuza were all dead, and my parents lived. Right now, my parents were probably sound asleep. For some reason, when I thought of them, I remembered the face of the woman who was my mysterious benefactor in the detention center—not my mother, but the mother of the robber who had killed me. But maybe it was all the same for me now.

"Come on, let's go," the woman at my arm said. She felt warm beside me.

I was struck by the temptation to steal this man's life. If I did, I wouldn't have to live on the run. That's right. I have the power now to steal someone else's life and become them. Are there others with this same ability? Are some of them living these lives of comfort?

But then came the doubt. If what's inside this shell is only me, then I'll never be able to be "him." The social status, the routine, the pleasures that this body had grasped—those things belonged to him. All I can capture are their vestiges. Only this body's former owner could look at these fleeting traces and find happiness. Not me. I'll only be happy with a life of my own making. Maybe it didn't look that way, but before all this—and even now—ladling out beef bowls for some hourly pay gave me all the satisfaction I needed. I liked beef bowls.

I glanced up and saw, in front of the flaming van, a man desperately pushing at the chest of a dead body. He was big. Steam rose from his bulging T-shirt. The big man looked on the verge of tears as he kept on pressing with his thick arms the center of the corpse's chest. The dead body was mine, from when I rammed the van into the building. You're wasting your time. I'm already dead—that's how I'm standing here. But the big man didn't know that.

I recognized his face. He was that hero of the night—the man who had caused the death of my original, irreplaceable self.

I approached the man and said, "Thank you."

"Huh?"

"Never mind. It's nothing."

Tears ran down my cheeks. I had simply wanted to express my gratitude to the man who was doing all he could for what once had been my body, and now in death was just a thing.

His attempt to rescue me in the beef bowl restaurant may have ended with my death, but he had risked his one—and only— life for me. Out there in the world were people like him, far too good. He was my opposite: a human being of a different kind, one that deserved deep admiration.

The woman asked me, "What's wrong?"

I shook off her hand and brushed aside her attempts to stop me as I walked away on my own. After a while, my cell phone started to buzz persistently, so I threw it on the ground and crushed it with my shoe.

All I wanted was to return to being me, a man whose face was already becoming hazy in my memory. I didn't want to be anyone else. My job at the beef bowl joint may have been monotonous, but at least I had done it myself, and not under the command of some other me. But that body—my body— was long since cremated and put into a grave. I would have to force myself to let go of the past. I wanted to be without a past. Death would never smile upon me, and so I could have nothing of substance, nothing to tie me down, nothing at all.

Then a realization came to me. I'm powerless. I'm not anyone. I'm just a lousy dog crawling through the dirt to my death. No, not even a dog. I'm a bone or a broken stick for the wandering dog to find. I'm a stick that hits any dot that comes toward me just because I feel like it. In the Old Testament, didn't man evolve from a stick? Or do I have that wrong? Whatever. It doesn't matter right now. Because this world is occupied almost entirely by my kind. Ninety percent—no, maybe even 99 percent—are the same as me, with nothing of their own, no past, no ties, no hopes for the future. Despite this—or because of it—they and I are invincible.

I found myself standing in front of a beef bowl joint in the middle of the night. It wasn't the place where I had worked, but like my store, it was bright and warm and clean, if only a feeding trough with dingy, mass-produced decor.

Adjacent was a vacant lot. On the other side of a wire fence, a single stick stood in the earth. In the past, the stick had provided support for a sign of some sort, but the plywood sign had fallen to rot in the dirt.

For some reason, I couldn't help but feel excited. The time had come to begin my next worthless life. At least that's how I felt. The feeling came as no surprise—I've been the same all along. The me who served up beef bowls, the me who was a robber, the me who was a convict and a killer, they were all me.

I roared at the night sky and pulled up the stick.

Inside the beef bowl joint, a lone charmless man interchangeable with my former self was serving up beef bowls.

Resting the stick on my shoulder, I strode inside.

My nose only itches in critical moments.

"Give me your money," I said.

Taking aim at this good-for-nothing world, I swung my stick as hard as I could.

Hiroshi Sakurazaka was born in Tokyo in 1970. After a career in information technology, he published his first light novel, *Modern Magic Made Simple*. With 2004's *All You Need Is Kill*, Sakurazaka earned his first Seiun Award nomination for best Japanese science fiction. His 2004 short story, "Saitama Chainsaw Massacre," won the 16th SF Magazine Reader's Award. In 2009, *All You Need Is Kill* was the launch title for Haikasoru, an imprint dedicated to publishing Japanese science fiction and fantasy for English-speaking audiences. The book also formed the basis for the international hit film *Edge of Tomorrow*, starring Tom Cruise. Sakurazaka's other novels include *Characters* (cowritten with Hiroki Azuma) and *Slum Online*, which was published in English by Haikasoru. In 2010, Sakurazaka started an experimental digital magazine, *AiR,* with Junji Hotta. He remains one of Japan's most energetic writers of both light novels and adult science fiction.

DESERT WALK

S. R. Mastrantone

Sam Atherstone had played nearly every computer game on the planet—he'd worked out the exact number not long ago and written about it on the blog that paid his bills—yet the excitement he felt when his housemate, Jamie, handed him the gray Jiffy bag that had come in the Saturday morning post caused his hands to shake so much that he couldn't get it open, and Jamie, tired of waiting, grabbed the bag from him and opened it on Sam's behalf.

"Is it the one?" Jamie said, holding out the black game cartridge on his chubby hand, bringing to Sam's mind a chocolate on a hotel pillow.

Sam took the cartridge and inspected it. The slightly faded logo of *Games World*, the magazine that had given the game its very limited distribution back in 1992, was the only sign of wear. Providing it still worked, he considered it half-a-grand well spent.

He gave Jamie both a smile and a nod.

While Sam retrieved the Sega Master System II from a cupboard filled with ancient consoles, Jamie went around clearing away the clutter of the MSII's modern brethren, shoving all the sleek new units and their myriad controllers beneath the huge flat screen that dominated the room.

"Right," said Sam, crossing the room with the MSII in hand. "Your first job—"

"I already did a job," Jamie said, pointing at the space he'd created on the floor. He sounded out of breath and his plump cheeks were red.

"Your second job, should you choose to accept it, is to get the tea in."

"I already *did* a job."

"No tea, no game."

Jamie left the room with a dramatic harrumph and Sam set up the MSII while listening to Jamie's disgruntled clattering in the kitchen directly below.

Once the wires were connected, Sam flicked the *On* switch. The pent-up anxiety that had been building for a week, ever since an anonymous gamer had contacted Sam on a forum and offered to sell him the rare game, melted away when the familiar blue Sega logo lit up the screen. He sat down on the single mattress that he slept on every night, control pad in hand. It had all worked out. It was real.

A menu appeared on the flat screen bearing the *Games World* logo and beneath, a list of six games. The game that Sam had been waiting for was the last on the list. He flicked down and selected it, the sweat of his anticipation greasing the pad.

The following screen was a pixel painting of a man standing alone in the middle of a desert looking across miles of empty terrain at a purple mountain range far on the horizon. Crude as the rendering was, Sam felt a shiver shoot up his spine and dissipate across his shoulders. Above the purple mountains were two words in bright green capital letters that were as much responsible for his reaction as the image: DESERT WALK.

At the bottom of the screen, in smaller text, were the flashing instructions: PRESS START TO WALK! Sam pressed *Start*.

Immediately the screen was filled with a yellow-pixel desert, seen from the point of view of the game's main character. On the ground were gray-pixel stones and on the horizon were purple-pixel mountains just below a blue-pixel sky. Sam pushed the *Up* arrow on the control pad, and on-screen the character he was embodying took a step in the direction of the mountain range. The game simulated the sound of footsteps on sand, *chshh*, *chshh*, *chshh*. Other than that, it made no noise. When Sam stopped walking, the game was silent.

"I'm really playing it," he said. "I'm bloody playing *Desert Walk*."

He was six steps in when the screen went black.

From downstairs Jamie shouted: "I've got it." Sam looked over at the blank face on the clock on his mattress side table and concluded that for the second time in the last few days, the kettle had caused a power cut. He shook his head.

While he waited for the power to come back on, Sam reached over and picked up the envelope in which the game had come. He looked inside the envelope and noticed a small square of paper. He retrieved it and saw the sender had sent him a handwritten note. It read: *Enjoy the game, but not too much. Don't forget to eat!*

When Jamie finally came in with the tea, Sam had the game back up and running, the power restored. "Mate," Sam said. "New house rule. When I'm playing this game, we can't use the kettle."

"Get out," Jamie said. "I need my caffeine."

"Look, you can't save this game, you can't even pause it. If I'm fifteen hours in and you start an explosive brew, I'm making you homeless."

"We could buy a new kettle."

"Or *you* could."

Jamie flapped his hand dismissively. "Sod off, you know I can't afford that." Sam did know this: Jamie had been staying with him rent-free for six months while he tried to get back on his feet following his "redundivorce." The simultaneous blows in quick succession had made his childhood best friend a figure of maddening pity, but Sam's patience was on the wane of late.

"No job, no tea," Sam said. Jamie looked crestfallen, and Sam felt a twinge of regret. Had he been too harsh? He was about to apologize when Jamie gave him the finger.

"Lovely," Sam said. "You done? Good. Now shut up and watch me play the best computer game ever made."

Ten minutes of walking later, Sam having made no visible ground on the mountains, Jamie said: "Is this literally it? The whole game."

Sam shrugged, his gaze fixed on the television. "That's the point," Sam said. "No one really knows—that's what's so exciting about it."

"Yeah, I can barely contain myself," Jamie said, and Sam sighed. "You said this was the game that you'd been waiting your whole life to play."

After a moment of reflection, Sam spoke softly: "You need to understand what you're looking at. This is possibly in the top five of the all-time rare games—"

"I know that, I'm just saying it's probably rare for a reas—"

"Listen first, and then learn. The game's rare because it was only ever released as part of this *Games World* sampler. The other games on the sampler were all demos that later got a proper release, but due to a manufacturing balls-up, the full game of *Desert Walk* was featured instead of the demo version. So the magazine had to recall the issue, which means loads of the samplers got destroyed. However, *Desert Walk* never got its official release in the end because Sega pulled it for no reason that anyone's been able to properly ascertain, meaning those few who bought the sampler before it was recalled were the only people to ever play *Desert Walk*."

"Well, it's obvious why it never got an official release, isn't it? It's rubbish."

"That's not the reason. No one knows exactly why it was pulled, but there's all sorts of cool rumors about it doing the rounds. Go look it up. The game causes epilepsy, it causes blindness, it causes madness. I'd never have put much stock in all that, but on one of the forums someone posted a link to a BBC article from two years ago about some bloke who apparently got a copy off eBay and died of dehydration after playing the game for a week straight."

"I'm the only one that's going to die of dehydration if you're serious about that kettle," Jamie said. Sam ignored him. Up on the screen, the passing desert looked the same as it had at the start of the game.

chshh, chshh, chshh

"And it isn't rubbish," Sam continued. "It was ahead of its time. It might look simple at first, but those stones on the floor aren't being regenerated from previous screens. The arrangements don't repeat. They're all completely unique. That means the designer made every square inch of this huge, endless desert."

"Why did he bother?"

"She. The designer's a woman, you pig. That's the question, isn't it? And that's what I intend to ask *her* when I go to Manchester to meet *her* on Thursday to interview *her* for the blog."

"You're going to ask *him* point-blank why *he* bothered making a game where nothing happens?"

"Obviously not. And anyway, it isn't like nothing happens. Some people—"

"Forum people?"

"Yes, they're people too. Some people who've played it a while say they've come across different objects after walking for long enough. A small shoe, a mailbox, a skeleton. One guy says he came across a van half-buried in the sand. It's, like, widely believed that if you keep walking long enough, you can complete the game by finding a main road. No one's done it, though, so that's what I want to ask her: Can it be completed? Why the attention to detail? Is there a cheat? Why was it pulled from the— Holy bum flaps."

Jamie, who was slouching on the mattress, sat up and looked at the screen. "What? What is it?"

"Look," Sam said. On the horizon a dark shape had appeared. At first it looked like a person, arms wide open. When they drew closer to it, the dark shape became green, and in doing so, revealed its true identity.

"It's a cactus. Yessss." Sam pumped a fist in the air, his voice high and excited. "Other people have found those too. Ten minutes in, and we've found our first object."

He flattened out his fist and offered it to Jamie for a high five. Jamie raised his eyebrows, stood up, and left Sam hanging. "Sorry, mate. I don't think I've got another minute of this in me."

"Fine," Sam said. "But don't cry to me when you miss me making history."

Jamie mumbled something on his way out the door but Sam didn't hear; he was already focused on putting the cactus behind him and finding the next secret of the game.

The alarm clock on the bedside table continued to flash uselessly on the default setting of 12:00, depriving Sam of a meaningful relationship with the correct time of day. He'd been too engrossed to get up and open the curtains. After what felt like an hour of playing, he hadn't come across any more objects, and the purple mountains still looked ominously distant.

He didn't mind, though. The gentle *chshh*, *chshh* and the undemanding graphics had lulled Sam into a deep contemplative state where he'd been able to think clearly for the first time in a long while. In addition to his biweekly blog, there had been numerous commissioned pieces he'd been writing that took up a substantial amount of his time, not to mention the monthly column he was writing for one of the national newspapers. It had been almost a year since Afshan left him, and it was only out here in the make-believe desert that he simultaneously reasoned and believed that it had probably been for the best. He wouldn't have had time for all the demands of gaming had they still been together. He'd have had to go back to work on the shop floor at PC Planet.

Certainly there wouldn't have been enough time or goodwill for the demands of a blog about *Desert Walk*.

Sam's stomach growled. He put down the controller and up on the screen the walker stopped. The room went quiet and Sam felt an unexpected stab of loneliness. He ran down to the kitchen, eager to return to the game. He opened the fridge and pulled out a bowl of leftover Balti from the night before. Only after he'd put the bowl in the microwave did he notice that the light coming through the kitchen window was much weaker than he'd expected it to be. He looked at the clock on the oven. It was flashing 12:00 too.

He went into the lounge, where Jamie was sitting, watching television. "What's the time, mate?" Sam said.

"Dunno. Can I use the kettle yet?"

"What do you mean, you don't know? Seriously, what's the time?"

Jamie sighed and flicked the button on the remote that brought up the menu. "It's twelve minutes past four."

"Get out." Sam went over to the screen to see for himself. He snorted out a laugh to hide his genuine shock. "Bloody hell, I thought it was, like, lunchtime."

"Nope, you missed that. You been playing that game the whole time?" Sam nodded. "Why don't you take a break, mate. Come watch this unbelievably fascinating documentary about the 1876–78 Indian famine. Next up's one about the fastest car in the world."

"Sorry, I'd love to, but I've got to get on with work."

"Yeah, of course. *Work.* You found anything else out in the desert yet?"

"No. Not yet. Can't believe it's been nearly six hours. That's insane."

"What's insane is you've been playing it for six hours and nothing's happened yet. You haven't even found another cactus? Or an anthill? Or a dried-up twig or a bit of leaf?"

Sam shook his head and grinned. "Nope. It's brilliant."

After devouring his curry, Sam went back upstairs. He was nearly at the landing when he heard the familiar noise of the game coming from his room: *chshh, chshh, chshh*. Wondering if he'd left the controller the wrong way up, he went inside and saw everything was as he had left it. The control pad was the right way up, and, on the screen, his character was standing still.

chshh, chshh, chshh

It was a glitch. It must be. Perhaps he'd uncovered the real reason the game had been pulled, and it was nothing more fantastic than a useless bit of programming.

Sam reached for the control pad to check that the buttons weren't stuck. They weren't. Two things occurred to him then. The first was that the *chshh, chshh* sound emanating from the television was slightly different from the one he had grown accustomed to over the course of the day. This sound was softer, and somehow more distant. And the spaces between footsteps sounded irregular, less rhythmic and robotic. The second was that there was a small dark shape on the desert horizon that hadn't been there when he left the room earlier.

More unnerved by both these realizations than he dared acknowledge, Sam laughed and went over to the television to look at the object more closely.

chshh, chshh, chshh

The object had already grown larger by the time Sam got close to the screen. He could make out that it was a small figure now. He could see its arms, and legs, its shaggy yellow hair.

Puzzled, Sam took a step back. The graphics used to render the figure were much more like those from the start screen than the surrounding blocky desert and mountains.

It was a toddler, dressed in a red romper suit and carrying some flat, rectangular object in its left hand.

"Hel-lo," Sam said, his voice soft.

chshh, chshh

Had he done it? Was this advancing child some sort of clue to the end of the game? His game-player's instinct told him it might be; he recalled a certain randomness to many of the solutions to old-school games. Even better: How funny would it be if after all that walking, the solution to the game was to just stand still?

He thought about the small shoe that someone had reported on one of the forums. Sam stepped toward the screen and saw that the child, now a third of the way between the top and bottom of the television, was wearing only one shoe.

Sam didn't feel a rush of excitement upon piecing this together. He'd noticed something unsettling about the child on the screen. He couldn't be sure if it was just bad design, but the boy—it was obviously a boy now—looked almost skeletal. The romper suit wasn't packed with pixelated puppy fat. Instead, it hung so loosely on the child that it appeared to be blowing to the left in a nonexistent desert wind.

There was something wrong with the child's face too. And this, unless the creator was unhinged, had to be some mistake in the programming. The drawn skin and the gaping mouth were reminiscent of famine victims that Sam had only ever seen on news items and in documentaries.

The child raised its one empty hand and reached toward Sam.

Appalled, Sam stepped backward and put his foot squarely on top of the MSII. The desert was replaced by a series of wavy lines, then the screen went black. Sam got his footing and realized he'd turned the console off.

He fought the urge to yell. He couldn't believe what he'd just done, the time he'd wasted. But when the rage subsided,

Sam was surprised to find he was also relieved: he could start the game afresh and wouldn't accidentally play all night without a stock of supplies. He thought of the note that had come with the game—*Don't forget to eat!*—and smiled. He was starving. He could grab a cup of tea now too.

He went to tell Jamie about his exploits but when he stepped out of his room, he found the whole house was pitch-black. He turned on the landing light and went downstairs. Jamie wasn't in the lounge and when Sam turned on the television to bring up the menu, he realized why. It was half past four in the morning.

"The game was meant to be a satire," the woman opposite Sam said. She took a sip of her coffee and pushed a loose strand of gray hair away from her eyes.

Sam typed *satire* into a document entitled "Lorna Fry Interview" on his laptop. He nodded, took a sip of his own coffee, then shook his head after understanding what it was she was saying. "Really?"

"Oh yeah. I wanted to bring down the industry from inside. Very idealistic stuff. Seems a long time ago now." Her eyes flicked down to the nurse's uniform she was wearing. "So I sold a game called *Duck Shot*, which I made enough money from to start my own little company. And when I say little, I mean it was just me and one other bloke. Because of *Duck Shot*, we were never short of offers for the games we made. Nintendo put out *Means of Production*, a Mario-style game where you had to overthrow your capitalist overlords."

"Yeah, I loved that one."

"You've played it? Interesting and impressive. What about *Freedom*?"

"Oh, I loved that."

"You know, the only thing they didn't let us do with that one was call it *The Nazi Killer*."

Sam laughed and typed *The Nazi Killer*. "No way. They were fine with the other stuff, the violence, et cetera?"

"Oh yeah, just not the literal description of the main character's job." Lorna took another sip and looked at her watch. "With *Desert Walk* we wanted to be subtle. We wanted to satirize game playing itself. My worry was that we were seeing kids spending more and more time playing games as a hobby. Great for the industry, but what about the kids?"

"Never harmed me," Sam said, offering a confident grin that definitely did not say "I've just spent every night since Saturday wandering around your satirical desert."

"Don't get me wrong: I'm not anti-gaming or anything. I think these people taking their shoot-'em-ups into the real world more than likely had a screw loose in the first place. But I reasoned if Moore's Law continued to hold through the nineties, soon consoles would be able to simulate real life, and I wanted to raise philosophical questions about that. So we designed a game where nothing happened. Literally nothing. And worse, it happened in the middle of nowhere."

Not knowing what else to say, feeling suddenly very self-conscious, Sam said: "So *Desert Walk* is, sort of, a practical joke?"

"Not *sort of*. It was."

It felt like a cork had just been pulled from him, and weeks, months, and years of enthusiasm were gushing out. He forced a laugh that sounded more bitter than he'd intended.

"So all those people on forums, all their theories, the legends . . . There are going be some pissed-off geeks out there."

Oblivious, Lorna carried on: "Looking at all the games around now, especially the ones with clocks telling you how much time you've spent playing . . . Wow, I mean, we're a step away from plugging ourselves into *The Matrix*, really."

"So can *Desert Walk* be completed?"

"Oh, now, if I told you that, I'd have to kill you," she said.

"It can't, can it?" There was desperate hope in his voice. Lorna mimed closing a zipper across her lips. "Okay, well, tell me what all the objects in the desert are about. Do they have a point? Are they clues?"

Lorna shook her head. "No, before we released the game we decided we needed a way to sell it to the suits; they wouldn't have been happy with a game where nothing happens, so we hinted at a possible ending and put in a few objects that players could 'find' if anyone did decide to check it: a cactus, a rusty old van—"

"A kid's shoe."

She frowned. "Don't remember that one. I remember a cricket bat . . . There's a few others. Maybe there was a shoe."

"What about the hungry kid?" Since Saturday, Sam hadn't managed to find the gaunt child again, although he'd traveled in much the same direction he had done before and even stumbled across the same cactus—or at least he thought it was the same cactus.

"Pardon?" Lorna said, although from her tone, Sam understood she'd heard him the first time.

"The hungry kid. What's he about?"

Lorna sat up straight, her face stiff and wary. "Are you being funny?"

Not liking the rapid shift in the tone of the interview, and feeling protective of his remaining enthusiasm, Sam tried changing the subject. "Let me ask something else, then: Why was the game pulled?"

She glared at him and said nothing.

He tried changing the subject again, not understanding what was happening, what he had done wrong. "Okay, you're a nurse now, I take it? Why did you leave gam—"

Lorna stood up and put on her coat. She was leaving.

Sam panicked. He tried to say something to rescue the situation. "Sorry, did I say—"

"You're a piece of work, aren't you?" she said, ejecting the words like insects that had flown into her mouth. "Hungry child? Why was the game pulled? Did someone put you up to this?"

"Honestly," Sam said, holding up both hands. "I don't know what I've said."

Lorna looked down at her coffee mug, then back to Sam, then at the laptop, then back to the coffee. Sam knew exactly what she was thinking, so he shut his laptop and turned to put it down on the floor out of harm's way. He heard her sigh, but when he turned back to face her, she was already through the coffee shop door and out onto the high street.

In the following days Sam wrote three apologetic emails to Lorna. It wasn't that he felt anything remotely close to guilt over what had happened in Manchester (how could he if he had no idea what he done?), he just didn't want anything to affect the publication of his blog about *Desert Walk*. Her revelations were going to generate a lot of traffic and there was potential for them to etch his name in the history of gaming, even if on a personal level they had deeply upset him.

He couldn't bear to play the stupid thing now. He packed up the MSII and put it back in the cupboard. Even if there really was a way to complete the game, he had no intention of being the subject of a stupid prank anymore. Two decades was long enough. He came close to throwing the game away, standing over the kitchen bin for a good minute with the cartridge in his hand before reminding himself how much it had cost him in both sleep and cash. Perhaps he'd sell it on for a profit when his blog revived interest in the game.

The game wasn't done with Sam, though. The sheer amount of time he'd put in during the first week had scarred him to the point of it dominating his dreams. More than once he awoke in the dark hours before dawn, his hands still clutching an invisible controller, the sound of electronic footsteps echoing in his mind.

He hadn't seen much of Jamie. Days after his last email to Lorna, he bumped into him in the kitchen and reported that the kettle was back in commission. "Did you complete it in the end?" he said when Sam broke the news that the *Desert Walk* days were done.

"Yeah, pretty much," Sam said. "Now you can loaf around here all day *and* get your caff-buzz on again."

Jamie flicked two fingers in Sam's direction, but Sam became distracted by an email on his phone. It was a response from Lorna. All it contained was an Internet link to a BBC news article. With Jamie still wittering away, he went upstairs to open it on his laptop.

JOHN TAYLOR RETURNED TO PRISON

The headline meant nothing to him, so he read the article. The first few paragraphs were equally confusing, the details of a drug bust in a rough part of Newcastle. It was only when he reached the fourth paragraph that he felt something close to understanding.

> *Taylor served a fifteen-year sentence after causing or allowing the death of his 3-year-old son Jeffrey. Taylor, along with his partner Amanda, was jailed following Jeffrey's death in 1992. Jeffrey was found dead by Taylor after a self-confessed five-day "computer game and drug binge," during which Jeffrey was locked in an upstairs bedroom unattended. Hospital staff alerted authorities when the condition of the child's body showed signs of severe dehydration and malnutrition.*

It took a number of reads to process what Lorna Fry was trying to tell him; each time his brain filtered out more and more of the words around the phrase *computer game and drug binge* until that was all he could focus on.

His limbs feeling heavy and weak, Sam searched online for anything more about the death of Jeffrey Taylor and found very little outside of John Taylor's rearrest. After scrolling through pages and pages of articles from earlier in the year, he found an article dated 2002 from a local Manchester paper.

AUNT URGES TOWN TO NEVER FORGET JEFFREY TAYLOR

In an interview on the tenth anniversary of Jeffrey's death, his aunt, the patron of a charity dedicated to helping families in inner-city areas, recalled her feelings about the case:

> *I think about him all the time. The horror of that room. They found a copy of a book,* The Tiger Who Came to

Tea, in with him. His favourite. They said he'd started eating the pages. I mean, it's just unthinkable, how hungry he must have been. And how lonely, all that time wondering what he'd done wrong and wondering why no one was coming to help him. I still wonder that now, I mean, the bedroom was at the front of the house. How can no one have heard him? All that time? Why did no one help Jeffrey? He must have been so hungry.

For a while, Sam stared at the wall beyond the flat screen television. Later, he found himself staring at the console cupboard.

Jamie clicked *Send* at the bottom of the online job application form with a practiced carefulness that came with owning large fingers in the digital age. When the screen confirmed the form had successfully sent, Jamie relieved his spine of his considerable weight by leaning back from the coffee table and collapsing onto the sofa.

This would show Sam.

Using the remote, Jamie brought up the television menu screen. It was nearly one a.m. It had taken an hour. Three down, one to go, he thought. But there was no way he'd get through another one without refreshment. With a groan he got to his feet and went to the kitchen. He switched on the light, took out the tea bags, then flicked on the kettle.

Living with Sam had been all right at first. They'd had some good laughs, seen some decent movies, smoked some excellent herb. Sam had really helped him get his head straight about the divorce, and in return he felt he'd helped Sam deal with all the baggage left behind after Afshan. There had been a good balance and it had been like old times, before jobs and money and partners. It wasn't the same now, though. Sam's little comments had been growing more and more barbed of late, and Jamie knew he had to get out before he threw a punch at the bloke. That Sam would rather spend time playing a computer game where you walked about in an endless, empty desert for no real reason than spend time with Jamie really was the final nail.

The kettle hissed as the water started to boil. Seconds later both the light and the kettle went off.

"Oh, for f—" He stopped when he heard a high-pitched shriek somewhere above him that ended so quickly his mind immediately began to doubt he'd heard it. His cholesterol-smothered heart started to work harder than it was used to. Jamie hadn't liked that sound at all. He fumbled his way to the electricity box in the downstairs hall. "Sorry, mate," he yelled in the direction of the stairs. "Just the kettle again." He didn't care if he woke Sam up. He didn't want to be the only one awake in the house after having heard that noise.

"It was a fox," he said out loud and flicked the master switch back on. "Outside."

It was a child, his mind taunted. You know it was a child.

Jamie went upstairs, not to find the cause of the upsetting cry, but to wake Sam up so he didn't feel so alone. He turned on every light he passed, though it didn't help.

He knocked on the door when he reached Sam's bedroom. "Sam, you awake, mate?" He didn't wait very long for a reply. He pushed the door open and walked inside.

Sam's mattress was immaculate but for a small indentation on the blanket where it looked like someone had recently been sitting. On the floor was the MSII control pad at the end of its fully stretched cable. Jamie followed the cable up to the console, which was resting on the floor beneath the flat screen. When he looked at the flat screen, what Jamie saw was so incongruous that at first all he could do was stare.

Eventually he walked over to the television. A triangular shape was jutting from the center of the otherwise black screen. When Jamie pulled at it, the whole television threatened to topple forward. It was stuck there, as if the glass had set around the protruding object.

He saw Sam then, huddled in the corner by the cupboard, clutching his knees. His wide eyes were fixed on the dead television. "I didn't think he could come through," Sam said, his voice riding the juddering of his chest. "I thought I could help—Jamie—but he was too hungry. I didn't think he could come through, though. I don't, I don't . . ." His words ended in a series of deep breaths.

Jamie looked back at the thing poking out from the television like a paper shark's fin. The object had no meaning to Jamie in that moment, although it would mean something to him later. It was the corner of a thin children's book. He couldn't see all the words on the cover, because some were clearly on the part of the book that resided on the other side of the glass, inside the television, perhaps. But it didn't take a great leap of logic to work out the title from what he could see, and from the cover image of a young girl, sitting at a table sharing a cup of tea with a tiger.

S. R. Mastrantone writes and lives in Oxford in the UK. His short fiction has won the Fiction Desk Writer's Award and been featured internationally in venues such as *Shock Totem*, *LampLight*, and *carte blanche*. He is currently working on his first novel. His favorite games are *Castle of Illusion Starring Mickey Mouse* and all of the Oliver Twins' Dizzy games (except *Fast Food Dizzy*, give that one a miss); he is painfully aware of just how old-school he is on this matter. You can find him at www.srmastrantone .com and @srmastrantone.

RAT CATCHER'S YELLOWS

Charlie Jane Anders

1.

The plastic cat head is wearing an elaborate puffy crown covered with bling. The cat's mouth opens to reveal a touch screen, but there's also a jack to plug in an elaborate mask that gives you a visor, along with nose plugs and earbuds for added sensory input. Holding this self-contained game system in my palms, I hate it and want to throw it out the open window of our beautiful faux-Colonial row house to be buried under the autumn mulch. But I also feel a surge of hope: that maybe this really will make a difference. The cat is winking up at me.

Shary crouches in her favorite chair, the straight-backed Regency made of red-stained wood and lumpy blue upholstery. She's wearing jeans and a stained sweatshirt, one leg tucked under the other, and there's a kinetic promise in her taut leg that I know to be a lie. She looks as if she's about to spring out of that chair and ask me about the device in my hands, talking a mile a minute the way she used to. But she doesn't even notice my brand-new purchase, and it's a crap-shoot whether she even knows who I am today.

I poke the royal cat's tongue, and it gives a yawp through its tiny speakers, then the screen lights up and asks for our Wi-Fi password. I give the cat what it wants, then it starts updating and loading various firmware things. A picture of a fairy-tale castle appears with the game's title in a stylized wordmark above it: THE DIVINE RIGHT OF CATS. And then begins the hard work of customizing absolutely everything, which I want to do myself before I hand the thing off to Shary.

The whole time I'm inputting Shary's name and other info, I feel like a backstabbing bitch. Giving this childish game to my life partner, it's like I'm declaring that she's lost the right to be considered an adult. No matter that all the hip teens and twentysomethings are playing *Divine Right of Cats* right now. Or that everybody agrees this game is the absolute best thing for helping dementia patients hold on to some level of cognition, and that it's especially good for people suffering from leptospirosis X, in particular. I'm doing this for Shary's good, because I believe she's still in there somewhere.

I make Shary's character as close to Shary as I can possibly make a cat wizard who is the main adviser to the throne of the cat kingdom. (I decide that if Shary was a cat, she'd be an Abyssinian, because she's got that sandy-brown-haired sleekness, pointy face, and wiry energy.) Shary's monarch is a queen, not a king—a proud tortoiseshell cat named Arabella IV. I get some input into the realm's makeup, including what the nobles on the Queen's Council are like, but some stuff is decided at random—like, Arabella's realm of Greater Felinia has a huge stretch of vineyards and some copper mines, neither of which I would have come up with.

Every detail I enter into the game, I pack with relationship shout-outs and little details that only Shary would recognize, so the whole thing turns into a kind of bizarre love letter. For example, the tavern near the royal stables is the Puzzler's Retreat, which was the gray-walled dyke bar where Shary and I used to go dancing when we were both in grad school. The royal guards are Grace's Army of Stompification. And so on.

"Shary?" I say. She doesn't respond.

Before it mutated and started eating people's brain stems, before it became antibiotic-resistant, the disease afflicting Shary used to be known as Rat Catcher's Yellows. It mostly affected animals, and in rare cases, humans. It's a close cousin of syphilis and Lyme, one that few people had even heard of ten years ago. In some people, it causes liver failure and agonizing joint pain, but Shary is one of the "lucky" ones who only have severe neurological problems, plus intermittent fatigue. She's only thirty-five years old.

"Shary?" I hold the cat head out to her, because it's ready to start accepting her commands now that all the tricky setup is over with. Queen Arabella has a lot of issues that require her Royal Wizard's input. Already some of the other noble cats are plotting against the throne—especially those treacherous tuxedo cats!—and the vintners are threatening to go on strike. I put the cat head right in front of Shary's face and she shrugs.

Then she looks up, all at once lucid. "Grace? What the fuck is this shit? This looks like it's for a five-year-old."

"It's a game," I stammer. "It's supposed to be good for people with your . . . It's fun. You'll like it."

"What the fucking fuck?"

She throws it across the room. Lucidity is often accompanied by hostility, which is the kind of trade-off you start to accept at a certain point. I go and fetch it without a word. Luckily, the cat head was designed to be very durable.

"I thought we could do it together." I play the guilt card back at her. "I thought maybe this could be something we could actually share. You and me. Together. You know? Like a real couple."

"Okay, fine." She takes the cat head from me and squints at Queen Arabella's questions about the trade crisis with the neighboring duchy of meerkats. Queen Arabella asks what she should do, and Shary painstakingly types out, "Why don't you go fuck yourself." But she erases it without hitting send, and then instead picks SEND AN EMISSARY from among the options already on the screen. Soon, Shary is sending trade representatives and labor negotiators to the four corners of Greater Felinia, and beyond.

2.

After a few days, Shary stops complaining about how stupid *Divine Right of Cats* is and starts spending every moment poking at the plastic cat's face in her lap. I get her the optional add-on mask, which is (not surprisingly) the upper three-quarters of a cat face, and plug it in for her, then show her how to insert the nose plugs and earbuds.

Within a week after she first starts playing, Shary's realm is already starting to crawl up the list of the one thousand most successful kingdoms—that is, she's already doing a better job of helping to run the realm of Felinia than the vast majority of people who are playing this game anywhere, according to god knows what metrics.

But more than that, Shary is forming *relationships* with these cats in their puffy-sleeve court outfits and lacy ruffs. In the real world, she can't remember where she lives, what year it is, who the President is, or how long she and I have been married. But she sits in her blue chair and mutters at the screen, "No you don't, Lord Hairballington. You try that shit, I will cut your fucking tail off."

She probably doesn't remember from day to day what's happened in the game, but that's why she's the adviser rather than the monarch—she just has to react, and the game remembers everything for her. Yet she fixates on weird details, and I've started hearing her talking in her sleep, in the middle of the night, about those fucking copper miners and how they better not try any shit because *anybody* can be replaced.

One morning, I wake up and cold is leaking into the bed from where Shary pulled the covers back without bothering to tuck me back in. I walk out into the front room and don't see her at first, and worry she's just wandered off into the street by herself, which has been my nightmare for months now and the reason I got her RFID'd. But no, she's in the kitchen, shoving a toaster waffle in her mouth in between poking the cat face and cursing at Count Meesh, whom I named after the friend who introduced Shary and me in the first place. Apparently Count Meesh—a big fluffy Siberian cat—is hatching some schemes and needs to be taught a lesson.

After that, I start getting used to waking up alone. And going to bed alone. As long as Shary sleeps at least six hours a night—which she does—I figure it's probably okay. Her neurologist, Dr. Takamori, was the one who recommended the game in the first place, and she tells me it's healthy for Shary to be focused on something.

I should be happy this has *worked* as well as it has. Shary has that look on her face—what I can see of her face, under the cat mask—that I used to love seeing when she was writing her diss. The lip-chewing, the half smile, when she was outsmarting the best minds in Melville studies. So what if Shary's main relationship is with these digital cats, instead of me? She's relating to *something*; she's not just staring into space all day anymore.

I always thought she and I would take care of each other forever. I feel like a selfish idiot for even feeling jealous of a stupid plastic cat face, with quivering antennae for whiskers.

One day, after Shary has already been playing *Divine Right of Cats* for four or five hours, she looks up and points at me. "You," she says. "You there. Bring me tea."

"My name is Grace," I say. "I'm your wife."

"Whatever. Just bring me tea." Her face is unreadable, half terrifying cat smile, half frowning human mouth. "I'm busy. There's a crisis. We built a railroad, they broke it. Everything's going to shit." Then Shary looks down again at the cat screen, poking and cursing.

I bring her tea, with a little honey, the way she used to like it. She actually thanks me, but doesn't look up.

3.

Shary gets an email. She gave me her email password around the same time I got Power of Attorney, and I promised to field any questions and consult her as much as I could. For a while, the emails were coming every day, from her former students and colleagues, and I would answer them to the best of my ability. Now it's been weeks since the last email that wasn't spam.

This one is from the Divine Righters, a group of *Divine Right of Cats* enthusiasts. They've noticed that Shary's realm is one of the most successful, and they want to invite Shary to some kind of tournament or convention . . . or something. It's really not clear. Some kind of event where people will bring their kingdoms and queendoms together and form alliances or go to war. The little plastic cat heads will interface somehow, in proximity to each other, instead of being more or less self-contained.

The plastic cat head already came with some kind of multiplayer mode, where you could connect via the Internet, but I disabled it because the whole reason we were doing this was Shary's inability to communicate with other humans.

I delete the email without bothering to respond to it, but another email appears the next day. And they start coming every few hours, with subject lines like "Shary Please Join Us" and "Shary, we can't do it without you." I don't know whether to be pissed off or freaked out that someone is cyber-stalking my wife.

Then my phone rings. Mine, not hers. "Is this Grace?" a man asks.

"Who is this?" I say without answering his question first.

"My name is George Henderson. I'm from the Divine Righters. I'm really sorry to take up your time today, but we have been trying to reach your partner, Shary, on email and she hasn't answered, and we really want to get her to come to our convention."

"I'm afraid that won't be possible. Please leave us alone."

"This tournament has sponsorship from"—he names a bunch of companies I've never heard of—"and there are prizes. Plus, this is a chance to interface with other people who love the game as much as she obviously does."

I take a deep breath. Time to just come clean and end this pointless fucking conversation. We're standing in the kitchen, within earshot of where Shary is sitting on a duct-taped bean-bag with her cat mask and her cat-face device, but she shows no sign of hearing me. I realize Shary is naked from the waist down and the windows are uncovered and the neighbors could easily see, and this is my fault.

"My wife can't go to your event," I say. "She is in no condition to 'interface' with anybody."

"We have facilities," says George. "And trained staff. We can handle—" Like he was expecting this to be the case. His voice is intended to sound reassuring, but it squicks me instead.

"Where the fuck do you get off harassing a sick woman?" I blurt into the phone, loudly enough that Shary looks up for a moment and regards me with her impassive cat eyes.

"Your wife isn't sick," George Henderson says. "She's . . . she's amazing. Could a sick person create one of the top one hundred kingdoms in the entire world? Could a sick woman get past the Great Temptation without breaking a sweat? Grace, your wife is just . . . just amazing."

The Great Temptation is what they call it when the nobles come to you, the Royal Wizard, and offer to support you in overthrowing the monarch. Because you've done such a good job of advising the monarch on running Greater Felinia, you might as well sit on the throne yourself instead of that weak figurehead. This moment comes at different times for differ-ent players, and there's no right or wrong answer—you can continue to ace the game whether you sit on the throne or not, depending on other circumstances. But how you handle this moment is a huge test of your steadiness. Shary chose not to take the throne, but managed to make those scheming nobles feel good about her decision.

Neither George nor I have said anything for a minute or so. I'm staring at my wife, whom nobody has called "amazing" in a long time. She's sitting there wearing a tank top and absolutely nothing else, and her legs twitch in a way that makes the whole thing even more obscene. Her tank top has a panoply of stains on it. I realize it's been a week since Shary has gotten my name right.

"Your wife is an intuitive genius," George says in my ear after the pause gets too agonizing on his end. "She makes connections that nobody else could make. She's utterly focused, and processing the game at a much deeper level than a normal brain ever could. It's not like Shary will be the only sufferer from Rat Catcher's Yellows at this convention, you know. There will be lots of others."

I cannot take this. I blurt something, whatever, and hang up on George Henderson. I brace myself for him to call back, but he doesn't. So I go find my wife some pants.

4.

Shary hasn't spoken aloud in a couple of weeks now, not even anything about her game. She has less control over her bodily functions and is having "accidents" more often. I'm making her wear diapers. But her realm is massive, thriving; it's annexed the neighboring duchies.

When I look over her shoulder, the little cats in their

Renaissance Europe outfits are no longer asking her simple questions about how to tax the copper mine—instead, they're saying things like, "But if the fundamental basis of governance is derived from external symbols of legitimacy, what gives those symbols their power in the first place?"

She doesn't tap on the screen at all, but still her answer appears somehow, as if through the power of her eyeblinks: "This is why we go on quests."

According to one of the readouts I see whisk by, Shary has forty-seven knights and assorted nobles out on quests right now, searching for various magical and religious objects as well as for rare minerals—and also, for a possible passage to the West that would allow her trading vessels to avoid sailing past the Isle of Dogs.

She just hunches in her chair, frowning with her mouth, while the big cat eyes and tiny nose look playful or fierce depending on how the light hits them. I've started thinking of this as her face.

I drag her away from her chair and make her take a bath, because it's been a few days, and while she's in there (she can still bathe herself, thank goodness) I examine the cat mask. I realize that I have no idea what is coming out of these nose plugs, even though I've had to refill the little reservoirs on the sides a couple of times from the bottles they sent. Neurotransmitters? Pheromones? Stimulants, that keep her concentrating? I really have no clue. The chemicals don't smell of anything much.

I open my tablet and search for "divine right of cats," plus words like "sentience," "becoming self-aware," or "artificial intelligence." Soon I'm reading message boards in which people geek out about the idea that these cats are just too frickin' smart for their own good and that they seem to be drawing something from the people they're interfacing with. The digital cats are learning a lot, in particular, about politics, and about how human societies function.

On top of which, I find a slew of economics papers—because the cats have been solving problems, inside the various iterations of Greater Felinia, that economists have struggled with in the real world. Issues of scarcity and resource allocation, questions of how to make markets more frictionless. Things I barely grasp the intricacies of, with my doctorate in Art History.

And all of the really mind-blowing breakthroughs in economics have come from cat kingdoms that were being managed by people afflicted with Rat Catcher's Yellows.

I guess I shouldn't be surprised that Shary is a prodigy; she was always the brilliant one of the two of us. Her nervous energy, her ability to get angry at dead scholars at three in the morning, the random scattering of note cards and papers all over the floor of our tiny grad-student apartment—as if the floor were an extension of her overcharged brain.

It's been more than a week since she's spoken my name, and meanwhile my emergency sabbatical is running out. And I can't really afford to blow off teaching, since I'm not tenure-track or anything. I'll have to hire someone to look after Shary, or get her into day care or a group home. She won't know the difference between me or someone else looking after her at this point, anyway.

A couple of days after my conversation with George Henderson, I look over Shary's shoulder, and things jump out at me. All the relationship touchstones that I embedded in the game when I customized it for her are still in there, but they've gotten weirdly emphasized by her gameplay, like her cats spend an inordinate amount of time at the Puzzler's Retreat. But also, she's added new stuff. Moments I had forgotten are coming up as geological features of her Greater Felinia, hillocks, and cliffs.

Shary is reliving all of the time we spent together, through the prism of these cats and their stupid politics. The time we rode bikes across Europe. The time we took up Lindy-hopping and I broke my ankle. The time I cheated on Shary, and thought I got away with it, until now. The necklace she never told me she wanted, that I tracked down for her. It's all in there, woven throughout this game.

I call George Henderson back. "Okay, fine," I say, without saying hello first. "We'll go to your convention, tournament, whatever. Just tell us where and when."

5.

I sort of expected that a lot of people at the "convention" would have RCY after the way George Henderson talked about the disease. But in fact it seems as though *every* player here has it. Either because you can't become a power player of *Divine Right* without the unique mind state of people with Rat Catcher's, or because that's whom they were able to strong-arm into signing up.

"Here" is a tiny convention hotel in Orlando, Florida, with fuzzy bulletin boards that mention recent meetings of insurance adjusters and auto parts distributors. We're a few miles from Disney World, but near us is nothing but strip malls and strip clubs, and one sad-looking Arby's. We get served Continental breakfast, clammy individually wrapped sandwiches, and steamer trays full of Stroganoff every day.

The first day, we all mill around for an hour, with me trying to stick close to Shary on her first trip out of New Hampshire in ages. But then George Henderson (a chunky white guy with graying curly hair and an 8-bit T-shirt) stands up at the front of the ballroom and announces that all the players are going into the adjoining ballroom, and the "friends and loved ones" will stay in here. We can see our partners and friends through an opening in the temporary wall bisecting the hotel ballroom, but they're in their own world, sitting at long rows of tables with their cat faces on.

Those of us left in the "friends and family" room are all sorts of people, but the one thing uniting us is a pall of weariness. At least half the spouses or friends immediately announce they're going out shopping or to Disney World. The other half mostly just sit there, watching their loved ones play, as if they're worried someone's going to get kidnapped.

This half of the ballroom has a sickly sweet milk smell clinging to the ornate cheap carpet and the vinyl walls. I get used to it, and then it hits me again whenever I've just stepped outside or gone to the bathroom.

After an hour, I risk wandering over to the "players" room and look over Shary's shoulder. Queen Arabella is furiously negotiating trade agreements and sending threats of force to the other cat kingdoms that have become her neighbors.

Because all of the realms in this game are called "Greater Felinia" by default, Shary needed to come up with a new name for Arabella's country. She's renamed it "Graceland." I stare at the name, then at Shary, who shows no sign of being aware of my presence.

"I will defend the territorial integrity of Graceland to the last cat," Shary writes.

Judy is a young graphic designer from Toronto, with a long black braid and an eager, narrow face. She's sitting alone in the "friends and loved ones" room, until I ask if I can sit at her little table. Turns out Judy is here with her boyfriend of two years, Stefan, who got infected with Rat Catcher's Yellows when they'd only been together a year. Stefan is a superstar in the Divine Right community.

"I have this theory that it's all one compound organism," says Judy. "The leptospirosis X, the people, the digital cats. Or at least, it's one system. Sort of like real-life cats that infect their owners with *Toxoplasma gondii*, which turns the owners into bigger cat lovers."

"Huh." I stare out through the gap in the ballroom wall, at the rows of people in cat masks all tapping away on their separate devices, like a soft rain. All genders, all ages, all sizes, wearing tracksuits or business-casual white-collar outfits. The masks bob up and down, almost in unison. Unblinking and wide-eyed, governing machines.

At first, Judy and I just bond over our stories of taking care of someone who barely recognizes us but keeps obsessively nation building at all hours. But we turn out to have a lot else in common, including an interest in Pre-Raphaelite art, and a lot of the same books.

The third day rolls around, and our flight back up to New Hampshire is that afternoon. I watch Shary hunched over her cat head, with Judy's boyfriend sitting a few seats away, and my heart begins to sink. I imagine bundling Shary out of here, getting her to the airport and onto the plane, and then unpacking her stuff back at the house while she goes right back to her game. Days and days of cat-faced blankness ahead, forever.

This trip has been some kind of turning point for Shary and the others, but for me nothing will have changed.

I'm starting to feel sorry for myself with a whole new intensity when Judy pokes me. "Hey." I look up. "We need to stay in touch, you know," Judy says.

I make a big show of adding her number to my phone, and then without even thinking, say: "Do you want to come stay with us? We have a whole spare bedroom with its own bathroom and stuff."

Judy doesn't say anything for a few moments. She stares at her boyfriend, who's sitting a few seats away from Shary. She's taking slow, controlled breaths through closed teeth. Then she slumps a little, in an abortive shrug. "Yes. Yes, please. That would be great. Thank you."

I sit with Judy and watch dozens of people in cat masks, sitting shoulder to shoulder without looking at each other. I have a pang of wishing I could just go live in Graceland, a place of which I am already a vassal in every way that matters. But also I feel weirdly proud, and terrified out of my mind. I have no choice but to believe this game matters, the cat politics is important, keeping Lord Hairballington in his place is a vital concern to everyone—or else I will just go straight-up insane.

For a moment, I think Shary looks up from the cat head in her hands and gives me a wicked smile of recognition behind her opaque plastic gaze. I feel so much love in that moment, it's almost unbearable.

━━━━━━━━

Charlie Jane Anders's novel *All the Birds in the Sky* is forthcoming in early 2016 from Tor Books. Her story "Six Months, Three Days" won a Hugo Award and was shortlisted for the Nebula and Theodore Sturgeon Awards. Her writing has appeared in *Mother Jones*, *Asimov's Science Fiction*, *Lightspeed*, Tor.com, *Tin House*, ZYZZYVA, *The McSweeney's Joke Book of Book Jokes*, *The End is Nigh*, and elsewhere. She is the editor of io9.com and runs the long-running Writers With Drinks reading series in San Francisco. More info at www.charliejane.net.

1UP

Holly Black

When people die in games, you just press a couple of buttons and bring them back to life. You reset. That's how games work. Restore from your last save point. Restore from the beginning. Start over.

Your people are never just gone.

That's what I think as I look at the photograph of Soren resting on top of a coffin. His family is Jewish—well, other than his stepmother—so they don't have open-casket funerals. I've never been to a closed-casket one before. I'm used to seeing the waxy faces of my dead relatives, made up with red lips and red cheeks, like they're waiting for true love's kiss to wake them. According to my phone, Jewish law prohibits embalming or removing any organs or doing anything but wrapping him in a shroud and putting him in the ground. That's why we aren't allowed to see him, I guess. He'd look too dead.

I can't help being sad, though. We've never met in person. And now I guess we never will.

In games, we know we're not supposed to give up, not until we've won out against the big boss and the credits start rolling. We know that if we don't give up, we'll win. There's always a solution. There's always a way. That's why games are great and this sucks.

Even as I listen to the rabbi talk, even as I watch Soren's grandmother dab her rheumy eyes with Kleenex, even as I hear everyone say his nickname—Sorry, Sorry, Sorry—over and over, I can't help trying to figure out how to *fix this*.

Just last week, he sent me a message: YOU HAVE TO COME FOR THE FUNERAL. PROMISE ME. It was the first message I'd gotten from him in more than two weeks. Still, I messaged back that there wouldn't be any funeral, that he was going to get better and we were going to meet up at PAX East in the winter like we'd all planned. But then there was the death notice. That's why me and Decker and Toad met up in Jersey and made the drive down to Florida together.

We'd never even met Soren in person, be we were still his three best friends in the whole world. Even if no one from his real life knows us.

Black ribbons get torn and pinned onto mourners. After they lower the casket into the ground, dirt gets tossed, and we go over to his house to visit his family while they sit shiva.

It's mostly old people. A graying great-uncle with bristling nose hairs. A hysterically weeping second cousin. Aunts who run the coffeemaker and take the plastic off trays of cold cuts. Uncles who smoke outside with a girl who tells us she's Sorry's cousin, back from art school for the funeral. No one else talks to us.

Sorry's stepmother sits in the center of a sofa, her shoulders rigid as relatives comfort her, tell her what a wonderful nurse she was to Sorry those last months, when things went from bad to worse, talk about her inner core of strength. Someone has given her coffee in a paper cup. I wonder if it's hot. I wonder if the coffee is burning her hand and she hasn't even noticed yet.

Sorry's father sits alone in a corner, looking at his phone. He's wearing a black pin-striped suit with a paisley tie that looks more appropriate for a business meeting than burying a kid.

We obviously didn't know what to wear either. Decker dressed in a too-small black blazer over black jeans and a black T-shirt. He looks like he's going to a concert.

Toad is about what I expected from his avatars and message-board signature. Big and shy, with a small, untrimmed goatee that extends to his neck. Wears the same thing every day—jeans, funny/ironic nerd shirt, and a flannel open over it. It doesn't even occur to me he might change for the funeral, and he doesn't.

I'm in a black shirtdress that my mother lent me. It's boring, which is apparently the point. I have on panty hose too—medium brown, to match my legs—and my big clunky black boots. Mom told me I couldn't wear boots to a funeral, but I left the pumps she loaned me in the trunk of Decker's car. Maybe I shouldn't have.

None of us fit in at Sorry's place. I can't imagine Sorry fitting in here either—not the Sorry that we knew. Of course, he was sick for so long that maybe it didn't matter.

Three years, stuck in his bedroom, too ill to go to high school or do anything teenagers are supposed to do but play games and hang out online.

Me and Decker and Toad drift toward that bedroom, not sure what else to do. We've never been there before, but we know it instantly by his posters of *Resident Evil*, *Arkham City*, *Left 4 Dead*, and *Warcraft*. We talk in hushed voices about how weird it is to be in his room for the first time.

"Maybe we shouldn't have come," Toad says.

I sit down on his bed. "I know what you mean."

Decker flops on the plush-carpet-covered floor and rests his head against a plush alien chestburster.

I can't quite put my finger on what I think of Decker now that we've met in person. He's some bizarre combination of cute and pretentious. He has a put-on British accent and insisted we navigate our way here with real maps, instead of just using the navigation on our cell phones. We got lost twice, until finally Toad turned off the sound on his phone and pretended not to be looking at it.

I wonder if Decker notices that I'm a girl. I wonder if he likes girls. Before Sorry died, we would sometimes send each other flirty messages, so maybe it's not okay that I wonder that.

Maybe it's not okay that we're going to have a long drive back and we're going to argue about which Marvel movie they should make next and stop for junk food and fast food and we're going to be sad about Soren, but happy that we went on a road trip together.

My mom insists that my friendships online aren't real. She says that until you meet someone in person, you don't *really* know them. I don't agree, but I think that belief is part of the reason she let me come on a three-day road trip with two boys. I'm supposed to call her every night at seven and text her three times a day, plus she spoke with Decker's and Toad's mothers before she agreed to let me come; I think she believes this is my one shot at having IRL friends before college.

Sitting there, I wonder how I am supposed to feel. I cried when I first heard Sorry was dead, but I haven't cried since. My eyes were dry when they lowered the coffin into the ground, even though I told Sorry things I never told anyone, things that I don't know if I will tell anyone ever again.

It just doesn't seem real that he's gone.

It's hard to cry when my brain still can't accept the truth.

After a while, Toad turns on Sorry's computer. "Lot of parental controls on this thing. And it's not connecting to the Internet."

"That sucks," I say. I wonder if there's something wrong with it. I wonder if that's why he didn't message us more or come online to game these last few weeks. I thought it was because he was tired from being sick, but the idea that we couldn't be there for him—that *I* couldn't be there for him near the end of his life—because of a stupid broken cable modem makes me want to punch something.

Across from me a corner of one poster has peeled back, rolling up. I wonder if Sorry's dad is going to box all this stuff up and put it in the attic. I wonder if his dad is going to box all this stuff up and just throw it out.

Toad opens a few more things and types a little. "Weird," he says, frowning at the screen.

"What?" demands Decker from the floor.

"I don't know," says Toad, rubbing his head. "Look."

He's opened up a game on Sorry's computer. It's an interactive fiction game—what people used to call text games, like *Zork*—but not one I've ever seen before. But no matter what it is, Toad shouldn't be messing around on his computer, opening his files and stuff.

"What are you doing?" I ask.

"I was trying to find his password for *Diamond Knights*," Toad says without missing a beat.

"You were going to make him donate his whole inventory

to one of your characters, weren't you?" Decker says. "Asshole. We're at his fucking funeral."

"I'm an asshole," says Toad. "This is known. But I didn't find his passwords, did I? I found this, right on the desktop. Look."

We crowd around the computer, peering at the screen.

"THE LAZARUS GAME"
by Soren Carp

```
You are sad.
>|
```

"He wrote a game?" Decker says. "Did any of you guys know he wrote a game?"

Toad shakes his head. "I didn't even know he liked this kind of thing."

Neither did I. Interactive fiction games aren't all that impressive to look at. They're just blocks of text with a blinking cursor after, waiting for you to make the right choice—the clever command—that will unlock the rest of the story. They used to be made and sold by big companies, but they don't make enough money for that anymore. Now they're pretty much just made by the people who love them.

"Look around," I say. "Type in 'L' for 'look.'"

He does.

```
You are wearing black, standing in a kid's bedroom. There are
nerdy posters on the walls and nerdy stuff all around you. One
of the posters is curled up at one corner and you think you might
be able to see writing on the other side.
>|
```

The poster I was looking at just a moment before.

I slide off the bed while the other two are still staring at the screen. I gently pull the poster free of the blue sticky stuff adhering it at three out of four points. Then I turn it over.

The back has been written on in Sharpie.

YOU HAVE FIVE HOURS TO WIN.

THE CLOCK STARTED WHEN I WENT IN THE GROUND.

GRAB THE FLASH DRIVE AND GO.

GO NOW BEFORE SHE FINDS YOU.

My heart starts hammering in my chest. Decker starts to roll up the poster.

"What are you doing?" Toad says. "They'll notice it's gone."

"So what?" Decker keeps rolling, crinkling the poster in his haste. "So they think we're poster thieves."

"Where's the flash drive?" I demand. "We need to find the flash drive."

"No, wait, this doesn't make sense." Toad looks around the room, like he's wondering if there's going to be some kind of hidden camera.

I go over to the desk, ignoring Toad. Loose change, breath mints, paperbacks, nerdy toys (including a figurine I sent him of a brown-skinned manga girl I wanted him to think looked like me), and a Hot Wheels car that had clearly been modified so that a USB connection stuck out of its rear bumper.

"Got it," I say, picking up the car.

"Wait," Toad says, and I pause. "Shouldn't we check what's on it first?"

"Don't worry about that," Decker says. He tries to push open the window—I guess so we can slip out in the most criminal way possible—but it doesn't budge. Toad turns off the computer.

I shove the flash drive in the pocket of my dress. As I am shutting the desk drawer, the door to the room opens.

Sorry's stepmother is standing in the hall, a startled smile pulling at her face. "What are you three doing in here?" she asks.

"We just—" I start, but I don't know what to say. This is the exact kind of situation that I'm bad at. This is why I started staying inside and talking to people over the Internet in the first place. My tongue feels heavy in my mouth. I want to crawl deep in my clothes, curl up, and hide.

Her gaze goes to the wall where there isn't a poster anymore, and then to the drawer she saw me close. Her expression sharpens and she stops smiling. "Who are you?"

"We're Soren's friends," Decker says.

"None of you ever visited here before." After a moment of silence, she steps back from the doorway and continues in her brusque voice. "I am going to ask you to leave. Now. We're all very upset, and whatever you're doing—we don't have time for it. Be glad I don't have the energy to pursue this further."

"Sorry," Toad says, sliding past her into the hall, head down. I follow him, unable to do anything else. I feel shamed, even though I know we weren't doing anything wrong. Sorry made us promise to come. Sorry left us the flash drive. He wrote a message just for us: *go now before she finds you.*

Out in the hall, I feel like a coward.

Decker is standing in the middle of the room, staring at Sorry's stepmother, eyes blazing. He looks like he's trying to swallow words before they crawl out of his mouth.

"Come on," I say.

Finally Decker makes a motion like he's zipping his lips closed and swings toward us. I keep glancing back to make sure he stays with us, and as I do my gaze falls on something I didn't notice before. There's a lock on Sorry's door—a brass dead latch—on the wrong side. The side that would have locked Sorry in.

My head starts to pound and I can feel the sweat under my armpits. As I walk out the door, my gaze sweeps over the black-clad people in the living room.

It occurs to me that maybe Sorry was sure he was going to die because he thought that someone was about to murder him.

We get back in Decker's car—a beat-up Impala with inside upholstery held together mostly with duct tape. We don't speak. Decker starts the engine and drives in what appears to be a random direction.

Finally, after long minutes of silence, Toad says, "I'm sorry. I freaked out."

Decker says, "I wanted to punch that bitch in the face."

And I say, "We need to see whatever is on that flash drive."

A few minutes later, Toad and I are on our smartphones, trying to find a place with Internet that also serves food. There's not a lot of choices, but there's always Starbucks. We head to the nearest one. This time Decker doesn't say anything about us navigating with our phones.

We all have laptops, but there's only one free outlet, so I pull out my MacBook Pro, and Decker and Toad crowd around. My laptop is covered in stickers; just the familiar sight of them makes me feel better. I flip open the case, type in my password, and shove the flash drive into the USB.

The game starts up again.

Words appear on the screen of my computer.

```
You are sad.
>|
```

I type in "L" again.

```
You are wearing black, standing in a kid's bedroom. There are
nerdy posters on the walls and nerdy stuff all around you. One
of the posters is curled up at one corner and you think you might
be able to see text on the other side.
>|
```

I try something else this time. *Why am I sad?* I type.

```
Some guy you know from the Internet is dead.
>|
```

I raise my eyebrows and look at Toad and Decker. Sorry had clearly intended for us to find this, just the way we did, but why? *X poster*, I type, "X" being standard shorthand for examine.

```
The back of the poster looks like a crazy person has written on
it. It seems to indicate that you have a deadline to complete
this game. I guess you'd better hurry.
>|
```

Decker raises his eyebrows. "I don't like this. I don't like anything about this."

"What do I do next?" I ask them.

"Take the flash drive from his desk," says Toad. "I mean, that's what we really did, right?"

"Right," I say, my fingers on the keys.

```
You've already taken it or you wouldn't be playing this.
>|
```

"I don't think there's anything else here. Exit the room," Decker says, blowing out a frustrated breath.

Toad stands up, heading toward the counter. "I need cake for this," he says. "And caffeine."

"Good idea," says Decker, reaching into his pocket for wadded up cash. "Get me a latte. And get Cat . . . What do you want, Cat?"

"Cappuccino with a lot of extra shots," I say, and start typing to exit the room in the game.

```
You are in the living room. More sad people wearing black. One
of them isn't as sad as she seems, however.
>|
```

Talk to Sorry's stepmother, I type without anyone needing to suggest it.

```
What would you like to ask her? Type the number to ask the ques-
tion or type "X" to say nothing.
1. Do you still have your MasterCard?
2. How come you tried to murder your stepson?
3. How come Sorry's father is never home anymore?
4. Did something happen three weeks ago?
5. Are you a diabetic?
>|
```

I turn the computer so Decker can see the screen. Toad comes back with our order. His pink-and-white piece of cake is enormous.

"Uh, two, obviously," Toad says, taking a big bite of it.

Sorry's stepmother looks at you like you're a worm stranded in
a puddle after rain.

"That's ridiculous," she says. "Surely if I did that, there
would be proof. Surely someone would have noticed. Just because
he got sick a few months after I married Aaron and then got
progressively sicker until he died, just because I was in sole
control of his care, just because I love the attention I get
when he's unwell, just because I locked him in his room and
disconnected his cable modem three weeks before he died, none
of that means anything."
>|

"Do you think that's what his game is? The proof?" Decker
says between swigs of latte. "Are we supposed to take his game
to the police?"

"Then why would we need to play quickly?" I shake my
head.

"Maybe his stepmother's going to destroy evidence,"
Toad replies. "Maybe the game is going to tell us how to
stop her."

"Then why doesn't it?" I ask, frustrated and sick to my
stomach. All those times we chatted while playing and he
never said a thing—not *one single thing* about what was going
on. "Why not just spell it out? Why all of this?"

"I think he made the game for us," Decker says. "His
stepmother wouldn't understand it, but we would. I don't
think there is any proof. I think he just wanted somebody to
know."

The idea of that being true is awful. "Why not tell us in
chat?"

Decker shrugs.

"Remember what I said about the parental controls?" Toad said. "I bet she was tracking what he said."

I type, *Talk to Sorry's stepmother*, again. I pick number three.

```
Sorry's stepmother gives you a kindly smile.
    "You have to understand how hard it is to have a sick son
and not be able to do anything to help him. I think he thought
it was easier to concentrate on his work."
>|
```

No real information there.

I go through the options again and ask about the diabetes.

```
Sorry's stepmother looks surprised.
    "Is this about all the insulin I ordered from Canada? That
was for my cat! What cat? Oh, she's around here somewhere."
>|
```

Disturbing.

My next question is about what happened three weeks ago, although I am not sure I can bear knowing.

```
Sorry's stepmother actually looks troubled.
    "You should have seen the expression on his face when I came
into the hospital room. He'd been feeling better that day and I
guess he'd seen me inject something into the bag attached to his
drip. It was just vitamins, but I think he—well, never mind. I
was bringing him green Jell-O. He looked at me and it was like
he was seeing me for the first time."
>|
```

I go through the options one more time and choose the only one left, the question about her credit card.

```
Sorry's stepmother looks surprised.
    "Do you know something about those fraudulent charges? I swear
I never ordered tetrodotoxin. I don't even know what that is."
>|
```

"What's with the tetro-whatever?" Decker eats a piece of the strawberry cake Toad procured and takes another sip of his latte. "Is that what she killed him with?"

I open up my browser, log in to the Internet, and search for "tetrodotoxin." I frown at the screen. "It's some kind of toad neurotoxin. Poisonous."

"But what about the insulin?" Toad asks. "I don't get this. Which one did she use? Does he not know? Are we supposed to figure it out, like in a murder mystery? Doesn't Sorry remember how dumb we are? He's got to just spell shit out."

"Yeah," I say, barely paying attention. Typing words in the game is enough like chatting to Sorry online that it allows me to—almost—pretend he's not dead. And yet, the whole game is a reminder that he is.

The Lazarus Game. I guess this is Sorry's way of rising from the grave to name his murderer.

Find proof, I type in, but the game doesn't seem to know what I am looking for.

Go to dining room, I type in. It still doesn't know what I am looking for.

Go to kitchen, I type. Still, nothing.

Go to funeral home, I type, which seems morbid. I'm almost relieved when it doesn't work.

Exit house, I type. Finally, this time I get something else, a menu of options.

```
You are standing outside on the patchy lawn in front of Sorry's
house. Cars are parked out front, like there's a party going on
inside, although you know it's a pretty grim party. It's after-
noon and the Florida sun is beating down mercilessly. You're
starting to sweat.

Where would you like to go? Type the number to travel or type
"X" to stay where you are.
1. The Police Station
2. The Hospital
3. The Graveyard
4. The Hardware Store
>|
```

"What the hell?" I say. "The hardware store?"

Toad and Decker were discussing something in low voices, but they stop abruptly when I speak. They both lean in to look at the screen.

Toad whistles. "I can't believe you think having the option of going to the hardware store is worse than going to the graveyard."

"Uh," Decker says, blinking at the screen a few times. "Can you google that toad poison again?"

"How come?" I ask.

Instead of answering, he opens his bag and pulls out his own laptop. "Spell it?"

I do and he starts clicking. After a few minutes, his face goes blank, then an expression of horror flashes across it. I can't even fathom what he could have found. What's worse than being poisoned by your own stepmother? In fairy tales, stepmothers are wicked, jealous, untrustworthy bitches with poisoned apples, but my mom remarried six years ago, so I am pretty sure not all stepparents are like that. My stepdad drops me off at school most mornings. Some days we get coffees and donuts and sit in the parking lot eating them until the bell rings, just talking. I couldn't imagine him wanting to hurt me. But I guess Sorry's stepmother seemed nice too, until she didn't.

"I think you better look at this," Decker says, turning his computer and pointing to the screen. "Read that part."

I look where he's pointing. There were cases of people being given tetrodotoxin and seeming to die, but actually being in a state of near-death, conscious the whole time. For a while, it was even alleged that tetrodotoxin was an essential ingredient to brainwash people into thinking they were zombies.

"Now read this part," he says, and pulls up another window. It has the amount of time a person can last with the air in a coffin. Five and a half hours.

"Fuck you," I say. "He's dead. We saw him buried."

But I am thinking of the message he left for us on the back of the poster. The one with the time limit we didn't understand.

YOU HAVE FIVE HOURS TO WIN.

THE CLOCK STARTED WHEN I WENT IN THE GROUND.

And I think about the options of places to go—the police station, where we could report his stepmother (if we had proof) for making him sick; the hospital, where we could go to try to find that proof and might stumble on something else, something that would send us to the hardware store and then the graveyard.

The graveyard.

Decker snorts. "But if he faked his own death, then he'd have to seem—"

"Whoa," says Toad, interrupting him. "What? Faked his own death? Both of you need to stop communicating brain-to-brain and spell things out for me."

"No," I say, standing up and jerking my power cord out of the wall. "We need to go. We need to go now!"

We get to the graveyard just as the sun is starting to set. The sky is shimmering with gold, gleaming on our Home Depot shovels in the backseat. I feel like we're on a real adventure, the kind that people in real life don't go on. This is the kind of thing that only happens in video games, and right now, I get why. No one in real life would ever want to feel like this.

I am scared we're going to be arrested, and I am terrified of what we're going to find inside his casket. We get out. We get our brand-new shovels.

The dirt is fresh, easy to scoop. My heart is hammering.

We're awkward at first, none of us used to this kind of physical work. We're the kids who spend our free time in front of our computers. We're the kids whose moms are always going on about "needing fresh air and vitamin D." My arms hurt and I don't know how to swing the dirt away in the right rhythm. Also, it spills back in if we don't toss it far enough from the side. We smack our shovels into one another's more often than not, sometimes hard enough to sting my hand. Still, we keep going.

"What if he comes back as a zombie?" Toad asks.

I give him a look.

"It could happen! He's using some kind of zombie drug and we don't know what else is in his system. This is how outbreaks happen."

I just keep digging. Decker shakes his head.

Sweat rolls down my neck. I keep hearing the noises of cars going by in the distance and nearly jumping out of my skin. We realize that we're going to have to make the hole wider if we're going to get down there and prize open the top, which spurs a round of groans.

"Okay, well, what if he's not awake yet?" Toad asks. I realize that he's talking to talk, that it's his way of managing his nerves. It's funny, on the drive down he was quiet and I figured that was how he normally was. But robbing a graveyard turned him into a chatterbox. "Like, we know this stuff wears off, but how long does it take? And won't he look dead until then? How are we going to get him out of here if he looks dead? I don't want to touch him if he's like that."

"Let's just try not to get arrested," Decker says quietly. "I heard Florida jails are no joke."

"My mom will kill me if I get picked up by the cops for messing with a grave," I say, and Decker laughs.

For a moment, it occurs to me that this is crazy. That maybe my mother is right about friendship, because I do feel differently about Decker and Toad now that we've been together in real life. Now that we've heard the timbre of one another's laughter. Now that we've learned one another's Starbucks order and how we like our burritos at Chipotle and who can burp the loudest. Now that I learned how far they were willing to go for someone they never met. After all this, it makes me realize that we didn't know Sorry at all.

We're putting ourselves in the way of a whole lot of trouble for someone we've never met.

Then my shovel hits wood.

"Sorry?" Toad calls softly. His voice shakes.

But either Sorry can't hear us or he can't reply, because there's no sound but traffic from the nearby road and wind ruffling the thick leaves of the nearby palms.

Squatting down, we start to clear dirt so that we can open the casket itself. By now, I am one big ball of sweat and my mother's dress is caked in dirt. My stockings ripped at the knee without my even noticing.

As I move earth, I have these moments of total immersion in what I'm doing and these other moments where I am totally aware that this is a crazy thing to be doing and I must be crazy for doing it.

Then the casket is cleared and there's no way to avoid our real purpose. We're going to open up a coffin and it's possible we're going to see a corpse. In fact, as we get ready to wedge open the wood with our Home Depot crowbar, even though I know exactly why we decided to do this, it seems inconceivable to me that we're going to see anything but a corpse.

"Stay back," Toad says, hopping down into the hole, wedging the crowbar under the lid. Decker and I hover above him.

And then, with a splintering sound, the lid is off and I am seeing Soren Carp in the flesh for the first time. His eyes are closed, long black lashes sweeping his cheeks. His hair is kind of a mess and he's wrapped in linen. He looks pale, his lips tinted blue.

"He sure doesn't smell dead," Toad says.

And even though it sounds rude coming out of his mouth, it's a relief that it's true. There is no scent of rot blooming in the air.

"We've got to call 911," Decker says, looking down at Soren's face. "He poisoned himself. He could still die."

I shake my head. "We can't. If he's in a hospital, his parents would get notified."

His stepmother was his guardian, the one who'd been making all his medical decisions. We have no legal right to make any decisions and, in fact, the police would probably take us away for questioning. They might not even really listen to what we were saying until it was too late.

"We should have played the rest of the game," Toad says. "I thought it was stupid that we could go to all those places, but we probably should have figured out what he wanted us to do."

Decker hops down, going on one knee next to Sorry's body. "What do you want us to do, buddy?" he whispers.

I almost expect Sorry to get up and tell us, but he doesn't. He doesn't move at all.

Toad climbs out of the hole and indicates I should get down. "Say something to him."

"Me?" I edge over to the casket, stumbling a little. I look up. "What should I say?"

Toad clears his throat. "He liked you."

I am too surprised to know how to respond.

Toad waits for me to say something and when I don't, goes on. "I'm not sure if he ever even went out with a girl. I mean, he's fifteen and he's been sick for three years. So unless he was making it with girls at twelve, probably not."

"What's that supposed to mean?" I ask.

Toad shrugs. "I don't know. I just mean, he had good reasons for not telling you—one of those reasons being that he's got no game. But I know he liked you . . . *likes* you, so he'd be more likely to listen if you were the one talking to him."

I glance toward Decker. He looks like he wants to ask me something, but he doesn't. Instead, he climbs out of the hole too, sending a shower of dirt raining down on Soren's face.

I squat and put my hand on Sorry's arm. His skin is cold from being deep in the ground. "Hey," I say. "It's Cat. We played the game, but now it's your turn. Time to wake up."

He doesn't move.

"We're risking our asses for you," I say.

"Nice," Decker calls down. "How about saying we love him?"

"How about saying *you* love him, Cat? How about 'If you wake up, I will give you a big, fat, sloppy kiss,' " Toad says.

"Shut up," I tell him.

"Soren," Decker says. "Listen, if you wake up, *one* of us will give you a big, fat, sloppy kiss. I can't guarantee it will be Cat, but one of us will definitely do it. I am ready."

"Soren," Toad says. "Listen, how about this—if you *don't* wake up, one of us will give you a big, fat, sloppy kiss and I can guarantee it *won't* be Cat."

We can't help it, we start laughing. We laugh helplessly, the relief like the release of a leg cramp.

Then, abruptly, Soren starts to cough.

I suck in my breath so sharply that I nearly choke. Toad yelps. Decker falls backward onto his ass.

A moment later, Sorry is half sitting, turned on his side, puking his guts up. I have never been so happy to see someone vomit. I crawl over to smooth his hair out of his face. His skin feels cold and clammy and when he turns to look at me, his eyes are bright with something like fever.

"You guys are insane," he says, the words slurred, then flops down face-first in the dirt.

It turns out that I do know him, even though we've never met before in person. It turns out that he knows us too. "You're one to talk," I tell him.

And it turns out that sometimes, you really do get to start from your save point. You do get another life.

You are standing in the graveyard with your friend, who until very recently, you thought was dead. Soon the police are going to come. Soon, he's going to have to go to a hospital, even though he hates hospitals. Soon, he's going to have to explain how he did it, how he knew he was going to die and why he decided to try to trick his way out of a locked bedroom in the most gruesome way possible. Soon he is going to have to thank you, even though there is no way to ever really thank you enough. But for right now, he just stands next to you and you all look up a little, into the middle distance. The wind blows your hair back from your faces and you strike a super badass pose.

<<You win the game.>>

To play again from the beginning, press "X."

———————

Holly Black is the author of bestselling contemporary fantasy books for kids and teens. Some of her titles include the Spiderwick Chronicles (with Tony DiTerlizzi), the Modern Faerie Tale series, the Curse Workers series, *Doll Bones*, *The Coldest Girl in Coldtown*, the Magisterium series (with Cassandra Clare), and

The Darkest Part of the Forest. She has been a finalist for an Eisner Award and the recipient of the Andre Norton Award, the Mythopoeic Award, and a Newbery Honor. She currently lives in New England with her husband and son in a house with a secret door.

SURVIVAL HORROR

Seanan McGuire

SOME THINGS ARE MYSTERIES NOT BECAUSE THEY
ARE IMPOSSIBLE TO UNDERSTAND, BUT BECAUSE
WHEN THEY STOOD UP AND SAID "GET OUT," THE
SENSIBLE PEOPLE ALL DID AS THEY WERE TOLD. NOT
EVERYTHING NEEDS SOLVING.

—Alice Healy

**A COMFORTABLY RENOVATED BASEMENT IN PORTLAND, OREGON
NOW**

Artie was burning scented candles again. It wasn't the real eye-watering stuff that he sometimes used when he got desperate—strictly Yankee Candle, artificial fruit and cliché Halloween all the way—but it was bad enough that I was breathing through my shirt as I tried to focus on the latest exploits of the X-Men, and not on the increasingly strong sensation of drowning in candied pumpkin and mango smoothies.

I tried making some theatrical gagging noises. Artie, his

attention focused entirely on his laptop, ignored me. He didn't even turn around to find out whether something was actually wrong. He just kept typing. I wrinkled my nose at his oblivious back and returned to my comic book, where Emma Frost—telepath with no time for this shit—was not murdering Cyclops—energy manipulator who caused way too much shit. Fun for the whole family.

If I was going to read comic books and marinate in the fumes from an entire scented-candle outlet, Artie's room was the place to do it. Most of the guys from my comic book store would have happily stabbed one or more family members in the throat if it got them sole ownership of Artie's basement lair, which had been converted for his use years before. Apart from the bed where I was reading and the desk where he was . . . well, whatever he was doing, there were shelves upon shelves loaded with comics, books, collectables, and his not-insubstantial DVD collection. If there was ever some sort of disaster that forced us to stay inside for six months, we might actually make a dent in his unwatched TV boxed sets. Until then, they lined the walls and helped keep the heating bills down.

"Scott's a tool," I said, not really expecting a response. "I mean, why does he keep getting otherwise intelligent women interested in him? It can't be the hair. He may be the only person in the entire Marvel Universe who's never had a decent haircut."

"Uh-huh," said Artie.

That was something: that meant he at least was still aware that I was in the room. "And they're all telepaths, have you noticed that? Maybe he could give you dating tips. Explain how you and Sarah can make things work."

"Uh-huh," said Artie.

"Not that you really need any help. You just need to stop denying your raw animal passions and allow yourselves to go at it like rabid weasels in a sack."

"Uh-huh."

"Okay, *what* can possibly be so interesting that me theorizing about your sex life doesn't even rate a 'stop that'?" I slid off the bed, leaving my comic book open on his pillow, and stalked over to loom behind him. "What are you doing?"

"Installing a new game." Artie tilted his head back to look at me. "Sorry, Annie, did you say something?"

I sighed. "Apparently not." Arthur Harrington—Artie—was my first cousin, but you'd never have guessed, looking at us. Where I got Grandpa Thomas's genes, tall and rangy with cheekbones you could use to cut bread, Artie got a combination of the usual Healy package (average height, compact, good-looking enough, yet still capable of disappearing into a crowd) and his father's incubus bonus stats, leaving him with thick black movie-star hair and big brown puppy-dog eyes that made basically everyone he met either want to hand over their wallets or beat the living crap out of him. My reaction to him was somewhere in between. As an immediate family member, his magical woo-woo incubus "you want me, you know you want me, I'm too sexy for this narrative" pheromones didn't do anything for me, which was why I was allowed in his bedroom. Nonfamily girls weren't even allowed in the *house*. Such were the trials and tribulations of raising a half-incubus child.

Artie frowned. "You said something, and I missed it, because I'm a terrible cousin," he guessed.

"Something like that," I said. "I was mostly just complaining about the X-Men again. I can't blame you for tuning that out. What's the game?"

"It's a new survival horror puzzle game. Solve the puzzles or Cthulhu's off-brand cousin comes through a rip in the fabric of the universe and eats you. Sarah would love it." He paused, apparently realizing what he'd just said, and grimaced before looking back to his screen. "I think the download is finished. Let's see how this baby launches."

"Artie . . ."

"Can't have a heart-to-heart about Sarah right now. Playing video games."

"Artie, you invited me over so we could talk about Sarah."

"Too late look I clicked the button." He clicked, making himself a liar. I didn't really have the chance to call him on that, though.

The lights going out as soon as he pressed the "launch" button was a much larger concern.

My name is Antimony Price, and the fact that my cousin is a half-incubus on his father's side has probably already made it pretty clear that my family is more Addams than Brady. That doesn't mean we're raised to enjoy being suddenly plunged into total darkness. I squawked like an angry duck, fumbling in my pocket for my phone. "Dammit, Artie, what did you *do*? You know you're not supposed to overload the fuses down here."

"I didn't do anything!" he protested from directly in front of me. Good: at least he wasn't trying to move around. Everyone has their strengths in this world, and while I loved my cousin dearly, physical coordination wasn't one of his.

"Well, somebody did *something*," I said, pulling out my

phone and pressing the button on the side to activate the screen.

Nothing happened.

I froze, staying silent for so long that Artie cleared his throat nervously and asked, "Annie? Are you still there, or should I be panicking right now?"

"Do you have your phone?"

"What?"

"My phone screen won't turn on. I know I have a full battery. It's just not working. Do you have your phone?"

"Um, sure, one second." There was a rustling noise, followed by silence. Then: "Shit."

"Yours isn't working either, huh." I touched his shoulder, reassuring myself of his location. "Okay, you stay here. I'm going to head for the stairs, go up, and see if the street is blacked out all over, or if we just got lucky."

"I should play the lottery," he said, deadpan.

"You should," I agreed, and took a step backward . . . or tried to, anyway. Moving my feet was like wading through tar, thick and resistant. I nearly overbalanced, and had to grab the back of Artie's chair at the last moment to keep myself from falling. If the floor had suddenly started trying to keep my feet, I didn't want to think about what it would do to the rest of me. "Shit!"

"Annie?"

"Artie, can you move? Can you stand up?" I did my best to keep my voice steady. If I let myself start panicking—much as I genuinely wanted to—I would have a hard time stopping, and that was a good way to wind up eaten by whatever had turned the floor to tar.

"Of course. Why, are you not wearing shoes or something?" The chair shifted under my hands as Artie moved, or attempted to, anyway. He was silent for a long moment before he said, "Uh . . ."

"Can't stand up, can you?"

"No, I can't." He sounded more puzzled than panicked. Even if his chair was refusing to let him up and I was inexplicably unable to move, he was still in his space, in his home, and he didn't feel like anything could threaten him here. I knew how wrong he was. In the interests of keeping him calm, I wasn't going to point it out. "It feels like someone's glued me to the chair."

"I'm having the same problem with the floor."

"Uh. That's pretty weird, right?"

I swallowed a peal of unhelpful, borderline mocking laughter. "I don't know, Artie. It's your room. Did you replace the carpet with the Blob and not tell me?"

The screen flickered before he could answer me, the change in illumination instantly visible in the dark room. Words swam up through the blackness:

THE JESTER'S PRISON

START NEW GAME? Y/N

"Because *that's* not creepy at all." There was a soft tapping sound, as if Artie had pressed a single key. I closed my eyes for a moment, not that it made much difference, given the room's absolute blackness. "Artie, what did you just do?"

"I said we wanted to start a new game."

I opened my eyes just in time to see the words disappear, ghosting away into CGI mist before a new block of text replaced them, glowing white and somehow menacing against the darkened screen:

THE JESTER OF THE DIVINE, ROBIN GOODFELLOW, IS BOUND BETWEEN THE WORLDS BY THE WORD OF MERLIN, LAST OF THE GREAT WIZARDS. RESTORE AND REFRESH THE WARDS WHICH KEEP HIM BOUND, LEST THE JESTER ONCE AGAIN RUN RAMPANT OVER THE BROKEN BODIES OF MANKIND.

"Jeez, Artie, what the fuck kind of game is this?"

"I don't know! I got it from a guy on my forum."

The text disappeared, replaced by another block:

YOUR WILLINGNESS TO PLAY HAS ACTIVATED ONE OF MERLIN'S FAIL-SAFES. SHOULD YOU FAIL TO RESTORE THE WARDS, ROBIN WILL NOT BE FREED.

"Oh," said Artie, sounding relieved. "Well, that's good."

YOU WILL BE SENT TO JOIN HIM IN EXILE, AND CAN HELP IN MERLIN'S BATTLE TO KEEP THE JESTER CONTAINED.

"And that's *not* good," I said. "Goddammit, Artie, what have you gotten us into?"

"We don't *know* that the game is doing anything," said Artie weakly. The words on the screen disappeared, replaced by a complicated illustration that looked like three triskelions that had been twisted together into a single tangled mass. At the same time, something in the shadows sparked green, and the darkness was filled with distant moaning. "Okay, yeah, the game is doing this," amended Artie. "Sorry."

"Who the hell was this 'guy' and what forum are you talking about?"

"It's a support ground for crossbreeds. You know, like me and Elsie? Half-humans talking about how difficult it can be sometimes to deal with living in a mostly human world. It's educational." His tone turned slightly distant. "I think I can manipulate these lines. How do you think it's supposed to fit together?"

"See if you can rotate the triskelions so that they line up," I said. "Okay, look, is there *any* chance this was targeted? Did someone figure out who you were and decide that we should really be sucked into a bad pocket dimension for our sins? Because I don't know about you, but I do *not* want to meet Robin Goodfellow. That guy was bad news before the Covenant banished him from this plane of reality."

"I don't see how they could have." There was a clicking sound as Artie did something with his mouse. The images on the screen began to rotate slowly. "My profile isn't connected to my real name, I don't have a Facebook, my Twitter account goes to a different email address—"

"What's your handle?"

"Um." The image kept rotating as Artie admitted, sounding mortified, "Incuboy."

"How many Lilu crossbreeds are there living in the Pacific time zone, that you know of?" Incubi and succubi were technically just male and female Lilu. We continued to refer to them as if they were separate species in part because it was tradition—which somehow was supposed to make it less confusing—and in part because their natural abilities were so radically different that they might as well have *been* different species on any practical level.

"Two. Me and Elsie."

"And does your profile give your time zone?"

Artie's silence was all the answer I needed. I managed, barely, to resist the urge to clock him one in the back of the head. It might have made me feel better—violence almost always did—but it wouldn't have helped anything. The conjoined triskelions were still rotating, flashing in and out of alignment with one another.

In and out of alignment . . . "Are they rotating around the places where they connect?"

"Yeah," said Artie, sounding relieved that I was apparently done quizzing him. He was going to be really disappointed in a few minutes. "I can stop them by right-clicking, but I'm not sure what I'm supposed to do with them."

"Try switching to a top view while they spin."

"Okay." More clicking sounds followed. The game might not have come with a tutorial, but with as many video games as Artie played, he didn't really need one. Not for a straightforward point-and-click puzzle game that might or might not be planning to suck us both into an unspeakable hell dimension if we did it wrong.

No pressure.

The view gradually shifted to show the triskelions from above, and as I had hoped, the change in perspective made it clear that each of the three, as it spun, would briefly appear to form a single branch on the three-part symbol. "There," I said. "If you free the pieces while you're looking at them like this, you'll get something that doesn't look so broken."

Artie hesitated. The graphics continued to spin. "Are we sure that's a good idea?" he asked.

"What do you mean?"

"Maybe completing the runes is what sends us off to hang with Robin Goodfellow."

"The instructions said to fix the runes if we *didn't* want to hang with him. Since they appear to be broken currently, and the room is filled with creepy moaning and mysterious darkness, I'm going to go with 'fix them.'" I tightened my hands on the back of his chair. I don't like things I can't hit. "Now."

"All right, all right, I'm fixing them." I heard the mouse click, and the runes on the screen slowed, finally freezing in a perfect triskelion. The image gleamed bright, etching itself on my eyes, so that when I blinked I still saw it floating on the inside of my eyelids. It hung there for a moment, doing nothing, before it began to spin lazily, the image remaining perfect from all angles. The moans in the darkness stopped, replaced by giggling.

"Okay, that's not an improvement," I muttered. "Artie?"

"I don't know! There were no instructions, remember?" The mouse clicked again. "Nothing's happening."

"So this must be the next puzzle," I said. "We have a rotating protection symbol and giggling in the shadows. What can you extend a triskelion into?"

"Annie, I don't do runic gingerbread." Artie sounded like he was on the verge of snapping. I couldn't blame him. This was a pretty terrifying situation, and at least I was armed. Artie wasn't much of a fighter. He was more of the "stay home and research and don't get shot at" school. "I have the book of runes and everything, but it's not like I've ever learned how to *use* them."

"Okay, okay, sorry. I just . . . triple spiral!"

"What?"

"It's an earlier form of the triskelion. See if you can pull the lines apart or anything like that. You'll need to get rid of the interior dots, too—try dragging them into the lines."

"Just a second." Artie hunched forward, focusing on the screen. One of the dots moved, merging into the nearest curving line of the figure, and the line promptly stretched, twisting outward into one arm of a triple spiral. "Got it!" Whatever he'd done, he repeated it twice more, and the triskelion morphed entirely, becoming a triple spiral before beginning to spin, faster and faster, like a portal opening.

"Oh, fuck," I said, unable to feel more than dull disappointment. This was supposed to have been a perfectly normal Saturday. Even we Prices (and Price-Harringtons) don't normally have to deal with evil video games threatening to suck us into portal dimensions if we don't play along. "Artie, if we get pulled through, grab my hand. You don't want to lose track of me."

"Okay," he said glumly.

The image continued to spin, morphing into a white disk that filled with static before becoming a clear picture of a dark-haired, pale-skinned woman. It was black-and-white, except for her eyes, which were a shade of clear ice blue that looked more like it belonged on a beetle's wings than on a person's face. I gasped. So did Artie.

"Sarah?" he asked, sounding equal parts hopeful and horrified.

The image smiled. "Hello," she said, and it wasn't our cousin Sarah, which was a relief but also somehow sad—Sarah was convalescing in Ohio with our grandparents, and while trying to suck us into another dimension wasn't exactly a *nice* way of saying "I'm feeling better," it would have been a wonderful indication of her recovery. "I'm so pleased that you were able to solve the first rune. Robin Goodfellow is a tricky sort, and he needs to be contained."

"That's a cuckoo," I said. "There is a cuckoo in your computer." Math-obsessed telepathic ambush predators. Again, we have an interesting family.

"I know," said Artie.

The cuckoo woman—who was clearly a video file, and couldn't see us, thank God—continued, "There are twenty runes ahead of you, each more complicated than the last. Complete them all, and Robin stays contained. Fail, even once, and you'll share his fate."

"There has to be a catch here," I murmured. "Cuckoos don't go around refreshing the wards on ancient evils for shits and giggles."

"They also don't have the magic to do this kind of programming," said Artie. He leaned forward, until his nose was almost brushing the computer screen. The cuckoo woman was smiling at him beatifically, her part in this little production finished, at least until we did something to trigger another video clip. I couldn't tell whether the video was still going. She could have become a still frame.

Artie stabbed his finger at the screen. "Look there: behind the door. That's a hand. She's working with the hidebehinds."

"Or the hidebehinds are working with her," I said. "Shit."

There's no such thing as magic, according to my grandma Alice, and since she married a witch and has spent the last thirty or so years jumping from reality to reality looking for him, I guess she'd know. Magic is just a sort of physics we don't fully understand yet, the kind that allows men to turn into monsters and semi-visible humanoid cryptids to use their uniquely folded perspective on reality to code video games that conceal dimensional portals. Hidebehinds are oddly refractive, and their way of seeing the world doesn't match up with anything else we've encountered, either in this dimension or the ones that they occasionally disappear into. They're usually harmless. The thought of them joining forces with the cuckoos, who were anything *but* harmless, was enough to make me want to hide under Artie's bed and wait for the nice video game to eat us. At least then I wouldn't be in a world where the hidebehinds and the cuckoos were going to gang up on me in the night.

"No, no, this is a good thing," said Artie. He leaned forward again, this time focusing on the corner of the screen. "See, if the cuckoos had made this by themselves, it would have been all math problems. The hidebehinds like hidden-eye stuff—naturally—and concealing puzzles in plain sight." He clicked something. The game's camera zoomed in on what I'd taken for a smudge, revealing a cobweb with several large swaths missing. The spider was perched in the top corner, black and gleaming.

"So what do we do?" I asked.

"Patch the web." I couldn't see Artie's face, but I could hear his frown. "The question is, do we need to do it in a single pass, or can we strategically choose our moves?"

"Let me see." I leaned forward. Artie shifted his head a little to the side, giving me a clear view of the puzzle. "Hidebehinds are big on barrow imagery, which tends to be Celtic in nature—not always, but something like eighty, ninety percent of the time. Celtic knots depend on the unbroken strand, or at least the illusion of the unbroken strand."

"And hidebehinds are all about illusions," Artie agreed. "Okay. So where's the move?"

I frowned, leaning closer still. My feet were still stuck to the floor, which created the bizarre sensation that someone was holding me down as I tried to see how to draw the correct line. Finally, I reached up and touched the bottom left corner of the broken web. "Here to . . . here," I said, drawing the first line. "Then here, here . . ." I kept moving my finger, repeating the path Artie would need to send the spider along over and over again as I waited for him to give me the okay to stop.

After the fifth repetition, Artie said, "All right. I think I have it." He began moving his mouse, replicating the motion of my finger. Finally, he released it, said, "Cross your fingers," and hit the space bar.

The spider began to move. It raced along the path Artie had traced, leaving a line of gleaming silver behind it. The newly patched web began to glow, and then the camera pulled out again, leaving us looking at the motionless cuckoo, the open closet door, and the otherwise featureless little room.

No: not completely featureless. "Left side, wainscot," I said. "Is that another puzzle?"

Artie tilted his head. "I think so." The giggling from the shadows got louder when he tapped on the left side of the screen, and a message popped up:

YOU ARE NOT READY FOR WHAT YOUR ACTIONS WOULD UNLEASH.

The camera didn't move. Artie sighed. "Okay, well, on the plus side, it's not going to let us try an advanced puzzle before we clear out the basic ones."

"Yeah, and on the negative side, we're stuck here until we either get sucked into another dimension with an ancient evil—which is *so* Syfy Saturday night, I can't even—or until we finish the whole game. How big is this thing?"

"I don't know. A few gigabytes. And hey, we could always die of mysterious causes before we do either." Artie began mousing around the screen, looking for something clickable.

I groaned. "Way to look on the bright side."

"I try."

I resisted the urge to strangle my cousin. It wouldn't have done either one of us any good, and I couldn't reach the keyboard from where I was stuck. "All right, while you find the next accessible puzzle, how about you tell me why a bunch of hidebehinds would be targeting you via evil video game. That doesn't feel like the sort of thing that happens at random, you know?"

"I don't know! I haven't done anything!"

I smacked him in the back of the head.

"Ow!" Artie twisted as much as he could, trying to look at me. "What did you do that for?"

"You're not thinking. You're supposed to be the smart one. One of the smart ones. Smarter than your sister, or mine. So *think*. Why would someone be out to get you? What have you been posting on that forum of yours?"

"Nothing." Something about his tone made it pretty clear that he was lying. I stayed silent. Artie sighed. "Nothing *important*. There's a forum about cryptid injuries is all. You know, like 'how do you patch a tear in the webbing between your fingers,' or 'what kind of mange treatments work for therianthropes.' That sort of thing." His voice took on a defensive note as he added, "It's hard not being the dominant species. You don't always know where to turn for information, you know? So sometimes we turn to each other."

"What were you posting, Artie?"

He clicked a stripe in the wallpaper. The camera zoomed

in, showing another knotwork puzzle, as he said miserably, "Sarah. I was posting about Sarah. How there was this Johrlac girl I knew, and she'd managed to hurt herself pretty bad, and did anyone know what I could do to help her get better."

I bit the inside of my cheek to stop myself from smacking him again. It wouldn't have done any good, and more, it wouldn't have been fair. He was asking the same questions we'd all been asking for months. He'd just taken them to a new forum. The fact that he might have gotten us killed in the process was almost irrelevant.

"I guess maybe someone could have gotten upset by me talking about taking care of a cuckoo like she was a person, even though she *is* a person," Artie concluded morosely. "I didn't mean to."

"I know you didn't mean to," I said. "Given that there's a cuckoo in the game, I'm going to bet that it wasn't talking about Sarah like a person that got you into trouble. It was admitting that you knew she existed at all. This is an assassination attempt."

"Really? Cool." Artie dragged something down the side of the line of knotwork, which warped into another series of figures. He began swapping them around, exchanging them for each other at a speed that made it clear he knew what he was doing, even if I didn't. "I mean, bad and terrible and probably something I'm going to get yelled at for, but you know. Also cool. I don't get many assassination attempts aimed in my direction."

"Yes, you're the family wallflower, I know," I deadpanned. "What are you doing?"

"This is something Sarah showed me once. It's a series of mathematical transformations. Fun, huh?"

"Yeah, fun," I said uneasily. "Okay: cuckoos can't use magic, at least not runic magic, which means our mystery cuckoo didn't design the game."

"No, the hidebehinds did that," agreed Artie. He clicked his mouse. The figure went through another transformation, going smooth and blending into the wallpaper. The camera pulled out again, and the cuckoo's lips curled upward in a warm smile.

I jumped—or tried to, anyway, and had to grab for Artie's chair to keep myself from going sprawling on the tarry floor. I'd grown so accustomed to the cuckoo woman being a still picture that I hadn't expected to see her move.

"You're smart; that's good," she said, and the disturbing part was that she sounded like she *meant* it. It was more fun for her if we were smart. "This room has been used to keep Robin imprisoned for generations. Every piece is a puzzle. Every puzzle has a solution. If you can complete them all, the runes will be redrawn, and your release will be at hand."

"Sounds good," said Artie, and he started to move his mouse again. I grabbed his arm, freezing him in mid-motion.

"The video hasn't finished," I said softly. "She's still watching you. Look at her nostrils." The cuckoo woman's nostrils were very slightly flared, like she smelled something unpleasant. That was the only sign that the feed was still live.

"So?"

"So she said that everything in the room was a puzzle, and *she's* in the room. I think . . . I think if you try to trigger another puzzle while she's active, it may count as losing. I'd really rather not lose, if it's all the same to you."

"Yeah, no, getting sucked into some unknown dimension to hang with Robin, not my idea of a good time." Cautiously,

Artie brought the mouse back around to the cuckoo woman, and clicked on her nose.

Her face split into a grin even wider than the one she'd been wearing before. "Fearless questers, brave and true, what gift can I give to you?" She stopped then, and appeared to be waiting.

"What?" I demanded. "That's not a riddle. That's barely even a question. That can't be the whole puzzle."

"Sure it can," said Artie philosophically. "She's a cuckoo, and cuckoos are all assholes. I bet that's a super long, easy riddle by their standards. I mean, really, the question is whether or not she's playing fair. If she *is*, then there's an answer we can guess from what we already know. If she's *not*, I might as well just do a keyboard smash, because we're about to be eaten by a video game."

"Hidebehinds are inherently fair," I said. "Assume that since they programmed the game—"

"We don't know that for sure."

"Assume that since they *probably* programmed the game, they're making her play fair. That means the riddle has an answer. I can't promise we won't be penalized for capitalization or anything, but at least we have something resembling a fighting chance."

"Oh. In that case . . ." Artie leaned forward and typed something in before I could object. We both focused our attention on the screen, barely breathing as we waited to see what would happen next.

The cuckoo's smile faded. "Really? That's what you want from me, out of everything in this world? I won't forget." Then she turned and stormed out of the picture, opening the door on the far wall to reveal a hallway beyond. The door swung slowly shut behind her, but the screen remained lit, and no dread portals appeared. We hadn't lost the game yet.

Artie let out a slow breath. "Whew," he said.

I smacked him in the back of the head. "What did you type?" I demanded.

"The only thing I could type. When a cuckoo that isn't Sarah or Grandma Angela asks what she can do for you, the answer is 'leave.'"

I blinked. And then I laughed. "God, I love you."

"I know," said Artie, and he clicked on another puzzle.

What felt like hours later, we were still playing, and the darkness still held absolute dominion over the room. The giggles from the shadows had been replaced by moans, except when they were replaced by hellish screams that made it difficult for us to concentrate on the puzzles we were struggling to solve. The cuckoo woman did not return. I had to view that as a good thing, since otherwise, it would have been proof that we had already lost, and that the game was just toying with us. I didn't like being toyed with.

"I need to pee," said Artie glumly.

"Yeah, and my feet hurt," I said. "How many puzzles do you think we have left?"

"I don't know. Every time I think we're done, two more pop up." Artie hesitated before asking the question I'd been fighting not to ask myself for the last four puzzles: "Do you think they're ever going to end? Because I'm not sure starving to death in my bedroom is any better than being sucked into a prison dimension."

"We won't starve to death," I said. "We'll die of dehydration long before that point."

"I knew there was a reason you were my favorite cousin."

The fear in Artie's voice was getting clearer with every word. "Annie . . . what if this never ends?"

"It'll end. You'll see. We just need to figure out why we're playing. You posted about Sarah, and there's a cuckoo in the game: I think it's pretty clear that the cuckoos sent this for you, after getting the hidebehinds to program it, which explains the fairness. You said you downloaded this from your forum? That means it's pretty new, right?"

"Yeah. It's still being play-tested. I guess if I never log on again, they know it works."

"Okay. So that means they're not completely sure it does what it's supposed to. They're testing. We're going to have to track them down and kick their teeth in after we get done with this, you realize, but . . . have you tried hitting 'escape'?"

"What." It wasn't a question. It was a statement of utter disbelief, like I had just said the most ridiculous thing anyone had ever uttered.

"They can't have played all the way through every time they decided to test a new puzzle. There has to be a way out."

"Annie—"

"Can you think of a better one?"

There was a long pause before Artie said, sounding somewhat sullen, "If we get sucked into a localized equivalent of hell for a hundred years, I am blaming you."

"Maybe we can find Grandpa Thomas while we're there." I squeezed his shoulder. "Just try it."

Artie sighed, raised his hand, and pressed the "escape" key. Words appeared on the screen:

EXIT AND SAVE?

Y/N

"Oh my God say yes Artie say yes *right now*," I said.

"Yes!" Artie stabbed his finger at the keyboard. The screen went black. The moaning in the shadows stopped.

The lights came back on.

Without the tarry floor holding me in place, I automatically adjusted my position, and then toppled over as my long-asleep feet refused to hold my weight any longer. I had never been so grateful to get a face full of carpet. I heard Artie's chair creak, followed by the sound of the bedroom door slamming open and his feet pounding up the stairs, presumably heading for the bathroom.

"Shouldn't drink so much Pepsi," I muttered, and began the laborious process of peeling myself off the floor. Artie's computer screen had returned to an innocuous view of browser and wallpaper—a picture of Sarah taken the summer before she followed my sister Verity to New York. No signs of an ancient evil waiting to either break free or swallow us whole. That was a nice change.

I staggered up the stairs on shaking legs, and passed the closed bathroom door on my way to the kitchen. Either Artie had needed to pee more than I thought, or he was having a quiet cry in the bathtub before he came back out to face the world. If I faulted him for that at all, it was only because *I* couldn't be crying in the tub while he was locked in there.

The kitchen clock said that it was almost seven. Artie had launched the game shortly after noon. I'd never been more exhausted in my life.

Aunt Jane turned away from whatever she was stirring on the stove to look over her shoulder at me and smile. "There you are," she said. "I was just getting ready to send a search party."

"I don't think that would have worked." I walked to the

fridge, opened it, and extracted a can of Dr Pepper. After a pause to consider, I made that two. As I walked over to the table, I continued, "They would just have gotten sucked into the magically generated shadows that were holding us captive as we tried to complete a series of complicated puzzles and refresh the wards that were holding Robin Goodfellow in his eternal prison." I collapsed into the chair across from Uncle Ted and cracked open the seal on my first soda.

Uncle Ted and Aunt Jane both stared at me, not saying a word. I took a long drink of Dr Pepper.

"So, what's for dinner?" I asked.

"Magically generated shadows?" asked Aunt Jane.

"Robin Goodfellow?" asked Uncle Ted.

Artie appeared in the doorway, eyes red, wiping his hands on a towel. "Oh," he said. "You told them."

I took another drink of Dr Pepper.

Uncle Ted eyed Artie's laptop like he expected it to grow teeth and start biting him at any moment. Honestly, that would have been easier to understand than "remotely executable runic magic embedded in the game program by hidebehinds working with a cuckoo for some unknown and probably unpleasant reason." Even for us, that was pushing the bounds of comprehensibility a bit. "And you say you just downloaded the game, and then the shadows came?"

"Yeah, Dad," said Artie. He sighed. "I swear there was no 'contains actual evil' warning on the file."

"There rarely is."

Aunt Jane walked back into the kitchen, waving her phone like it had just unlocked the secrets of the universe. "All right, my contact with the local bogeymen confirmed that some hidebehinds have been taking contract work from whoever's willing to put down the cash. Something about establishing a competitive multimedia company in a human-dominated market. They specialize in puzzle games and phone apps for cryptids—which does sometimes mean executable magic."

"Great," I said. "Let's go punch them a lot."

"No can do, my darling, overly violent niece," she said. "They're down in Silicon Valley. Even if we could convince your parents to let us take you to California on no notice for the sole purpose of punching people, I can't get the time off work."

"Your brother would probably let us take Antimony to California in order to punch people," said Uncle Ted, giving the laptop another poke. "He'd view it as a bonding exercise."

Aunt Jane snorted. "No one is crossing state lines in order to commit assault today, all right?"

"But they nearly sucked us into a pocket dimension," I said. "Don't they deserve *some* punching?"

"I'll set up a conference call and have some words with their CEO about taking money from cuckoos," said Aunt Jane. "That's really the best I can do right now. Sometimes you have to explore nonviolent solutions."

I crossed my arms and leaned back in my seat, glowering sullenly. "I hate nonviolent solutions."

"Even the X-Men sometimes resolve things without punching," said Artie.

I swiveled around so that I was glowering directly at him. He quailed.

"I mean, punching would be better, we should really go with punching."

"See, look there, Annie got her way without punching you, clearly diplomatic methods can work." Uncle Ted pushed Artie's laptop across the table toward him. "Uninstall the evil software and you should be fine."

"That's it?" I abandoned glaring at Artie in favor of staring at my uncle Ted. "Just 'uninstall the evil software'? We don't even have to kill a chicken?"

"Why would you? It's not like you installed Windows 7." Uncle Ted started laughing at his own joke. I groaned, which just made him laugh harder.

"You'd think someone would be at least a *little* upset about us nearly getting sucked into an unidentified pocket dimension," I grumbled.

"I'm upset," offered Artie. "Come on. I'll let you help me write the game review. That'll make you feel better."

"The really pathetic part is that you're right." I sighed and stood, grabbing my soda. "Let's go."

"Awesome." Artie picked up his computer. "Mom, when's dinner?"

"About twenty minutes," said Aunt Jane.

"Great, plenty of time." He went trotting off toward his basement. I followed him more slowly. My feet still hurt.

The last thing I heard before I slammed the basement door was Uncle Ted saying, far too calmly, "I told those kids video games were going to get them in trouble one day."

Artie was back at his desk by the time I finished stomping down the stairs. He had a browser open and was typing something into a forum window. I stopped, eyeing first his screen, and then him. He reddened.

"I'm just . . . reporting . . . that the game is sort of evil," he said.

"Uh-huh. And then?"

"I'm uninstalling the game."

"And then?"

"I'm deleting my forum account before I accidentally

invite any more assassination attempts from pissed-off Johr-lac who don't like people knowing that they exist."

"And then?"

"I'm being grateful that it wasn't the Covenant of St. George."

"And then?"

He sighed deeply. "I'm apologizing to my wonderful, brilliant, totally not going to punch me in the throat cousin for endangering her life."

"Good." I walked back to the bed, where my comic book was still waiting for me. "Let me know when you want to start." I stretched out on my stomach, getting comfortable, and turned the page. All in all, the afternoon hadn't been *that* unusual.

———————

Seanan McGuire was born and raised in Northern California, resulting in a love of rattlesnakes and an absolute terror of weather. She shares a crumbling old farmhouse with a variety of cats, far too many books, and enough horror movies to be considered a problem. Seanan publishes about three books a year and is widely rumored not to actually sleep. When bored, Seanan tends to wander into swamps and cornfields, which has not yet managed to get her killed (although not for lack of trying). She also writes as Mira Grant, filling the role of her own evil twin, and tends to talk about horrible diseases at the dinner table.

REAL

Django Wexler

The big black car pulls up outside Shinjuku Station against the line of concrete posts that marks the edge of the domain of automobiles. Beyond, it's bikes and pedestrians only, so I get out of the back and tell the driver to wait. From the station it's only a couple of blocks' walk to Kabuki-cho, with its famous red archway outlined in pulsing neon.

Ichibanchou-dori is packed at this hour. All the buildings are tall and thin, with a different business on each floor, and their big vertical signboards looming overhead: 1F BAR, 2F MASSAGE, 3F KARAOKE, lights flashing in a desperate plea for attention. Both sides of the street are lined with touts shouting the advantages of their clubs at the men walking by, trying to draw them into conversation with "special offers."

I can't help but stand out in a crowd in Japan—too tall, too blond, too foreign. It repels some of the shouting men—no point in trying to get a foreigner into a hostess club, he won't speak Japanese anyway—and draws others like a magnet. I wave off invitations to drinks, to sushi, whatever else they think will appeal to a touring American. One of the salesmen, a big black guy with an impressive Afro, gives me a little nod of shared understanding. We're both oddities here. I smile at him.

The door I'm looking for is unmarked. It leads down a half flight of steps into a little *izakaya*, sort of a pub that serves fried snacks. There's a long bar top, half-occupied by some really serious drinkers, and a scattering of empty tables. It's oddly shaped, bending around one of the building's support columns, so half the floor is out of sight. Around here, no empty space goes unused.

"*Irasshaimase*," the man behind the bar mutters, not looking up from watching some unmentionable chicken component crisp up in a pan. He's one of these stocky, solid older guys that seem to be standard equipment for places like this, as though there were a press somewhere stamping them out. His hair is frosted white at the temples.

He doesn't really pay attention to me until I step up to the bar. Then he takes me in and gets a look I'm very familiar with—it's the slightly panicked expression of someone trying to dredge up enough high school English to speak to a foreigner.

"I'm looking for Aka-sensei," I tell him. My Japanese is not quite perfect, with a trace of unplaceable accent I can't quite eradicate. It bothers me: professional pride; I'm a translator, after all.

Relief is written all over his face, though he tries to hide it. He grunts an acknowledgment and points to a back corner.

I nod. "Send us over another of whatever he's drinking, and a soda water."

Another grunt. He keeps his eyes on the frying chicken parts.

I thread my way through the empty tables and around the intrusive pillar. Aka-sensei is in the very back, tucked away in the dark, bent over a bottle with the air of a dedicated drunk.

There's only one chair at his table, so I grab one and carry it with me, setting it down opposite him with a clatter.

He looks up. He's in his thirties, long-faced and thin, with weird, gangly limbs and a spray of dark hair tipped with the remnants of a blond dye-job. He wears jeans and a sport coat that has seen better days.

"Who the hell are you?" he rasps at me as I sit down.

"I wanted to talk to you, Aka-sensei," I say.

His face goes sly. "So somebody finally tracked me down."

"It wasn't easy."

"No kidding. It's not supposed to be easy." He picks up the bottle in front of him, takes a pull that empties it, sets it back on the table. "You with the cops?"

"No."

"The papers, then?"

"Something like that."

"I'm not supposed to talk to the papers," he says. "Not supposed to talk to anyone, they told me. You know I'm still getting a salary?" He gestures around the dingy bar and laughs. "I'm at work! This is work. Who says lifetime employment is dead?"

A waitress arrives, an older woman who conspicuously avoids Aka-sensei's gaze. He gives her a long, unashamed stare as she bends over to put a new bottle in front of him and hand me a glass of bubbling water. She nods politely and leaves, and his eyes stay glued to her ass until she's out of sight.

"Bitch," he mutters. "Asked her out once. As a joke. She got all serious about it." He barks a laugh. "Women, eh?"

"I wondered," I say, "if I could ask you a few questions."

"I could get in trouble if you write about it," he says. "Lose this sweet gig."

"It's not for publication. Call it professional curiosity."

"Curiosity is a goddamned curse, let me tell you. I know better than anybody." He eyes me sidelong, but I can already tell he's going to talk. He *wants* to tell his story, so badly he's practically panting at the opportunity. Finally, awkwardly, he shrugs. "What the hell. You won't believe me anyway. Nobody believes me. I don't even believe me, some days."

"Let me confirm a few things." I sip my drink. "Your *real* name is Nakamura Takumi. You were born in—"

"Skip the biographical bullshit. I know what you want." He sits back in his chair, bottle dangling from his hand. "You want to know about *REAL*."

I offer him a tight smile.

"*REAL*" is what you might call a loanword, although in this case it hasn't been so much borrowed as abducted. Pronunciation changed (it's "REE-ah-ru," or close enough), and it was twisted from an adjective to a noun. It means the flesh-and-blood world we all live in, as opposed to the electronic fantasyland of the Net.

"You built a game," I say, going through the facts as though I really were a journalist. "A game that people don't believe is only a game."

"Come on. Nobody *really* believes that." He smiles, a bit sickly around the edges. "A few weirdos, maybe. Everyone just . . . pretends. Like a mass hallucination. It's a joke."

"Isn't that what you intended from the start, though? *REAL* was never announced in public, and no one has officially claimed responsibility for it. It just appeared."

Aka-sensei laughs again. "You think that just happens? I had six social media guys working overtime to make sure it 'just appeared.' We were hardly the first, either. Remember that *Halo* thing in the States? And that movie—"

I nod. "Maybe you should start at the beginning."

Aka-sensei lets out a long sigh. He pats his pockets like he's suddenly remembered something, comes out with a rumpled pack of cigarettes and extracts one with a practiced tap. He makes a show of looking for a light, but I'm way ahead of him, pulling my brushed-steel lighter from my inside jacket pocket and extending it across the table. It lights on the first try, and the end of the cigarette glows bright. I put the lighter away, and Aka-sensei takes a long drag.

"The beginning," he muses. "That must be Shiki. You know Shiki?"

I shake my head. He takes another pull from his beer, cigarette dangling limply from his fingers.

"He's probably your boss's boss's boss's boss's boss. We were buddies in college. Nerds together, at the time, but after graduation, he straightened up and I went hard-core. Shiki went straight to the top. Works at the big publisher now, head executive vice president of something or other. Nice big office with his own bathroom. But he still calls me now and then, or he used to. Throws me work, like he's doing me a favor.

"A couple of years ago, he called me up and said he had a project for me. They were doing a new game, a networked phone game. Real pie-in-the-sky stuff. He had no goddamn idea what he was talking about, but there was a lot of money behind the project, so I told him I'd run the thing for him if that's what he wanted. I sent him a spec of what I wanted to do, and right there and then he kicked out his corporate programmers and put me in charge.

"It's a pretty simple idea, honestly. Demons are invading

the world, and there's this special phone app that lets you see them. I ripped it off from that old movie *They Live*. You remember *They Live*, with the glasses?" I shrug, and he shakes his head. "Nobody watches the classics anymore."

"Was it your idea to keep the origin of the game a secret?"

"Of course. Shiki could never come up with anything so ballsy. He went for it, though, I have to give him that. We 'leaked' it, made sure it got spread around, got a little buzz going. When you start the thing up, it doesn't show you everything all at once. You get these little glimpses, you know? You look through your phone, and there's glowing runes on a wall, or you see a flash of something moving in the distance. You get pulled in. After a while, you get a message from Mari."

"Mari?" I ask, though of course I know all about Mari.

"Mariko. The heroine. I wrote all this myself. Outcast fighting to save an uncaring world, the middle school kids eat that up. Mariko was supposed to be the one who'd written the program in the first place. She needs your help to stop the bad guys. There's a secret message board, with information, the demonic hierarchy, all this stuff. We had this guy—"

He stops, cigarette halfway to his lips, staring into space for a moment. Then he shakes his head. "Mariko, though. She was perfect. The agency sent us this actress. Smart as whip, and she got the role down perfectly, first try. Determined, but just a little scared. Strong, but vulnerable. *Moé*. They eat that up, I told you. God, and the body on her . . ."

Aka-sensei stops, pulls in smoke, lets it out in a languorous puff.

"We signed her to a long-term contract, ironclad. We would run her whole life until it was over. Shiki talked her into it. He must have paid a fortune. Or maybe not. She was smart. She could see how big this was going to be when we finally pulled the cover off.

"After about a year of dev, we launched it. Started letting people in, a few at a time. My guys got rumors started. Shiki even had some stuff put in the papers, unexplained disappearances, that kind of thing." He chuckled. "You know that's why I'm talking to you, right? It doesn't really matter what I say. Shiki will never let you print anything that blows the secret. He runs the whole show now."

"I'd like to hear it anyway," I say. "Like I said, professional curiosity."

Aka-sensei stares at me as he grinds the cigarette out in the ashtray. He *wants* to tell me everything, I can see it in his eyes. He wants to tell someone what he knows, so badly it hurts. It can be hard, keeping secrets.

"You won't believe me," he says.

"That's my problem."

He shrugs. "Fair enough. After six months, we were doing great. Everyone was excited, the community was growing, people were working on the little mysteries I threw them. We hired people to go out and plant things—dead drops, spy stuff. And then if you looked through the phone, you could see they were 'possessed,' with weird mirror eyes and a green aura. I loved it. I used to sit in the command center, watching all the screens—we could track everyone who used the app, follow them around—and I thought this must be what it's like to be a god. I speak a word, and something gets created. You have no idea how much fun it was."

Aka-sensei stops, looking down at the table, the ashtray and the dead cigarette. I signal the waitress over my shoulder for another beer.

"Something went wrong," he says very quietly. "That's when it all went bad. People started dying."

"I read about that in the papers," I say. "The kid they called Boy A, who killed himself—"

"You don't know *shit*." Aka-sensei slams his hand on the table, hard enough to make the empty bottles jump. "Shiki was happy to let people talk about stuff like that. Sure, a kid killed himself. So what? Kids do that all the time. Some other guy fell in front of a train while he was looking through his phone, and they talked about banning us. We laughed and laughed. That's all just *publicity*. If it hadn't happened, Shiki would have made something up."

"Then I'm not sure what you mean."

He hesitates, shakes his head. His hand is tight on his latest beer. "We were getting ready for the big reveal. The endgame. We had this elaborate setup, all these demons, and right at the top there was the big, bad boss. The Dark Queen. I *drew* her, I sketched her out in pencil on a goddamn cocktail napkin and gave her to my assistant to copy over. We had just started looking for an actress, since she was going to have some video with Mariko. After that . . ."

Aka-sensei sighs. "I told Shiki it was time to thinking about going public. We'd had a good run, but we couldn't expect the secret to hold forever, and it was time to monetize. Take all the buzz we'd created and turn it into something people could buy. That's the whole point, right? And the big shots at the publisher were getting anxious to see some return on investment. So I figured once we ran through the Dark Queen stuff, we'd wind it up—Mariko defeats the Queen, right, the heroes always win. Darkness driven back but not truly defeated, and we get a spin-off anime, manga, video game, figurines, the works. I thought I was going to be set for life." He looks around the bar and gives a weak chuckle. "Heh. I guess I was right about that."

"But who died?"

"I told you we had a guy who wrote out all the backstory for us. Kabbalic symbolism, ancient secrets, that sort of thing. Anytime we needed a big chunk of text. We all called him the Professor, but his real name was—" He names an author, a well-known professor of philosophy with several popular volumes to his credit. I raise an eyebrow, and he smiles. "I guess spouting bullshit doesn't pay as well as it used to. He never wanted to be associated with us in public, but he was happy enough to take our money. Until they found him dead."

"I thought he died of a heart attack."

"That's what they told us. Natural causes, very tragic. Especially since he was barely fifty. Shiki sent me to his house to make sure he hadn't left anything behind that would blow the project—he was already getting paranoid—but there was nothing. I mean, *nothing*. No notes, no computer files. Like he'd written a book's worth of demonic history for us without ever scribbling something down. Or like someone else had already cleaned the place out. Shiki was relieved to hear it. You know what he told me? 'Thank goodness he'd already finished up.'"

"It doesn't sound like you and Shiki got along."

"We used to. But he was *obsessed* with *REAL*, with keeping it secret. He wouldn't even talk about going public. And he kept fighting with the agencies about who would play the Dark Queen, wouldn't accept anyone they sent over but wouldn't say why. Then Gopher died."

I frown. "Who was Gopher?"

"In the game he was a friend of Mariko's. A fat, nerdy guy who helped her out with stuff. He never got a name, so we called him Gopher. We used to send him out on trips, just walking around where there were a lot of players, so people would see him and think he was running errands for their heroine. Well, one day he went out and didn't come back. The cops found him in an alley, stabbed about fifty times."

"That I *didn't* hear about."

"Of course not. You think Shiki would let that get out? We'd have to say what he'd been doing; it would blow the whole thing. He became convinced someone was on to us, one of the other publishers maybe, and they were trying to sabotage him. Murder people so that *REAL* got shut down. He was going crazy! Nobody would do that, not for a goddamn game."

"You must have had your own theory."

"Yeah." Aka-sensei holds his beer cupped in front of him, in both hands. "Yeah, I did. I guessed Shiki might not be the only crazy one. See, on the message boards for *REAL*, there was a group of people who had decided that Mariko was lying to everyone, and that the demons were really the good guys. I loved it, tried to encourage them whenever I got the chance. That was the idea, right? That people would react in their own way. But after Gopher died, that part of the boards was celebrating, and I thought, maybe one of these guys is taking this seriously.

"I started looking through the tracking data. I had this idea that if someone from the boards really had killed Gopher, I could track their phone and figure out who. We had a ton of data on everyone who used the app, and the hard-core *REAL* players kept it running all the time so they could get alerts on anything nearby. So I pulled a bunch of information on the top players."

"One of them was the killer?" I lean forward, expectant.

"I wish. God, that would have been easy. I could have been the hero." He shook his head, slowly. "No, I forgot all about that. What I found was that the top players were *disappearing*. One by one, everyone who had made the most progress toward, you know, uncovering the demon conspiracy, they were quitting the game. Or not even quitting, just going dark. I found one guy who had the app on, just sitting still, for seventeen hours. After that his phone must have died."

"Maybe he left it on the train."

"That's exactly what I said. But it was *still happening*. I could watch the list in real time, watch them disappear one by one. Even people on the message boards were starting to clue in. When I told Shiki about it, he thought it confirmed his conspiracy theory. He put us all in lockdown. Everyone associated with the project was hustled off to a block of company apartments while he sorted it out.

"I spent a lot of time with Mariko. You would have thought she'd have lost her shit, but she was braver than any one of us. She wanted to move on, incorporate it into the story and run with it. God, that girl." He sighs. "I was fucking her by then. Honestly, it was just a favor to her. She couldn't go out, not ever, since Shiki couldn't take the chance she'd be recognized, so I was one of the only people she ever got to see. She needed *some* kind of entertainment, right?

"After a week, I couldn't stand it anymore. I snuck out of the building, past the rent-a-cops Shiki posted all around it, and went out to a bar to get blasted. I was feeling . . . well, scared, maybe, and pissed off, so I overdid it a bit. That was a hell of a night." A shiver runs through him. "I didn't think I'd be able to sneak back in, so I got a room at a hotel. I was so drunk, I barely made it up the stairs, and . . ."

He pauses to look me in the eye.

"Aka-sensei?" I prompt.

"I've never told anyone this," he says. "Not anyone. Who would believe me?"

"I'm listening."

"When I got into the hotel room . . ." He takes a breath. "*She* was waiting for me."

"Mariko?"

"Not Mariko," he says. "The fucking Dark Queen."

"An actress, you mean," I say. "Someone Shiki hired."

"No! I mean, yes, sure. I don't know. I don't *know*." He puts his hands to his head, pressing the half-full bottle against his skull. "Why would Shiki send an actress to do that? How would he even know I was there?" He closed his eyes. "She looked exactly like the Dark Queen. *Exactly.* As though she'd stepped out of my head, off my fucking napkin, and into my room. She has these eyes—they're like mirrors, like she's wearing reflective lenses under her skin. You look at her and you see tiny versions of yourself staring back at you. I thought I was hallucinating. Or else that I'd passed out on the floor, and now I was dreaming."

I sip my soda water. The ice has long ago melted. "That also seems possible."

"The Queen doesn't speak our language," he says. "That's what the Professor wrote, anyway. I just thought it would make her a little stranger if she didn't talk to you directly. She has this voice, like she's singing a four-part melody all by her-self. It's beautiful. When I heard it, I thought I would cry. And then—she has this *thing*, a twisted little goblin creature, and it tells you what she means. I knew our CG guys were still working on it, but it was *there*, in the room. It hopped up on the bed and spoke to me."

My smile is strained. I try to convey disbelief. "What did it say?"

"It said, 'The Queen wishes to convey her thanks, mortal.'

"I laughed at it. I couldn't help it. I've always been crap at writing that epic, mythic dialogue. At that point I'd about convinced myself I was dreaming anyway, so I bowed and got all formal.

" 'My Queen,' I said, 'I'm honored, but I'm not sure you should be thanking me.'

"She sang another note, and the little imp said, 'Why do you say so?'

" 'If not for me,' I told her, 'you wouldn't have to wear that outfit.' " Aka-sensei smiles, a bit wan. "I mean, okay, I didn't draw the Dark Queen's gear for practicality. She looks like she came from a cross between a Victorian dress ball and a bond-age shop. It shows off her tits—*great* tits—but I can't imagine it's easy to get into.

" 'If I were you,' I told her, 'I'd ditch the fetish outfit for something a little more comfortable.' Then I pushed past the little imp and into the bathroom, 'cause I didn't think I could wait any longer. Dream or not, you don't want to piss all over a Queen's shoes. By the time I came out, they were gone."

"I can see why you never told anyone about this," I say.

"I told you you wouldn't believe me." He waves the nearly empty beer bottle in my face. "Honestly, I don't give a fuck. I didn't believe it at the time, either. I woke up the next morning feeling like shit, of course. Clicked on the TV while I was washing up, and every station was talking about the fire."

"Fire?" I say.

"At the apartments." Aka-sensei drains the rest of his beer in a gulp. "I don't know where Shiki found that old building, but it went up like a fucking torch. Burned to the ground. Only a few people made it out. I was on the top floor—if I hadn't snuck out, I would have died for sure."

I wait, in silence. Aka-sensei's hand tightens on the bottle.

"Mariko made it," he says. "I heard the story from the firefighters later. She came out half carrying one of the others. Maybe *she* started to take *REAL* too seriously, thought she was an actual hero instead of an actress. She said there was another guy in there, passed out, one of our social media kids, and before anybody could stop her she turned around and went back in after him. A couple of minutes later the roof went and the whole building came down." Aka-sensei's eyes glitter for a moment, and he squeezes them shut. "Stupid bitch."

I let him have the moment, then clear my throat. "What did you do?"

"I think I went a little crazy," he says. "Like Shiki. Paranoid. Can you blame me? I went back to the control room and grabbed as much data as I could, then ran for it. Found a shithole apartment to stay in, spent all my time in a Net café, running correlations. Tracking down who all those top players were, and trying to figure out what had happened to them in real life. It wasn't easy, but what I managed to find scared the hell out of me.

"They were dying. At least, that's what I thought at the time. I built this whole case, cross-referencing dates and tracking locations. Pulled up all the mysterious deaths and disappearances from the police reports. There were too many. *Way* too many, I couldn't believe no one had noticed. I felt like a reporter tracking down some government conspiracy, waiting for the Men in Black to kick down my door.

"Finally I called Shiki. He was frantic, said they'd been trying to find me, that nobody knew if I'd died in the fire or what. I told him I had something I wanted to show him, and he told me to come up to the office the next day. I brought all my stuff—data, printouts, newspaper clippings. I felt like a loon walking into the publisher with this big fat file under one arm.

"Shiki listened, I'll give him that. I told him we had to shut it down, that the players were going crazy and killing each other, that something creepy was happening and I was scared out of my mind. I thought he'd understand, since he'd been acting crazy all along, but he was like a different person now. Calm, smart, reasonable. Asking questions that made it clear how half-assed my 'research' really was."

"Did you tell him about the Queen?"

Aka-sensei snorted. "Of course not. I told you, I didn't believe it myself. And he would have just thrown me in a hospital. I thought the disappearances would be plenty, but he folded his hands and told me how it was going to be. *REAL* would go on, he said. They'd gotten new funding, a new investor who was very interested in the project. They were going to put together a new team, working remotely to help protect the secret. Mariko would 'mysteriously disappear,' in the story, and we'd get a new heroine.

"I got angry with him. Shouted a bit. Told him I wasn't going to be a part of it. That was when he told me there wasn't a place for me on his new team. He was grateful to me for creating *REAL*, and I'd keep getting paid, but they didn't want me to be a part of it anymore. Then he got up and left.

"I just sat there for a while. In shock, I guess. This thing had been my *life* for more than a year, and I was half out of mind with fear, and now he was saying, 'Go home, you're done.' After a while I decided I wasn't going to take it, and I went to find him. I asked one of the office ladies where he'd gone, and she told me he was in the conference room. I was going to storm right into his meeting, I thought. Get in his face.

"The conference room was the kind with glass walls, with blinds all around so you can get some privacy when you need it. Shiki had the blinds shut. I could see a little light, though, where something had gotten tangled up. A little peephole. I took a look.

"Shiki was there, all right. And so was *she*."

"The Dark Queen," I say, deadpan.

"The Dark fucking Queen. She'd traded the stupid outfit for a nice black suit, with sunglasses to cover up her eyes. But I could tell it was her. Same face, same body, same long black hair. I *drew* her, of course I could recognize her. And she looked at me, when I put my eye to the window, and *smiled*. Then Shiki started to look around, too, and I ran for it."

"That's it," Aka-sensei says, leaning back in his chair. He looks like a man who has had a weight lifted from his shoulders. "That's the whole story. They keep paying my salary, and I keep turning it into booze and cigarettes. I stay the hell away from anything to do with that game."

"But *REAL* is still running."

"So I hear. I also hear they're on their fourth new heroine." He shakes his head. "Maybe they just don't enjoy the work? But . . ."

"You don't think so."

"I told you the story. It's done. What else do you want?"

"I want to know what you think, Aka-sensei." I finish my drink and set the empty tumbler down. "Do you really believe it? The murders? The Dark Queen?"

He laughs. "Do I look crazy to you? Of course I don't believe it. I was on two hours' sleep a night, running that god-damn game, drinking whenever I got the chance, and Shiki with his goddamn paranoia . . ." He shakes his head. "Just accidents, that's all. Stupid accidents, and people who got bored of a game, and a woman who looked like some drawing I made. That's all it can be, obviously."

A long, silent moment passes. He meets my eyes. His hand tightens on the tabletop, knuckles going white.

"You *do* believe it, don't you?" I say, very quietly.

"She was *there*," he whispers. "I don't know how. It doesn't make any sense. But it was *her*. No one who saw her could think she was . . ." He swallows. "Human. No matter what she looks like—she isn't. And Mariko's dead."

Another pause, and he shakes his head.

"Get out of here," he says. "I'm done with this. Go write your goddamn story. Shiki will never let you print it."

I don't move. He cocks his head, staring at me.

"You're not from the paper, are you," he says, flatly.

"Not exactly."

"Then . . ."

Just for a moment, I let him see my true face. He takes it

surprisingly well. His hands clench into fists, and his face goes pale, but he doesn't scream.

"Can I ask you something?" he says when he manages a breath.

I nod.

"Is this really my fault? All of this. If I hadn't created *REAL . . .*"

"It's about belief, Aka-sensei. My kind has always fed on belief. When people play your game, they *believe*, even if it's only for a while, and that opens the door."

"So I created you. I *designed* you. I wrote the script."

"In a way. I am ancient, and I am newborn."

"But that's *bullshit.*" His hand slams down on the tabletop. One of the beer bottles topples over, rolls to the floor, and shatters. "You're not playing by the rules."

"Oh?"

"The good guys win." There are tears in his eyes. "Everyone *knows* the good guys win, they always win. Mariko sends the Dark Queen back to hell. I wrote the goddamn ending! So if I created you—" He cuts off, his voice thick, and swallows. "If it's all my fault, then why didn't she win?" His voice drops to a whisper. "Why did Mari die?"

"No one really believes in heroes these days, Aka-sensei." I smile. "But *everyone* believes in monsters."

He opens his mouth to reply, pauses as though he doesn't know what to say. I send my power across the table, fast and deadly. Life pulses between us, and I drink it in greedily. I stand up in time to catch him as he slumps forward and lower him gently to the tabletop.

I leave a stack of bills on the table and walk out the bar. No one notices me go. Outside, the crowds have thinned a little, but the touts are still hard at work. It may be my imagination, but the revelry carries a strained, desperate note. There's an anxiety in the air, the nervous tension of the herd in the presence of the predator. I walk back up Ichibanchou-dori and under the Kabuki-cho sign, to where the big black car is waiting.

I slide into the back. *She* is in the other seat, her mirror eyes reflecting the flashing neon of Shinjuku Station for a moment before I pull the door closed behind me. She's dressed in sweatpants and a too-large T-shirt, her river of long, dark hair pulled up and pinned behind her head in a no-nonsense tail.

She speaks in her native tongue, the musical language of a fallen angel, the speech of creation. I understand perfectly. I am, after all, a translator. It's no surprise Aka-sensei didn't recognize me. A twisted little goblin creature—once, perhaps. But I have fed, and grown *strong*.

"Did you find him?"

"Yes, my Queen."

"And is he . . ."

"Yes, my Queen."

She nods, mirror eyes gleaming. "Well done."

The Queen taps the window with her knuckle, and the driver clacks his mandibles in acknowledgment. The black car pulls away from the station, and out into the darkness.

———————

Django Wexler graduated from Carnegie Mellon University in Pittsburgh with degrees in creative writing and computer science. Eventually he migrated to Microsoft in Seattle, where he now lives with two cats and a teetering mountain of books. When not writing, he wrangles computers, paints tiny soldiers, and plays games of all sorts. He is the author of military fantasies *The Thousand Names* and *The Shadow Throne* and the middle-grade fantasy *The Forbidden Library*. His website is djangowexler.com.

OUTLIERS

Nicole Feldringer

Fix your climate model! Join scientists in digging through climate model output from more than thirty international research centers. Your mission: decide whether each file contains interesting information, and identify the key factors contributing to global warming.

Some simulations will be control runs to create a historical baseline. Others will be generated from emissions scenarios with varying burdens of greenhouse gases and aerosols, reflecting alternative socioeconomic pathways.

Complexities in our cloud microphysics scheme are potentially producing unphysical realizations. And who knows what else may turn up? By validating models against actual observations, citizen scientists like yourself will help us better predict, and plan for, climate change where you live!

Esme Huybers-Smith resents taking on the work of some drudge graduate student who should have made better life choices, but her fingers keep flexing to navigate back to the browser tab. The ad, copied to the gamer message board she frequents, is festooned with enough university logos that she thinks maybe they ponied up money for good designers. Could be a slick game. In her apartment, her leg jitters in anticipation; without a full haptic suit, the motion doesn't register on her avatar. She isn't sold on saving the world—isn't sure what that world would look like. The talking heads on the media outlets wax nostalgic about plenty, prosperity, and stretches of peaceful coastline that sound like bullshit to Esme. But a game . . . well, she'll try any game once.

Esme closes windows to clear real estate on her display. She has a vague feeling that she's forgetting to be somewhere but the "Play Now" button beckons, and anyway it's the weekend. She shakes off the feeling and dives into the tutorial.

Gameplay centers around comparing model output ("simulation") with satellite observations ("data").

Step 1: A simulated climate field (temperature, humidity, etc.) will be plotted on the left.

Step 2: Compare the simulation to real-world satellite data automatically loaded on the right.

Step 3: In the comment form, make any specific observations about why the data deserve further scrutiny. Look for areas where the simulation disagrees with the data: Water droplets that are too big or too small, or icy where they should be liquid. Rain that is too heavy or too drizzly. Temperatures that are too cold or too warm. Clouds that form in the wrong place. Links to extensive satellite data archives can be found under the menu bar.

You also have the option to fix the climate model of the nearest modeling center by entering your postal code. Or hit "random."

Esme types in her postal code and is surprised to find a modeling center in New Jersey. There's an FAQ on how climate models work too, with an eye-numbing list of equations. Maybe she'll read it over later.

She's about to pull up her first simulation when a jingle erupts in her earbud. Esme's gaze flicks to the notification icon. Her father. She ignores it, but the ringtone trills a second time. Esme taps to accept.

"Dad, I'm a little busy right now."

"Because you're on the train?"

"What? No."

He continues as if she hasn't said anything. "You're busy because you're on the train to your brother's wedding. Your mother is waiting at the station to pick you up." His voice is dangerously even.

"Ah, about that . . . I'm not going to make the wedding after all."

She listens to him breathe on the other end of the connection. They both know that if she hasn't left by now, she's already missed the wedding. The high-speed train down the coast is six hours minimum. "Jacob will be so busy he won't even notice I'm—"

"Attending virtually," he interrupts.

"But—"

"Nonnegotiable, if you want a second chance with Huybers-Smith. Your family deserves better and so does your new brother-in-law. Wear something nice."

That's rich. She opens her mouth to say she's not particularly inclined to give *him* a second chance, but he's already logged out of chat. She worked for the family corporation out of college, but her father wanted an assistant, and Esme isn't assistant material. To say they butted heads is an understatement.

Esme shrinks the game window to a thumbnail. She pulls up the wedding invitation (re-sent by her father so she couldn't claim she lost it) and taps the door icon in the corner.

Her avatar materializes at her brother's wedding extravaganza on St. Pete Island. She thinks she looks just fine in black jeans and a ripped tank—otherwise how will her brother recognize her? She makes a concession to the occasion by painting on some lipstick. Her aunts' inane greetings wash over her. Esme provides the aunts with equally inane responses. It must be so nice in New Jersey, they say.

Esme imagines her apartment. Her body, visored and gloved and sprawled across rumpled bedsheets. The slit of a window, curtains drawn tight to keep out the glare even though it makes her room stuffy as hell. When the apartment was subdivided decades ago, the contractors ran drywall down the middle of the window so each unit got a bit of natural light. They bisected the shower as well, not that she has the water rations to use it. Balanced on the windowsill and nearly buried by curtain is a withered jade plant that Esme's been meaning to trash for weeks.

"How's the beach?" she asks instead of answering. As long as the aunts don't start in on Jacob's latest triumph at the corporation, maybe she'll survive the family gathering. He always did play well with others. She loves her brother. It's the rest of them who lack subtlety.

"We have an amazing view from the dome, and the margaritas are divine. It's too bad you couldn't make it here for the ceremony." They wear sweaters tossed over their shoulders, the dome's climate control being another, unspoken selling point. Esme licks the salt from her upper lip.

Sure, she could have gone to Florida. But the idea of touristing on the broken back of a hurricane-slammed economy makes her feel like a vampire. In the corner of her display, *Fix Your Climate Model!* beckons.

The guests file into rows of white folding chairs, their avatars auto-tracking their devices for the benefit of Esme and those too infirm to attend in person. NPCs fill out the back rows. Up near a palm tree arbor, Esme's father scans the crowd. Esme waggles her fingers at him. He frowns when he takes in her appearance.

When the minister clears his throat, Esme toggles the windows, bringing up the game and shrinking the wedding to a thumbnail.

She links her hands over her head to stretch, checking the wedding progress bar. The vows are over; the reception has begun. Sunlight sparkles on the Gulf beyond and below the dome, and the tarps of a distant shanty town flap in the breeze. Esme tries to remember if she's ever met her brother's boyfriend—husband—outside of a chat room but draws a blank.

On the game, she hits "Start" and is presented with her first climate simulation. A colorful, meaningless plot fills the window. Satellite data appear on the right with the same height-latitude axes. The two plots look the same, near as she can tell. Esme swipes for the next image and hopes that the difficulty setting ramps up.

It's soothing, she decides, like listening to music. She scans through ten in rapid succession. Then twenty. She gets points for every simulation she looks at, and double points for submitting comments.

"Esme?"

At the top of the display, her name populates the bottom of the high-score board. The first stirrings of game obsession flutter in her chest.

"Esme?"

Her gaze snaps down to the wedding thumbnail, and she hastily maximizes it. A sea of avatar faces stare back at her from a shining, air-conditioned dome overlooking the sea. Esme squints. They all hold champagne flutes aloft. Her father, still trim and rather dapper—at least according to his avatar—stares at her steadily. Her brother, sitting before a gargantuan cake, tugs at their father's coat sleeve, already seeing how this will play out and trying to stop it.

"Esme, the toast?"

Shit. Esme chews her lip, considering whether she can make something up on the fly. Her father's frown deepens, and she shrugs helplessly at her brother.

Days later, boxes of empty Cheez-Its and rehydration packets surround her bed like shrapnel as Esme swipes through simulation after simulation. With her paychecks cleared from the last couple of freelance jobs, she can afford to devote herself to the hunt for the elusive outlier.

She likes outliers. She identifies with outliers.

Unfortunately, the game developers, or climate modelers, don't.

She's been monitoring outlier frequency. The game is converging. If she's right, soon all the models will be tuned to produce the same cookie-cutter output, and extreme weather events won't even be projected. Which means the game can't be won the way Esme plays it.

It also means the other players are being duped. Perhaps

they wouldn't care. With each simulation taking less than a minute to complete, the game is obviously designed to appeal to do-gooders in their spare moments. But the unfairness of it burns in Esme.

The data formats have become more familiar to her than family. Eight times daily instantaneous, monthly mean, lat-lon, lat-height, 500 millibar pressure level. For most players the game probably begins and ends at pattern recognition, but Esme makes a point of paying attention to the plot axes. In a separate window, the satellite data archives are open and ready, in case she wants to double-check the simulation against yet more data.

Her gaze zeros in on a wash of magenta, and she checks the values on the color bar. She barely glances at the data and already she can tell the ice droplet concentration is too high, and the cloud too deep. Esme flags the simulation, typing a quick note in the comment box. As she hits submit, her gaze is trained on the scoreboard. She scowls when her username doesn't budge. Second place. Always the bridesmaid.

She broods at the name above hers: dc2100.

Esme knows she's good. A folder on her desktop is filled with screen captures of her best finds. If someone is scoring higher than she is, they must be following a different MO, flagging minutiae on simulations that Esme skips and racking up double points that way.

She's already mentally composing the message she'll leave on the gamer boards—blowing the whistle on the rigged game. But if the project is canned, what then? No more climate forecasting and it's all on her? No thank you.

Esme pulls up the About page, this time reading more carefully. She considers the contact form but isn't in the mood to wait out a reply. The project scientist is listed as Dr. Derya Çok. A moment later, Esme has accessed her webpage at the nearby lab, complete with contact information.

She'll just call her up and straighten this out.

Esme considers her skin inventory. Her hand hovers over her white male avatar, her go-to when it doesn't suit her to be underestimated. On the other hand, Derya Çok is a woman, and not senior staff. Authenticity could go a long way. With a sigh, Esme pulls off her VR headset and haptic gloves. She leverages herself out of bed and rummages around in her closet for a nice shirt. While her outdated laptop boots, she kicks food wrappers out of the camera field-of-view and initiates the connection as herself.

As she waits for Dr. Çok to accept or reject the call, Esme hopes she won't have to track her down in person. The streets are clogged with refugees, and they make her feel helpless. Meanwhile, ads tout romantic gondola rides around the flooded streets of Atlantic City, or cruises out to the storm-surge barriers. She avoids leaving her apartment.

To Esme's surprise, someone picks up.

"This is Derya Çok." She pronounces it like "choke." Her expression is serious and composed.

Esme straightens. "Hello, Dr. Çok. I'm contacting you about *Fix Your Climate Model!*"

Dr. Çok raises her brows in silent inquiry.

Esme forges on. "I've identified a bug. Initially, whenever I flagged a good outlier, my score would go up, and the game would get harder. But lately, I'm barely seeing any game adjustment at all. It's like the outliers are being tuned away."

Dr. Çok smiles reassuringly. "We have a graduate student who's addressing each report submitted by the public."

"But my score doesn't go up."

"We appreciate your participation. To be clear, you're upset that you haven't won?"

Yes. "No. I'm upset because the game is rigged to reward conservative thinking."

"The game is *designed* to reduce uncertainty in climate change projections. This is what the funding agencies want and the policymakers demand. A single number, or as close as we can give them. Not a wide range that governments can use to argue for inaction. Given the opportunity, they would happily bank on the slim chance that the low estimate is the right one, and leave later generations in the lurch."

"Precise doesn't mean accurate."

Patience has fled Dr. Çok's voice. "I am well aware of the distinction," she says. "*Fix Your Climate Model!* isn't just a game, and winning is not just about one individual. I'm sorry if that offends your aesthetics. For decades, we've struggled to get a handle on cloud variability, and we're actually making progress now."

"But you're preconditioning to predict the answer you want," Esme says.

"It's not about what I want." Dr. Çok makes an arrested motion, as if to pinch the bridge of her nose. "I have a meeting to attend. Good day."

Esme lounges in her chair and steeples her fingers. The image of Dr. Derya Çok lingers on her screen until she keystrokes out of the program.

Should have gone with the avatar, she thinks as she spins in a circle.

Esme needs a hacker.

She doesn't have the computer skills to do what needs doing, and she doesn't have the people skills to convince a random person (or project scientist) to help. Which leaves family. Her father's out of the question. She logs into her private chat room and pings Jacob.

"Hey, bro," she says when his avatar materializes. "I need a hacker."

He mills around the sectional sofa and quirks an eyebrow at the media screen that covers most of one wall. "And you're telling me this why?"

"More specifically, I need your husband."

"I need my husband too," he says. "Too bad you made a scene at our wedding."

She checks to make sure she didn't actually call her father. "You don't really care about that, do you? Toasts are lame. Better that I talked too little—"

"Try not at all."

"—than too much. I saved you the embarrassment."

"That's really not how I . . ." He sighs. "When are you going to stop playing games and grow up, Esme?"

"What do you care how I spend my time anyway? You have your pretty apartment and your pretty husband. Isn't that enough to keep you occupied?"

"It would be, if not for Dad," he says. "I'm sick of being the responsible heir. Take some of the fucking pressure off me for once."

"Reality is one big game to Dad. At least I'm honest about what I'm doing."

An orange tabby leans into Jacob's leg. Jacob starts, then bends over to scratch the cat behind its ears. The beast starts to purr. Esme programmed it to put her guests at ease.

Esme relents. "If you help me with this," she says, "I'll do my best to make up with Dad."

"Deal. If Manuel agrees, of course."

"I agree," a cheery voice calls, picked up by the mic in Jacob's headset.

"You had us on *speaker*?" Esme says in disgust.

"Just grant Manuel access." Jacob logs off, and Manuel appears a moment later.

"So, I'm pretty?" Manuel settles on the sofa, and the cat jumps into his lap.

"Sure, but can you code?"

They share a grin, and Manuel cracks his knuckles.

"Do you know where the code repository is?" He pulls up a window in the space in front of him and leaves it visible to her.

"The lab in New Jersey."

"Give me the address. Let me run a pentest on it." His hands flex in a flurry of keystrokes, and a moment later he groans. "This is a government computer."

"Technically it's a government-*funded* computer. Nonessential, nondefense."

"I don't think they see the distinction."

Esme thinks of Dr. Çok. "They never do."

Manuel lowers his voice. "Do you know any staff account usernames?"

Esme's gaze strays to the open window of *Fix Your Climate Model!*, hidden from Manuel's view. The scoreboard taunts her. "Try dc2100."

"I'll attempt to brute force the password first. Give me a minute."

"Does my father know you can do this?" Esme says.

"He hired me."

Smart. Sense of humor. Maybe Jacob landed a good one after all.

She leaves off pondering her brother's love life when Manuel's hands still. "I have write access. Tell me how you want the game to work."

Esme explains about the convergence. She gets pissed off all over again thinking about it.

"So they're weighting entries more heavily that fall within some preferred range? And then the models are tuned to those output, and provide more of the same?" Manuel asks.

"Exactly that," Esme says, grateful he grasps the problem immediately. "I don't want to break the physics of the models. I just want them to sample the full range of variability."

"I think I can reset the thresholds."

He makes it sound so easy. Esme shakes her hands nervously, and her stomach grumbles. "How long is this going to take?"

"Don't know," he says without looking away from the window.

"Do you mind if I grab something to eat?"

Manuel gives a distracted nod, and Esme puts her avatar on standby. As she slips out of VR, she plucks her sweat-soaked shirt away from her skin and fans herself. It's only three o'clock but she grabs a box of noodle soup and switches on the hotplate. By the time Manuel resurfaces, she's licked the bowl clean.

"I uploaded the patch," he says. "You know network security might question dc2100 and clue in to the backdoor?"

Esme restarts *Fix Your Climate Model!* "As long as they don't catch it till Monday. I have a game to win."

Manuel glances to the side, presumably to a hidden display. "Jacob sent me some articles . . . This game has sparked a wave of climate mitigation policies. It's a good thing they're doing," he says softly. "You're not out to destroy the world, are you?"

Esme recalls what Dr. Derya Çok said. How the policy-makers want an answer, and it doesn't so much matter if the answer is right or wrong as long as they're seen trying to do something. It's not good enough.

"I'm *fixing* the world."

She's nervous to resume the game. What if Manuel's patch didn't fix the problem? What if an overzealous network tech was paying attention and undid the changes to the source code? Esme gives her display the side eye as she selects the first simulation.

It's a boring one. She swipes through the output until she finds something worth flagging.

Chills run along her spine, and she knows Manuel's hack worked.

The image spread before her is a surface map, which is her favorite, because continents. Most of the simulations in the game focus on cloudy skies up in the troposphere, but the problem with big data—the reason the global community of scientists crowdsourced gamers to troll through it in the first place—is that there's too much of it and it's too complex to winnow automatically. And occasionally she runs across surface maps.

It takes her a moment to identify what's different about this particular simulation, a sweep of blues across the whole northeast quadrant of North America. Esme squints at the color bar, then finds New Jersey for reference. It's *colder*. By about five degrees Celsius, and the temperature gradient between the equator and pole is out of whack. From hours spent playing *Fix Your Climate Model!*, Esme knows the warming pattern has a profound effect on the circulation of the atmosphere, the distribution of clouds, the intensity of rain. The boundaries of deserts.

She stares at the display. With the original thresholds back in place, this find will send her to the top of the scoreboard, but so what? Who does that help other than her own ego? Not the homeless encampments up and down the Eastern Seaboard.

Esme's hand flexes in an aborted keystroke. If only she had a way to pull up the matching precipitation file, or the emissions cocktail, or the daily extremes. She wants access beyond that doled out by the game, the kind of access that no one will grant a gamer. She also has more resources than most, much as she hates to admit it.

Dr. Derya Çok was right about one thing. Fixing the game world is the lesser goal. Esme scares herself, a little, even contemplating manipulating the actual climate. Engineering hurdles don't daunt her but unintended consequences do. As does the ethical dilemma of optimizing one region's climate at the expense of another's, and what does "optimize" even mean. But it would be irresponsible not to study these cases. If some models are simulating more amenable climates, she wants to know why, and if that can be replicated in the real world.

Esme sends a chat request to her father. If her family wants her back in the fold, they'll have to take her on her own terms.

Her father is quiet for a long moment after she makes her proposition. "How do I know you won't bail on this project too?"

"I didn't leave last time," Esme says, encouraged that he hasn't said no outright. "You pushed me out."

"I expected you to want to learn the ropes from me, not try to take over."

Esme shrugs. "I had my own ideas. I *have* my own ideas."

She finishes the conversation with her father and turns her attention back to *Fix Your Climate Model!* Into the comment box, she types:

Dear Derya/dc2100,

I know you'll tell me it's way more complex than I realize. That this one (awesome) simulation spit out by one climate model doesn't represent a panacea. That's okay.

But if there's one outlier, there can be another. It's beautiful, what's out here in the fringe.

I'm involved in a new geoengineering working group at Huybers-Smith, and we could use your expertise. I've already okayed your consulting fees.

The more I think about it, the more I wonder if you seeded that simulation for someone to find. Either way, I'm pretty sure shilling your precisely accurate predictions to the government gets old, though I've done what I can to alleviate that. Besides, where's the fun if you're always in first place?

Esme Huybers-Smith

———————

Nicole Feldringer holds a PhD in atmospheric sciences from the University of Washington and a master's degree in geological sciences. In 2011, she attended the Viable Paradise Writer's Workshop, and her first published short story appeared in the *Sword & Laser Anthology*. She currently lives in Los Angeles, where she is a research fellow at the California Institute of Technology. Find her on Twitter @nicofeld or at www.nicofeld.com.

<end game>

Chris Avellone

Your bedroom. (In the bed)
You are in your bed. You are cold and trembling under the thin sheet.

The alarm is beeping loudly.

The sound is like blades in your head.

:<turn off alarm>
You can't reach the alarm from the bed.

The thin sheet covering you is coarse, and scratches at your skin like sandpaper.

The alarm is beeping loudly.

:<get up>
You crawl out of the bed. You feel nauseous. Your bare feet crunch against what feels like layers of papers, books, and cardboard.

The room is freezing, even colder than the bed. You are shuddering.

It is dark in the room.

The alarm is beeping loudly.

:<tiurn off alarm>
I don't understand the word "tiurn."

:<turn off alarm>
It is too dark to see.

:<turn on light>
With a trembling hand, you fumble for the lamp switch. The lamp
bursts to life, momentarily blinding you.

    You notice your hand is shaking.

Your bedroom.
You are in your bedroom. It has not been cleaned in some time.
The bed you have just left is covered with a thin sheet flecked
with red, and a small lamp rests on a nightstand near the bed.
Through the narrow window you can see the dark street outside.
It is snowing. Books, unopened mail, and trash are scattered on
the floor, blanketing it completely.

    More papers and book pages are pinned to the walls, burying
the wall underneath.

    The lamp on the nightstand is on (providing light).

    There is a locked door to the hall to the west, and a closed
door to the bathroom is to the east.

    An old computer sits on a table against the wall. On the
computer table are empty soda cans, a pizza box, a pill bottle,
and even more drifts of papers and books. In front of the table
is a chair.

    There is a phone on the computer table. A red light, indi-
cating a message, is flashing.

    The alarm is beeping loudly. Even with the light on, you
cannot see it.

:<listen>

The beeping is coming from beneath a pile of papers on the floor beneath the nightstand.

:<examine pile>

The pile is a mass of unopened letters, blank paper, and pages torn from books. Every blank space on every paper you see is covered with marks in black pen: rectangles joined by arrows, all at right angles to each other.

    An electrical cord snakes into the pile from the wall.

:<search>

You must tell me what to search.

:<search pile>

You cannot search the pile without disturbing the patterns drawn across the pages.

:<pull cord>

You jerk the cord from the wall, and the buried alarm clock falls silent.

    You notice your hand is shaking.

:<look>

Your bedroom.

You are in your bedroom. It has not been cleaned in some time. The bed you have just left is covered with a thin sheet flecked with red, and a small lamp rests on a nightstand near the bed. Through the narrow window you can see the dark street outside. It is snowing. Books, unopened mail, and trash are scattered on the floor, blanketing it completely.

More papers and book pages are pinned to the walls, burying the wall underneath.

The lamp on the nightstand is on (providing light).

There is a locked door to the hall to the west, and a closed door to the bathroom is to the east.

An old computer sits on a table against the wall. On the computer table are empty soda cans, a pizza box, a pill bottle, and even more drifts of papers and books. In front of the table is a chair.

There is a phone on the computer table. A red light, indicating a message, is flashing.

:<examine door>
Which door do you mean, the bathroom door or the hall door?

:<hall door>
There was no verb in that sentence!

:<examine hall door>
The thick wooden door to the hall bears the same symbols as the papers by the nightstand and the papers on the walls, except the symbols are scratched directly into its surface.

The door is triple-locked, the top lock a large dead bolt. There is a mail slot (closed). A pile of unopened mail lies beneath the mail slot. The hall door does not look like it's been opened in some time.

:<examine computer>
The computer is substandard, and so old it is surprising it still works. A thick CRT green-and-black monochrome monitor rests on top of the CPU/keyboard unit. The fans inside are silent.

The computer screen is on. There is something written on the screen.

You can't make it out from where you are standing.

:<sit in chair>
Your' bedroom. (In the chair)
You are now sitting in the chair.

The computer table is covered in papers, pages torn from books, and unopened envelopes, all with marks similar to the pages layering the floor and walls.

Every one of the papers on the desk has been carefully arranged so the marks make a continuous path across the pages and even onto the stained cardboard interior of the pizza box, the same arrow and box pattern repeating, always at right angles.

The keyboard is in front of you, and the computer screen is at eye level.

The computer screen is on.

There is something written on the screen.

:<read computer>
You must tell me how to do that with the computer.

:<read screen>

Warren slumped upon the floor of the steam tunnel, exhausted, the cold eating its way into his jacket. His joints were stiff and his muscles painfully sore—he must have drifted off. He checked his watch and with a start, saw that he had been asleep for hours. His heart began to beat frantically.

He couldn't allow himself to fall asleep again. Not down here.

:<look>

The tunnel he was in was dirty, cold, and dark. He had had to crouch in order to move through it, and even still, he banged his head occasionally when he rose too high.

Heavy pipes ran along the walls and ceiling, vanishing into the darkness ahead.

He couldn't remember how he had gotten here.

:<take inventory>

Warren checked himself over to make sure nothing was missing. His hands were burdened with a penlight (providing light) and a heavy iron crowbar; in the folds of his jacket, he had a tiny pocketknife and a small box of crackers.

:<get up>

Warren rose from his sitting position into a low crouch and rubbed his hands together to ward off the chill. Pointing his light down the darkened tunnel, he tried to make out what was ahead. The penlight shed only a small beam, but it was surprisingly strong.

Warren clutched his jacket tightly around himself as he shivered. It had never been this cold before. His teeth chattered, and he fought to control the noise.

Sounds carried far—too far—down here.

:<go east>

Bent forward, Warren made his way down the darkness of the tunnel. As he moved, his hair brushed one of the pipes

above him, and he instinctively ducked while keeping his eyes
firmly fixed ahead, the beam like a compass.

After a few seconds, he found himself in a section of tunnel identical to the one he had just left. Ahead of him, there
was nothing but blackness.

These tunnels seemed to go on forever.

:<go east>

Warren took another few steps forward, and suddenly
stopped. He could hear a scraping noise . . . feet? . . . farther
down the tunnel, but he couldn't quite make it out.

He could feel his heart beating faster.

:<listen>

Warren froze and strained to make out the noise. It
sounded like it was coming closer.

The drumming of his heart fell out of rhythm, skipping
beats, and he took a breath as quietly as he dared.

:<go east>

Warren advanced, toward the noise. He tried to move
as quietly as possible, but the crowbar scraped against the
ground and echoed down the tunnels.

The sound stopped.

:<listen>

Warren strained to pick up the noise again but heard
nothing. He knew he hadn't imagined it. Switching the pen-

light to his left hand, he kept it pointed down the tunnel and transferred the crowbar to his right. Although reassured by the cold iron, he did not fool himself—if it came down to it, he couldn't use the crowbar to good effect in the cramped tunnel.

Still, he might get in a good hit before someone . . . *something* . . . got past his guard.

He hoped it wouldn't come to that. He had been lucky to get this far.

:<go east>

Warren advanced slowly and as quietly as he could manage down the tunnel. The penlight lit his way, and Warren noticed the darkness seemed thicker ahead. Maybe the tunnel opened up into a maintenance room—the pipes must lead somewhere.

He froze as he heard the scraping sound again, then silence.

:<save game: scraping noise>
Saved.

Warren shivered again and gripped the crowbar.

He was scared. Terribly scared. For the hundredth time, he cursed his stupidity. He hadn't wanted to come down here. But he had to. He had spent years mapping its chambers. He had to see what lay at the end.

Someone had built this place for a reason. They must have . . . Everything about it felt *wrong*, and it was up to him to fix it.

He clutched the crowbar tighter.

`:<wait>`

Whatever was ahead, he wasn't going to rush out and meet it. The hairs on the back of Warren's neck rose as he watched the blackness ahead of him. It seemed to roll nearer, thicker somehow, but the light revealed nothing.

It was difficult to hear past the thudding of his heartbeat struggling in his chest. The beats were driven even more out of rhythm as adrenaline coursed through him.

`:<listen>`

As Warren strained to listen, the darkness ahead of him came alive. With a yelp of fear, Warren dropped the penlight as the *thing* seized him with its cold talons.

He had no room to run as it engulfed him.

`:<hit thing>`
`(With the crowbar)`

Warren flailed in its embrace, and swung the crowbar wildly. It missed the *thing* completely, and he screamed as he felt talons tear at his throat and it began to feed.

His crowbar fell from his grasp, and warm blood flowed from Warren as the *thing* feasted.

`You are dead. You have scored 0 points.`
`    Do you wish to Restore, Restart, or Quit?`

`:<quit>`
`Are you sure you want to Quit? (Y = Affirmative)`

:<>

Are you sure you want to Quit? (Y = Affirmative)

:<n>

Do you wish to Restore, Restart, or Quit?

:<get up>

You are standing. Your legs are trembling. Your throat is dry.

It is difficult to catch your breath. Your heart is beating rapidly.

The room is colder than before.

:<take breath>

You close your eyes and try to steady yourself.

Your heartbeat slows.

You are trembling. Your throat is dry.

:<look>

Your bedroom.

The lamp on the nightstand is on (providing light).

There is a locked door to the hall to the west, and a closed door to the bathroom is to the east.

An old computer sits on a table against the wall. On the computer table are empty soda cans, a pizza box, a pill bottle, and even more drifts of papers and books. In front of the table is a chair.

There is a phone on the computer table. A red light, indicating a message, is flashing.

You are trembling. Your throat is dry.

:<get soda>
You have the soda can.

    You are trembling. Your throat is dry.

:<drink soda>
The can is empty.

:<drop can>
Dropped.

:<get another can>
I don't understand the word "another."

:<open door>
Which door do you mean, the bathroom door or the hall door?

:<open the bathroom door>
With a trembling hand, you turn the knob. The bathroom door
opens with a slow creak.

    The bathroom door is now open.

:<go into bathroom>
You can't go there.

:<go east>
The bathroom.
You are in a tiny bathroom.

    There is a toilet, a sink, and a mirror. Beside the sink is
a small white plastic trash can.

    There is a faint sickly smell to the room.

:<turn on water>
You can't do that.

:<examine sink>
The sink is a small porcelain sink, with a faucet and two han-
dles marked "Hot" and "Cold."

There is dried vomit and blood in the sink.

:<turn handle>
Which handle do you mean, the Hot handle or the Cold handle?

:<turn cold>
Your hand trembles on the handle as you turn it. Cold water flows
from the faucet. The water turns a brownish red as it washes
away the vomit and blood.

:<get water>
You'll need a container.

:<go west>
Your bedroom.
The lamp on the nightstand is on (providing light).

There is a locked door to the hall to the west, and a closed
door to the bathroom is to the east.

An old computer sits on a table against the wall. On the computer
table are empty soda cans, a pizza box, a pill bottle, and even
more drifts of papers and books. In front of the table is a chair.

There is a phone on the computer table. A red light, indicating a message, is flashing.

An empty soda can lies on the floor.

You are trembling. Your throat is dry.

:<get can>
Taken.

    Your hand is trembling.

:<examine hand>
Your hand is trembling.

:<examine self>
You are tired, cold, and your body is trembling. Your throat is
dry. You are naked.

    You are carrying:

    An empty soda can.

:<go east>
The bathroom.
Cold water is running from the faucet.

:<go west>
Your bedroom.
The lamp on the nightstand is on (providing light).

    There is a locked door to the hall to the west, and an open
door to the bathroom is to the east.

    An old computer sits on a table against the wall. On the computer
table are empty soda cans, a pizza box, a pill bottle, and even
more drifts of papers and books. In front of the table is a chair.

    There is a phone on the computer table. A red light, indi-
cating a message, is flashing.

    You are trembling. Your throat is dry.

:<get pill>
You don't see a pill here.

:<get bottle>
You have the pill bottle. It rattles as you pick it up. It continues to rattle as you hold it.

    Your hands are trembling.

:<examine bottle>
The pill bottle is a prescription bottle of sickly brown plastic. It is sealed with a twist-off white cap with a warning label stuck to the top. You do not recognize the name of the medication on the label. The name on the prescription is not yours.

    The bottle rattles in your trembling fingers.

:<go east>
The bathroom.
Cold water is running from the faucet.

:<fill can with water>
The soda can is now filled with water.

:<take pill>
The pill bottle is closed.

:<open bottle>
You twist the cap off. Inside the bottle are twenty-three red pills.

:<get pill>
You have the pill.

    Your hands are trembling.

:<eat pill>
The pill has a bitter taste. You try to choke it down, but it burns your tongue and lodges in your throat.

:<dtrink water>
I don't understand the word "dtrink."

:<drink water>
The soda can is now empty. The refreshingly cold water enables
you to wash down the pill.

:<wait>
Time passes . . .

:<wait>
Time passes . . .
    You feel a rush of warmth.

:<examine self>
You are alert, warm, and you are no longer trembling. You are
naked.
    You are carrying:
    An empty soda can.
    A pill bottle. The pill bottle is open. In the pill bot-
tle are:
    Twenty-two red pills.

:<look in mirror>
In the mirror, you see Warren.

:<look at warren>
I don't understand the word "Warren."

:<examine warren>
I don't understand the word "Warren."

:<take inventory>

You are alert, warm, and you are no longer trembling. You are naked.

   You are carrying:

   An empty soda can.

   A pill bottle. The pill bottle is open. In the pill bottle are:

   Twenty-two red pills.

:<drop can>

The can clatters to the hard floor and rolls to rest next to the trash can.

:<examine trash>

In the trash can is a dried, bloody washcloth, a snapped ballpoint pen (black), and five empty pill bottles.

   The pen has bled into the washcloth, the black mixing with the red.

:<go west>

Your bedroom.

The lamp on the nightstand is on (providing light).

   There is a locked door to the hall to the west, and a closed door to the bathroom is to the east.

   An old computer sits on a table against the wall. On the computer table are empty soda cans, a pizza box, and even more drifts of papers and books. In front of the table is a chair.

   There is a phone on the computer table. A red light, indicating a message, is flashing.

:<sit in chair>
Your bedroom. (In the chair)
You are now sitting in the chair.

The computer table is covered in papers, pages torn from books, and unopened envelopes, all with marks similar to the pages layering the floor and walls.

Every one of the papers on the desk has been carefully arranged so the marks make a continuous path across the pages and even onto the stained cardboard interior of the pizza box, the same arrow and box pattern repeating, always at right angles.

The keyboard is in front of you, and the computer screen is at eye level.

The computer screen is on.

There is something written on the screen.

:<read screen>
Do you wish to Restore, Restart, or Quit?

:<restore>
Name of Restored Game:

:<scraping noise>
Restored.

Warren shivered again and gripped the crowbar.

He should feel scared. But he wasn't. He had to keep going. He had spent years mapping its chambers, testing each route, going ever onward. But this place . . . It was falling apart. Whatever was wrong here, he would fix it. He was near the end, he could feel it.

He clutched the crowbar tighter.

`:<listen>`

Warren strained to listen, but heard nothing from the blackness ahead.

But he was more certain than ever there was a space ahead, a room—and a room meant enough space to swing a crowbar freely. He felt a rush of warmth at the thought, and his heart thudded tightly in his chest, harder, faster. A smile crawled to his lips as he raised the crowbar.

Whatever stood in his way, he was going to kill it.

`:<go east>`

The narrow tunnel walls fell away to the sides as Warren entered the chamber and drew himself up from his crouch to a ready stance.

He swung his small light quickly around the room, his crowbar gripped tightly.

Warren was sure the noise had come from here, but the room was empty.

`:<examine room>`

The walls were crumbling brick, each brick framed by hollow black lines where the mortar had cracked away, leading like steps down to the broken concrete of the floor, where the surface became a mass of ragged, perpendicular cracks.

Almost on instinct, Warren caught himself following the lines of the wall and floor where they led—all to the opposite side of the room, where the concrete and brick fell away into a wall of blackness . . . into what seemed an even larger space.

He could feel the chill from the opening, but his body fought off the shiver, his heart beating even faster to drive heat to his limbs. He had come too far to turn back, had spent too long down here.

Had the *thing* gotten behind him somehow?

He risked a glance over his shoulder at the tunnel he'd just left, stabbing it with the light.

As he did, Warren heard the scraping of feet behind him as the *thing* rushed from the darkness of the maw.

```
:<hit thing>
(With the crowbar)
```

With a rush of adrenaline, Warren rolled to the side, and the *thing* hissed as its talons tore at empty air. The penlight fell to the floor and rolled across the ground.

Laughing triumphantly, Warren gripped the crowbar high with both hands and swung down at where he imagined the *thing*'s head would be.

There was a sickening crunch, like an eggshell cracking, and the *thing* crumpled to the ground.

```
:<hit thing>
(With the crowbar)
```

Warren brought the crowbar down again and again, covering it with black ichor. His laughter possessed him as he smashed at the *thing* repeatedly in the darkness, his crowbar finding solid body wherever it landed.

When he found his breath catching, he stepped back. The floor was slick, and he almost fell.

```
:<get light>
```

Warren picked up the penlight and shone it on the *thing*.

Where he had struck, there was only black ichor spill-ing across the floor, slowly filling the cracks in the concrete around him.

```
:<examine thing>
```

Warren looked for any solid remains, but found none—only the ichor that ran across the dirty floor like spilled ink. He gave a last, nervous laugh. His hands were clenched white around the crowbar.

Ichor dripped down the shaft and coated his hands. He didn't care. He'd never felt more alive. This was the last obsta-cle, he was sure of it.

It had to be.

```
:<save game: killed thing>
Saved.
```

```
:<go east>
```

Warren, his resolve strengthened by his victory, gripped the crowbar as he advanced on the only exit from the cham-ber. The depth of the maw grew as he approached.

He felt the same chill as before, stronger, and this time, he found he could not shake it off. His heart felt dull in his chest, slow, as if trying to hold him back.

His steps slowed as his heartbeat slowed, then stopped dead as he reached the edge. His light found no walls in the space ahead . . . at least none the light could reach.

The brick walls, even the concrete floor ... all fell away into darkness.

:<examine floor>

As he studied the floor, the ichor from the *thing* rolled through the jagged veins of the floor toward the maw, as if drawn to it. As it touched the edge of the darkness, the two bled together seamlessly.

The cold was sharper now, and he drew the jacket around him.

He had crossed countless chambers and tunnels, had mapped them, move by move. He had spent years down here, exploring. But he had never encountered anything like this.

As before, he felt a wrongness well up within him, but this time was different: he could not go back.

This was the only path left to him if he wanted to continue.

Yet he could not move his feet, and stood rooted, afraid, facing the only exit.

:<exit>
Game exited. You have scored 0 points.
    Do you wish to Restore, Restart, or Quit?

:<quit>
Are you sure you want to Quit? (Y = Affirmative)

:<n>
Do you wish to Restore, Restart, or Quit?

:<get up>
You are standing. You feel dizzy.

It is difficult to catch your breath. Your chest feels tight. The room is colder than before.

:<take breath>
You close your eyes and try to steady yourself but your chest continues to shake.

Your heart feels tight, like a fist.

You are trembling. Your throat is dry.

:<look>
Your bedroom.
The lamp on the nightstand is on (providing light).

There is a locked door to the hall to the west, and a closed door to the bathroom is to the east.

An old computer sits on a table against the wall. On the computer table are empty soda cans, a pizza box, and even more drifts of papers and books. In front of the table is a chair.

There is a phone on the computer table. A red light, indicating a message, is flashing.

:<pick up phone>
You pick the phone off the cradle.

There is small click and a gender-neutral voice states, "You have one new message."

:<listen>
You hear nothing.

:<press playt>
I don't understand the word "playt."

:<press play>

The answering machine comes to life. The same gender-neutral voice as before speaks.

"First message."

:<listen>

There is only silence.

:<listen>

There is only silence. The machine recorded something, but there are no words.

:<listen>

"Warren."

:<listen>

"The next time you go below, you will never return."

:<listen>

The voice is your own.

:<smash phone against wall>

You can't do that with the phone.

:<hit phone>

(With fist)

You hit the phone and knock it from the table, scattering the papers around it and breaking the carefully drawn lines bridging the pages.

The phone falls to the floor. The message light is dark.

Your hands are shaking.

:<examine self>
You are hallucinating, warm, and your hands are shaking. You
are naked.

    You are carrying:

    An empty soda can.

    A pill bottle. The pill bottle is open. In the pill bottle are:

    Twenty-two red pills.

:<eat pills>
You aren't holding them.

:<get pill>
You have the pill.

    You notice your hands are shaking.

:<eat pills>
How many pills do you want?

:<all>
The pills have a bitter taste.

    You try to choke them down, but they burn your tongue and
lodge in your throat.

:<eat pills>
With effort, you swallow all the pills. Your head spins.

    You begin to feel nauseous.

:<sit in chair>
Your bedroom. (In the chair)
You are now sitting in the chair.

    The papers, once carefully arranged, are now a mass of broken
lines that break at the edge of the pages, going nowhere.

The keyboard is in front of you, and the computer screen is
at eye level.

The computer screen is black.

:<examine computer>
The computer and the monitor do not look like they've worked for
a long time. There is no heat coming from them, and the fans are
silent, just as they were before.

Dust covers the top of the monitor but the letters on the
keyboard have worn away from use.

:<examine screen>
The computer screen is black.

:<wait>
Time passes . . .

You feel a rush of warmth, stronger than before.

You can feel your heart beating fast.

:<look>
Your bedroom. (In the chair)
You are sitting in the chair in front of the computer table.

The papers, once carefully placed, are now a mass of broken
lines that break at the edge of the pages, going nowhere.

They seem to bleed off the table and onto the floor, crossing
the lines on the papers there and up onto the walls.

The keyboard is in front of you, and the computer screen is
at eye level.

There is something written brightly on the screen, so bright
it hurts your eyes.

```
:<redscreen>
I don't understand "redscreen."


:<read screen>
Do you wish to Restore, Restart, or Quit?


:<restore>
Name of Restored Game:


:<killed thing>
Restored.
```

Warren looked for any solid remains, but found none—only the ichor that ran across the dirty floor like spilled ink. He had the urge to laugh, but it died in his throat. His hands clenched around the crowbar slowly relaxed. He could feel his heart hammering in his chest, but he wasn't afraid.

Ichor coated his hands. This was the last obstacle, he was sure of it.

It had to be.

```
:<look east>
```

Warren turned to the maw. He didn't raise his light; instead, he simply stared into the blackness. There was no sound, not even the whisper of his breathing.

There had to be something beyond, but Warren felt apprehension begin to seep into him. He had come all this way. His heart hammered, harder, in his chest.

There had to have been a reason.

```
:<look east>
```

He continued to stare into the darkness ahead of him. There was nothing there.

He fought the urge to look back the way he had come. He had lost his map. Retracing his steps, finding his way back . . . It would take too long. He was lost.

```
:<go east>
```

Warren advanced toward the maw and stopped at the edge. Ichor pooled around his feet, rising from the cracks in tandem with the pounding in his chest.

Don't, Warren begged.

I don't have to do this. I can go back. Back to my room.

I can piece it all together again.

```
:<go east>
Warren's hand trembled.
    He felt a rush of warmth.
    Then, almost against his will, his body fell into darkness.
```

———————

Chris Avellone is the creative director of Obsidian Entertainment. He started his career at Interplay's Black Isle Studios division, and he's worked on a whole menagerie of RPGs throughout his career, including *Planescape: Torment*, *Fallout 2*, the Icewind Dale series, *Dark Alliance*, *Knights of the Old Republic II*, *Neverwinter Nights 2: Mask of the Betrayer*, *Alpha Protocol*, *Fallout: New Vegas*, *FNV DLC: Dead Money*, *Old World Blues*, and *Lonesome Road*. He just finished working on inXile's *Wasteland 2*, the *Legend of Grimrock* movie treatment, and the *FTL: Advanced*

Edition, and is currently doing joint work on Obsidian's Kickstarter RPG, *Pillars of Eternity,* and inXile's *Torment: Tides of Numenera.* His story was inspired by the fine Infocom game *The Lurking Horror,* one of the first games to ever frighten him.

SAVE ME PLZ

David Barr Kirtley

Meg hadn't heard from Devon in four months, and she realized that she missed him. So on a whim she tossed her sword and scabbard into the backseat of her car and drove over to campus to visit him.

She'd always thought that she and Devon would be one of those couples who really did stay friends afterward. They'd been close for so long, and things hadn't ended that badly. Actually, the whole incident seemed pretty silly to her now. Still, she'd been telling herself that the split had been for the best—with her working full-time and him still an undergrad. It was like they were in two different worlds. She'd been busy with work, and he'd always been careless about answering email, and now somehow four months had passed without a word.

She parked in the shadow of his dorm, then grabbed her sword and strapped it to her jeans. She approached his building. A spider, dog-sized, iridescent, rappelled toward her, its thorned limbs plucking the air. She dropped a hand to the hilt of her sword. The spider wisely withdrew, back to its webbed lair amid the eaves.

She had no key card, so she waited for someone to open

the door. She checked her reflection. Eyes large, hips slender, ears a bit tapered at the tips. She looked fine. (Though she'd never be a match for the imaginary elf-maid Leena.)

Finally someone exited, an unfamiliar brown-haired girl. Meg caught the door and passed into the lobby. She climbed the stairs and walked down the hall to Devon's door. She knocked.

His roommate, Brant, answered, looking half-asleep or maybe stoned. "Hey, Meg," Brant mumbled—casually, as if he'd just seen her yesterday. "How's the real world?"

"Like college," she said, "but with less art history. Is Devon here?"

"Devon?" Brant seemed confused. "Oh. You don't know." He hesitated. "He dropped out."

"What?" She was startled.

"Just packed up and left. Weeks ago. He said it didn't matter anymore. He was playing that game all the time." Brant didn't need to say *which* game. Least of all to her. "He said he found something huge. In the game. Then he went away."

"Went away where? Is he all right?"

Brant shrugged. "I don't know, Meg. He didn't tell me. You could email him, I guess. Or try to find him online. He's always playing that game." Brant shook his head. "And I mean *always*."

Meg strode to her car. She chucked her sword in back, slid into the driver's seat, and slammed the door.

Devon was the smartest guy she'd ever met, and the stupidest. How could he drop out with just one year left? Sadly, she wasn't all that surprised.

She'd met him at an off-campus party her junior year.

They'd ended up on the same couch. Before long he was on his third beer and telling her, "I didn't even want to go to college. My parents insisted. I had a whole other plan."

She said, "Which was?"

"To be a prince." He gave a grandiose shrug. "I think I'd make a pretty good prince." He noted her skeptical expression, and added, "But not prince of like, England. I'm not greedy. Prince of Monaco would be fine. Wait, is that even a country?"

"Yes," she said.

"Good," he declared, thumping his beer on the end table. "Prince of Monaco. Or if that's taken . . ."

"Liechtenstein," she suggested.

"Liechtenstein, great!" he agreed, pointing. "Or Trinidad and Tobago."

She shook her head. "It's not a monarchy. No princes."

"No princes?" He feigned outrage. "Well, screw *them* then. Liechtenstein it is."

After that she noticed him everywhere. He seldom went to class or did coursework, so he was always out somewhere—joking with friends in the dining hall, pacing around the pond, or sitting under a tree in the central quad, doodling. His carefree independence was oddly endearing, especially to her, who was always so conscientious, though later his indifference to school worried her. She'd ask, "What'll you do after you graduate?"

He'd just shrug and say, "Grades don't matter. Just that you have the degree."

And now he'd dropped out.

Angry, she started her car. She drove back to her apartment.

She emailed him repeatedly, but got no response. Mutual friends hadn't heard from him. His mom thought he was still in school. Meg got really worried. Finally, she resorted to something she'd promised herself she'd never do—she drove over to the mall to buy the game.

It was called *Realms of Eldritch*, a groundbreaking multiplayer online game full of quests and wizards and monsters. Some of the game was based on real life: People carried magic swords, and many of the enemies were real, such as wolves or goblins or giant spiders. And like in real life, there was a gnome who sometimes appeared to give you quests or hints or items. But most of it was pure fantasy: dragons and unicorns and walking trees and demon lords.

And elves. In the game store, Meg eyed the box art. Leena, the golden-haired and impossibly buxom elf-maid, grinned teasingly.

Meg had a complicated relationship with Leena (especially considering that Leena wasn't real). The year before, Meg had been riffling through Devon's notebook and had come across a dozen sketches of Leena. The proportions were off, but each sketch came closer and closer to being a perfect representation. Meg had begun teasing Devon that he was in love with Leena. Meg had also once, foolishly, dressed up as Leena in bed, for Devon's twenty-first birthday. It was just a campy gag, but he'd seemed way too into it. He'd even called her "Leena." She'd never worn the costume again, and he'd never brought it up. He'd been pretty drunk that night, and she'd wondered if he even remembered her looking like someone else.

She bought the game (planning to return it the next day) and started home. In the rearview mirror she saw a flock of giant bats tailing her. She tensed, ready to slam on the brakes and reach for her sword, but finally the bats veered off and vanished into the west.

Back at her apartment, she opened the game box and dumped its contents out on her coffee table. Half a dozen CDs, a thick manual, some flyers, a questionnaire. It seemed so innocuous. Hard to believe that this little box could destroy a relationship. She and Devon had been so happy together for almost a year before he got caught up in this game.

She installed it. As progress bars chugged, she thumbed through the manual, which described the rules in mind-numbing detail—races, classes, attributes, combat, inventory, spells. She'd never understood how someone as smart and talented as Devon could waste so much time on this stuff.

Maybe she could have understood if the game at least featured some brilliant story, but Devon spent all his time doing "level runs"—endlessly repeating the same quest over and over in hopes of attaining some marginally more powerful magical item. And even after he'd become as powerful as the game allowed, he still kept playing, exploiting different bugs so that he could duplicate superpowered items or make himself invincible. How could someone who read Heidegger for fun so immerse himself in a subculture of people too lazy or daft to type out actual words, who instead of "Someone please help" would type "sum1 plz hlp"?

Meg, on the rare occasions that she permitted herself solitary recreation, preferred Jane Austen novels or independent films. She'd once told Devon, "I'm more interested in things that are *real*."

He'd been playing the game. Monitor glow made his head a silhouette. He said, "What's *real* is just an accident. No one designed reality to be compelling." He gestured to the screen.

"But a fantasy world *is* so designed. It takes the most interesting things that ever existed—like knights in armor and pirates on the high seas—and combines them with the most interesting things that anyone ever dreamed up—fire-breathing dragons and blood-drinking vampires. It's the world as it *should* be, full of wonder and adventure. To privilege reality simply because it *is* reality just represents a kind of mental parochialism."

She knew better than to debate him. But she still thought the game was vaguely silly, and she refused to play it, though he often bugged her to join in. He'd say, "It's something we could do together."

And she'd answer, "I just don't want to."

And he'd say, "Give it a try. I do things *I* don't want to because they're important to you. Sometimes I even end up liking them."

But by then Meg had already spent far too many hours sitting on the couch watching him play the game, or hearing about it over candlelit dinners, and she didn't intend to do anything to justify his spending any more time on it.

It was hard some nights, after they'd made love, to lie there knowing that he was just itching to slip from her embrace and go back to the game. To know that a glowing electronic box full of imaginary carnage beckoned him in a way that her company and conversation and even body no longer could.

Finally, she couldn't take it anymore. Though she knew she might lose him, she announced, "Devon. Look. I don't know how else to say this. It's that game or me. I'm not kidding."

He released the controls and swiveled in his chair. He gave her a wounded look and said, "That's not fair, Meg. I'd never make you give up something you enjoyed."

She stood her ground. "This is something I'm asking you to do. For me."

"You really want me to delete it?"

"Yes," she said. Oh God, yes.

He bit his lip, then said, "Fine." He fiddled with the computer, then turned to her and added, "There, it's gone. All right?"

"All right," she said, euphoric. And for a few weeks things were great again, like they used to be.

But one night she came over and found him playing it again. She stared. "What are you doing?"

He glanced at her and said, "Oh, hi." He noticed her agitation, and explained, "My guild really needed me for this one quest."

"You told me you deleted it."

He turned back to the screen. "Yeah, I had to reinstall the whole thing. Don't worry, I'll delete it again tomorrow."

Meg was furious. "You *promised.*"

"Come on," he said, "I haven't played for *three weeks*. It's just this one time."

She stomped away. "I told you, Devon. That game or me. Isn't that what I said?"

"Meg, don't leave, okay? Would you just—" Something happened in the game, and he jumped. "Shit! He got me."

She left, slamming the door. Devon called out, "Meg, wait." But he didn't run after her.

She expected him to call and apologize, beg her forgiveness, but he didn't. Days passed, then she sent him a curt email saying that maybe it would be better if they just stayed friends from now on, and—disappointingly—he had agreed.

The game finished installing. Meg hovered the mouse

pointer over the start icon. She felt strangely ambivalent. She'd fought so hard against this damn game, and now she was actually going to run it. She also felt an inexplicable dread, as if the game would suck her in the way it had sucked in Devon, and she'd never escape. But that was silly. She was just using it to contact him. She double-clicked.

The game menu loaded. She created a character and chose all the most basic options—human, female, warrior. The name Meg was taken, so she added a random string of numbers, Meg1274, and logged in. The game displayed a list of servers. Meg did a search for his character, Prince Devonar. He was the only player listed on a server named Citadel of Power. She connected to it.

She typed, "Hi Devon." No response.

She tried again. "Devon? It's me, Meg. Are you there?"

Finally, he answered. "Meg?"

She typed, "Are you OK?"

A long pause. "I found something. In the game. Unbelievable. But now I'm stuck. Need help."

Was this whole situation some elaborate setup to get her to play the game with him? But that was crazy. Not even Devon would drop out of school as part of such a ruse. She typed, "Devon, call me. OK?"

Another pause. "Can't call. Trapped. Plz, Meg, help me. You're the only one who can."

"I can't help," she typed. "I'm only level 1."

"Not in the game," he typed back. "In real life. Ask the gnome. Plz, Meg. I really need you. Can't stay. Meg, save me plz."

She typed frantically. "Devon, wait. What's going on? Where are you???"

But Prince Devonar was gone.

Devon had said to ask the gnome. But that wasn't so easy.

No one really understood what the gnome was. He seemed to wander through time and space. He was usually benevolent, appearing to those in need and offering hints or assistance or powerful items. But he was also fickle and enigmatic. He seemed to only appear after you'd given up hope of finding him. He also seemed to prefer locales with corners that he could pop out from and then disappear around.

So Meg parked downtown and wandered the back alleys. She couldn't stop thinking of Devon's final words: "Save me plz." If only the gnome would show himself. Hours passed.

Forget it. She was going home. She crossed the street—

And then the gnome, before her.

Crimson-robed, white-bearded, flesh like dry sand. One eye brown, kindly. The other blue, inscrutable. In a soft and alien voice he observed, "On a quest."

Finally. She wanted to grab him. "Where's Devon? Tell me."

"This is your path." The gnome pointed to the road at her feet, then westward.

Meg nodded. "I'll follow it."

The gnome turned his kindly brown eye upon her. "Have no fear, though obstacles lie in your way. Your victory is assured, foretold by prophecy: 'When the warrior-maid with love in her heart sets out, sword in her right hand, wand in her left, nothing shall stand before her.'"

"Wand?" she said.

The gnome reached up his sleeve and drew forth a thin black rod, two feet long. He whispered, "The most dire artifact in all the world, the Wand of Reification." He handed it to her. It chilled her fingers, and was so dark that it seemed to have no surface. He said, "Imbued with the power to give form to dreams. It may only be used three times."

Devon had said once that in the game there were items that vanished after you used them. So he never used them. He'd beat quest after quest without them, though they would've aided him considerably. He was always afraid he'd need them later. He'd asked, "What does that say about me?" and she'd said, "You're afraid of commitment?" and he'd laughed. It wasn't so funny now though, as she clutched this wand, so potent yet so ephemeral. How could she ever use it?

When she looked again, the gnome had vanished.

Meg retrieved her car and set off the way the gnome had pointed. The road: a double yellow line and two lanes of black asphalt, bordered by sidewalks. She drove. Skyscrapers and then suburbs fell away behind her. She passed clusters of thatched-roof cottages. Men farmed and cows grazed and windmills turned. Sometimes ancient oaks pressed in close to the road. Sometimes she saw castles on distant hills.

The needle on her gas gauge sank, and she hoped to find a station, but there were none. Finally, the engine died. She left her car and set off down the sidewalk.

Twilight came. Then the long line of streetlamps lit up, casting eerie white splotches on the darkened street and creating a tableau somehow dreamlike and unreal. She thought of how Devon and Brant would sometimes smoke pot and then get into long, rambling discourses on the nature of existence. During one such conversation, Devon had said, "Do you know anything about quantum mechanics?"

"Not really," Brant had replied.

So Devon said, "Well, in the everyday world, things exist. If I leave a book on this table, I know for sure that it's there. But when you get down to the subatomic level, things don't exist in the same way. They only exist as *probabilities*, until directly observed. How do you explain that?"

Brant countered, "How do *you* explain it?"

Devon smirked. "Like this: Our world isn't real. It's a *simulation*. An incredibly sophisticated one, but not without limits. It can keep track of every molecule, but not every last subatomic particle. So it estimates, and only starts figuring out where specific particles are when someone goes looking for them."

"That's so weird," Brant had said.

Meg heard a vehicle approaching from behind. Then its headlights lit the street. She glanced back into the glare, then kept walking. The vehicle slowed. It followed, in a way she didn't like. Finally, it pulled even with her. A black SUV, its windows open. From the darkness came a rasping, lascivious voice, "Hey, where you going?"

She ignored it, walked.

"Need a ride?" The voice waited. "Hey, I'm talking to you." A long pause. "What, you too good to talk to us?" When Meg didn't answer, the voice hissed, "Bitch," and the driver gunned the engine. The truck sped off.

Meg watched it go, then watched its taillights flare a sudden red challenge, watched it swing around, its headlights sweeping the trees, watched it come on, two coronas of searing white. Cackles rose from its windows. Meg drew her sword and stepped into the street. The car horn shrieked.

She slashed upward, between the lights, and the truck split. Its two halves swept past on either side. Its right half sped into a tree. Its left half flipped over and rolled thirty yards along the pavement.

Meg followed after. She neared the wreckage. A scraggly vermillion arm reached up through one window, then a face appeared—hairless, dark-eyed, ears like rotting carrots. A goblin. He squirmed free and dropped to the ground. A second goblin crawled from beneath the wreck.

The first drew a long, wavy dagger. "Look what you did to my truck!"

But before he could start forward, the second grabbed him and leaned in close. "It's *her*. The Facilitator."

The first goblin studied Meg, and his eyes widened. He sheathed his dagger. "So it is." He touched two knuckles to his gnarled red brow. "I apologize, my lady. We owe you much."

The goblins edged around her, then hurried over to the other half of their vehicle. They dragged out two more goblins, who were seriously injured, and departed together.

And then they were gone. But their words stayed with Meg, and perplexed her, and troubled her greatly.

She had other adventures, vanquished other foes, and the road led ever on. Finally, she came to the peak of a rocky prominence and looked out over a mile-long crater. The street ran downhill until it reached the gates of a dark and forbidding fortress. She knew that this must be the Citadel of Power and that Devon must be within. She hiked down to it.

The drawbridge had been lowered. She eased across, sword in her right hand, Wand of Reification in her left. The portcullis was up and the gate lay open. She slipped into the yard.

Empty. She crept sideways, keeping the wall at her back. She held her breath, heard nothing.

She peeked into the central yard and saw a grand stone altar. She crept closer. An object lay upon it. A wand.

The Wand of Reification.

She glanced at her left hand, which still held *her* wand. She'd thought it unique. She already had a Wand of Reification, and hadn't even used it. She shrugged, took the second wand and tucked it in her belt, then moved on.

She searched bedchambers, kitchens, a great hall, a cavernous ballroom, all empty. She entered an ancient armory. Crossbows, shields, pikes—

Wands.

Rack after rack of wands. Hundreds of wands. A thousand? Wands of Reification all, she felt sure. She didn't understand.

She went outside and crossed the yard again. The sky had begun to dim, and now she saw faint light in a tower window. She ran toward it.

Which hall? Which way? She dashed through rooms and under arches and up spiral stairs. Finally she found it—a door, shut, wan light spilling from beneath. She hurled herself against the door, and burst into the room with her sword raised.

A bedchamber. Posters on the walls. Devon's posters, from his old dorm room.

Light from a computer monitor. Someone sat before it. He turned. Devon.

He smiled and said, "Meg. Hey!"

She ran to him, enfolded him in her arms along with sword and wand and everything, and said, "Are you all right? I was so worried."

"I'm fine." He squeezed her and chuckled. "Everything's fine." He pulled back, brushed aside a lock of her hair, and kissed her. He was so tall and handsome, tawny-haired and emerald-eyed. He wore a gold medallion over a purple doublet with dagged sleeves. "Come on. You're exhausted." He led her to the bed, and they sat down together. He took her sword and wand and laid them on the nightstand.

She rested her cheek against his shoulder. She stared at the familiar posters (the nearest was an Edmund Leighton print) and whispered, "Aren't you in trouble? I thought you were. Devon, I don't understand what's happening."

"Shhh." He stroked her hair. "Just relax, okay? I'll explain everything."

He said that the real world was just a simulation, like a game. He didn't know who'd made it, but whoever they were they didn't seem to show themselves or ever interfere. Like any game, it had bugs. Many of these involved *Realms of Eldritch*, which was itself a new, fairly sophisticated simulation, and sometimes things got confused, and an item from the game got dumped into the real world. That's how he'd gotten the Wand of Reification, which could be used to alter almost anything. With it he'd set things in motion. He said, "Do you understand so far?"

She nodded, tentatively. It was all so strange.

He said that since the wand could only be used three times, he'd had to go looking for another bug, some way to duplicate the wand. Fortunately, there *was* one. But it was very specific: if a female warrior set out to rescue a man she loved, and was given the wand by the gnome, the game set a quest tag wrong and let her acquire the wand again at the Citadel of Power, leaving her with two. Devon said, "Ah, speak of the devil." Meg raised her head.

The gnome, his head canted so that his mysterious blue

eye watched her. Devon reached toward the nightstand, took the wand, and handed it to the gnome.

Meg murmured, "Why are you giving it to him?"

Devon said, "So he can give it to you again."

The gnome stuck the wand in his sleeve, gave a curt nod, and hobbled from the room.

Meg was mystified. "You said this bug creates an extra wand?"

"Yes."

She thought of the armory. "But you have *hundreds* of wands."

"Over a thousand," Devon said. He took the spare wand from her belt and placed it on the bed. "One for each time you've come here. One thousand two hundred and seventy-four wands."

She was stunned. "But . . . I don't remember . . ."

He told her, somewhat cryptically, "When you restart a quest, you lose all your progress."

Meg stood, pulling from his embrace. "Devon, you *lied* to me. You said you were trapped here."

He stood too. "I'm sorry. I had to. You had to be on a quest to save me, otherwise it wouldn't work."

She fumed. "I was in danger. I was attacked!"

He held back a smile. "And what happened?"

"I . . ." She hesitated. "I beat them."

"Of course. Meg, you're level sixty. You have the most powerful sword in the game. Nothing can harm you. There was never any danger. Didn't you get my prophecy?"

"*Your* prophecy?"

"That's why I wrote it," he said. "That's why I made the gnome recite it. So you wouldn't be afraid."

She paced to the window and looked out. This was all too much. "So now you've got a thousand wands. Why? What are you planning to do?"

He came and put his arm around her, and said softly, "To remake the world. To make it what it should have been all along—a place of wonder and adventure, without old age or disease. A place where death is only temporary—like in the game."

"You're going to make the game real," she said.

"Yes."

She felt apprehension. "I don't know, Devon. Maybe you shouldn't be messing around with this. I like the world just fine the way it is."

"Meg." His tone was affectionate. "You always say that."

She felt a sudden alarm. "What?"

Again, he suppressed a smile. "It's already begun. Ages ago. You think the world always had goblins and giant spiders and a gnome running around handing out magic items? That's all from the game. *I* made that happen."

She felt adrift. "I . . . don't remember."

"No one does," he said. "The wand makes things real. Not just physical, but *real*. Only *I* know that things used to be different, and now so do you."

And the goblins, Meg thought. They knew.

Devon kept going. "That's what's so funny, Meg. No matter what I do, no matter what crazy, incongruous reality I create, you always want things to stay exactly the way they are. That's just your personality. But we can't stop now. There's still so much to do. And you'll love it when I'm done, you'll see. You have to trust me."

"I don't know," she said. "I . . . need to think about it."

"Of course," Devon replied. "Take all the time you need."

So she stayed with Devon at the Citadel of Power, and they ate meals together in the dining hall and danced together in the grand ballroom, and after that first night they slept together again too. She was still in love with him. She always had been. Even the game knew it.

They hiked together around the crater's rim, and he told her of the world as it *had* been, when there'd been no magic at all, and humans were the only race that could speak, and adventure was something that most people only dreamt of. It sounded dismal, and yet Meg wondered, "Could you reverse the process? Put everything back the way it was?"

Devon was silent a while. "It would take a long time. But yes, I could. Is that what you want?"

"I don't know," she said.

That night, Devon told her, "I want to show you something." He led her to their tower chamber and turned on his computer. Meg was suddenly nervous. The monitor flickered. Icons appeared. Devon said softly, "Look at my background."

It showed two students sitting on a couch at a party. Meg didn't know them. The girl was pear-shaped and frizzy-haired and wore thick glasses. The guy wore glasses too, and was gangly, with thin lank hair and blotchy skin. The two of them looked happy together, in a pathetic sort of way. Meg said, "Who are they?"

Devon said, "That's the night we met."

Meg was horrified. She looked again, and suddenly she *did* recognize traces of themselves in the features of those strangers on the couch.

Devon explained, "I used the wand on us. Nothing drastic. I could do a lot more. I could make us anything we want. But you need to understand, Meg, when you talk about putting things back the way they were, exactly what you're saying."

Meg could accept the way she looked now—merely a pale shadow of Leena. But to think that she might not even be pretty, might be *that* girl . . .

"I thought you should know," Devon said, apologetic.

The next day at lunch, Meg asked him, "What is it you want me to do?"

He lowered his utensils. "Start the quest over."

"How?"

He nodded in the direction of the tower. "On my computer. I can show you."

"So that you'll get another wand?" she said.

"Yes."

"And I won't remember any of this?"

"No," he said.

She leaned back in her seat. "How many more times, Devon? My God, how many more wands?"

"As many as it takes," he said, without equivocation.

She stood up from the table, and said, "I need to think. Alone." He nodded. She went and paced the castle walls.

Devon wanted his new world more than anything. If she went along, then together they could have immortality and adventure and opulence and wonder. What had the old world offered? Crappy jobs and student loans, illness and death. What kind of a choice was that? She'd been here before, even if she didn't remember, and had sided with Devon one thousand two hundred and seventy-four times. Who was she now, to doubt the wisdom of all her past choices?

He was still sitting there when she returned and said, "Fine. Show me."

He led her to the tower and loaded the game. He selected a

character named Meg, who looked exactly like her. The character was level 60, and carried a Sword of Ultimate Cleaving +100. Devon clicked through a few menus, then stood. "Okay, *you* have to do it."

Meg sat down at the computer. A box on the screen said: "Citadel of Power—Are you sure you want to start this quest over from the beginning?" The mouse pointer hovered over "Yes."

Devon leaned down next to her. "Are you ready?"

"Yes," she whispered.

He kissed her cheek. "I'll see you again soon, okay?"

"Okay," she said, and clicked.

Meg hadn't heard from Devon in four months, and she realized that she missed him. So on a whim she tossed her sword and scabbard into the backseat of her car and drove over to campus to visit him.

Ages passed.

And now Leena the elf-maid is the most beautiful woman in all the world, and her lover is the most handsome man, Prince Devonar. They journey onward together, battling giants, riding dragons to distant lands, and feasting in the halls of dwarven kings. The prince is incandescent with joy. He was born for this, and Leena enjoys seeing him so happy. She loves him.

They ride two white unicorns down a forest path blanketed with fresh snow, and by some strange twist of magic or fate they come upon something that should not exist.

It lies half-buried in the drifts, but Leena can see that it was once a sort of carriage made from black metal. It has a roof, and its underside is all manner of piping, rusted now. Long ago, someone had sliced it in half. Where its other half may now lie, none can say.

The prince leaps from his mount and circles the strange object. "What foul contraption is this?"

Leena drops to the ground too, and staggers forward. A strange feeling passes over her, and a teardrop streaks her cheek. She can't say why. Soon she is sobbing.

The prince takes her in his arms. "My lady, what's the matter?" He scowls at the object. "It's upset you. Here, it shan't trouble us any longer." He pulls the Wand of Reification from his belt and aims.

"No!" She pushes his arm aside. "Leave it! Please."

He shrugs. "As you wish. But come, let's away. I mislike this place." He mounts his unicorn.

Leena stares at the strange carriage, and for a moment she remembers a world where countless such things raced down endless black roads. A world of soaring glass towers, of medallions that spoke in the voices of friends a thousand leagues distant, and where tales were told with light thrown up on walls the size of giants. Film, she remembers. Independent film. Jane Austen.

But the moment passes, and that fantastic world fades, leaving only the present, leaving only this odd, lingering sensation of being trapped in someone else's dream. She mounts her unicorn, and three words stick in her head, an incantation from a forgotten age. She no longer remembers where she heard the words, only that they now seem to express a feeling that surges up from somewhere deep inside her.

Save me plz.

———

David Barr Kirtley's short fiction appears in magazines such as *Realms of Fantasy*, *Weird Tales*, *Light-*

speed, and *Intergalactic Medicine Show*, on podcasts such as "Escape Pod" and "Pseudopod," and in books such as *The Living Dead*, *New Cthulhu*, *The Way of the Wizard*, and *The Dragon Done It*. His story "Save Me Plz" was picked by editor Rich Horton for the 2008 edition of the anthology series *Fantasy: The Best of the Year*. Kirtley is also the host of *The Geek's Guide to the Galaxy* podcast on Wired.com, for which he's interviewed more than one hundred authors, including George R. R. Martin, Richard Dawkins, and Paul Krugman. He lives in New York.

THE RELIVE BOX

T. C. Boyle

Katie wanted to relive Katie at nine, before her mother left, and I could appreciate that, but we had only one console at the time, and I really didn't want to go there. It was coming up on the holidays, absolutely grim outside, nine thirty at night—on a school night—and she had to be up at six to catch the bus in the dark. She'd already missed too much school, staying home on any pretext and reliving all day, while I was at work, so there really were no limits, and who was being a bad father here? A single father unable to discipline his fifteen-year-old daughter, let alone inculcate a work ethic in her?

Me. I was. And I felt bad about it. I wanted to put my foot down and at the same time give her something, make a concession, a peace offering. But, even more, I wanted the box myself, wanted it so baldly it was showing in my face, I'm sure, and she needed to get ready for school, needed sleep, needed to stop reliving and worry about the now, the now and the future. "Why don't you wait till the weekend?" I said.

She was wearing those tights that all the girls wear like painted-on skin, standing in the doorway to the living room, perching on one foot the way she did when she was doing her dance exercises. Her face belonged to her mother, my ex, Christine, who hadn't been there for her for six years and counting. "I want to relive now," she said, diminishing her voice to a shaky, hesitant plaint that was calculated to make me give in to whatever she wanted, but it wasn't going to work this time, no way. She was going to bed, and I was going back to a rainy February night in 1982, a sold-out show at the Roxy, a band I loved then, and the girl I was mad crazy for before she broke my heart and Christine came along to break it all over again.

"Why don't you go upstairs and text your friends or something?" I said.

"I don't want to text my friends. I want to be with my mom."

This was a plaint, too, and it cut even deeper. She was deprived, that was the theme here, and my behavior, as any impartial observer could have seen in a heartbeat, verged on child abuse. "I know, honey, I know. But it's not healthy. You're spending too much time there."

"You're just selfish, that's all," she said, and here was the shift to a new tone, a tone of animus and opposition, the subtext being that I never thought of anybody but myself. "You want to, what, relive when you were, like, my age or something? Let me guess: you're going to go back and relive yourself doing homework, right? As an example for your daughter?"

The room was a mess. The next day was the day the maid came, so I was standing amid the debris of the past week, a healthy percentage of it—abandoned sweat socks, energy-drink cans, crumpled foil pouches that had once contained biscotti, popcorn, or Salami Bites—generated by the child standing there before me. "I don't like your sarcasm," I said.

Her face was pinched so that her lips were reduced to the smallest little O-ring of disgust. "What *do* you like?"

"A clean house. A little peace and quiet. Some privacy, for Christ's sake—is that too much to ask?"

"I want to be with Mom."

"Go text your friends."

"I don't have any friends."

"Make some."

And this, thrown over her shoulder, preparatory to the furious pounding retreat up the stairs and the slamming of her bedroom door: "You're a pig!"

And my response, which had been ritualized ever since I'd sprung for the five-thousand-dollar, second-generation Halcom X1520 Relive Box with the In-Flesh Retinal Projection Stream and altered forever the dynamic between me and my only child: "I know."

Most people, when they got their first Relive Box, went straight for sex, which was only natural. In fact, it was a selling point in the TV ads, which featured shimmering adolescents walking hand in hand along a generic strip of beach or leaning in for a tender kiss over the ball return at the bowling alley. Who wouldn't want to go back there? Who wouldn't want to relive innocence, the nascent stirrings of love and desire, or the first time you removed her clothes and she removed yours? What of girlfriends (or boyfriends, as the case may be), wives, ex-wives, one-night stands, the casual encounter that got you halfway there, then flitted out of reach on the wings of an unfulfilled promise? I was no different. The sex part of it obsessed me through those first couple of months, and if I drifted into work each morning feeling drained (and not just figuratively) at least I knew that it was a problem, that it was adversely affecting my job performance, and, if I didn't cut back, threatening my job itself. Still, to relive Christine when we first met, to relive her in bed, in candlelight, clinging fast to me and whispering my name in the throes of her passion, was too great a temptation. Or even just sitting there across from me in the Moroccan restaurant where I took her for our first date, her eyes like portals, as she leaned into the table and drank up every word and witticism that came out of my mouth. Or to go farther back, before my wife entered the picture, to Rennie Porter, the girl I took to the senior prom and spent two delicious hours rubbing up against in the backseat of my father's Buick Regal—every second of which I'd relived six or seven times now. And to Lisa, Lisa Denardo, the girl I met that night at the Roxy, hoping I was going to score.

I started coming in late to work. Giving everybody, even my boss, the zombie stare. I got my first warning. Then my second. And my boss—Kevin Moos, a decent enough guy, five years younger than me, who didn't have an X1520, or not that he was letting on—sat me down in his office and told me, in no uncertain terms, that there wouldn't be a third.

But it was a miserable night, and I was depressed. And bored. So bored you could have drilled holes in the back of my head and taken core samples and I wouldn't have known the difference. I'd already denied my daughter, who was thumping around upstairs with the cumulative weight of ten daughters, and the next day was Friday, TGIF, end of the week, the slimmest of workdays, when just about everybody alive thinks about slipping out early. I figured that even if I did relive for more than the two hours I was going to strictly limit myself to, even if I woke up exhausted, I could always find a way to make it to lunch and just let things coast after that. So I went into the kitchen and fixed myself a gin and tonic, because that was what I'd been drinking that night at the Roxy, and carried it into the room at the end of the hall that had once been a bedroom and was now (Katie's joke, not mine) the reliving room.

The console sat squarely on the low table that was the only piece of furniture in the room, aside from the straight-backed chair I'd set in front of it the day I brought the thing home. It wasn't much bigger than the gaming consoles I'd had to make do with in the old days, a slick black metal cube with a single recessed glass slit running across the face of it from one side to the other. It activated the minute I took my seat. "Hello, Wes," it said in the voice I'd selected, male, with the slightest bump of an accent to make it seem less synthetic. "Welcome back."

I lifted the drink to my lips to steady myself—think of a conductor raising his baton—and cleared my throat. "February 28, 1982," I said. "Nine forty-five p.m. Play."

The box flashed the date and time and then suddenly I was there, the club exploding into life like a comet touching down, light and noise and movement obliterating the now, the house gone, my daughter gone, the world of getting and doing and bosses and work vanished in an instant. I was standing at the bar with my best friend, Zach Ronalds, who turned up his shirt collars and wore his hair in a Joe Strummer pompadour just like me, only his hair was black and mine choirboy blond (I'd dye it within the week), and I was trying to get the bartender's attention so I could order us G and Ts with my fake ID. The band, more New Wave than punk, hadn't started yet, and the only thing to look at onstage was the opening band, whose members were packing up their equipment while hyper-vigilant girls in vampire makeup and torn fishnet stockings washed around them in a human tide that ebbed and flowed on the waves of music crashing through the speakers. It was bliss. Bliss because I knew now that this night alone, out of all the long succession of dull, nugatory nights building up to it, would be special, that this was the night I'd meet Lisa and take her home with me. To my parents' house in Pasadena, where I had a room of my own above the detached garage and could come and go as I pleased. My room. The place where I greased up my hair and stared at myself in the mirror and waited for something to happen, something like this, like what was coming in seven and a half real-time minutes.

Zach said what sounded like "Look at that skank," but since he had his face turned away from me and the music was cranked to the sonic level of a rocket launch (give credit to the X1520's parametric speaker/audio-beam technology, which is infinitely more refined than the first generation's), I wasn't quite sure, though I must have heard him that night, my ears younger then, less damaged by scenes like this one, because I took hold of his arm and said, "Who? Her?"

What I said now, though, was "Reset, reverse ten seconds," and everything stalled, vanished, and started up once more, and here I was trying all over again to get the bartender's attention and listening hard when Zach, leaning casually against the bar on two splayed elbows, opened his mouth to speak. "Look at that skank," he said, undeniably, and there it was, coloring everything in the moment, because he was snap-judging Lisa, with her coat-hanger shoulders, Kabuki makeup, and shining black lips, and I said, "Who? Her?," already attracted, because in my eyes she wasn't a skank at all, or if she was, she was a skank from some other realm altogether, and I couldn't from that moment on think of anything but getting her to talk to me.

Now, the frustrating thing about the current relive technology is that you can't be an actor in the scene, only an observer, like Scrooge reliving his boarding-school agonies with the Ghost of Christmas Past at his elbow, so whatever howlers your adolescent self might have uttered are right there, hanging in the air, unedited. You can fast-forward, and I suppose most people do—skip the chatter; get to the sex—but, personally, after going straight to the carnal moments the first five or six times I relived a scene, I liked to go back and hear what I'd had to say, what she'd had to say, no matter how banal it might sound now. What I did that night—and I'd already relived this moment twice that week—was catch hold of the bartender and order not two but three G and Ts, though I only had something like eighteen dollars in my wallet, set one on the bar for Zach and cross the floor to where she was standing, just beneath the stage, in what would be the mosh pit half an hour later. She saw me coming, saw the drinks—two drinks—and looked away, covering herself, because she was sure I was toting that extra drink for somebody else, a girlfriend or a best bud, lurking in the drift of shadow that the stage lights drew up out of the murky walls.

I tapped her shoulder. She turned her face to me.

"Pause," I said.

Everything stopped. I was in a 3-D painting now, and so was she, and for the longest time I just kept things there, studying her face. She was eighteen years old, like me, beautiful enough underneath the paint and gel and eyeliner and all the rest to make me feel faint even now, and her eyes weren't wary, weren't *used*, but candid, ready, rich with expectation. I held my drink just under my nose, inhaling the smell of juniper berries to tweak the memory, and said, "Play."

"You look thirsty," I said.

The music boomed. Behind me, at the bar, Zach was giving me a look of disbelief, like *What the?*, because this was a violation of our club-going protocol. We didn't talk to the girls, and especially not the skanks, because we were there for the *music*, at least that was what we told ourselves. (Second time around I did pause this part, just for the expression on his face—Zach, poor Zach, who never did find himself a girlfriend, as far as I know, and who's probably someplace reliving every club he's ever been in and every date he's ever had, just to feel sorry for himself.)

She leveled her eyes on me, gave it a beat, then took the cold glass from my hand. "How did you guess?" she said.

What followed was the usual exchange of information about bands, books, neighborhood, high school, college, and then I was bragging about the bands I'd seen lately and she was countering with the band members she knew personally—like John Doe and the drummer for the Germs—and letting her eyes reveal just how personal that was, which only managed to inflame me till I wanted nothing more on this earth than to pin her in a corner and kiss the black lipstick right off her. What I said then, unaware that my carefully sculpted pompadour was collapsing across my brow in something very much like a bowl cut (or worse—*anathema*—a Beatles shag), was "You want to dance?"

She gave me a look. Shot her eyes to the stage and back, then around the room. A few people were dancing to the canned music, most of them jerking and gyrating to their own drugged-out beat, and there was no sign—yet—of the band we'd come to hear. "To this?"

"Yeah," I said, and I looked so—what was it?—*needy*, though at the time I must have thought I was chiseled out of a block of pure cool. "Come on," I said, and I reached out a hand to her.

I watched the decision firm up in her eyes, deep in this moment which would give rise to all the rest, to the part I was about to fast-forward to because I had to get up in the morning. For work. And no excuses. But watch, watch what comes next . . .

She took my hand, the soft friction of her touch alive still somewhere in my cell memory, and then she was leading me out onto the dance floor.

She was leading. And I was following.

Will it surprise you to know that I exceeded my self-imposed two-hour limit? That after the sex I fast-forwarded to our first date, which was really just an agreed-upon meeting at Tower Records (March 2, 1982, 4:30 p.m.), and then up to Barney's Beanery for cheeseburgers and beers and shots of peppermint schnapps (!), which she paid for, because her father was a rich executive at Warner Bros.? Or that that made me feel so good I couldn't resist skipping ahead three months, to when she was as integral to my life as the Black Flag T-shirt that never left my back except in the shower? Lisa. Lisa Denardo. With her cat's tongue and her tight, torquing body that was a girl's and a woman's at the same time and her perfect, evenly spaced set of glistening white teeth (perfect, that is, but for the incisor she'd had a dentist in Tijuana remove, in the spirit of punk solidarity). The scene I hit on was early the following summer, summer break of my sophomore year in college, when I gave up on my parents' garage and Lisa and I moved into an off-campus apartment on Vermont and decided to paint the walls, ceiling, and floors the color of midnight in the Carlsbad Caverns. June 6, 1982,

2:44 p.m. The glisten of black paint, a too-bright sun caught in the windows, and Lisa saying, "Think we should paint the glass, too?" I was oblivious of anything but her and me and the way I looked and the way she looked, a streak of paint on her left forearm and another, scimitar-shaped, just over one eyebrow, when suddenly everything went neutral and I was back in the reliving room, staring into the furious face of my daughter.

But let me explain the technology here a moment, for those of you who don't already know. This isn't a computer screen or a TV or a hologram or anything anybody else can see—we're talking retinal projection, two laser beams fixed on two eyeballs. Anybody coming into the room (daughter, wife, boss) will simply see you sitting there silently in a chair with your retinas lit like furnaces. Step in front of the projector—as my daughter had done now—and the image vanishes.

"Stop," I said, and I wasn't talking to her.

But there she was, her hair brushed out for school and her jaw clenched, looking hate at me. "I can't believe you," she said. "Do you have any idea what time it is?"

Bleary, depleted—and guilty, deeply guilty—I just gawked at her, the light she'd flicked on when she came into the room transfixing me in the chair. I shook my head.

"It's six forty-five a.m. In the morning. The *morning*, Dad."

I started to say something, but the words were tangled up inside me, because Lisa was saying—had just said—"You're not going to make me stay here and watch the paint dry, are you? Because I'm thinking maybe we could drive out to the beach or something, just to cool down," and I said, or was going to say, "There's, like, maybe half a pint of gas in the car."

"What?" Katie demanded. "Were you with Mom again? Is that it? Like, you can be with her and I can't?"

"No," I said, "no, that wasn't it. It wasn't your mom at all . . ."

A tremor ran through her. "Yeah, right. So what was it, then? Some girlfriend, somebody you were gaga over when you were in college? Or high school? Or, what, *junior* high?"

"I must have fallen asleep," I said. "Really. I just zoned out."

She knew I was lying. She'd come looking for me, dutiful child, motherless child, and found me not up and about and bustling around the kitchen, preparing to fuss over her and see her off to school, the way I used to, but pinned here in this chair, like an exhibit in a museum, blind to anything but the past, my past and nobody else's, not hers or her mother's, or the country's or the world's, just mine.

I heard the door slam. Heard the thump of her angry feet in the hallway, the distant muffled crash of the front door, and then the house was quiet. I looked at the slit in the box. "Play," I said.

By the time I got to work, I was an hour and a half late, but on this day—miracle of miracles—Kevin was even later, and when he did show up I was ensconced in my cubicle, dutifully rattling keys on my keyboard. He didn't say anything, just brushed by me and buried himself in his office, but I could see that he was wearing the same vacant pre-now look I was, and it didn't take much of an intuitive leap to guess the reason. In fact, since the new model had come on the market, I'd noticed that randy, faraway gaze in the eyes of half a dozen of my fellow employees, including Linda Blanco, the receptionist, who'd stopped buttoning the top three buttons of her blouse and wore shorter and shorter skirts every day. Instead of breathing "Moos and Associates, how may I help you?" into the receiver, now she just said, "Reset."

Was this a recipe for disaster? Was our whole society on

the verge of breaking down? Was the NSA going to step in? Were they going to pass laws? Ban the box? I didn't know. I didn't care. I had a daughter to worry about. Thing was, all I could think of was getting home to relive, straight home, and if the image of a carton of milk or a loaf of bread flitted into my head, I batted it away. Takeout. We could always get take-out. I was in a crucial phase with Lisa, heading inexorably for the grimmer scenes, the disagreements—petty at first, then monumental, unbridgeable, like the day I got home from my makeup class in calculus and found her sitting at the kitchen table with a stoner whose name I never did catch and didn't want to know, not then or now—and I needed to get through it, not to analyze whether it hurt or not but because it was there and I had to relive it. I couldn't help myself. I just kept picking at it like a scab.

Ultimately, this was all about Christine, of course, about when I began to fail instead of succeed, to lose instead of win. I needed Lisa to remind me of a time before that, to help me trace my missteps and assign blame, because, as intox-icating as it was to relive the birds-atwitter moments with Christine, there was always something nagging at me in any given scene, some twitch of her face or a comment she threw out that should have raised flags at the time but never did. All right. Fine. I was going to go there, I was, and relive the minutiae of our relationship, the ecstasy and the agony both, the moments of mindless contentment and the swelling tide of antipathy that drove us apart, but first things first, and, as I fought my way home on the freeway that afternoon, all I could think about was Lisa.

In the old days, before we got the box, my daughter and I had a Friday-afternoon ritual whereby I would stop in at the

Italian place down the street from the house, have a drink and chat up whoever was there, then call Katie and have her come join me for a father-daughter dinner, so that I could have some face time with her, read into her, and suss out her thoughts and feelings as she grew into a young woman herself, but we didn't do that anymore. There wasn't time. The best I could offer—lately, especially—was takeout or a microwave pizza and a limp salad, choked down in the cold confines of the kitchen, while we separately calculated how long we had to put up with the pretense before slipping off to relive.

There were no lights on in the house as I pulled into the driveway, and that was odd, because Katie should have been home from school by now—and she hadn't texted me or phoned to say she'd be staying late. I climbed out of the car feeling stiff all over—I needed to get more exercise, I knew that, and I resolved to do it, too, as soon as I got my head above water—and as I came up the walk I saw the sad, frosted artificial wreath hanging crookedly there in the center panel of the front door. Katie must have dug it out of the box of ornaments in the garage on her own initiative, to do something by way of Christmas, and that gave me pause, that stopped me right there, the thought of it, of my daughter having to make the effort all by herself. That crushed me. It did. And as I put the key in the lock and pushed the door open I knew things were going to have to change. Dinner. I'd take her out to dinner and forget about Lisa. At least for now.

"Katie?" I called. "You home?"

No response. I shrugged out of my coat and went on into the kitchen, thinking to make myself a drink. There were traces of her there, her backpack flung down on the floor, an open bag of Doritos spilling across the counter, a

Diet Sprite, half-full, on the breadboard. I called her name again, standing stock-still in the middle of the room and listening for the slightest hint of sound or movement as my voice echoed through the house. I was about to pull out my phone and call her when I thought of the reliving room, and it was a sinking thought, not a selfish one, because if she was in there, reliving—and she was, I knew she was—what did that say about her social life? Didn't teenage girls go out any-more? Didn't they gather in packs at the mall or go to movies or post things on Facebook, or, forgive me, go out on dates? Group dates, even? How else were they going to experience the inchoate beginnings of what the Relive Box people were pushing in the first place?

I shoved into the room, which was dark but for the lights of her eyes, and just stood there watching her for a long moment as I adjusted to the gloom. She sat riveted, her body present but her mind elsewhere, and if I was embarrassed—for her, and for me, too, her father, invading her privacy when she was most vulnerable—the embarrassment gave way to a sorrow so oceanic I thought I would drown in it. I studied her face. Watched her smile and grimace and go cold and smile again. What could she possibly be reliving when she'd lived so little? Family vacations? Christmases past? Her biannual trips to Hong Kong to be with her mother and stepfather? I couldn't fathom it. I didn't like it. It had to stop. I turned on the overhead light and stepped in front of the projector.

She blinked at me and she didn't recognize me, didn't know me at all, because I was in the now and she was in the past. "Katie," I said, "that's enough now. Come on." I held out my arms to her, even as recognition came back into her eyes and she made a vague gesture of irritation, of pushing away.

"Katie," I said, "let's go out to dinner. Just the two of us. Like we used to."

"I'm not hungry," she said. "And it's not fair. You can use it all you want, like, day and night, but whenever I want it—" And she broke off, tears starting in her eyes.

"Come on," I said. "It'll be fun."

The look she gave me was unsparing. I was trying to deflect it, trying to think of something to say, when she got up out of the chair so suddenly it startled me, and, though I tried to take hold of her arm, she was too quick. Before I could react, she was at the door, pausing only to scorch me with another glare. "I don't believe you," she spat before vanishing down the hall.

I should have followed her, should have tried to make things right—or better, anyway—but I didn't. The box was right there. It had shut down when she leaped up from the chair, and whatever she'd been reliving was buried back inside it, accessible to no one, though you can bet there are hackers out there right now trying to subvert the retinal-recognition feature. For a long moment, I stared at the open door, fighting myself, then I went over and softly shut it. I realized I didn't need a drink or dinner, either. I sat down in the chair. "Hello, Wes," the box said. "Welcome back."

We didn't have a Christmas tree that year, and neither of us really cared all that much, I think—if we wanted to look at spangle-draped trees, we could relive holidays past, happier ones, or, in my case, I could go back to my childhood and relive my father's whiskey in a glass and my mother's long-suffering face blossoming over the greedy joy of her golden boy, her only child, tearing open his presents as a weak, bleached-out California sun haunted the windows and the turkey crackled in the oven. Katie went off (reluctantly, I thought) on a skiing vacation to Mammoth with the family of her best friend, Allison, whom she hardly saw anymore, not outside of school, not in the now, and I went back to Lisa, because if I was going to get to Christine in any serious way—beyond the sex, that is, beyond the holiday greetings and picture-postcard moments—Lisa was my bridge.

As soon as I'd dropped Katie at Allison's house and exchanged a few previously scripted salutations with Allison's grinning parents and her grinning twin brothers, I stopped at a convenience store for a case of eight-ounce bottles of spring water and the biggest box of PowerBars I could find and went straight home to the reliving room. The night before, I'd been close to the crucial scene with Lisa, one that was as fixed in my memory as the blowup with Christine a quarter century later, but elusive as to the date and time. I'd been up all night—again—fast-forwarding, reversing, jumping locales, and facial expressions, Lisa's first piercing, the evolution of my haircut, but I hadn't been able to pinpoint the exact moment, not yet. I set the water on the floor on my left side, the PowerBars on my right. "May 9, 1983," I said. "Four a.m."

The numbers flashed and then I was in darkness, zero visibility, confused as to where I was until the illuminated dial of a clock radio began to bleed through and I could make out the dim outline of myself lying in bed in the back room of that apartment with the black walls and the black ceiling and the black floor. Lisa was there beside me, an irregular hump in the darkness, snoring with a harsh gag and stutter. She was stoned. And drunk. Half an hour earlier, she'd been in the bathroom, heaving over the toilet, and I realized I'd come too far. "Reset," I said. "Reverse ninety minutes."

Sudden light, blinding after the darkness, and I was alone in the living room of the apartment, studying, or trying to. My hair hung limp, my muscles were barely there, but I was young and reasonably good-looking, even excusing any bias. I saw that my Black Flag T-shirt had faded to gray from too much sun and too many washings, and the book in my lap looked as familiar as something I might have been buried within a previous life, but then this *was* my previous life. I watched myself turn a page, crane my neck toward the door, get up to flip over the album that was providing the sound track. "Reset," I said. "Fast-forward ten minutes." And here it was, what I'd been searching for: a sudden crash, the front door flinging back, Lisa and the stoner whose name I didn't want to know fumbling their way in, both of them as slow as syrup with the cumulative effect of downers and alcohol, and though the box didn't have an olfactory feature, I swear I could smell the tequila on them. I jumped up out of my chair, spilling the book, and shouted something I couldn't quite make out, so I said, "Reset, reverse five seconds."

"You fucker!" was what I'd shouted, and now I shouted it again, prior to slapping something out of the guy's hand, a beer bottle, and all at once I had him in a hammerlock and Lisa was beating at my back with her bird-claw fists and I was wrestling the guy out the door, cursing over the sound track ("Should I Stay or Should I Go"—one of those flatline ironies that almost make you believe everything in this life's been programmed). I saw now that he was bigger than I was, probably stronger, too, but the drugs had taken the volition out of him, and in the next moment he was outside the door and the three bolts were hammered home. By me. Who now turned in a rage to Lisa.

"Stop," I said. "Freeze." Lisa hung there, defiant and guilty at the same time, pretty, breathtakingly pretty, despite the slack mouth and the drugged-out eyes. I should have left it there and gone on to those first cornucopian weeks and months and even years with Christine, but I couldn't help myself. "Play," I said, and Lisa raised a hand to swat at me, but she was too unsteady and knocked the lamp over instead.

"Did you fuck him?" I demanded.

There was a long pause, so long I almost fast-forwarded, and then she said, "Yeah. Yeah, I fucked him. And I'll tell you something"—her words glutinous, the syllables coalescing on her tongue—"you're no punk. And he is. He's the real deal. And you? You're, you're—"

I should have stopped it right there.

"—you're *prissy*."

"Prissy?" I couldn't believe it. Not then and not now.

She made a broad, stoned gesture, weaving on her feet. "Anal-retentive. Like, who left the dishes in the sink or who didn't take out the garbage or what about the cockroaches—"

"Stop," I said. "Reset. June 19, 1994, 11:02 p.m."

I was in another bedroom now, one with walls the color of cream, and I was in another bed, this time with Christine, and I'd timed the memory to the very minute, postcoital, in the afterglow, and Christine, with her soft aspirated whisper of a voice, was saying, "I love you, Wes, you know that, don't you?"

"Stop," I said. "Reverse five seconds."

She said it again. And I stopped again. And reversed again. And she said it again. And again.

Time has no meaning when you're reliving. I don't know how long I kept it up, how long I kept surfing through those moments with Christine—not the sexual ones but the loving ones, the companionable ones, the ordinary day-to-day moments when I could see in her eyes that she loved me more than anybody alive and was never going to stop loving me, never. Dinner at the kitchen table, any dinner, any night. Just to be there. My wife. My daughter. The way the light poured liquid gold over the hardwood floors of our starter house, in Canoga Park. Katie's first birthday. Her first word ("Cake!"). The look on Christine's face as she curled up with Katie in bed and read her *Where the Wild Things Are*. Her voice as she hoarsened it for Max: "I'll eat you up!"

Enough analysis, enough hurt. I was no masochist.

At some point, I had to get up from that chair in the now and evacuate a living bladder, the house silent, spectral, unreal. I didn't live here. I didn't live in the now with its deadening nine-to-five job I was in danger of losing and the daughter I was failing and a wife who'd left me—and her own daughter—for Winston Chen, a choreographer of martial-arts movies in Hong Kong, who was loving and kind and funny and not the control freak I was. (*Prissy*, anyone? *Anal-retentive*?) The house echoed with my footsteps, a stage set and nothing more. I went to the kitchen and dug the biggest pot I could find out from under the sink, brought it back to the reliving room, and set it on the floor between my legs to save me the trouble of getting up next time around.

Time passed. Relived time and lived time, too. There were two windows in the room, shades drawn so as not to interfere with the business of the moment, and sometimes a faint glow appeared around the margins of them, an effect I noticed when I was searching for a particular scene and couldn't quite pin it down. Sometimes the glow was gone. Sometimes it wasn't. What happened then, and I may have been two days in or three or five, I couldn't really say, was that things began to cloy. I'd relived an exclusive diet of the transcendent, the joyful, the insouciant, the best of Christine, the best of Lisa, and all the key moments of the women who came between and after, and I'd gone back to the intermediate algebra test, the very instant, pencil to paper, when I knew I'd scored a perfect one hundred percent, and to the time I'd squirted a ball to right field with two outs, two strikes, ninth inning and my Little League team (the Condors, yellow Ts, white lettering) down by three, and watched it rise majestically over the glove of the spastic red-haired kid sucking back allergic snot and roll all the way to the wall. Triumph after triumph, goodness abounding—till it stuck in my throat.

"Reset," I said. "January 2, 2009, 4:30 p.m."

I found myself in the kitchen of our second house, this house, the one we'd moved to because it was outside the L.A. city limits and had schools we felt comfortable sending Katie to. That was what mattered: the schools. And, if it lengthened our commutes, so be it. This house. The one I was reliving in now. Everything gleamed around me, counters polished, the glass of the cabinets as transparent as air, because details mattered then, everything in its place whether Christine was there or not—especially if she wasn't there, and where was she? Or where had she been? To China. With her boss. On film business. Her bags were just inside the front door, where she'd dropped them forty-five minutes ago, after I'd picked her up at the airport and we'd had our talk in the car, the talk I was going to relive when I got done here, because it was all about pain now, about reality, and this scene was the capper, the coup de grâce. You want wounds? You want to take a razor blade to the meat of your inner thigh just to see if you can still feel? Well, here it was.

Christine entered the scene now, coming down the stairs from Katie's room, her eyes wet, or damp, anyway, and her face composed. I pushed myself up from the table, my beginner's bald spot a glint of exposed flesh under the glare of the overhead light. I spoke first. "You tell her?"

Christine was dressed in her business attire, black stockings, heels, skirt to the knee, tailored jacket. She looked exhausted, and not simply from the fifteen-hour flight but from what she'd had to tell me. And our daughter. (How I'd like to be able to relive *that*, to hear how she'd even broached the subject, let alone how she'd smoke-screened her own selfishness and betrayal with some specious concern for Katie's well-being—let's not rock the boat and you'll be better off here with your father and your school and your teachers and it's not the end but just the beginning, buck up, you'll see.)

Christine's voice was barely audible. "I don't like this any better than you do."

"Then why do it?"

A long pause. Too long. "Stop," I said.

I couldn't do this. My heart was hammering. My eyes felt as if they were being squeezed in a vise. I could barely swallow. I reached down for a bottle of water and a PowerBar, drank, chewed. She was going to say, "This isn't working," and I was going to say, "*Working?* What the fuck are you talking about? What does work have to do with it? I thought this was about love. I thought it was about commitment." I knew I wasn't going to get violent, though I should have, should have chased her out to the cab that was even then waiting at the curb and slammed my way in and flown all the way to Hong Kong to confront Winston Chen, the martial-arts genius, who could have crippled me with his bare feet.

"Reset," I said. "August, 1975, any day, any time."

There was a hum from the box. "Incomplete command. Please select date and time."

I was twelve years old, the summer we went to Vermont, to a lake there, where the mist came up off the water like the fumes of a dream and deer mice lived under the refrigerator, and I didn't have a date or time fixed in my mind—I just needed to get away from Christine, that was all. I picked the first thing that came into my head.

"August nineteenth," I said. "Eleven thirty a.m. Play."

A blacktop road. Sun like a nuclear blast. A kid, running. I recognized myself—I'd been to this summer before, one I remembered as idyllic, messing around in boats, fishing, swimming, wandering the woods with one of the local kids, Billy Scharf, everything neutral, copacetic. But why was I running? And why did I have that look on my face, a look that fused determination and helplessness both? Up the drive now, up the steps to the house, shouting for my parents: "Mom! Dad!"

I began to have a bad feeling.

I saw my father get up off the wicker sofa on the porch, my vigorous young father, who was dressed in a T-shirt and jeans and didn't have even a trace of gray in his hair, my father, who always made everything right. But not this time. "What's the matter?" he said. "What is it?"

And my mother coming through the screen door to the porch, a towel in one hand and her hair snarled wet from the lake. And me. I was fighting back tears, my legs and arms like sticks, striped polo shirt, faded shorts. "It's," I said, "it's—"

"Stop," I said. "Reset." It was my dog, Queenie, that was what it was, dead on the road that morning, and who'd left the gate ajar so she could get out in the first place? Even though he'd been warned about it a hundred times?

I was in a dark room. There was a pot between my legs, and it was giving off a fierce odor. I needed to go deeper, needed out of this. I spouted random dates, saw myself driving to work, stuck in traffic with ten thousand other fools who could only wish they had a fast-forward app, saw myself in my thirties, post-Lisa, pre-Christine, obsessing over *Halo*, and I stayed there through all the toppling hours, reliving myself in the game, boxes within boxes, until finally I thought of God, or what passes for God in my life, the mystery beyond words, beyond lasers and silicon chips. I gave a date nine months before I was born, "December 30, 1962, 6:00 a.m.," when I was, what—a zygote?—but the box gave me nothing, neither visual nor audio. And that was wrong, deeply wrong. There should have been a heartbeat. My mother's heartbeat, the first thing we hear—or feel, feel before we even have ears.

"Stop," I said. "Reset." A wave of rising exhilaration swept over me even as the words came to my lips, "September 30, 1963, 2:35 a.m.," and the drumbeat started up, *ba-boom, ba-boom*, but no visual, not yet, the minutes ticking by, *ba-boom, ba-boom*, and then I was there, in the light of this world, and my mother in her stained hospital gown and the man with the monobrow and the flashing glasses, the stranger, the doctor, saying what he was going to say by way of congratulations and relief. A boy. It's a boy.

Then it all went dead, and there was somebody standing in front of me, and I didn't recognize her, not at first, how could I? "Dad," she was saying. "Dad, are you there?"

I blinked. Tried to focus.

"No," I said finally, shaking my head in slow emphasis, the word itself, the denial, heavy as a stone in my mouth. "I'm not here. I'm not. I'm not."

=====

T. C. Boyle is the author of twenty-four books of fiction, including, most recently, *After the Plague*, *Drop City*, *The Inner Circle*, *Tooth and Claw*, *The Human Fly*, *Talk Talk*, *The Women*, *Wild Child*, *When the Killing's Done*, *San Miguel*, *T. C. Boyle Stories II*, and *The Harder They Come*. He received a PhD in nineteenth-century British literature from the University of Iowa in 1977, his MFA from the University of Iowa Writers' Workshop in 1974, and his BA in English and history from SUNY Potsdam in 1968. He has been a member of the English Department at the University of Southern California since 1978, where he is Distinguished Professor of English. His stories have appeared in most of the major American magazines, including *The New Yorker*, *Harper's*, *Esquire*, *The Atlantic Monthly*, *Playboy*, *The Paris Review*, *GQ*, *Antaeus*, *Granta*, and *McSweeney's*, and he has been the recipient of a number of literary awards, including the PEN/Faulkner Award for best novel of the year (*World's End*, 1988); the PEN/Malamud Prize in the short story (*T. C. Boyle Stories*, 1999); and the Prix Médicis Étranger for best foreign novel in France (*The Tortilla Curtain*, 1997). He lives near Santa Barbara with his wife and three children.

ROGUELIKE

Marc Laidlaw

Good morning, Agent @, and congratulations on acceptance into the Academy of Assassins. Your first assignment may also be your last. The Emperor of Antagonia, having already depleted our resources and left the Resistance with almost nothing we can use in our struggle, is drawing up secret orders to accelerate our extermination. He must be stopped before these orders are finalized. And by stopped we mean assassinated.

All our more experienced agents have died in the attempt to eliminate the Emperor. Despite your junior status, you are the finest agent we have left.

Your mission is to infiltrate the Palace of Heaven, ascend to the Penthouse, and kill the Emperor. One hundred floors of bodyguards, attack dogs, rabid leopards, great white shark tanks, whirling blades, and other dangers yet unenumerated lie in your path. Be sure to study the case files of the agents who have gone before you, that you may learn from their failures.

The fate of the Resistance is in your hands.

Good luck, Agent @!

You enter the lobby of the Palace of Heaven.
A security camera turns to note your presence.
The camera emits a laser beam and burns a hole through you.

```
          HERE
          LIES

        Agent @

     Perforated by
     a Laser Camera

        Floor 1
```

Good morning, Agent b, and congratulations on acceptance into the Academy of Assassins. Your first assignment may also be your last. The Emperor of Antagonia, having already depleted our resources and left the Resistance with almost nothing we can use in our struggle, is drawing up secret orders to accelerate our extermination. He must be stopped before these orders are finalized. And by stopped we mean assassinated.

All our more experienced agents have died in the attempt to eliminate the Emperor. Despite your junior status, you are the finest agent we have left.

Your mission is to infiltrate the Palace of Heaven, ascend to the Penthouse, and kill the Emperor. One hundred floors of bodyguards, attack dogs, rabid leopards, great white shark tanks, whirling blades, and other dangers yet unenumerated lie in your path. Be sure to study the case files of the agents who have gone before you, that you may learn from their failures.

The fate of the Resistance is in your hands.
Good luck, Agent b!

You enter the lobby of the Palace of Heaven.
A security camera turns to note your presence.
You step behind a column.
You enter a door marked SECURITY.

You destroy the security camera controls.

A security guard shoots you in the face.

```
         HERE
         LIES

       Agent b

      Shot by
   a Security Guard

      Floor 1
```

Good morning, Agent c . . .

You enter the lobby of the Palace of Heaven.

A security camera turns to note your presence.

You step behind a column.

You enter a door marked SECURITY.

You shoot a security guard.

You destroy the security camera controls.

The other security guard shoots you in the back.

```
         HERE
         LIES

       Agent c

      Shot by
   a Security Guard

      Floor 1
```

Good morning, Agent k . . .

You enter the lobby of the Palace of Heaven.

A security camera turns to note your presence.

You step behind a column.

You enter a door marked SECURITY.

You shoot a security guard.

You shoot a security guard.

You destroy the security camera controls.

You enter the lobby of the Palatial Tower.

You shoot a security guard.

You shoot a security guard.

You shoot a security guard.

You shoot a security guard.

You find stairs going up.

You step onto the second floor.

An attack dog tears your throat out.

```
                  HERE
                  LIES

                Agent k

            Throat Torn Out by
              an Attack Dog

                Floor 2
```

Good morning, Agent v . . .

You enter the lobby of the Palace of Heaven.

You shoot a security camera.

You shoot a security guard.

You shoot a security guard.

You shoot a security guard.

You shoot a security guard.

You shoot a security guard.

You shoot a security guard.

You shoot a security guard.

You shoot a security guard.

You are feeling hungry.

You find stairs going up.

You step onto the second floor.

You shoot an attack dog.

You shoot an attack dog.

You shoot an attack dog.

You are feeling hungry.

You shoot a security guard.

You enter an elevator.

You exit an elevator.

You search a security guard.

You search a security guard.

You take an elevator key.

You take a handful of change.

You enter an elevator.

You are feeling faint.

You descend in the elevator.

You step into a parking garage.

You see a snack vending machine.

You put change in the snack vending machine.

You are killed by the snack vending machine.

Good morning, Agent @@ . . .

You enter the parking garage.

You garrote a security guard.

You search a security guard.

You take an elevator key.

You take a security robot remote control unit.

You deactivate all parking robots.

You enter an elevator.

You take the elevator to floor 25.

You exit the elevator.

You are pricked in the neck by a ninja.

Good morning . . .

Good morning . . .

Good morning . . .

Good morning . . .

Good morning . . .

Good morning . . .

Good morning . . .

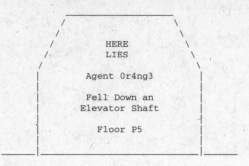

```
              HERE
              LIES

          Agent 0r4ng3

          Fell Down an
          Elevator Shaft

          Floor P5
```

Good morning . . .

```
              HERE
              LIES

        Agent $923498U

        Eviscerated by
    a Window Washer Thingie

        Floor 37-1/2
```

Good morning . . .

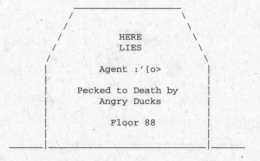

```
              HERE
              LIES

          Agent :'{o>

      Pecked to Death by
        Angry Ducks

          Floor 88
```

Good morning . . .

```
          HERE
          LIES

       Agent @@7

     Something to Do
       with Kittens

         Floor 56
```

Good morning . . .

```
          HERE
          LIES

      Agent +7&43

     Carried Off by
        an Ague

         Floor 90
```

Good morning . . .

```
           HERE
           LIES

    Agent 00010001.001

 Died of Rag-Picker's Disease
  Inflicted by a Rag-Picker


          Floor 98
```

Good morning . . .

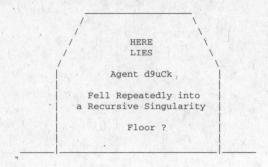

```
          _____
         /                    \
        /       HERE           \
       /        LIES            \
      |                          |
      |     Agent d9uCk          |
      |                          |
      |    Fell Repeatedly into  |
      |   a Recursive Singularity|
      |                          |
      |        Floor ?           |
      |                          |
    __|_____|__
```

Good morning . . .

```
          _____
         /                    \
        /       HERE           \
       /        LIES            \
      |                          |
      |    Agent &*$02.33e       |
      |                          |
      |        Died by           |
      |       Own Hand           |
      |                          |
      |        Floor 1           |
      |                          |
    __|_____|__
```

Good morning, Agent @bc@x1vvYz%#1$ . . .

You enter the Visitors' Garden at the base of the Palace of Heaven.

You step between two elephants in a topiary hedge.

You twist a sprinkler counterclockwise.

You enter a secret passage.

You enter a secret elevator.

You take the elevator to the Penthouse.

You step behind a column.

You intercept a patrolling ninja and strangle him with his own poisoned garrote.

You don the ninja's stylish hooded filter mask.

You lob the ninja's full complement of toxin bombs down the corridor.

You liberate a sword from a dead GMO-samurai.

You enter a security ring and decapitate the controllers.

You power down the Emperor's Robot Escort.

You step in the Emperor's Suite.

You step on the Emperor's marmoset.

You kill the Emperor.

Congratulations!

The Resistance is victorious!

Imagine reading these victory messages In Real Life!

To be clear, you have not actually assassinated the Emperor IRL. This has been a simulation, meant to train you (and all your predecessors) in some of the challenges you can expect to face as we attempt to assassinate the Emperor. As previously disclosed, the Resistance has been left with virtually no resources—not even virtual ones. Once, in our glorious past, we possessed state-of-the-art simulators that allowed our finest killers to develop their skills against a believably responsive set of dynamic, procedurally generated foes. But such simulators are expensive, enormous, and require the kind of technological infrastructure that the Resistance can no longer maintain in its current impoverished state. Once, in our glorious past, we created digital scenarios so convincing that would-be assassins would often complete a training session only to discover that they had assassinated not a virtual enemy but a real one! Sadly, this glorious past of ours is now ingloriously in the past. We retain but the one laptop, a few solar panels, a rack of batteries, and the recalcitrant wooden wheel of the Old Mill.

We are aware that—the assassin gossip network being what it is—you probably believed that by running through this primitive simulator, you were actually engaged in assassinating the Emperor. Naturally we regret to disappoint you, just as we have disappointed all the trainees before you, from Agent @ onward.

On the other hand, you have one advantage not enjoyed by previous trainees: you are still alive. While victory in the simulator is ephemeral, defeat is quite real. We have remained steadfast and true to our code. As educators of killing machines, we insist that death be lethal. (Assassin death, that is. No guard dogs or ninjas were harmed by you in the apparent execution of your simulated duties.)

So take this moment to relax and enjoy being alive. But keep in mind that the Emperor, a greater threat than ever, still awaits.

Also please note that due to inadequate network access and a resulting inability to download patches, all floor plans, shortcuts, and hazards represented in the simulation you have just survived may bear no resemblance to conditions in the actual Palace of Heaven. To name but one example, the Visitors' Garden was removed four years ago, due to its vulnerability to assassins.

Now please exit the game, Agent @bc@x1vvYz%#1$, and proceed to the Palace of Heaven—

===

Marc Laidlaw is best known as one of the creators of and the lead writer on the Half-Life video game series, but he initially got that gig on the strength of his short stories and novels of fantasy, horror, and science fiction. His novel *The 37th Mandala* won the International Horror Guild Award for Best Novel. Laidlaw has been a writer at Valve since 1997, and his short stories continue to appear in various magazines and online venues.

ALL OF THE PEOPLE IN YOUR PARTY HAVE DIED

Robin Wasserman

It was the day of the mock election at Armstrong Elementary, Dukakis losing to Bush by more than two hundred votes, when Lizzie Kepler finally had to admit to herself she'd made a serious mistake.

Only forty-two of the ballots had been cast for Dukakis—twelve of those by Lizzie herself. (Given that half the people she knew from college were out on the campaign trail, while she herself was a suburbanite teacher molding the minds of young future Republicans and apparently doing a piss-poor job of it, stuffing the ballot box seemed the literal least she could do.)

All those boozy nights watching dawn break through the dorm's cracked windows, spilling bong water and gnawing on cold pizza, dreaming together about how they would change the world, she and Paula and Sam and Fish, all those plans for revolution and a grown-up life free of commercials, religious taboos, sexual hang-ups, suburban mores, the crap that had hollowed out their parents' '60s souls—and now Sam was a Wall Street hack and Fish was dead and Paula, who'd kissed Lizzie's toes and pledged forever love, was off fucking her way across California.

And Lizzie? Lizzie was very much not saving inner-city youth from a life of violence and poverty, nor was she bringing literacy to the oppressed daughters of some third-world village. Lizzie was a glorified babysitter to overprivileged fourth graders who didn't give a shit what she thought about trickle-down economics or the likelihood the so-called crack epidemic was a collaboration between the White House and the CIA; Lizzie was doing her parents proud with a plum job at a *nice* suburban school and an efficiency apartment in a *nice* neighborhood, because when her father said, "Over my dead body will you live in the ghetto," and her mother said, "We didn't send you to college so you could get shot in a gang war," and her aunt's rabbi's wife forwarded her name to the Armstrong school board without asking permission, she'd caved.

She'd promised herself: one year, maybe two, just enough to put away some savings, pay off some student loans, pacify her parents, and then she could return to the life she was supposed to live.

That was September.

By the end of October, after the weeks of mock campaigning, the little bastards dressing up as Reagan and Nixon for Halloween, after she'd served carpool duty enough times to know which kids came by Audi and which by BMW, which by Volvo and which by Jag, after she'd promised Lauren G.'s mother that yes, of course, the little princess could retake her math test as many times as she liked and let Robbie J.'s father lecture her about system-abusing freeloaders (like, say, Lauren G. and co.) while peeking shamelessly down her cleavage, she was forced to accept that two years, maybe even *one* year, was asking too much. She didn't belong in a school like this. She was starting to doubt she belonged in any school—it was turning out she liked the idea of children substantially more than she appreciated the real (germy, snotty, squirrelly) thing.

She lived for the hours she could dump them off in someone else's lap: gym, art, music, recess. These were her oases of sanity, precious moments to close herself into the silence of the empty classroom and try to imagine herself into a different life. Which is why she so resented the twice-a-week computer labs, because for incomprehensible reasons, she was expected to stay with the class, sitting in a corner monitoring their behavior while the computer teacher instructed them on basic typing skills for five or ten minutes, then let them piss away the rest of the hour on whatever ostensibly educational game they wanted.

Lizzie resented the sparkling new computer lab, its whirring monitors and tangles of wire representing the district's disgusting surplus of funds; while other, worthier districts were scrounging to pay for pencils and chalk, Armstrong had stocked itself up with twenty-two state-of-the-art computers, to teach computer literacy to a bunch of rich kids who all, as far as Lizzie could tell, had even more state-of-the-art computers at home. (Unlike Lizzie, who made do with the hand-me-down electric typewriter with broken space bar that only a couple of years before had seemed a technological miracle.) Most of all, she resented the computer lab supervisor, Rebecca Grady, who either couldn't be bothered or wasn't permitted to actually supervise the children, and who had a barbed wire tattoo ringing her taut bicep and a diamond stud in her nose and had held Lizzie's hand for a beat too long when they first met, which was an invitation to complication that Lizzie could very much not afford . . . but also, some treasonous inner voice complained, *not long enough.*

Every Tuesday and Thursday at four p.m., Lizzie trooped her class down to the computer lab, stationing them in front of the monitors and herself in whatever corner was farthest from Rebecca Grady, which seemed safest. But that day, mock election Thursday, Rebecca came to her.

"That election's a bitch, isn't it?" She said it in a low voice, but even if she'd screamed it, the kids were too immersed in their stupid computer games to hear.

"Excuse me?"

"Oh god, you're not a Republican? I mean, you dress like one, but I assumed—"

"I dress like a *Republican*?" Lizzie forgot herself, forgot even, for a second, the soft tufts of hair curling at the nape of Rebecca's neck and the hint of cinnamon gum on her breath. "Fuck no."

Rebecca smiled, as if to say: *I knew you were in there somewhere.* Then she pressed on. "You even have a Republican name, come to think of it. Elizabeth Kepler. Ann Taylor WASP, three generations back." She rolled it around in her mouth like she was tasting each syllable, and approved.

"*Lizzie* Kepler. Proud Kmart shopper. Jew. And just for the record, I voted Dukakis. Twelve times."

"Only twelve?" She tapped her chest. "Thirty."

"Miss Grady!" It was the high-pitched squeal of Keith Stoneapple, who Lizzie had known upon first sight would be the most shit-upon kid in the class. His concave, wart-speckled face was a kick-me sign, and neither the inhaler nor the Garbage Pail Kids obsession helped, especially with the latter's tendency to call attention to the unsubtle eau de Keith, an unfortunate mixture of sweat and rotting fruit. "Miss Grady!" He was waving his hand wildly, bouncing in his seat like he needed to pee, which was a distinct possibility and one that had been known to end in disaster.

Lizzie nudged her. "Rebecca, I think—"

"Who are you asking for, Keith?" the lab teacher asked, without turning to look.

"Uh, *Ms.* Grady?"

"Yes, Keith?"

"The screen froze."

"Turn the computer off and on again."

"But I just shot a buffalo!"

"And America thanks you for it."

"What? Ms. Grady, what do I *doooo*?"

"Off and on, Keith. Think like an early settler: there are always more buffalo." She turned her attention back to Lizzie, who was trying to direct *her* attention anywhere else. Lizzie liked this too much, all of it. "They have to learn that names matter," she said, and Lizzie, who answered to Ms., Miss, and Mrs. indiscriminately, figuring it wasn't worth the effort, felt chastened. "Speaking of which, forget this Rebecca shit. You can call me Beck. Rebecca's a fat girl name."

Lizzie's gaze swung inadvertently toward Jordana Goldstein, a chunky girl whose inability to break into the popular crowd had turned her mean.

Beck rolled her eyes. "Trust me, they're in a world of their own. A bunch of ten-year-olds obsessed with Manifest Destiny? If it weren't a postcolonialist nightmare I'd say it was fucking adorable."

It was the first time since her graduation that Lizzie had heard the word *postcolonialist* spoken aloud, and it made her want to lunge at Beck tongue-first, gave her dangerous visions of the two of them tangled naked and sweaty arguing about

Foucault. Maybe, she thought, trying to force herself back to safer ground, if she ever went back to school, she could write her dissertation on the retro semiotics of *Oregon Trail*.

"You die of cholera!" Robby Kline shrieked, jabbing a finger into Keith's shoulder.

"No touching," Lizzie snapped automatically.

"Cholera! Cholera!" Robby cried, kicking out his legs in what Lizzie took to be his very own cholera dance. "Dead! Dead! Dead!"

Keith burst into tears.

"Fucking adorable," she murmured, then sprang into action to do her teacherly duty, she and Beck double-teaming the increasingly hysterical pack, perpetrators and victims punished alike, as was the way of elementary school life.

Robby Kline was a hyperactive monster, and Lizzie supposed she should muster some sympathy for the kid, whose mother forbid him all sugar in a futile effort to keep him on an even keel. But she couldn't. No sympathy for the little bastard, no sympathy for poor, wheezy Keith, no sympathy for fat Jordana or shy Lindsay or even Lauren G., who was surely only such a royal bitch because her mother taught her there was no other way.

In the beginning, Lizzie had tried to imagine herself into their world, pretending to be one of them in an attempt at empathy. Rookie mistake. It was an age before empathy; picturing herself as a ten-year-old only encouraged categorizing them as her young self would have: losers to shun, cool kids to envy, weirdos to mock, nerds to resent because they were the only ones who would have her. Next she tried imagining them all grown up, searching for the matured, wondrous adults they surely had the capacity to be, but that was even worse, because by the time they were the age she was now, she would be depressingly old. And the older they got, the older she would be.

She hated them for that.

"A teaching degree is safe," her father had advised her. "You'll always have a job."

Best not to dwell on that, lest she start hating him, too.

Beck put Robby out in the hall, while Lizzie escorted poor Keith, whose tears had erupted into a full-blown asthma attack, down to the nurse's office. But not before she agreed to meet Beck for lunch the next day. Which, by virtue of being limited to school grounds and daylight, could most definitely not be qualified as a date.

Lizzie avoided the faculty lounge whenever possible. She'd taken her lunch there the first couple days of the semester, assuming that this was what one did at a real, grown-up job—mingle, kibitz, gossip, whatever. She was still close enough to her own school years to remember the glamour of the faculty lounge, the suspicions of scandal unfolding just beyond the formidable door. It turned out that even at a school like Armstrong, where the bathrooms gleamed with new linoleum and the office boasted its very own fax machine and two copiers, the faculty lounge was a dump. Two moldy couches spotty with cigarette holes, a narrow row of windows that would have peered out over the playground were their curtains not perpetually drawn, and a sad, squat refrigerator that reminded Lizzie of the dorm, each Tupperware container marked by exclamation-point-studded Post-its, *mine, mine, mine.* The old ladies lunched together on the best of the couches, the two middle-aged men swapped baseball stats and tinkered with a beat-up old black-and-white TV, and Beck—at least on the two occasions Lizzie had ventured inside—sat with the school's one black teacher and the sixth-grade science teacher who no one else liked. It depressed Lizzie more than anything, the thought that wherever she went, however old she got, there would always be a table for the cool kids and one for the freaks.

After that, she'd eaten lunch in her classroom. But Friday, as promised, she met Beck at noon. Mercifully, Beck led them out onto the playground, staking out a shady spot beneath the low stone wall. The lower-grade kids used it for wall ball, but they were all back in class, and the upper-grade kids disdained the whole area as tainted by "babies." It was the closest they would get to a private picnic without playing hooky. Lizzie watched her kids chasing after one another, trying, as she occasionally did, to locate some affection for them. Wondering what it was about happy children that made them want to scream.

Today's charming hijinks seemed to involve chasing Keith around the playground, shouting that he was going to die of cholera, and wheezy Keith had apparently accepted his fate, foregoing tears for one impressively melodramatic death scene after another. Robby, the little playground dictator, presided over the funeral.

"That game is so fucked-up," Lizzie said. "Do you think they even know what cholera is?"

"That's what makes it educational," Beck said brightly.

Lizzie had watched over their shoulders long enough to dimly understand the deal: You bought your supplies and lit off for the territory, shooting buffalo and fording rivers in a doomed effort to make it to the West Coast, an apparent nirvana, for reasons never specified. You were encouraged to name your wagon party after your friends, and as far as Lizzie could tell, the whole endeavor was simply an excuse to watch them die off one by one, of cholera and typhoid and dysentery and the ever-mysterious "exhaustion," then crafting a loving epitaph for their tombstone, like "Keith sux."

"It's morbid," Lizzie said. "Not to mention boring as hell, except for the dying thing."

Beck offered her an Oreo. Lizzie loved her a little for eating real cookies, not the fat-free crap her friends had been shoveling down their throats for as long as she could remember. She took the Oreo, then on second thought, two Oreos, and tried not to stare as Beck split hers open and licked the cream out of the center. Her tongue was very pink. Once she'd dispatched with the cream, she dropped the bare cookies into her lunch bag.

"What are you doing?"

"Sorry, I know it's gross. I only like the cream."

"Are you insane?" Lizzie said. "The cream is just the part you have to tolerate to get to the cookies."

Beck shrugged, then reached into the bag and retrieved one of the chocolate disks. "Unless you think I have cooties."

It felt like a dare, and Lizzie took it.

"I think something in their little peanut-sized brains must recognize the game's fundamental similarities to life," Beck said as Lizzie crunched and swallowed. "It's practice."

She said *peanut-sized* with affection, which Lizzie found equal parts confusing and shaming.

"Practice? You mean in case they suddenly need to ford the Mississippi? Or figure out how many pounds of squirrel meat will get them through the winter?"

Beck gave her a light shove, her tattoo brushing against Lizzie's cheap rayon blouse, and Lizzie imagined the inked barbed wire tearing through the fake silk, seeking skin. Thirty yards away, beneath the worm tree, Robby and the two Matts drizzled dirt on Keith's still face, while the girls wailed at his untimely loss.

"Someone's got to teach them that sometimes bad shit happens," Beck said. "That you can't choose what kind of shit it's going to be, or when. You can only choose what you're going to do in between."

At twenty-two, Lizzie still believed everyone over thirty was full of crap, but Beck was an obvious few years short of that deadline and there was something about the way she spoke that made Lizzie take her words for wisdom. She said it like she knew, like a weathered movie cop in a buddy flick, with Lizzie playing the clueless rookie, desperate for any crumbs of information that would keep her from getting shot.

"Besides," Beck added, "it's probably good for them to get used to the idea that your friends can die. Otherwise, the first time it happens can break you. Not to mention the fucking next time and the one after that."

"You've had friends who—" Lizzie stopped herself, thinking through what Beck's life must be like based on what she knew, and of what the other teachers whispered, thinking through the bars and clubs Beck probably spent her time in, the friends she'd made, thinking about the things Lizzie had seen on the news, the things Lizzie's friend Paul had reported—from what he called "the front lines," his shit room in the East Village that he'd only scored because the guy who lived there was now dead—and shut her mouth.

The places her mind went, thinking about that life, about

Beck's life, were exactly the places she worried her parents' minds would go, if she told them certain uncomfortable truths, and that made her feel as vindicated as she did craven.

Beck shrugged. "Maybe you have to play it to understand."

"You're biased," Lizzie pointed out. "Blinded by your computer love."

"Computer love? Are you kidding? I'm a fucking luddite." She gestured to the horde of fourth graders, who'd gotten bored of their fake funeral and were now running wild again, some form of cholera tag in which poor Keith was the perpetual It. "Every one of these little idiots knows more about computers than I do. Don't tell."

"But you're the *computer teacher*," Lizzie pointed out.

"Yeah, you think that was my idea? I'm supposed to be teaching first graders how to read, or something useful like that. That was the plan, at least."

"What happened?"

Beck glared in the general direction of the administrative offices. "What happened is it turns out it's not as easy as I thought to convince people like *them* to leave someone like *me* alone with children. You have no idea."

Lizzie worked to maintain a neutral expression.

"Huh. Or maybe you do," Beck said. There was no judgment. "Anyway, my aunt Helen's on the school board here, and she's fucking terrifying. Bullied them into giving me a job. Just not one where I'll be around the kids unsupervised." She laughed. Lizzie loved the sound of it—no, she corrected herself, *liked* the sound of it, mildly and without any emotional tether *appreciated* the sound of it—angry and musical all at once, like a fist smashed against piano keys. "And one where I have no idea what I'm doing."

Lizzie confessed her own foiled plans and dreams deferred—the underfunded city school she'd intended to take by storm, the dragons of poverty and illiteracy she'd planned to slay, the young lives she'd planned to mold and save, and the more she talked, the dumber it all sounded, and the dumber she sounded, the more she talked, until finally she choked herself off and Beck didn't laugh.

"You need a new job," Beck said just before little Keith started shrieking with tears again and Lizzie had to take him on another trip to the nurse's office, all the while assuring him he didn't have cholera. "Which means you need a new résumé. Come to the lab after hours, you can use one of the computers. No one will ever know." She winked, her expression full of something that Lizzie didn't want to see. "Promise."

She didn't go to the lab after school. She went home, ate frozen pizza in front of the TV, listened to the Cure while staring moodily at a framed photo of her ex, graded a set of abysmally written book reports, tried not to think about Beck, *did* think about Beck, rubbed herself into moderate bliss, and then slept.

Monday morning, Keith Stoneapple was absent. Word came down by lunch: the poor kid had had the asthma attack to end all attacks, nearly died, was tubed up in a hospital bed, and if/when they released him, he would relocate with his family to some warm, lung-hospitable climate, like a nineteenth-century tubercular shipped off to the sanitarium. Lizzie had the class make a giant "get well" card, watching warily as Robby mashed a red crayon against the construction paper, scribbling what looked like a vampire bunny, blood dripping from his fangs. The little bastard had, obviously, not magicked Keith into a coma by sheer force of will, had not transmuted digital cholera into real-world plague like some alchemist of disease, but Lizzie couldn't shake the image of him forcing Keith to the ground and heaping dirt all over his "grave." Kids will be kids and all that shit, she supposed, but it was creepy nonetheless.

She decided it was time to try this game for herself, see how it felt to kill off some of her own and whether Beck was right that digital grief could be educational and therapeutic, and that, she told herself, was her sole reason for knocking at the computer lab door late that afternoon—that, and maybe the need to update her résumé, and nothing else.

Beck looked inordinately pleased to see her.

Lizzie was pleased to see that.

Beck set her up on the machine and teased only a little when Lizzie admitted she wanted to make her way across this infamous Oregon Trail before getting down to serious work. Then Beck said she had some copying to do and not to break anything, and, before Lizzie could come up with a clever response, slipped out the door and left Lizzie alone.

It's better this way, Lizzie told herself as she typed the names of her least-favorite students into the game and decided how much money to spend on imaginary supplies in the imaginary frontier supply shop. She couldn't afford a slipup *here*, of all places, she reminded herself as she watched the pixelated wagon chug along flat ground, oxen powering across the countryside, temperature rising and food supply falling, Kathleen inexplicably breaking a leg and then dying a few imaginary days later. This was Lizzie's workplace—not to mention a direct connection to her aunt's rabbi and, through that, to her mother; this was her job and her rent and her reputation. The game wanted to know whether she would like to hold a funeral, and Lizzie chose "no." Her crew's morale and health immediately plummeted. She shot a few deer and one buffalo, which yielded two thousand more pounds of food than the game allowed her to carry, and Jordana succumbed to dysentery; bored, Lizzie indulged a fantasy: the door creaking open, the lights going out, strong hands kneading her shoulders, the diamond stud tickling her lip. She wondered if Beck was pierced anywhere else. Lauren G. died of dysentery, no big loss—Lizzie figured she'd spent the whole trip lounging in the back of the wagon whining about the smell of oxen.

They lost two oxen while trying to cross the Kansas River and half their food supply to a thief in the night, and Lizzie would have liked to ask Beck what the hell she'd meant by getting to make choices between bad shit, because as far as she could tell, the game was entirely made up of unmotivated bad shit, punctuated by choices she was forced to make completely at random, because who the hell knew whether it was better to ford or float a river, or even if there was a difference? But she couldn't ask that, because Beck was still gone, photocopying, or hiding out, or maybe Lizzie's presence in the computer lab was such a nonissue for her that she'd forgotten and gone home, or maybe—

"Shit," Lizzie said. She'd had one job: *don't break anything.* But somehow, she must have, because the game's date had gone from June 7, 1848, to November 7, 1988—today. And Robby was dead, not of measles or typhoid, but an electrical fire. Which, Lizzie knew, despite scraping by with a C in every dull American history class she'd ever taken, was a highly unlikely prospect in the Missouri wilderness circa 1848.

She must have done something wrong, pressed some button, and it's not like the computer was smoking or sparking—

it was just the stupid game wigging out on her—but it wasn't something she wanted Beck to come back to see.

And it creeped her out a little to see Robby's name right there beside that night's date and the word *dead*.

She remembered Beck's advice about malfunctioning computers, and turned the thing on and off again. She rebooted the game, made all her choices again, superstitiously naming her wagon mates exactly as she had before, which seemed like the best way to reverse whatever bad juju she'd brought down on them, and then held her breath as they began dropping like flies. Measles again, and diphtheria, all well and good, and then Robby broke his leg, which would have been fine, except that the date was all fucked-up *again*, and Lizzie shut the computer down in disgust, replacing the disk where Beck had found it, deciding the whole night had been a mistake, Beck was never coming back, and she might as well go home.

It wasn't until she was back in her classroom the next morning that she thought of her résumé, still un-updated, and then Robby lumbered in on crutches, with his leg in a purple cast, and that was the end of rational thought for the day.

The cast made Robby more popular than ever—and more insufferable. Out of some insane guilt, Lizzie let him have pet-feeding duty for the week, which probably meant she'd soon end up with a dead hamster. Even more blood on her hands, she thought, then felt like an idiot. Coincidences weren't magic, and neither were computers.

Still, that day she unilaterally decided to cancel computer lab for the afternoon and instead threw an impromptu party, sugaring the kids with leftover Halloween candy. Even Robby got a Reese's; she figured there was a limit to the trouble he could cause with one leg.

When the final bell rang, she told herself she was only going to the computer lab to take another look at the game, to exorcise any foolish lingering superstitions, and that it had nothing to do with Beck. Midway down the emptying corridor, she changed her mind, told herself she didn't *actually* think an evil computer program had, with her help, broken Robby Kline's leg, and this was all her subconscious's devious ruse to drive her into Beck's arms.

Neither of these lines of thought felt wholly convincing.

"Where'd you go yesterday?" Beck asked. "I got back and you were gone. You left the room unlocked, too—you know how much trouble I'd get in if something happened to these things?"

"Sorry," Lizzie said weakly.

"No harm, no foul. But you owe me a drink."

"Done," Lizzie said, thinking: *Tonight? Someday? Never?* Was it a date or a hypothetical? Imaginary, like the oxen and the diphtheria, real like tequila-infused kisses, something in between like Robby's cast and the dreams she'd started having, the kind that made her wake up in sweaty sheets? Nothing had been this hard back in school. You drank, you ate greasy pizza, you went home together or you didn't, and without trying, you were suddenly living in someone else's dorm room, wearing her sweatshirts to class and hoping no one thought it was weird how you kept inhaling the cuffs, thinking of her.

"So?" Beck said.

"So . . ."

"Did you come here to see me, or . . . ?"

"The game," Lizzie blurted, remembering a second too

late that her résumé would have been a more plausible, not to mention practical, response.

"Ah, an addict already." Beck pulled out one of the *Oregon Trail* disks and slid it over to Lizzie. "You get one round. Then happy hour. Beer on you. Yes?"

Terrible idea, Lizzie reminded herself. Don't shit where you eat and all that, and the wicked witch of the third grade was already giving her knowing looks, like she suspected something dark.

"Yes," she said.

Beck settled herself behind the desk with a P. D. James novel and Lizzie played. This time the children all died as they were supposed to, when they were supposed to, and Lizzie gave each of them a funeral. She proceeded on her own, with one sickly oxen and a couple of extra axles, and made it as far as Soda Springs before the date changed to June 27, 2028, and the computer informed her:

You have died of throat cancer.

Lizzie yanked the plug. The screen went dark.

"What the hell are you doing?" Beck yelped, looking up from her book. "You can't turn it off that way."

She didn't know what the hell she was doing.

"That almost sounded like I cared." Beck sighed. "If I ever do, you have my permission to kill me. So, you really that eager for a drink?"

Lizzie nodded, not trusting herself to speak, and when Beck took her hand and pulled her to her feet, Lizzie held on, turned into her, *fell* into her, anchored herself with Beck's shoulders and Beck's waist and Beck's lips, felt steady against Beck's body, felt protected in Beck's arms, felt Beck, her muscle and her flesh and her tremble of barely contained desire.

Or maybe it was Lizzie who was shaking, Beck who was still. They were too entangled to know the difference, and Lizzie would not let go.

This was love: steaming hot chocolate spiked with bourbon on freezing November nights, the two of them cozy on the couch in Beck's flannel pajamas, listening to the rain. Licking tequila from Beck's bare stomach, memorizing her ticklish spots, the sensitive patch on the back of her left knee, the point on her spine where a grazing fingertip would make her squeal. Throwing the photos of Paula in the trash, then reneging and hiding them in the back of her closet instead, because Beck said the past made them the women they were and lovers past should be thanked for lovers present. Listening to Beck, believing Beck, who seemed to know so much. Listening to Beck's stories of the friends she needed to remember, men who were there and then suddenly weren't, going with Beck to a hospital and standing awkwardly by her side as she gossiped with a gaunt man, catching him up on other friends, dying and not, his hollow cheeks speckled, his body disappearing. Taking Beck's hand afterward as she cried and giving silent thanks that they were not men and so were maybe safe. Caravanning to school in separate cars so no one would know they'd rolled reluctantly out of the same bed, groped for conditioner and each other in the same shower, fed each other burnt cinnamon toast, flashed each other the bird at red lights, because *fuck you* was their unspoken way of saying the opposite. Passing in the school hallways without looking at each other so no one would know. Avoiding each other at lunch so no one would know. Enduring computer lab periods while trying not to fixate on the curve of Beck's shoulder or the tufts of hair at her ears or her tongue wetting her lips or the soft pads of her fingers touching keyboards, touching monitors, touching pencils, touching shoulders, touching everyone but Lizzie—all so no one would know. Was it love that made her think of nothing but Beck, that emptied her mind of all but the essentials—the tastes and smells and urgent needs—or was it obsession? Lizzie had no reference point, had never felt like this before, was unsure anyone had ever felt like this before, and didn't give a shit.

This was obsession: Going to the computer lab after the final bell. Going to the computer lab even though Beck carefully absented herself, *because* Beck carefully absented herself, because they couldn't afford to be seen together even after hours, but the lab smelled of Beck, embodied Beck, and Beck had GREs to study for, studying she couldn't do with Lizzie there pressing hands to flesh and whispering secrets into the hollow of neck or base of spine, so Beck went home with her book and Lizzie used Beck's key to get into the lab and imagined Beck until it was time to be with her again. And so: Going to the computer lab for totally reasonable reasons—staying in the computer lab because of the game. Playing the game. Dying in the game. Killing off her loved ones in the game. Playing the game again and again. The game malfunctioning, more frequently every day, the game murdering the people who mattered to her, mother with a heart attack in 2010, father in a construction accident in 1994, Beck with cancer in 1998, Beck with cancer in 2007, Beck with cancer in 2030—the game showed her so many ways to die, and so many were cancer. Naming her party, buying supplies, hunting for buffalo, fording the river, rolling asymptotically west, west, west, until, always: *You have died. You have died. You have died.*

Dying in a week, dying in a year, dying in twenty years, always a tombstone with her name on it, electrocution, fire, heart attack, cancer, mountaineering, car accident, cancer again, every choice changing the method, no choice changing the prognosis: terminal. Telling herself this was some programmer's idea of a joke, telling herself she should tell Beck and they could play together and laugh away all fear, telling herself it couldn't possibly matter whether she made it to Oregon, that no one in their right mind would expend all that effort on getting to Oregon, that there was no promised land, that a computer could not kill her, that the boy wobbling around her classroom on a cast and the asthmatic wheezing in a hospital bed were statistical outliers, that she should put the game away or light it on fire or forget it existed and go home. Playing again, trying again, one more time, just in case, just to be safe. Thinking about Beck when she was playing the game, thinking about the game when she was with Beck, lying awake nights, worrying through discovery and disease, dreaming of death, waking afraid.

This was fear: lying in bed, Beck snuggled into her shoulder or sprawled over her chest, blinking into the dark, thinking, *what if*. What if they fell in love, *even* more in love, what if Lizzie lost herself, fell down so deep she couldn't find her way out, and then Beck disappeared or Beck died or Beck simply got tired of her and went on her way and Lizzie was left alone. What if they didn't fall further in love, what if they grew bored of each other, what if this feeling was temporary, what if, *unthinkable*, it disappeared, and left an unfillable void in its place, turned her cold. What if someone at school found out, and she got fired, and ran out of money, and ended up on the street or in her parents' basement; what if no one found out, and Beck made her tell someone, what if she told her parents, and they couldn't love her anymore, they turned their backs to her, they thought she was disgusting, they made her choose, they cut her off. What if she wasn't the person Beck thought she was, couldn't be the person she wanted to be, what if she never left this job, never ventured into the terrifying heart of the city, never changed lives or helped people, was too selfish to bother or care. What if she did, what if she went, what if her parents were right and the city was no place for a nice girl like her and she was attacked in a dark corner, what if she was raped, what if she was shot, what if she was killed. What if she caught the thing she and Beck never talked about and knew they were probably safe from but no one knew enough about it to be so sure and if she did catch it she would die. What if she died like the game said she would die, in a fiery wreck or stumbling off a cliff, what if she was going insane, if the game was driving her crazy, if this burning that felt like love was actually insanity, or if they were enemies, if one would destroy the other, and she had to choose, which she could survive without, love or obsession, love or fear, love or life.

Lack of sleep wasn't exactly improving her teaching skills, and they hadn't been so strong to begin with. There was the day, hopped up on three cups of coffee and a caffeine pill, still blinking away exhaustion and realizing only once she got to school that she'd forgotten to put on underwear, that she decided it would be a good idea to give her class a dose of the *real* Oregon Trail, and described the symptoms of dysentery in all their shitting glory, then lectured her rapt fourth graders on the 1857 Mountain Meadows massacre, forty men, thirty women, seventy children, traveling through Utah—on some trail to Oregon, according to her book, if not the actual Oregon Trail, she was too bleary-eyed to tell—beset by a party of Mormons and Native Americans, bamboozled into surrendering, then shot, clubbed, hacked to death. Bloody, bloody death, she described it, just as she'd read about it in the hours before dawn, because she couldn't scrub it from her mind and was too tired to sanitize the horror, all of them dead but seventeen children drenched in the blood of their parents, crying the way her students·began to cry as Lizzie painted the picture.

It wasn't her most successful lesson, and in the end she bribed them with cookies and an indoor recess to shut them up. Bribery was her new hobby. She'd discovered that Robby Kline had an encyclopedic knowledge of the game, reeling off the shifting statistical probabilities of death. Robby knew which month it was best to set off, when it was worth fording a river or taking a ferry—dependent on dwindling food supplies and number of spare axles—when to hold a funeral and when to skip the ritual and press on, when squirrels were preferable to buffalo, whether being a banker was all it seemed cracked up to be. Robby taught her to be ruthless, to winnow her party down as quickly as she could, to press on alone in pursuit of salvation. And the ruthless little monster, upon realizing how desperately she wanted his advice, offered it only for a price. He hadn't handed in homework for more than two weeks, and despite borderline illiteracy, had already been guaranteed straight As.

So when the wicked witch, Mrs. Polanyi—this was how Lizzie thought of her, even though they were ostensibly colleagues, because there was nothing about the hunched woman with the brown teeth and the battle-axe attitude that invited a first-name basis—summoned her after the lunch bell rang, Lizzie expected to be chewed out for any number of sins. Everyone knew Polanyi was the principal's hatchet woman, and if she was to be fired for scaring the living shit out of her students, or if Robby had opened his big mouth to one of his asshole little friends, this was how it would begin.

The conversation took an unexpected turn. "Elizabeth, we all want to see you succeed here." The woman's breath smelled of tuna fish.

"Thank you?"

They spoke not in the faculty lounge or in Lizzie's empty classroom but, aptly enough, in the small utility room between upper and lower grades that was stocked with extra art supplies and known to all as, simply, the closet.

"I thought you should know that there are those who might draw unfortunate implications from your recent behavior."

"I'm not on drugs or anything." It was the first thing that popped into her head, and she was too tired not to voice it. *The things that come out of your mouth*, her mother said sometimes, in wonder, and Lizzie was inclined to agree. Someone should duct-tape her lips shut; it would be better for all. "I mean, I just haven't been sleeping very well, and I thought the kids could use a dose of real history, something to get them engaged with the topic, like an action movie or something. Some of the sensitive ones might have been upset, but I bet they'll all be a lot more . . ."

It was the deepening furrow in Mrs. Polanyi's gnarled brow that suggested she shut her mouth. "Excuse me?" Polanyi said. "Who was upset? About what?"

"Nothing." Lizzie felt ten years old. She reminded herself that feminists didn't cry in the workplace.

"Your friendship with Rebecca Grady," the witch said. "I suggest you reconsider it."

"Wait—what?" It took her a moment to shift gears, but only a moment, because this was the shoe she'd been waiting to drop, and she had her game face ready to go. "I barely know Rebecca."

Silently she congratulated herself for remembering. Rebecca, not Beck. It was easier, that way, to imagine she was talking about a stranger, to keep quiet as the witch went on about Rebecca's unsavoriness and Rebecca's unwholesomeness and Rebecca's precarious position at the school and Lizzie's similarly precarious position if she elected not to understand that people see, people judge, people draw conclusions Lizzie most certainly wouldn't want them to draw. It was easier that way, thinking of Rebecca as a stranger, to nod and agree that of course she understood, and—strained smile here, almost a curtsy—thank you.

That night, she stayed in the lab through dark, playing and dying, dying and playing. Beck was nearly asleep when Lizzie slid into bed beside her, but awake enough to say, "You can't stay out of the closet for a second, can you?"

Lizzie tensed, so much that Beck tugged her tighter, started kneading her shoulders. "Whoa, kidding," she said. "I just meant you and Polanyi in the closet today. I hear she tore you a new one. Everything okay?"

Lizzie nodded. Said nothing.

"The witch put a curse on you?" Beck said.

Lizzie shook her head. Said nothing.

The shoulder kneading stopped. "So what was she on about, then?"

Lizzie made something up, something about how she'd

skipped carpool duty and been chewed out, assigned double as punishment, lied without even thinking about it, without hesitation or stammer, and when Beck called her on it, admitted she already knew exactly what Polanyi wanted, because Polanyi was the kind of unsubtle nosy bitch to spread it around, Lizzie felt oddly unashamed.

Maybe I'm a sociopath, Lizzie thought when Beck asked why she lied, why the lie had come so easily to her, what this was all about, where she went in those hours after school, hours she supposedly spent in the computer lab but why would she do that and what was actually going on. *Maybe I can teach myself not to care.*

"I told you when this started that I'm not ready," Lizzie said. "And for the record I don't see any point in labeling myself, or any of that political shit."

"By *that political shit* you mean fighting for the rights and the lives of people slightly less cowardly than you? You mean peeking outside your own self-absorption for more than thirty seconds? Yeah, I'm pretty clear on you not seeing the point of that."

"Unlike you, bravely teaching rich brats and applying to grad schools while all your friends are dying off like flies? That's some political activism. They should give you a plaque."

She thought Beck might hit her; maybe she wanted that.

"You didn't mean that," Beck said.

Lizzie shrugged.

"I don't want to fight about . . . the bigger questions. I just hate that you can lie to me so easily," Beck said. "It makes it hard to trust anything. Can you understand that?"

"You're speaking in English. I get it."

"So . . . where were you tonight?"

"I told you," she said. "School."

"Working on your résumé. *Again.*"

"Yeah."

"And lesson planning."

"Sure."

She could tell Beck about the game. There was no reason not to. *Not* telling was giving it more importance than it deserved; telling might be the one thing that relieved her of its burden, turned the whole thing into a joke, but Lizzie couldn't risk that yet, not until she won. She was too tired to decide what was meant to be secret and what deserved to be open truth; she was too scared to pick the wrong things to speak aloud, because once you spoke, there was no taking it back.

"So did you tell Polanyi you'd stay away from me, like she wanted?"

"Do you want me to lie to you?" Lizzie asked.

"I want the truth to be different," Beck said.

It was their first fight.

They met for lunch on the playground, as they had done the first day. It was Lizzie's invitation, Lizzie's idea of an apology, after she had left Beck's place in the middle of the night, and spent the hours until morning wondering about the things she could live without and the things she couldn't. They had a picnic of vending machine snacks beneath the stone wall, in full view of the children and the gossipy recess monitors, and Lizzie thought maybe she could do this after all.

"I'm not trying to rush you," Beck said.

"I know."

"I know you think you need this job."

"I 'think' I need it?"

Beck sighed. "You keep saying how much you hate it here, Lizzie, but you don't do anything about getting out of here, you don't do anything to get this life of yours you keep saying you're supposed to have, so I guess I figure . . ."

"What?"

Beck shook her head. "I don't want to fight again."

"*What?*"

"If this is the life you have, Lizzie, it's because this is the life you're choosing to have. It's either what you want or it isn't. You don't get to pick and then pretend like someone else picked for you."

"I'm God now?" Lizzie said. "I have absolute control over everything that happens to me?" She pointed toward Jordana, lingering heartbreakingly near the popular kids' four-square game, waiting to be invited to play. "I smite thee." Jordana continued to stand there, unsmote, fists clenching and unclenching as she watched the game and poorly pretended not to care. "Somebody forgot to tell her I'm omnipotent."

"I told you, I don't want to fight."

Beck split an Oreo, licked out the cream, and handed the bare chocolate disks to Lizzie. It was what made them perfect for each other, Beck had once said. She'd spent her whole life looking for someone to split her Oreos with.

Lizzie crunched down on the cookie. The artificial chocolate always tasted better to her than the real thing.

"I love you, you know." Beck said it casually, like they said it to each other all the time, though they never had.

"You too," Lizzie said. Without thinking, she put her hand over Beck's.

Little Robby Kline saw her do it. She saw him see it, and yanked her hand away.

"I'm not contagious," Beck said. "I'm not going to give you cholera or something." She laughed, like she had made a joke, and Lizzie laughed, like it was funny, wondering whether she had anything left that Robby wanted, and if not, whether she could just return to the computer and keep playing the game until she found a set of choices that killed him off before he could ruin everything. It was okay to think like that, of course, because the game was a joke.

"You'll come over tonight?" Beck said.

"Don't I always?" Which they both knew wasn't an answer.

"No one saw," Beck promised.

"I know."

"Don't worry," Beck begged her.

"I'm not."

"I love you," Beck said, not casually this time.

"I love you," Lizzie echoed, meaning it and loving Beck all the more for believing it was all that mattered.

It took her until nearly midnight, but she did it. There was something about the night, right from the beginning, she sensed she was closing in. One game, she even made it as far as the Snake River before Beck succumbed to cancer in 2030 and Lizzie fell to Alzheimer's a few years later. They would both be in their sixties by then, and maybe, she thought, that was good enough; maybe she should go home—which was Beck's bed, Beck's arms—lay down this burden, and sleep.

But on the next game, she made it to Fort Boise, which was the farthest she'd ever got. Too far to give up. Finally, three games later, she made it to Chimney Rock with her whole party intact, and though thieves came in the night near Fort

Laramie, she had enough money to replace the stolen supplies once she got to town. She flipped the disk over, and both her parents succumbed to a plane crash at Independence Rock in 2004, but that was forever away; she pressed on. Paula OD'd at Soda Springs in 1992, but that was the farthest Lizzie'd gotten with her own health in good shape, and anyway, fuck Paula, who'd cheated on her all through senior year and then, after a teary confession and several weeks' begging for forgiveness, had dumped Lizzie the day after graduation to run off with her Deconstructing Shakespeare TA.

The wagon rolled on and on.

At the Snake River, she hired an Indian guide in exchange for clothes, just as Robby had recommended. She passed Fort Boise, then the Blue Mountains. When the trail divided, she proceeded to The Dalles. There Beck died. Car accident, January twenty-seventh, which happened to be tomorrow.

Lizzie skipped the tombstone epitaph, too eager now to keep going and knowing if she paused she would lose her nerve, start over again, but there was no need for that, she thought, not when she was so close, not when the whole thing was just a stupid digital prank, sound and fury and nothing, when, if she could just *win*, just make it through and out without dying herself, she could maybe let the whole thing fall away, go to Beck, say whatever it was she needed to say, start fresh. Start clean. She knew what to do; she would be ruthless. From The Dalles, she took the river, and it happened, as it had never happened before.

The Willamette Valley unfurled before her, electric green meadow beneath wildly blue sky.

Congratulations! You have made it to Oregon!

She was the only member of her party to survive. This is

what it feels like to survive, she told herself. It felt lonely in bed, in the dark, cold without a body pressed to hers, listening to the floors creak and the windows rattle, but for the first time in too long, Lizzie slept through the night.

It wasn't until morning that she played her messages, the machine full up, all of them from Beck, wondering where she was, wondering why she hadn't come home, Beck sad and then Beck drunk and then Beck threatening to come and find her, if not at her apartment then at the computer lab where she supposedly spent all her time. Beck had some trouble with the word *supposedly*, and when she got through it went on to slur more words on the topic of Lizzie's secret life, speculations of whores in bars or asshole football players hidden in the closet, her favorite place, and then she called back to apologize, but "I'm still coming" because "we need to talk" because "I love you and you love me, I know that you do."

Lizzie called, knowing Beck wouldn't answer her phone, and she didn't. Lizzie drove to school, certain she wouldn't be there, either, and she wasn't.

This is what it feels like to survive, Lizzie told herself. It felt lonely, but it was what she'd chosen, she thought, so she must have wanted it that way.

———————

Robin Wasserman is the author of *The Waking Dark* and the forthcoming *Girls on Fire*. Her short fiction has appeared in several anthologies, including *Oz Reimagined*, *Robot Uprisings*, and *The End Is Now*, and she has published nonfiction in *Tin House*, the *Los Angeles Review of Books*, and *The New York Times*.

She is a former children's book editor who lives and writes in Brooklyn, New York, and has fonder memories of elementary school than this story would suggest. Find her at www.robinwasserman.com or on Twitter @robinwasserman.

RECOIL!

Micky Neilson

Jimmy Nixon put a 7.62 mm bullet straight through the guard's head.

With practiced ease he slipped through the verandah into the villa's great room. He took the nearest flight on the imperial staircase. As he ascended the steps (all solid pink), he spotted the next sentry on the floor above. In one swift motion he scoped the sentry and popped a single round through his faceplate.

Who's next, motherfuckers?

He heard shouts. Someone had found the first guard's corpse. A knot of angry henchmen—their body armor solid pink—ran onto the floor below, their Mag 5s trained on Jimmy. With a voice command he engaged auto-assist, then turned and strafed. The system calculated trajectory for multiple head shots and adjusted his heads-up reticle as necessary; Jimmy dropped the thugs like targets at a carnival shooting gallery. An automated voice, as well as the readout on his display, revealed that his ammo was spent. He switched out the magazine and continued on to the second floor. Jimmy switched his goggles to IR and spotted the cartel leader's heat signature in the master bedroom. He raced down the hall, kicked in the boss's pink door, and . . .

The game crashed. Jimmy threw up his hands, nearly pulling the controller cable out of the console. "Shit!" He was nearly at the boss fight. In record time, too.

With a grunt of frustration he tossed the controller onto the coffee table.

A small digital clock next to the testing station told him that it was almost two a.m. *Damn, Kim's gonna be pissed.* She'd probably called him six times by now. Jimmy snapped up the TV remote and shut the set off, dropped the remote, and stood. The floor-to-ceiling window behind the testing setup offered a scenic view of the Bay Area. Jimmy stretched and shuffled over next to the entertainment unit to have a look. *You could have a view like this every day if you get the job.*

That was the plan. Jimmy had been hard at work since a little after nine, creating file after file of detailed texture maps for his portfolio. His buddy Ross McTiernan, the lucky bastard, had been working here at Full Metal Entertainment for six months. Ross was nice enough to not only promise Jimmy a referral but to offer up his own computer and software for him to use after hours, to create textures. If he played his cards right, he would get a job and be one of the guys making textures to replace the pink, untextured surfaces currently in the game.

Full Metal had developed one licensed game already—not a blockbuster, but a solid B title, and hordes of gamers were anxiously awaiting their next product, a first-person shooter.

It was currently in the alpha phase—playable by employees but not ready for beta, when it would be made available to public testers. *RECOIL!* was the name. "Pull the Trigger, Feel the Recoil!" It took place in a not-too-distant future where "multinational military forces, called Factions, have risen to prominence." Through the tutorial, testers could choose one of two player character types—Enforcers, who fought against terrorism as well as organized crime and international drug operations, or Peacekeepers, who performed hostage rescue and close protection and were often embedded in hostile territory. Jimmy had just been an Enforcer. He had played as both types, though, and still wasn't sure which he preferred.

Either way, the game was beyond badass and Jimmy wanted nothing more than to be a part of it. To be a texture artist at a promising new game developer before the age of twenty? How sick would that be?

Jimmy had taken a short break to play the game but had gotten swept away. Right about now it was time to shut off Ross's computer and get back to his mom's house, where Kim was no doubt still awake, waiting.

Just then a *click-click* echoed through the reception area outside. Jimmy leaned out and looked to his right, through the open office space to the main entry. Someone was opening one of the double doors. Did Ross come back? Another employee? The door swung open . . .

It was the building security guard.

Oh, shit. Jimmy *technically* wasn't supposed to be there. Ross told him it wouldn't be a big deal, but what if the guard was making rounds? Jimmy didn't have a badge.

Dumb ass, hide!

He ducked back into the small room and slipped behind the right side of the couch.

A voice called out, "Security, anyone on the floor?"

Shit. Shit, shit, shit . . .

Should he just go out and explain? But how would it look for Jimmy's chances at getting hired if he was discovered sneaking time on Ross's machine?

"Hellooo?"

The voice was at the other end of the floor space now. The guard was searching the entire office area. Footsteps approached the testing room. Jimmy curled up, made himself as small as possible, looking to see if he was being reflected in the opposite window. He wasn't, but he could see the reflection of the doorway.

The figure of the guard stepped closer, a black man, maybe in his late twenties. There was a creak of the security guard's belt as he leaned in. Jimmy's heart thundered up into his throat. He held his breath.

The guard leaned back out, turned, and walked away. Jimmy exhaled a long sigh of relief.

He heard the entry door, then the guard's voice again: "All clear, fellas."

There was a discussion between the guard and maybe two more people as they passed by. The other two sounded like the bad guys from that game *Cold War*. Russians? What the hell were Russians doing here?

The conversation receded as they made their way to the back of the office space. There was the sound of two heavy objects hitting the floor. Jimmy eased out from behind the couch and back to the testing room doorway.

He peeked around the corner. The office floor was one big rectangle, with the entry doors and reception desk to his right and, to his left, QA/IT cubicles (all personalized with action figures and merchandise ranging from *Star Wars* to *Doctor Who*). There were two large duffel bags on the floor next to the corner cubicle opposite him. One bag had square metal legs sticking out. The periphery of the space was lined with smaller rooms like the one he was in now, most of them offices or bullpens.

The security guard had used his electronic badge to open a door at the far corner, diagonal from Jimmy's position. This was the server room, and the door usually remained locked. The guard was inside, facing sideways, talking to the men who had moved into the room but were now out of Jimmy's line of sight. The guard said, "Well, if that's that, I'll take my cash and get outta your way."

A husky voice replied, "Yes, we should settle up."

The guard said, *"Hey!"* and reached for something on his belt. Jimmy saw the silencer-equipped barrel of a gun come into his field of view, saw the barrel twitch upward, and heard a muffled *Pop!* as the guard's head jerked back. The man collapsed.

Holy shit Jesus Christ what the fuck—

The barrel dropped out of sight. The same husky voice said, "Paid in full," then spoke to his unseen companion in Russian.

Was that—did I really just see that? I just saw someone get killed. Jimmy's hands covered his mouth. He was shaking all over, his heart jackhammering inside his chest.

Run, dumb ass!

The Russians were still inside the room, still out of sight. A loud, piercing noise blared out. To Jimmy it sounded like one of those big drills, the kind used to bore through concrete. If he could just make it to the entry doors . . .

Legs quivering, he took rapid steps out of the testing room and toward the main doors, trying desperately not to make a sound, eyes glued to the server room doorway as he went. His head spun back around just in time to avoid running straight into the reception desk. He was just a few feet away from the entry doors when the handle spun downward.

Someone was coming in.

Shit shit shit shit—

Jimmy dropped to all fours and scuttled past the rolling chair and secreted himself under the reception desk.

Maybe it's another guard, maybe it's the cops—

The drilling noise stopped. A man from the server room called out in Russian. The man who had just entered answered. Jimmy heard the sound of the front door locks engaging.

Jimmy's heart skipped as footsteps approached the reception desk . . .

. . . and passed by, heading toward the other end of the room. Jimmy tried to control his breathing so he wouldn't be heard. He peeked out just enough to see the new man, wearing a red jogging jacket, at the first cubicle on the right-hand side, rummaging through a long duffel bag he had placed on the cubicle desk. Behind his feet were the bags Jimmy had already seen on the floor.

Think, think . . .

If he tried to make a run for the entry doors, he would have to stop long enough to unlock them. Maybe he could outrun these guys but only to the elevators, and then he'd have to push the button and wait.

Then he'd be dead.

There was a small hallway and exit at the back of the room that led to stairs, but there was no way he could make it past the guy who had just come in.

Phones. You need a phone, he thought. *Call the police.*

Right. He had brought his own cell phone, but it was in the artists' bullpen, charging, and the artists' bullpen was right by the server room. So no dice. But if he could crawl into the level designers' bullpen, which was next to the testing room, he could use one of their desk phones. There was a stand-up of *RECOIL!*'s main character, Brock Johnson, behind the reception desk that could help block him from view as he relocated. Jimmy looked over at the Russian; the guy was still occupied with the bag.

Now or never.

Jimmy scurried on hands and knees across the short open space to the designers' bullpen doorway. Once inside, he tried again to slow his breathing as he listened for any indications that he'd been detected. There was none.

The long, rectangular room was filled with workstations and had entryways on either end. Jimmy ran to a desk that was situated in the middle of the room, where he couldn't be seen directly from either doorway. He picked up the receiver with a shaky hand, put it to his ear . . .

But there was no sound.

He looked at the base's display, which would normally show the time and have menu options, but the screen was blank. Jimmy replaced the receiver and looked at the displays on the surrounding phones. All blank as well. He looked at the computers. Some of the guys left their computers on all night, but they were all password protected and he didn't know any of their passwords.

The phones were all connected to the company's local network. They must have shut off the network to this floor. Even if he could get on to a computer, he'd have no Internet access.

Maybe . . . maybe he could just hide out here until they did whatever it was they came to do.

Jimmy backed up against the wall near the second entryway. He could hear a voice in Russian come through a walkie-talkie. A Russian voice in the office responded; he leaned out just enough to see Red Jacket finish talking and place the walkie-talkie in the bag on the desk.

A man with spiky hair came out from the server room, muttering. It wasn't the husky voice he'd heard before; this was someone else. How many trespassers was he dealing with at this point? Two on the main floor, another in the server room, and one more on the walkie. Four at least.

The new guy kneeled, opened one of the bags on the floor, and withdrew some kind of chainsaw. It had what looked like a collector or pan attached to it. The man pulled a plastic jug of water from the same bag.

He took the chainsaw and water and returned to the server room.

The floor . . . was that what the chainsaw was for, cutting through the floor? Jimmy's dad installed fire-suppression systems for a living and was a tool nut. He'd heard him talk about wet saws; that must be what he had just seen. Was there something in the floor these guys wanted, or . . . maybe the level below?

TechniCom.

Jimmy remembered Ross talking about the company, and he'd seen some of the employees downstairs in the coffee shop. They always wore polo shirts and khakis. The rumor was they were a university team working off of a Department of Defense grant. Whatever they were developing was top secret. No one was allowed in their work area. There had been some talk—where it came from, no one knew exactly—that the team was focused on cutting-edge learning augmentation: a direct neural interface. Kind of like virtual reality, but a giant leap forward.

Whatever TechniCom was working on, it looked like these Russians were breaking in to steal it.

Who cares? Leave it to the cops. Just hide out. If they don't know you're here . . .

All of a sudden LMFAO's "Sexy and I Know It" blared from the artists' bull pen.

Fuck! It was Jimmy's ringtone. Kim was calling. The two Russians shared a look. The man with the chainsaw said something and returned to the server room. Red Jacket walked into the artists' bullpen and came out a second later with Jimmy's now silent cell phone in his hand.

You gotta get out of here . . .

If he could just get to his vehicle. He scurried to the windows at the back of the room and looked down onto the parking lot. There was his piece-of-shit hand-me-down purple Festiva, sitting all alone save for a large, white, unmarked van. Just then another car pulled into the lot from around the back . . .

A cop car.

Jimmy balled his fists and had to physically restrain himself from pounding on the glass. The car passed by the van without stopping, then pulled onto the small access road and headed out toward the main street.

No!

A man emerged from the white van, holding a walkie-talkie. He pressed a button and spoke into it. His staticky voice sounded from the main floor.

There were several business buildings in this corporate park. The cop might remain close by. If only Jimmy had a way of signaling him . . .

He ran back to the doorway and peeked out.

Red Jacket replaced the radio in the duffel on the desk, then went to the server room and stood in the doorway. After a short conversation Red Jacket turned around, scanning the office space. Jimmy ducked back. He waited a second, runnels of sweat crawling down from his pits over his ribs. He dared to look back out and saw Red Jacket heading into the artists' bullpen.

He's searching the place to make sure no one's here.

Jimmy eyed the bag on the cubicle desk. That was where the radio was. If he could get the radio, sneak out the back exit, and hide somewhere, wouldn't he be able to use the radio to call the cops? He couldn't run to his car because of the guy from the van . . .

His thoughts were cut off by the sudden sound of heavy machinery. It was the wet saw powering up. They were starting to cut. That noise should cover the sound of him opening the exit door . . .

Red Jacket walked out of the artists' bullpen and into the next office on that side, a programmer's office. There were three more of those offices and then Red Jacket would be on this side of the floor space. Jimmy's side.

Whatever you're going to do, do it now.

Jimmy crawled through the doorway and to the cubicle adjacent to the one with the desk and bag. There was less than an inch of clearance between the carpet and the bottom of the cubicle wall, but Jimmy was able to scrunch down and flatten his cheek against the carpet so he could see Red Jacket's shoes as he walked out of the programmer's office and into the next one.

Two offices left.

Sweat running down his face, Jimmy crawled over to the next cubicle and reached up, feeling for the bag. He reached inside but couldn't feel the radio.

You're gonna be seen, shit head!

He groped frantically, felt something large and metal . . .

Screw it, just grab the whole bag.

Jimmy scrunched the bag's fabric together, pulled it off the table, and scooted back to the opposite cubicle.

He's going to notice the bag's missing when he comes out.

Once again Jimmy pressed his face to the floor. He saw the shoes again as Red Jacket walked into the last programmer's office.

It's now or never.

The bag was heavy and cumbersome as Jimmy snuck over to the short hallway at the rear corner opposite the server room. Once he reached the small passage, he ran, and as he pushed against the metal bar to open the door he glanced back, expecting for a heart-stopping second to see Red Jacket running toward him, gun drawn . . .

But there was no one. Jimmy slipped through the door and eased it closed behind him.

He turned so that he was facing the door and collapsed against the short wall that overlooked the second set of stairs, dropping the duffel on the ground. He sat quickly, still catching his breath, and looked into the open bag. His eyes grew wide and his breath caught.

So that's *why it was so heavy.*

Inside the bag was a rifle. A really heavy, really real rifle. Jimmy had memorized every weapon used in *RECOIL!*, though they were all future-tech. Plus, he had played a ton of other first-person shooters. The rifle looked a little like what the mercenaries used in the game *Cold War*. He lifted the weapon out, almost reverently. He had never held a real gun of any kind before. The barrel was pretty short, and the butt part that went against his shoulder didn't stick out like other rifles. He turned it over, and stamped on the left side was G3K A4 HK followed by some numbers.

HK . . . yeah that was what the mercs used in the game. When you killed them, you could take their gun and use it.

For an instant he almost forgot about the Russians, the cutting (still loud enough to be heard through the walls and closed door), the police cruiser, all of it. He was mesmerized by the killing machine in his hands.

There was a short burst of static from inside the bag, enough of a distraction to jolt him back to reality.

But when he reached into the bag, the radio wasn't the first thing his fingers brushed against. There was something much smaller. He grabbed it, withdrew, and opened his hand to see a red-and-black thumb drive. Multiple thoughts streamed through his mind at once: What was on it? Why did they need it? Did it have something to do with TechniCom? A few ideas took shape, one in particular that seemed most plausible given what little he knew. He filed these away for now, stuffed the thumb drive in his front jeans pocket, and reached back in for the walkie-talkie.

It was in the corner, a shiny black handheld device roughly the size of an iPhone but a good bit thicker. There were several buttons, a dial on top, a display screen . . . Jimmy had never used one before, and the whole thing looked intimidating at first glance. Still, how hard could it be?

He was all set to try using it when he smelled the smoke.

Cigarette smoke, coming from the stairwell. Jimmy's blood ran cold. He wasn't alone. *What if someone's coming up? One of* them? Jimmy set the radio down and lifted the gun. *Shit, how do you cock this thing?* He thought about *Cold War* . . . There was some metal piece on the side of the gun that his player character's hand would pull on and then slap down . . . There! He found the short handle and pulled. Nothing happened. *If one of them comes up now, you're dead.* He pulled harder and managed to move the handle back until it could go no farther.

He pushed the handle down, cringing at the sharp clicking noise. Praying the other person or persons hadn't heard it, he swung the weapon to his left, where the landing ended at a wall and a set of stairs lead down.

Nothing.

Whoever was down there either took off or was staying put. What if it's just a janitor? *Yeah, how would the Russians have gotten into the stairwell? Because the security guard unlocked the exit door for them, dummy.*

Jimmy maneuvered to his left side, to his knees, and slowly pulled himself up to peek over the short wall and down onto the first and then second turn of carpeted steps. Nobody on the stairs, but there was a foot poking out from the landing at the bottom, one floor below. Smoke puffed out and wafted up into Jimmy's face and for a split second he thought he might cough and give himself away, but he held it in.

Jimmy couldn't use the radio with that guy hanging out down there. He'd have to talk loud to be heard over the saw. What if that guy just stays down there, watching the door? Jimmy couldn't go back the way he came. Who knew how far away that cop was by now.

You have to do something! Three bad guys in the office, possibly one downstairs, and another outside. *Okay . . . so I point the gun at him, and tell him to . . . put his hands on his head and walk downstairs. If it's just a janitor, we both get the hell out of here. If it's one of them, we go out to the bottom of the stairs and I hold the gun on him while I radio for help.* That could work, right?

What choice do you have? Maybe just sit here and hope no one comes? *If that thumb drive is what you think it is, they'll know it's missing soon. And they'll come looking. You're running out of time.*

Jimmy's heart drummed against his chest. He left the bag behind, crouch-walking to the corner of the short wall, peeking around to look at the first, empty set of stairs. He positioned himself against the stair wall, his back against the handrail, and began descending one step at a time.

The weapon was suddenly slick in his hands as he reached the next turn. The smoker was at the bottom of these next stairs, just around this corner.

Okay, look tough, authoritative. Go!

Jimmy's knees were quaking as he turned the corner. The smoker wore a blue Windbreaker over a black T-shirt. His hair was shaved close to his head and he had eyes like a bloodhound. He was in the midst of coming up the stairs, was about halfway when he looked up to see Jimmy, three steps away. Those bloodhound eyes widened.

"Hands on your head! Now!" Jimmy blurted. His voice broke. The smoker mumbled something in Russian, tossed his cigarette down, and reached behind his back . . .

Shoot!

Jimmy pulled the trigger. Nothing happened.

Idiot! Safety!

He remembered seeing a lever on the left side, above the trigger. As Jimmy turned the rifle and flipped the lever down to "F," Smoker pulled a silencer-equipped pistol from the small of his back.

Jimmy pointed the weapon, closed his eyes, and pulled the trigger.

The rifle roared and bolted, kicking upward into Jimmy's chin. The impact knocked him back and into the wall, putting a nice crack in it with his skull. His ears were ringing. He shook his head to try to stop the world from spinning. He had barely held on to the gun, but lifted it now and held it out, repositioning himself to see down the stairs . . .

Smoker was lying in an awkward position at the landing for floor five. His handgun was lying on the stairs by the dropped cigarette, where the guy had been before Jimmy had . . .

Shot him.

Holy shit, I shot somebody.

Jimmy descended the stairs quickly, concerns over whether the others heard the gunfire set aside for the moment, because all he could think about was the human being whose existence he might have just ended.

The man was breathing, which was good, but he was also breathing so fast Jimmy thought he might hyperventilate . . . if he didn't bleed out first.

There was blood, a lot of it. Jimmy laid down his weapon on the stairs and got the larger man into a better position. It looked like there were three wounds: one high in the chest on the right side, one that punctured the muscle at the top of the shoulder, and one that clipped an almost perfect half circle shape out of his right ear. There were a couple more holes at the top of the entry door to floor five, and the wall just above.

Jimmy looked back down at the man and did the only thing he could think of: he removed his own T-shirt and pushed it against the hole in the man's chest.

"You're gonna be okay. Keep pressure on this."

The man's eyes were wide, and though he was looking at Jimmy, it didn't seem like he was *seeing* him.

Dude's in shock.

A Russian voice sounded over the radio. Jimmy could hear it both from his walkie-talkie and from the one on Smoker's belt. He couldn't understand what was being said but he could tell a question was being asked.

They heard it. They must have.

Jimmy took the man's radio and attached it next to the first on his own belt.

Hurry.

He grabbed the pistol, switched it to his left hand, and swept up the HK in his right. "I'm going to call for help. I'll make sure an ambulance gets here, okay?"

The man didn't respond, but Jimmy had no time to wait. He stepped over Smoker's waist and rushed down the next set of stairs, and the next . . .

He was breathing heavy, racing down the steps to floor three when he heard a door open somewhere below, followed by a voice. Russian.

Think, think . . .

Jimmy tried the access door to floor three. Locked. The voice was coming up the stairs. Heart pounding, he scrunched his shoulders and fired a burst point-blank at the door's lock. With a kick, the door flew open and Jimmy was inside, sprinting down a short hallway. Voices continued coming through the radios on his belt, and he could have sworn one said "Jimmy," but he was too freaked out to pay it much attention. He turned left into a much longer hallway with offices to either side, which came to a T. He turned right, fled down another short hall.

Dead end.

After a quick survey of his surroundings, Jimmy ran into a large office on one side. He slammed the pistol on the desk, ripped both radios from his belt and tossed them into the reclining office chair, then snatched the pistol back up and ran across to the room on the other side of the hall.

A conference room. One large table dominated the center of the space, surrounded by several chairs. The far wall was a series of floor-to-ceiling windows. Jimmy put his back to one of these and slid down, keeping the barrels of both weapons pointed at the office across from him, trying his best to slow his breathing, sweat running from his head down onto his neck and bare chest.

The last thing he wanted to do was shoot anyone else. In fact, his mind kept drifting back to the wide, unseeing, bloodhound eyes of the man he'd shot. Jimmy found himself wondering if the man would survive.

Right now you need to worry about your own ass.

There were no sounds coming from the hall, or beyond. Jimmy looked up at the conference table, where a cord trailed down to a jack in the wall. There was a phone up there. He set down the pistol, got to his knees, shuffled over, and looked. The display on the phone was lit. He grabbed it from the tabletop and as quietly as possible sat back where he had an unobstructed view of the hallway, setting the phone on the floor beside him. While keeping the HK pointed in that direction he flipped the receiver off onto the carpet, happy to hear a dial tone, and with his pointer finger he hit 9, 1—

"Jimmy."

He stopped. That voice had come from the radio in the office across the hall.

"Jimmy," the voice repeated. "I hope you are listening . . ." It was husky and thickly accented. "Your girlfriend was worried about you . . ."

Ice spread through Jimmy's veins. The voice continued: "One of my men was nice enough to let her in."

No no no no no . . .

Jimmy turned and looked out the window. His Festiva was there, along with the white van . . . and Kim's yellow VW. A long, defeated sigh gushed from Jimmy's lungs as he thumped his head against the glass.

Dammit, Kim.

"She is on her way here now. Why don't you join us? We monitor police channels, so we'll know if you call."

A kaleidoscope of emotions swirled within Jimmy: anger, frustration, hopelessness, and most especially fear. But there was something else as well, something indistinct and just barely taking shape . . .

The beginnings of a crazy, desperate plan.

When Jimmy opened the rear door and walked back into the Full Metal office space, he was holding the thumb drive in a death grip with his left hand. The pistol was tucked into his pants behind his back, and the HK was slung over his right shoulder. There was no one on the floor. Jimmy stepped out of the short hall and turned left, passed two offices, and came to the doorway of the server room. As he stepped to the threshold the noise of the saw ceased.

The walls of the room were lined with tall server racks. Red Jacket was there, to the far right, aiming his pistol at Jimmy. Next to him was the driver of the van. The spiky-haired Russian was pulling the wet saw from the floor, where he had cut a two-foot square block. The metal legs Jimmy had seen poking out of one of the bags earlier belonged to a tripod, positioned above the block. From the tripod's top, a chain hoist descended, hooked to a bracket anchored in the block's center. Spiky Hair set the saw down, removed a pair of safety goggles, and stared at Jimmy with small, close-set eyes.

Standing directly in front of Jimmy was the leader. He was dressed sharply, in a dark gray suit with a blue button-up. His left hand was on Kim's shoulder, and with his right he held a gun to her head, the same gun he had used to kill the security guard who was lying at his feet, head propped against the bottom row of server blades. The leader's eyes were cold, soulless. He looked down at Jimmy's scrawny bare chest and smirked.

Kim looked scared out of her mind, not that anyone could blame her. Her dark eyes were wide and glistening in the overhead lights, and the entirety of her five-foot three-inch frame was shaking, from her brown hair to her pink, laceless sneakers. She wore a T-shirt and sweats, clothes obviously thrown on hastily to come and retrieve Jimmy.

"Good choice," Husky Voice said. He nodded at the driver, who started to approach, then stopped as Jimmy revealed the torch lighter he had been concealing in his right hand, the one he had taken from Smoker on the way back up. He ignited it and held it just below the thumb drive in his outstretched left hand.

"This is important to you, right? I'm guessing it has some kind of decryption, for whatever it is you're going after down below."

Husky Voice smiled, revealing a row of uneven teeth. "Exciting new technology. Lots of security measures down there. Easier to get through this way." He nodded toward the tripod and block. "North Koreans will pay handsomely."

I was right about the thumb drive. Thank God.

"It's brave, what you're doing," Husky Voice continued. "But not very bright. By the time you heat up the drive enough to cause damage, I will put a bullet through your head . . ." He nodded toward Kim. "And hers."

Kim made an almost-squealing noise low in her throat. Jimmy swallowed. "I know," he said. "I just needed an excuse to have the lighter out." *Now!* He tossed the thumb drive high into the air, where it hit the far wall and fell behind a rack of servers.

All eyes had followed it, except for Kim's. She took advantage of the situation to knock the leader's hand away and run for the door. Jimmy grabbed onto the top of the nearest server rack, pulled himself up, and held the lighter beneath the ceiling sprinkler. For the first agonizing seconds nothing happened. Then a recorded voice, female, issued: "Warning: fire detected. Suppression system will activate in ten seconds . . ."

Jimmy dropped behind the rack and grabbed the door handle. "Please exit the room immediately," the voice continued. As Jimmy pedaled backward, pulling the door closed, he heard a sound like a small, keening insect and felt a sharp impact to the upper left side of his forehead. He slammed the door closed . . .

And was now standing on the other side, on the main floor. The world was spinning beneath him. He could hear Kim sobbing somewhere in the open space behind him. Side-stepping toward the wall, he pulled the HK from his shoulder. The door handle jostled but did not open. Right about now Husky Voice would be going for the key card . . .

Jimmy pointed the HK at the badge reader next to the door as three bullets tore through it from the other side and into the floor space. Kim yelped. He risked a quick glance over his shoulder and saw that she was unhurt, huddling somewhere out of sight behind the cubicles. Jimmy unloaded a burst into the badge reader. From the other side of the door he heard a whooshing sound. That would be the fire-suppression system engaging. Jimmy's dad had explained gaseous fire-suppression systems to him once—the kind used in server rooms, where water would cause damage to the electrical equipment. The gas being released into the server room now would push most of the oxygen out of the space, and the mercs inside would soon pass out.

The world teetered. Jimmy's head was swimming and darkness crept in. The voices on the other side of the door became frantic. There was coughing and shouting, but Jimmy thought the Russians would live. The fire department would get the alarm and be on their way shortly.

They'll live. Kim will live. But things aren't looking so good for me, he thought as the floor rushed up to meet him.

Jimmy awoke to bright lights, in a reclining chair. The circular room was a nest of holo-monitors and multi-touch interface stations. *Where the hell . . . ?* He attempted to draw his left hand up to feel his injured head and found that he was unable to move it. Same with the right.

"The restraints are for your own safety," a thin, bald man in a white coat said as he leaned over Jimmy and began fiddling with the straps. Standing a few feet away from the chair was a man in military uniform . . . A Faction uniform. From . . . the game?

No, not a game. Slowly, memories returned. At first it was difficult to sort what was real from what he had just experienced, like the confusion that lingers after waking up in the middle of a dream. The thin man removed the arm restraints, then he reached up and took something off Jimmy's head—a relatively simple-looking device with a few connection points. A single word on one side of it read TECHNICOM.

Jimmy lifted his right hand and felt his shaved head. No blood. No injury. The man in the military uniform was eyeing Jimmy, his expression unreadable.

The simulation. Before joining a Faction, all soldiers went through a simulation . . . to determine what camp they would fall into: Peacekeepers or Enforcers. It was all coming back to him now. Jimmy marveled at the direct neural interface technology, but he was most impressed with how it melded reality and his own subconscious. The Factions and subordinate Peacekeeper/Enforcer groups were reflected in the "game": *RECOIL!* TechniCom itself was integrated into the scenario as a kind of plot device. Even his girlfriend, Kim, was used to raise the stakes. On the subconscious side, Jimmy's fascination with the early years of the twenty-first century and his love of video games were baked into the simulation. Much of it even mirrored his favorite '80s action movie. It was all pretty amazing. However . . .

"I failed," he said.

"What's that, son?"

The officer approached as the thin man walked away. "I failed," Jimmy repeated. "I died."

The older man inclined his head. "The simulation is designed to push you to your limits; to approximate a test subject with zero military training and gauge response to violence and the threat of death, the ability to overcome fear. You saved your girlfriend's life. You demonstrated tactical aptitude, courage, and clear thinking under extreme duress. You proved capable of using deadly force and knowing when to do so, but, most important of all, you *felt* something when you pulled the trigger . . . something more than just the recoil."

The officer held out his hand. "Congratulations, son. And welcome to the Peacekeepers."

———————

Micky Neilson is the lead writer in publishing at Blizzard Entertainment, where he has worked since 1993. Neilson's game-writing credits include *World of Warcraft*, *StarCraft*, *Warcraft III*, and *Lost Vikings 2*. Micky's first comic book, *World of Warcraft: Ashbringer*, hit number two on the *New York Times* bestseller list for hardcover graphic books, and *World of Warcraft: Pearl of Pandaria* reached number three. In 2014, his Diablo III novella, *Morbed*, was published, as well as his long-awaited novella *Blood of the Highborne*. With the support of his wife, Tiffany, and daughter, Tatiana, Neilson looks forward to continuing his writing adventures for years to come.

ANDA'S GAME

Cory Doctorow

Anda didn't really start to play the game until she got herself a girl-shaped avatar. She was twelve, and up until then, she'd played a boy elf because her parents had sternly warned her that if you played a girl, you were an instant perv magnet. None of the girls at Ada Lovelace Comprehensive would have been caught dead playing a girl character. In fact, the only girls she'd ever seen in-game were being played by boys. You could tell, 'cause they were shaped like a boy's idea of what a girl looked like: hooge buzwabs and long legs all barely contained in tiny, pointless, leather bikini armor. Bintware, she called it.

But when Anda was twelve, she met Liza the Organiza, whose avatar was female but had sensible tits and sensible armor and a bloody great sword that she was clearly very good with. Liza came to school after PE, when Anda was sitting and massaging her abused podge and hating her entire life from stupid sunrise to rotten sunset. Her PE uniform was at the bottom of her schoolbag and her face was that stupid red color that she *hated* and now it was stinking maths, which was hardly better than PE but at least she didn't have to sweat.

But instead of maths, all the girls were called to assembly, and Liza the Organiza stood on the stage in front of Miss Cruickshanks, the principal, and Mrs. Danzig, the useless counselor.

"Hullo, chickens," Liza said. She had an Australian accent. "Well, aren't you lot just precious and bright and expectant with your pink upturned faces like a load of flowers staring up at the sky? Warms me fecking heart, it does."

That made her laugh, and she wasn't the only one. Miss Cruickshanks and Mrs. Danzig didn't look amused, but they tried to hide it.

"I am Liza the Organiza, and I kick arse. Seriously." She tapped a key on her laptop and the screen behind her lit up. It was a game—not the one that Anda played, but something space themed, a space station with a rocket ship in the background. "This is my avatar." Sensible boobs, sensible armor, and a sword the size of the world. "In-game, they call me the Lizanator, Queen of the Spacelanes, El Presidente of the Clan Fahrenheit." The Fahrenheits had chapters in every game. They were amazing and deadly and cool, and to her knowledge, Anda had never met one in the flesh. They had their own *island* in her game. Crikey.

On-screen, the Lizanator was fighting an army of wookie-men, sword in one hand, laser blaster in the other, rocket jumping, spinning, strafing, making impossible kills and long shots, diving for power-ups and ruthlessly running her enemies to ground.

"The *whole* Clan Fahrenheit. I won that title through popular election, but they voted me in 'cause of my prowess in *combat*. I'm a world champion in six different games, from first-person shooters to strategy games. I've commanded armies and I've sent armies to their respawn gates by the thousands. Thousands, chickens: my battle record is 3,522 kills in a single battle. I have taken home cash prizes from competitions totalling more than four hundred thousand pounds. I game for four to six hours nearly every day, and the rest of the time, I do what I like.

"One of the things I like to do is come to girls' schools like yours and let you in on a secret: girls kick arse. We're faster, smarter, and better than boys. We play harder. We spend too much time thinking that we're freaks for gaming, and when we do game, we never play as girls because we catch so much shite for it. Time to turn that around. I am the best gamer in the world and I'm a girl. I started playing at ten, and there were no women in games—you couldn't even buy a game in any of the shops I went to. It's different now, but it's still not perfect. We're going to change that, chickens, you lot and me.

"How many of you game?"

Anda put her hand up. So did about half the girls in the room.

"And how many of you play girls?"

All the hands went down.

"See, that's a tragedy. Practically makes me weep. Gamespace smells like a boy's *armpit*. It's time we girled it up a little. So here's my offer to you: if you will play as a girl, you will be given probationary memberships in the Clan Fahrenheit, and if you measure up, in six months, you'll be full-fledged members."

In real life, Liza the Organiza was a little podgy, like Anda herself, but she wore it with confidence. She was solid, like a brick wall, her hair bobbed bluntly at her shoulders. She dressed in a black jumper over loose dungarees, with giant goth boots with steel toes that looked like something you'd see in an in-game shop, though Anda was pretty sure they'd come from a real-world goth shop in Camden Town.

She stomped her boots, one-two, *thump-thump*, like thunder on the stage. "Who's in, chickens? Who wants to be a girl out-game and in?"

Anda jumped to her feet. A Fahrenheit, with her own island! Her head was so full of it that she didn't notice that she was the only one standing. The other girls stared at her, a few giggling and whispering.

"That's all right, love," Liza called, "I like enthusiasm. Don't let those staring faces rattle yer: they're just flowers turning to look at the sky. Pink-scrubbed, shining, expectant faces. They're looking at you because *you* had the sense to get to your feet when opportunity came—and that means that someday, girl, you are going to be a leader of women, and men, and you will kick arse. Welcome to the Clan Fahrenheit."

She began to clap, and the other girls clapped, too, and even though Anda's face was the color of a lollipop lady's sign, she felt like she might burst with pride and good feeling, and she smiled until her face hurt.

> Anda

her sergeant said to her,

> how would you like to make some money?
> Money, Sarge?

Ever since she'd risen to platoon leader, she'd been getting more missions, but they paid *gold*—money wasn't really something you talked about in-game.

The Sarge—sensible boobs, gigantic sword, longbow, gloriously orcish ugly phiz—moved her avatar impatiently.

> Something wrong with my typing, Anda?
> No, Sarge

she typed.

> You mean gold?
> If I meant gold, I would have said gold. Can you go voice?

Anda looked around. Her door was shut and she could hear her parents in the sitting room watching something loud on telly. She turned up her music just to be safe and then slipped on her headset. They said it could noise-cancel a Black Hawk helicopter—it had better be able to overcome the little inductive speakers suction-cupped to the underside of her desk. She switched to voice.

"Hey, Lucy," she said.

"Call me Sarge!" Lucy's accent was American, like an old TV show, and she lived somewhere in the middle of the country where it was all vowels, Iowa or Ohio. She was Anda's best friend in-game but she was so hard-core, it was boring sometimes.

"Hi, Sarge," she said, trying to keep the irritation out of her voice. She'd never smart off to a superior in-game, but v2v it was harder to remember to keep to the game norms.

"I have a mission that pays real cash. Whichever PayPal you're using, they'll deposit money into it. Looks fun, too."

"That's a bit weird, Sarge. Is that against Clan rules?" There were a lot of Clan rules about what kind of mission you could accept, and they were always changing. There were curb crawlers in gamespace, and the way that the Clan leadership kept all the mummies and daddies from going ape-poo about it was by enforcing a long, boring code of conduct that was meant to ensure that none of the Fahrenheit girlies ended up being virtual prozzies for hairy old men in raincoats on the other side of the world.

"What?" Anda loved how Lucy quacked *What?* It sounded especially American. She had to force herself from parroting it back. "No, geez. All the executives in the Clan pay the rent doing missions for money. Some of them are even rich from it, I hear! You can make a lot of money gaming, you know."

"Is it really true?" She'd heard about this but she'd assumed it was just stories, like the kids who gamed so much that they couldn't tell reality from fantasy. Or the ones who gamed so much that they stopped eating and got all anorexic. She wouldn't mind getting a little anorexic, to be honest. Bloody podge.

"Yup! And this is our chance to get in on the ground floor. Are you in?"

"It's not—you know, *pervy*, is it?"

"Gag me. No. Geez, Anda! Are you nuts? No—they want us to go kill some guys."

"Oh, we're good at that!"

The mission took them far from Fahrenheit Island, to a cottage on the far side of the largest continent on the game world, which was called Dandelionwine. The travel was tedious, and twice they were ambushed on the trail, something that had hardly happened to Anda since she joined the Fahrenheits: attacking a Fahrenheit was bad for your health, because even if you won the battle, they'd bring a war to you.

But now they were far from the Fahrenheits' power base,

and two different packs of brigands waylaid them on the road. Lucy spotted the first group before they got into sword range and killed four of the six with her bow before they closed for hand-to-hand. Anda's sword—gigantic and fast—was out then, and her fingers danced over the keyboard as she fought off the player who was attacking her, her body jerking from side to side as she hammered on the multibutton controller beside her. She won—of course! She was a Fahrenheit! Lucy had already slaughtered her attacker. They desultorily searched the bodies and came up with some gold and a couple of scrolls, but nothing to write home about. Even the gold didn't seem like much, given the cash waiting at the end of the mission.

The second group of brigands was even less daunting, though there were twenty of them. They were total noobs, and fought like statues. They'd clearly clubbed together to protect themselves from harder players, but they were no match for Anda and Lucy. One of them even begged for his life before she ran him through:

> please sorry u cn have my gold sorry!!!11!

Anda laughed and sent him to the respawn gate.

> You're a nasty person, Anda

Lucy typed.

> I'm a Fahrenheit!!!!!!!!!!

she typed back.

———

The brigands on the road were punters, but the cottage that was their target was guarded by an altogether more sophisticated sort. They were spotted by sentries long before they got within sight of the cottage, and they saw the warning spell travel up from the sentries' hilltop like a puff of smoke, speeding away toward the cottage. Anda raced up the hill while Lucy covered her with her bow, but that didn't stop the sentries from subjecting Anda to a hail of flaming spears from their fortified position. Anda set up her standard dodge-and-weave pattern, assuming that the sentries were non-player characters—who wanted to *pay* to sit around in gamespace watching a boring road all day?—and to her surprise, the spears followed her. She took one in the chest and only some fast work with her shield and all her healing scrolls saved her. As it was, her constitution was knocked down by half and she had to retreat back down the hillside.

"Get down," Lucy said in her headset. "I'm gonna use the BFG."

Every game had one—the Big Friendly Gun, the generic term for the baddest-arse weapon in the world. Lucy had rented this one from the Clan armory for a small fortune in gold and Anda had laughed and called her paranoid, but now Anda helped Lucy set it up and thanked the game gods for her foresight. It was a huge, demented flaming crossbow that fired five-meter bolts that exploded on impact. It was a beast to arm and a beast to aim, but they had a nice, dug-in position of their own at the bottom of the hill and it was there that they got the BFG set up, deployed, armed, and ranged.

"Fire!" Lucy called, and the game did this amazing and cool

animation that it rewarded you with whenever you loosed a bolt from the BFG, making the gamelight dim toward the sizzling bolt as though it were sucking the illumination out of the world as it arced up the hillside, trailing a comet tail of sparks. The game played them a groan of dismay from their enemies, and then the bolt hit home with a crash that made her point of view vibrate like an earthquake. The roar in her headphones was deafening, and behind it she could hear Lucy on the voice chat, cheering it on.

"Nuke 'em till they glow and shoot 'em in the dark! Yee-haw!" Lucy called, and Anda laughed and pounded her fist on the desk. Gobbets of former enemy sailed over the tree line dramatically, dripping hyper-red blood and ichor.

In her bedroom, Anda caressed the controller pad, and her avatar punched the air and did a little rugby victory dance that the All Blacks had released as a limited-edition promo after they won the World Cup.

Now they had to move fast, for their enemies at the cottage would be alerted to their presence and waiting for them. They spread out into a wide flanking maneuver around the cottage's sides, staying just outside of bow range, using scrying scrolls to magnify the cottage and make the foliage around them fade to translucency.

There were four guards around the cottage, two with nocked arrows and two with whirling slings. One had a scroll out and was surrounded by the concentration marks that indicated spell casting.

"*Go, go, go!*" Lucy called.

Anda went! She had two scrolls left in her inventory, and one was a shield spell. They cost a fortune and burned out fast, but whatever that guard was cooking up, it had to be bad news. She cast the spell as she charged for the cottage, and lucky thing, because there was a fifth guard up a tree who dumped a pot of boiling oil on her that would have cooked her down to her bones in ten seconds if not for the spell.

She power-climbed the tree and nearly lost her grip when whatever the nasty spell was bounced off her shield. She reached the fifth man as he was trying to draw his dirk and dagger, and lopped his bloody head off in one motion, then backflipped off the high branch, trusting to her shield to stay intact for her impact on the cottage roof.

The strategy worked—now she had the drop (literally!) on the remaining guards, having successfully taken the high ground. In her headphones, the sound of Lucy making mayhem, the grunts as she pounded her keyboard mingling with the in-game shrieks when her arrows found homes in the chests of two more guards.

Shrieking a berserker wail, Anda jumped off the roof and landed on one of the two remaining guards, plunging her sword into his chest and pinning him in the dirt. Her sword stuck in the ground, and she hammered on her keys, trying to free it, while the remaining guard ran for her on-screen. Anda pounded her keyboard, but it was useless: the sword was good and stuck. Poo. She'd blown a small fortune on spells and rations for this project with the expectation of getting some real cash out of it, and now it was all lost.

She moved her hands to the part of the keypad that controlled motion and began to run, waiting for the guard's sword to find her avatar's back and knock her into the dirt.

"Got 'im!" It was Lucy, in her headphones. She wheeled her avatar about so quickly it was nauseating and saw that Lucy was on her erstwhile attacker, grunting as she engaged him close-in. Something was wrong, though: despite Lucy's avatar's awesome stats and despite Lucy's own skill at the keyboard, she was being taken to the cleaners. The guard was kicking her arse. Anda went back to her stuck sword and recommenced whanging on it, watching helplessly as Lucy lost her left arm, then took a cut on her belly, then another to her knee.

"Shit!" Lucy said in her headphones as her avatar began to keel over. Anda yanked her sword free—finally—and charged at the guard, screaming a ululating war cry. He managed to get his avatar swung around and his sword up before she reached him, but it didn't matter: she got in a lucky swing that took off one leg, then danced back before he could counterstrike. Now she closed carefully, nicking at his sword hand until he dropped his weapon, then moving in for a fast kill.

"Lucy?"

"Call me Sarge!"

"Sorry, Sarge. Where'd you respawn?"

"I'm all the way over at Body Electric—it'll take me hours to get there. Do you think you can complete the mission on your own?"

"Uh, sure," she said, thinking, *Crikey*, if that's what the guards *outside* were like, how'm I gonna get past the *inside* guards?

"You're the best, girl. Okay, enter the cottage and kill everyone there."

"Uh, sure."

She wished she had another scrying scroll in inventory so she could get a look inside the cottage before she beat its door in, but she was fresh out of scrolls and just about everything else.

She kicked the door in and her fingers danced. She'd killed

four of her adversaries before she even noticed that they weren't fighting back.

In fact, they were generic avatars, maybe even non-player characters. They moved like total noobs, milling around in the little cottage. Around them were heaps of shirts, thousands and thousands of them. A couple of the noobs were sitting in the back, incredibly, still crafting more shirts, ignoring the swordswoman who'd just butchered four of their companions.

She took a careful look at all the avatars in the room. None of them were armed. Tentatively, she walked up to one of the players and cut his head off. The player next to him moved clumsily to one side and she followed him.

```
> Are you a player or a bot?
```

she typed.

The avatar did nothing. She killed it.

"Lucy, they're not fighting back."

"Good, kill them all."

"Really?"

"Yeah—that's the orders. Kill them all and then I'll make a phone call and some guys will come by and verify it and then you haul ass back to the island. I'm coming out there to meet you, but it's a long haul from the respawn gate. Keep an eye on my stuff, okay?"

"Sure," Anda said, and killed two more. That left ten. *One, two, one, two and through and through,* she thought, lopping their heads off. Her vorpal blade went snicker-snack. One left. He stood off in the back.

```
> no porfa necesito mi plata
```

Italian? No, Spanish. She'd had a term of it in Third Form, though she couldn't understand what this twit was saying. She could always paste the text into a translation bot on one of the chat channels, but who cared? She cut his head off.

"They're all dead," she said into her headset.

"Good job!" Lucy said. "Okay, I'm gonna make a call. Sit tight."

Bo-ring. The cottage was filled with corpses and shirts. She picked some of them up. They were totally generic: the shirts you crafted when you were down at level zero and trying to get enough skillz to actually make something of yourself. Each one would fetch just a few coppers. Add it all together and you barely had two thousand gold.

Just to pass the time, she pasted the Spanish into the chat-bot.

```
> no [colloquial] please, I need my [colloquial] [money|silver]
```

Pathetic. A few thousand golds—he could make that much by playing a couple of the beginner missions. More fun. More rewarding. Crafting shirts!

She left the cottage and patrolled around it. Twenty minutes later, two more avatars showed up. More generics.

```
> are you players or bots?
```

she typed, though she had an idea they were players. Bots moved better.

```
> any trouble?
```

Well, all right, then.

```
> no trouble
> good
```

One player entered the cottage and came back out again. The other player spoke.

```
> you can go now
```

"Lucy?"

"What's up?"

"Two blokes just showed up and told me to piss off. They're noobs, though. Should I kill them?"

"No! Geez, Anda, those are the contacts. They're just making sure the job was done. Get my stuff and meet me at Marionettes Tavern, okay?"

Anda went over to Lucy's corpse and looted it, then set out down the road, dragging the BFG behind her. She stopped at the bend and snuck a peek back at the cottage. It was in flames, the two noobs standing amid them, burning slowly along with the cottage and a few thousand golds' worth of badly crafted shirts.

That was the first of Anda and Lucy's missions, but it wasn't the last. That month, she fought her way through six more, and the PayPal she used filled with real, honest-to-goodness cash, pounds sterling that she could withdraw from the cashpoint situated exactly 501 meters away from the school gate, next to the candy shop that was likewise 501 meters away.

"Anda, I don't think it's healthy for you to spend so much time with your game," her dad said, prodding her bulging podge with a finger. "It's not healthy."

"Daaaa!" she said, pushing his finger aside. "I go to PE every stinking day. It's good enough for the Ministry of Education."

"I don't like it," he said. He was no movie star himself, with a little potbelly that he wore his belted trousers high upon, a wobbly extra chin, and two bat wings of flab hanging off his upper arms. She pinched his chin and wiggled it.

"I get loads more exercise than you, Mr. Kettle."

"But I pay the bills around here, little Miss Pot."

"You're not seriously complaining about the cost of the game?" she said, infusing her voice with as much incredulity and disgust as she could muster. "Ten quid a week and I get unlimited calls, texts, and messages! Plus play, of course, and the in-game encyclopedia and spell-checker and translator bots!" (This was all from rote—every member of the Fahrenheits memorized this or something very like it for dealing with recalcitrant, ignorant parental units.) "Fine, then. If the game is too dear for you, Da, let's set it aside and I'll just start using a normal phone, is that what you want?"

Her da held up his hands. "I surrender, Miss Pot. But *do* try to get a little more exercise, please? Fresh air? Sport? Games?"

"Getting my head trodden on in the hockey pitch, more like," she said darkly.

"Zackly!" he said, prodding her podge anew. "That's the stuff! Getting my head trodden on was what made me the man I are today!"

Her da could bluster all he liked about paying the bills, but she had pocket money for the first time in her life: not book tokens and fruit tokens and milk tokens that could be exchanged for "healthy" snacks and literature. She had real money, cash money that she could spend outside of the five-hundred-meter sugar-free zone that surrounded her school.

She wasn't just kicking arse in the game, now—she was the richest kid she knew, and suddenly she was everybody's best pal, with handfuls of Curly Wurlys and Dairy Milks and Mars bars that she could selectively distribute to her schoolmates.

"Go get a BFG," Lucy said. "We're going on a mission."

Lucy's voice in her ear was a constant companion in her life now. When she wasn't on Fahrenheit Island, she and Lucy were running missions into the wee hours of the night. The Fahrenheit armorers, non-player characters, had learned to recognize her and they had the Clan's BFGs oiled and ready for her when she showed up.

Today's mission was close to home, which was good: the road trips were getting tedious. Sometimes, non-player characters or Game Masters would try to get them involved in an official in-game mission, impressed by their stats and weapons, and it sometimes broke her heart to pass them up, but cash always beat gold and experience beat experience points: *Money talks and bullshit walks,* as Lucy liked to say.

They caught the first round of snipers/lookouts before they had a chance to attack or send off a message. Anda used the scrying spell to spot them. Lucy had kept both BFGs armed and she loosed rounds at the hilltops flanking the roadway as soon as Anda gave her the signal, long before they got into bow range.

As they picked their way through the ruined chunks of the dead player-character snipers, Anda still on the lookout, she broke the silence over their voice link.

"Hey, Lucy?"

"Anda, if you're not going to call me Sarge, at least don't call me 'Hey, Lucy!' My dad loved that old TV show and he makes that joke every visitation day."

"Sorry, Sarge. Sarge?"

"Yes, Anda?"

"I just can't understand why anyone would pay us cash for these missions."

"You complaining?"

"No, but—"

"Anyone asking you to cyber some old pervert?"

"No!"

"Okay, then. I don't know, either. But the money's good. I don't care. Hell, probably it's two rich gamers who pay their butlers to craft for them all day. One's fucking with the other one and paying us."

"You really think that?"

Lucy sighed a put-upon, sophisticated, American sigh. "Look at it this way. Most of the world is living on, like, a dollar a day. I spend five dollars every day on a frappuccino. Some days, I get two! Dad sends Mom three thousand a month in child support—that's a hundred bucks a day. So if a day's money here is a hundred dollars, then to an African or whatever my frappuccino is worth, like, *five hundred dollars*. And I buy two or three every day.

"And we're not rich! There's craploads of rich people who wouldn't think twice about spending five hundred bucks on a coffee—how much do you think a hot dog and a Coke go for on the space station? A thousand bucks!"

"So that's what I think is going on. There's someone out there, some Saudi or Japanese guy or Russian mafia kid who's so rich that this is just chump change for him, and he's paying us to mess around with some other rich person. To them, we're like the Africans making a dollar a day to craft—I mean, sew—T-shirts. What's a couple hundred bucks to them? A cup of coffee."

Anda thought about it. It made a kind of sense. She'd been

on hols in Bratislava where they got a posh hotel room for ten quid—less than she was spending every day on sweeties and fizzy drinks.

"Three o'clock," she said, and aimed the BFG again. More snipers pat-patted in bits around the forest floor.

"Nice one, Anda."

"Thanks, Sarge."

They smashed half a dozen more sniper outposts and fought their way through a couple of packs of suspiciously badass brigands before coming upon the cottage.

"Bloody hell," Anda breathed. The cottage was ringed with guards, forty or fifty of them, with bows and spells and spears, in entrenched positions.

"This is nuts," Lucy agreed. "I'm calling them. This is nuts."

There was a muting click as Lucy rang off and Anda used up a scrying scroll to examine the inventories of the guards around the corner. The more she looked, the more scared she got. They were loaded down with spells, a couple of them were guarding BFGs and what looked like an even *bigger* BFG, maybe the fabled BFG10K, something that was removed from the game economy not long after gameday one as too disruptive to the balance of power. Supposedly one or two existed, but that was just a rumor. Wasn't it?

"Okay," Lucy said. "Okay, this is how this goes. We've got to do this. I just called in three squads of Fahrenheit veterans and their noob prentices for backup." Anda summed that up in her head to a hundred player characters and maybe three hundred non-player characters: familiars, servants, demons . . .

"That's a lot of shares to split the pay into," Anda said.

"Oh, ye of little tits," Lucy said. "I've negotiated a bonus for us if we make it—a million gold and three missions' worth of cash. The Fahrenheits are taking payment in gold—they'll be here in an hour."

This wasn't a mission anymore, Anda realized. It was war. Gamewar. Hundreds of players converging on this shard, squaring off against the ranked mercenaries guarding the huge cottage over the hill.

Lucy wasn't the ranking Fahrenheit on the scene, but she was the designated general. One of the gamers up from Fahrenheit Island brought a team flag for her to carry, a long spear with the magical standard snapping proudly from it as the troops formed behind her.

"On my signal," Lucy said. The voice chat was like a wind tunnel from all the unmuted breathing voices, hundreds of girls in hundreds of bedrooms like Anda's, all over the world, some sitting down before breakfast, some just coming home from school, some roused from sleep by their ringing game-sponsored mobiles. *"Go, go, go!"*

They went, roaring, and Anda roared, too, heedless of her parents downstairs in front of the blaring telly, heedless of her throat lining, a Fahrenheit in berserker rage, sword swinging. She made straight for the BFG10K—a siege engine that could level a town wall, and it would be hers, captured by her for the Fahrenheits if she could do it. She spelled the merc who was cranking it into insensibility, rolled and rolled again to dodge arrows and spells, healed herself when an arrow found her leg and sent her tumbling, springing to her feet before another arrow could strike home, watching her hit points and experience points move in opposite directions.

HERS! She vaulted the BFG10K and snicker-snacked her sword through two mercs' heads. Two more appeared—they had the thing primed and aimed at the main body of Fahrenheit fighters, and they could turn the battle's tide just by firing it—and she killed them, slamming her keypad, howling, barely conscious of the answering howls in her headset.

Now *she* had the BFG10K, though more mercs were closing on her. She disarmed it quickly and spelled at the nearest bunch of mercs, then had to take evasive action against the hail of incoming arrows and spells. It was all she could do to cast healing spells fast enough to avoid losing consciousness.

"LUCY!" she called into her headset. *"LUCY, OVER BY THE BFG10K!"*

Lucy snapped out orders, and the opposition before Anda began to thin as Fahrenheits fell on them from behind. The flood was stemmed, and now the Fahrenheits' greater numbers and discipline showed. In short order, every merc was butchered or run off.

Anda waited by the BFG10K while Lucy paid off the Fahrenheits and saw them on their way. "Now we take the cottage," Lucy said.

"Right," Anda said. She set her character off for the doorway. Lucy's brushed past her.

"I'll be glad when we're done with this—that was bugfuck nutso." Her character opened the door and disappeared in a fireball that erupted from directly overhead. A door curse, a serious one, one that cooked her in her armor in seconds.

"SHIT!" Lucy said in her headset.

Anda giggled. "Teach *you* to go rushing into things," she

said. She used up a couple of scrying scrolls, making sure that there was nothing else in the cottage save for millions of shirts and thousands of unarmed noob avatars that she'd have to mow down like grass to finish out the mission.

She descended upon them like a reaper, swinging her sword heedlessly, taking five or six out with each swing. When she'd been a noob in the game, she'd had to endure endless fighting practice, "grappling" with piles of leaves and other nonlethal targets, just to get enough experience points to have a chance of hitting anything. This was every bit as dull.

Her wrists were getting tired, and her chest heaved and her hated podge wobbled as she worked the keypad.

```
> Wait, please, don't—I'd like to speak with you
```

It was a noob avatar, just like the others, but not just like it, after all, for it moved with purpose, backing away from her sword. And it spoke English.

```
> nothing personal
```

she typed.

```
> just a job
> There are many here to kill—take me last at least. I need to
talk to you.
> talk, then
```

she typed. Meeting players who moved well and spoke English was hardly unusual in gamespace, but here in the cleanup phase, it felt out of place. It felt *wrong*.

```
> My name is Raymond, and I live in Tijuana. I am a labor orga-
nizer in the factories here. What is your name?
> i don't give out my name in-game
> What can I call you?
> kali
```

It was a name she liked to use in-game: Kali, Destroyer of Worlds, like the Hindu goddess.

```
> Are you in India?
> london
> You are Indian?
> naw im a whitey
```

She was halfway through the room, mowing down the noobs in twos and threes. She was hungry and bored and this Raymond was weirding her out.

```
> Do you know who these people are that you're killing?
```

She didn't answer, but she had an idea. She killed four more and shook out her wrists.

```
> They're working for less than a dollar a day. The shirts they
make are traded for gold and the gold is sold on eBay. Once their
avatars have leveled up, they too are sold off on eBay. They're
mostly young girls supporting their families. They're the lucky
ones: the unlucky ones work as prostitutes.
```

Her wrists *really* ached. She slaughtered half a dozen more.

> The bosses used to use bots, but the game has countermeasures
against them. Hiring children to click the mouse is cheaper than
hiring programmers to circumvent the rules. I've been trying to
unionize them because they've got a very high rate of injury.
They have to play for 18-hour shifts with only one short toilet
break. Some of them can't hold it in and they soil themselves
where they sit.
> look

she typed, exasperated.

> it's none of my lookout, is it. the world's like that. lots
of people with no money. im just a kid, theres nothing i can do
about it.
> When you kill them, they don't get paid.

no porfa necesito mi plata

> When you kill them, they lose their day's wages. Do you know
who is paying you to do these killings?

She thought of Saudis, rich Japanese, Russian mobsters.

> not a clue
> I've been trying to find that out myself, Kali.

They were all dead now. Raymond stood alone among the
piled corpses.

> Go ahead

he typed.

> I will see you again, I'm sure.

She cut his head off. Her wrists hurt. She was hungry. She was alone there in the enormous woodland cottage, and she still had to haul the BFG10K back to Fahrenheit Island.

"Lucy?"

"Yeah, yeah, I'm almost back there, hang on. I respawned in the ass end of nowhere."

"Lucy, do you know who's in the cottage? Those noobs that we kill?"

"What? Hell no. Noobs. Someone's butler. I dunno. Jesus, that respawn gate—"

"Girls. Little girls in Mexico. Getting paid a dollar a day to craft shirts. Except they don't get their dollar when we kill them. They don't get anything."

"Oh, for chrissakes, is that what one of them told you? Do you believe everything someone tells you in-game? Christ. English girls are so naive."

"You don't think it's true?"

"Naw, I don't."

"Why not?"

"I just don't, okay? I'm almost there, keep your panties on."

"I've got to go, Lucy," she said. Her wrists hurt, and her podge overlapped the waistband of her trousers, making her feel a bit like she was drowning.

"What, now? Shit, just hang on."

"My mom's calling me to supper. You're almost here, right?"

"Yeah, but—"

She reached down and shut off her PC.

Anda's da and mum were watching the telly again with a bowl of crisps between them. She walked past them like she was dreaming and stepped out the door onto the terrace. It was nighttime, eleven o'clock, and the chavs in front of the council flats across the square were kicking a football around and swilling lager and making rude noises. They were skinny and rawboned, wearing shorts and string vests with strong, muscular limbs flashing in the streetlights.

"Anda?"

"Yes, Mum?"

"Are you all right?" Her mum's fat fingers caressed the back of her neck.

"Yes, Mum. Just needed some air is all."

"You're very clammy," her mum said. She licked a finger and scrubbed it across Anda's neck. "Gosh, you're dirty—how did you get to be such a mucky puppy?"

"Owww!" she said. Her mum was scrubbing so hard, it felt like she'd take her skin off.

"No whingeing," her mum said sternly. "Behind your ears, too! You are *filthy*."

"Mum, *owww*!"

Her mum dragged her up to the bathroom and went at her with a flannel and a bar of soap and hot water until she felt boiled and raw.

"What *is* this mess?" her mum said.

"Lilian, leave off," her dad said quietly. "Come out into the hall for a moment, please."

The conversation was too quiet to hear and Anda didn't want to, anyway: she was concentrating too hard on not crying—her ears *hurt*.

Her mum enfolded her shoulders in her soft hands again. "Oh, darling, I'm sorry. It's a skin condition, your father tells me, acanthosis nigricans—he saw it in a TV special. We'll see the doctor about it tomorrow after school. Are you all right?"

"I'm fine," she said, twisting to see if she could see the "dirt" on the back of her neck in the mirror. It was hard because it was an awkward placement—but also because she didn't like to look at her face and her soft extra chin, and she kept catching sight of it.

She went back to her room to google acanthosis nigricans.

> A condition involving darkened, thickened skin. Found in the folds of skin at the base of the back of the neck, under the arms, inside the elbow, and at the waistline. Often precedes a diagnosis of type 2 diabetes, especially in children. If found in children, immediate steps must be taken to prevent diabetes, including exercise and nutrition as a means of lowering insulin levels and increasing insulin sensitivity.

Obesity-related diabetes. They had lectures on this every term in health class—the fastest-growing ailment among British teens, accompanied by photos of orca-fat sacks of lard sat up in bed surrounded by an ocean of rubbery, flowing podge. Anda prodded her belly and watched it jiggle.

It jiggled. Her thighs jiggled. Her chins wobbled. Her arms sagged.

She grabbed a handful of her belly and *squeezed it*, pinched it hard as she could, until she had to let go or cry out. She'd left livid red fingerprints in the rolls of fat and she was crying now, from the pain and the shame and oh, God, she was a fat girl with diabetes—

"Jesus, Anda, where the hell have you been?"

"Sorry, Sarge," she said. "My PC's been broken—" Well, out of service, anyway. Under lock and key in her dad's study. Almost a month now of medications and no telly and no gaming and double PE periods at school with the other whales. She was miserable all day, every day now, with nothing to look forward to except the trips after school to the newsagents at the 501-meter mark and the fistfuls of sweeties and bottles of fizzy drink she ate in the park while she watched the chavs play footy.

"Well, you should have found a way to let me know. I was getting worried about you, girl."

"Sorry, Sarge," she said again. The PC Baang was filled with stinky, spotty boys—literally stinky, it smelt like goats, like a train-station toilet—being loud and obnoxious. The dinky headphones provided were greasy as a slice of pizza, and the mouthpiece was sticky with excited boys' saliva from games gone past.

But it didn't matter. Anda was back in the game, and just in time, too: her money was running short.

"Well, I've got a backlog of missions here. I tried going out with a couple other of the girls"—a pang of regret shot through Anda at the thought that her position might have been usurped while she was locked off the game—"but you're too good to replace, okay? I've got four missions we can do today if you're game."

"Four missions! How on earth will we do four missions? That'll take days!"

"We'll take the BFG10K." Anda could hear the savage grin in her voice.

The BFG10K simplified things quite a lot. Find the cottage, aim the BFG10K, fire it, whim-wham, no more cottage. They started with five bolts for it—one BFG10K bolt was made up of twenty regular BFG bolts, each costing a small fortune in gold—and used them all on the first three targets. After returning it to the armory and grabbing a couple of BFGs (amazing how puny the BFG seemed after just a couple of hours' campaigning with a really *big* gun!) they set out for number four.

"I met a guy after the last campaign," Anda said. "One of the noobs in the cottage. He said he was a union organizer."

"Oh, you met Raymond, huh?"

"You knew about him?"

"I met him, too. He's been turning up everywhere. What a creep."

"So you knew about the noobs in the cottages?"

"Um. Well, yeah, I figured it out mostly on my own and then Raymond told me a little more."

"And you're fine with depriving little kids of their wages?"

"Anda," Lucy said, her voice brittle. "You like gaming, right, it's important to you?"

"Yeah, course it is."

"How important? Is it something you do for fun, just a hobby you waste a little time on? Are you just into it casually, or are you *committed* to it?"

"I'm committed to it, Lucy, you know that." God, without the game, what was there? PE class? Stupid acanthosis nigricans and, someday, insulin jabs every morning? "I love the game, Lucy. It's where my friends are."

"I know that. That's why you're my right-hand woman, why I want you at my side when I go on a mission. We're badass, you and me, as badass as they come, and we got that way through discipline and hard work and really *caring* about the game, right?"

"Yes, right, but—"

"You've met Liza the Organiza, right?"

"Yes, she came by my school."

"Mine too. She asked me to look out for you because of what she saw in you that day."

"Liza the Organiza goes to Ohio?"

"Idaho. Yes—all across the U.S. They put her on the tube and everything. She's amazing, and she cares about the game, too—that's what makes us all Fahrenheits: we're committed to each other, to teamwork, and to fair play."

Anda had heard these words—lifted from the Fahrenheit mission statement—many times, but now they made her swell a little with pride.

"So these people in Mexico or wherever, what are they doing? They're earning their living by exploiting the game. You and me, we would never trade cash for gold, or buy a character or a weapon on eBay—it's cheating. You get gold and weapons through hard work and hard play. But those Mexicans spend all day, every day, crafting stuff to turn into gold to sell off on the exchange. *That's where it comes from*—that's where the crappy players get their gold from! That's how rich noobs can buy their way into the game that we had to play hard to get into.

"So we burn them out. If we keep burning the factories down, they'll shut them down and those kids'll find something else to do for a living and the game will be better. If no one does that, our work will just get cheaper and cheaper: the game will get less and less fun, too.

"These people *don't* care about the game. To them, it's just a place to suck a buck out of. They're not players, they're leeches, here to suck all the fun out."

They had come upon the cottage now, the fourth one, having exterminated four different sniper nests on the way.

"Are you in, Anda? Are you here to play, or are you so

worried about these leeches on the other side of the world that you want out?"

"I'm in, Sarge," Anda said. She armed the BFGs and pointed them at the cottage.

"Boo-yah!" Lucy said. Her character notched an arrow.

```
> Hello, Kali
```

"Oh, Christ, he's back," Lucy said. Raymond's avatar had snuck up behind them.

```
> Look at these
```

he said, and his character set something down on the ground and backed away. Anda edged up on them.

"Come on, it's probably a booby trap, we've got work to do," Lucy said.

They were photo objects. Anda picked them up and then examined them. The first showed ranked little girls, fifty or more, in clean and simple T-shirts, skinny as anything, sitting at generic white-box PCs, hands on the keyboards. They were hollow-eyed and grim, and none of them older than she.

The next showed a shantytown, shacks made of corrugated aluminum and trash, muddy trails between them, spray-painted graffiti, rude boys loitering, rubbish, and carrier bags blowing.

The next showed the inside of a shanty, three little girls and a little boy sitting together on a battered sofa, their mother serving them something white and indistinct on plastic plates. Their smiles were heartbreaking and brave.

> That's who you're about to deprive of a day's wages

    "Oh, hell *no*," Lucy said. "Not again. I killed him last time and I said I'd do it again if he ever tried to show me photos. That's it, he's dead." Her character turned toward him, putting away her bow and drawing a short sword. Raymond's character backed away quickly.

    "Lucy, don't," Anda said. She interposed her avatar between Lucy's and Raymond's. "Don't do it. He deserves to have a say." She thought of old American TV shows, the kinds you saw between the Bollywood movies on telly. "It's a free country, right?"

    "God *damn* it, Anda, what is *wrong* with you? Did you come here to play the game, or to screw around with this pervert dork?"

> what do you want from me raymond?
> Don't kill them—let them have their wages. Go play somewhere else
> They're leeches

    Lucy typed,

> they're wrecking the game economy and they're providing a gold-for-cash supply that lets rich assholes buy their way in. They don't care about the game and neither do you
> If they don't play the game, they don't eat. I think that means that they care about the game as much as you do. You're being paid cash to kill them, yes? So you need to play for your money, too. I think that makes you and them the same, a little the same.
> go screw yourself

Lucy typed. Anda edged her character away from Lucy's. Raymond's character was so far away now that his texting came out in tiny type, almost too small to read. Lucy drew her bow again and nocked an arrow.

"Lucy, *DON'T*!" Anda cried. Her hands moved of their own volition and her character followed, clobbering Lucy bare-handed so that her avatar reeled and dropped its bow.

"You *BITCH*!" Lucy said. She drew her sword.

"I'm sorry, Lucy," Anda said, stepping back out of range. "But I don't want you to hurt him. I want to hear him out."

Lucy's avatar came on fast, and there was a click as the voice link dropped. Anda typed one-handed while she drew her own sword.

```
> dont lucy come on talk2me
```

Lucy slashed at her twice and she needed both hands to defend herself or she would have been beheaded. Anda blew out through her nose and counterattacked, fingers pounding the keyboard. Lucy had more experience points than she did, but Anda was a better player, and she knew it. She hacked away at Lucy, driving her back and back, back down the road they'd marched together.

Abruptly, Lucy broke and ran, and Anda thought she was going away and decided to let her go, no harm, no foul, but then she saw that Lucy wasn't running away, she was running *toward* the BFGs, armed and primed.

"Bloody hell," she breathed as a BFG swung around to point at her. Her fingers flew. She cast the fireball at Lucy in the same instant that she cast her shield spell. Lucy loosed the bolt at her a moment before the fireball engulfed her, cooking her down to ash, and the bolt collided with the shield and drove Anda back, high into the air, and the shield spell wore off before she hit ground, costing her half her health and inventory, which scattered around her. She tested her voice link.

"Lucy?"

There was no reply.

> I'm very sorry you and your friend quarreled.

She felt numb and unreal. There were rules for Fahrenheits, lots of rules, and the penalties for breaking them varied, but the penalty for attacking a fellow Fahrenheit was—she couldn't think the word, she closed her eyes, but there it was in big glowing letters: EXPULSION.

But Lucy had started it, right? It wasn't her fault.

But who would believe her?

She opened her eyes. Her vision swam through incipient tears. Her heart was thudding in her ears.

> The enemy isn't your fellow player. It's not the players guarding the fabrica, it's not the girls working there. The people who are working to destroy the game are the people who pay you and the people who pay the girls in the fabrica, who are the same people. You're being paid by rival factory owners, you know that? THEY are the ones who care nothing for the game. My girls care about the game. You care about the game. Your common enemy is the people who want to destroy the game and who destroy the lives of these girls.

"Whassamatter, you fat little cow? Is your game making you cwy?" She jerked as if slapped. The chav who was speaking to her hadn't been in the Baang when she arrived, and he had mean, close-set eyes and a football jersey, and though he wasn't any older than she, he looked mean, and angry, and his smile was sadistic and crazy.

"Piss off," she said, mustering her braveness.

"You wobbling tub of guts, don't you *dare* speak to me that way," he said, shouting right in her ear. The Baang fell silent and everyone looked at her. The Pakistani who ran the Baang was on his phone, no doubt calling the coppers, and that meant that her parents would discover where she'd been and then—

"I'm talking to you, girl," he said. "You disgusting lump of suet—Christ, it makes me wanta puke to look at you. You ever had a boyfriend? How'd he shag you—did he roll yer in flour and look for the wet spot?"

She reeled back, then stood. She drew her arm back and slapped him, as hard as she could. The boys in the Baang laughed and went *Whoooooo!* He purpled and balled his fists and she backed away from him. The imprint of her fingers stood out on his cheek.

He bridged the distance between them with a quick step and *punched her*, in the belly, and the air whooshed out of her and she fell into another player, who pushed her away, so she ended up slumped against the wall, crying.

The mean boy was there, right in front of her, and she could smell the chili crisps on his breath. "You disgusting whore—" he began, and she kneed him square in the nadgers, hard as she could, and he screamed like a little girl and fell backward. She picked up her schoolbag and ran for the door, her chest heaving, her face streaked with tears.

"Anda, dear, there's a phone call for you."

Her eyes stung. She'd been lying in her darkened bedroom

for hours now, sniffling and trying not to cry, trying not to look at the empty desk where her PC used to live.

Her dad's voice was soft and caring, but after the silence of her room, it sounded like a rusting hinge.

"Anda?"

She opened her eyes. He was holding a cordless phone, silhouetted against the open doorway.

"Who is it?"

"Someone from your game, I think," he said. He handed her the phone.

"Hullo?"

"Hullo, chicken." It had been a year since she'd heard that voice, but she recognized it instantly.

"Liza?"

"Yes."

Anda's skin seemed to shrink over her bones. This was it: expelled. Her heart felt like it was beating once per second, time slowed to a crawl.

"Hullo, Liza."

"Can you tell me what happened today?"

She did, stumbling over the details, backtracking and stuttering. She couldn't remember, exactly—did Lucy move on Raymond, and Anda asked her to stop, and then Lucy attacked her? Had Anda attacked Lucy first? It was all a jumble. She should have saved a screenmovie and taken it with her, but she couldn't have taken anything with her, she'd run out—

"I see. Well, it sounds like you've gotten yourself into quite a pile of poo, haven't you, my girl?"

"I guess so," Anda said. Then, because she knew that she was as good as expelled, she said, "I don't think it's right to kill them, those girls. All right?"

"Ah," Liza said. "Well, funny you should mention that. I happen to agree. Those girls need our help more than any of the girls anywhere in the game. The Fahrenheits' strength is that we are cooperative—it's another way that we're better than the boys. We care. I'm proud that you took a stand when you did—glad I found out about this business."

"You're not going to expel me?"

"No, chicken, I'm not going to expel you. I think you did the right thing—"

That meant that Lucy would be expelled. Fahrenheit had killed Fahrenheit—something had to be done. The rules had to be enforced. Anda swallowed hard.

"If you expel Lucy, I'll quit," she said, quickly, before she lost her nerve.

Liza laughed. "Oh, chicken, you're a brave thing, aren't you? No one's being expelled, fear not. But I wanta talk to this Raymond of yours."

Anda came home from remedial hockey sweaty and exhausted, but not as exhausted as the last time, nor the time before that. She could run the whole length of the pitch twice now without collapsing—when she'd started out, she could barely make it halfway without having to stop and hold her side, kneading her loathsome podge to make it stop aching. Now there was noticeably less podge, and she found that with the ability to run the pitch came the freedom to actually pay attention to the game, to aim her shots, to build up a degree of accuracy that was nearly as satisfying as being really good in-game.

Her dad knocked at the door of her bedroom after she'd showered and changed. "How's my girl?"

"Revising," she said, and hefted her maths book at him.

"Did you have a fun afternoon on the pitch?"

"You mean 'Did your head get trod on?'"

"Did it?"

"Yes," she said. "But I did more treading than getting trodden on." The other girls were *really* fat, and they didn't have a lot of team skills. Anda had been to war: she knew how to depend on someone and how to be depended upon.

"That's my girl." He pretended to inspect the paintwork around the light switch. "Been on the scale this week?"

She had, of course: the school nutritionist saw to that, a morning humiliation undertaken in full sight of all the other fatties.

"Yes, Dad."

"And—?"

"I've lost a stone," she said. A little more than a stone, actually. She had been able to fit into last year's jeans the other day.

She hadn't been in the sweetshop in a month. When she thought about sweets, it made her think of the little girls in the sweatshop. Sweatshop, sweetshop. The sweetshop man sold his wares close to the school because little girls who didn't know better would be tempted by them. No one forced them, but they were *kids*, and grown-ups were supposed to look out for kids.

Her da beamed at her. "I've lost three pounds myself," he said, holding his tum. "I've been trying to follow your diet, you know."

"I know, Da," she said. It embarrassed her to discuss it with him.

The kids in the sweatshops were being exploited by grown-ups, too. It was why their situation was so impossible: the adults who were supposed to be taking care of them were exploiting them.

"Well, I just wanted to say that I'm proud of you. We both are, your mum and me. And I wanted to let you know that I'll be moving your PC back into your room tomorrow. You've earned it."

Anda blushed pink. She hadn't really expected this. Her fingers twitched over a phantom game controller.

"Oh, Da," she said. He held up his hand.

"It's all right, girl. We're just proud of you."

She didn't touch the PC the first day, nor the second. The kids in the game—she didn't know what to do about them. On the third day, after hockey, she showered and changed and sat down and slipped the headset on.

"Hello, Anda."

"Hi, Sarge."

Lucy had known the minute she entered the game, which meant that she was still on Lucy's buddy list. Well, that was a hopeful sign.

"You don't have to call me that. We're the same rank now, after all."

Anda pulled down a menu and confirmed it: she'd been promoted to sergeant during her absence. She smiled.

"Gosh," she said.

"Yes, well, you earned it," Lucy said. "I've been talking to Raymond a lot about the working conditions in the factory, and, well—" She broke off. "I'm sorry, Anda."

"Me too, Lucy."

"You don't have anything to be sorry about," she said.

They went adventuring, running some of the game's standard missions together. It was fun, but after the kind of campaigning they'd done before, it was also kind of pale and flat.

"It's horrible, I know," Anda said. "But I miss it."

"Oh, thank God," Lucy said. "I thought I was the only one. It was fun, wasn't it? Big fights, big stakes."

"Well, poo," Anda said. "I don't wanna be bored for the rest of my life. What're we gonna do?"

"I was hoping you knew."

She thought about it. The part she'd loved had been going up against grown-ups who were not playing the game but *gaming* it, breaking it for money. They'd been worthy adversaries, and there was no guilt in beating them, either.

"We'll ask Raymond how we can help," she said.

"I want them to walk out—to go on strike," he said. "It's the only way to get results: band together and withdraw your labor." Raymond's voice had a thick Mexican accent that took some getting used to, but his English was very good—better, in fact, than Lucy's.

"Walk out in-game?" Lucy said.

"No," Raymond said. "That wouldn't be very effective. I want them to walk out in Ciudad Juárez and Tijuana. I'll call the press in, we'll make a big deal out of it. We can win—I know we can."

"So what's the problem?" Anda said.

"The same problem as always. Getting them organized. I thought that the game would make it easier; we've been trying to get these girls organized for years: in the sewing shops, and the toy factories, but they lock the doors and keep us out and the girls go home and their parents won't let us talk to them. But in the game, I thought I'd be able to reach them—"

"But the bosses keep you away?"

"I keep getting killed. I've been practicing my swordfighting, but it's so hard—"

"This will be fun," Anda said. "Let's go."

"Where?" Lucy said.

"To an in-game factory. We're your new bodyguards." The bosses hired some pretty mean mercs, Anda knew. She'd been one. They'd be *fun* to wipe out.

Raymond's character spun around on the screen, then planted a kiss on Anda's cheek. Anda made her character give him a playful shove that sent him sprawling.

"Hey, Lucy, go get us a couple BFGs, okay?"

Cory Doctorow is a science fiction author, activist, journalist, and blogger. He serves as coeditor of Boing Boing (boingboing.net) and is the author of several novels, including *Homeland*, *For the Win*, and *Little Brother*. He is the former European director of the Electronic Frontier Foundation and cofounded the UK's Open Rights Group. Born in Toronto, Canada, he now lives in London. Learn more about Doctorow's work at www.craphound.com.

COMA KINGS

Jessica Barber

So I guess the story begins, fittingly, with someone handing me a *Coma* rig and saying, *play me.*

Two a.m. and I'm at this party in somebody's trailer out in the trashy part of town. I'm stoned out of my mind and there's something on the television, either one of those cheesy infomercials or some sort of comedy thing making fun of those cheesy infomercials, and I'm trying to figure out which. I keep turning to the kid sprawled out beside me and saying, "Is this for real? Or is this like, a joke?" and he keeps blinking at me and going, "What? I don't . . ." and then trailing off. And so I'm deep into this important cultural assessment when somebody shoves a *Coma* rig into my hands.

"Fuck off," I say, even though my fingers automatically curl into the wires. "I'm stoned, I don't wanna play."

"Come on," says the guy who handed me the rig. "You're Jenny, right? I hear you're really good," he says. True. "I hear you're like, the best in the state, easy." Not true, because of Annie, but I guess he's not counting her. "I've wanted to play you like, forever."

Either I'm really susceptible to flattery when stoned, or I actually just want to be playing *Coma* all the time, twenty-four/seven, no matter what, but either way I say fine and start to pull on the rig.

In each of my temples there are three distinct depressions, dents where the electrodes of my own rig have sat for hours on end. When I play *Coma* using my own gear, pulling on the headpiece feels like slotting a puzzle piece into place, but this kid's rig is too big for me, not broken in. I try my best to align the electrodes properly, but in the end I just can't get it to sit right, so I say fuck it and let it go all crooked. If you've played *Coma* you know this is a dumb idea, because it means the calibration will be all off and it will make you play like a spaz, but this is a throwaway game and I figure, who cares. I slide the opaque goggles over my eyes, fumble for the headphones and settle their huge soft cups over my ears, and the world disappears.

This is the point where usually I'd access my own personal *Coma* account, but like I said, I'm stoned, the rig doesn't fit, and I don't want some stupid throwaway game to drop me in the rankings. So I log in as a guest on the kid's account instead.

Which is what fucks me over so badly, in the end.

When *Coma* first came out, it was this gimmicky thing, a rich kid's game, nothing I cared about or could have afforded if I did. I played for the first time at a mall. One of those demo booths set up spanning the food court, and the only thing I noticed about it then was that it was blocking my way to Sbarro. I hadn't been interested, but Annie thought it looked like the coolest thing ever, and she begged me to let her play.

Forget it, I'd said, it looks stupid, I'm hungry, but she whined until I told her fine, get in line. Tough luck for her, though, you had to be thirteen and at the time she was only eleven. I played just to spite her, since I was fourteen and made the age cutoff.

I love how you can do these things that fuck you over forever, that change your goddamn life, and not even care at the time, not even know.

I won that first game at the mall easily, even though I had no clue what I was doing. Then I won the next game, and the game after that too, and by the end of the day I had more wins than anybody else and guess what that meant? Two free *Coma* rigs for the trouble.

I planned on selling them. They were going for five hundred bucks apiece, I mean, shit. But when we got home, Annie goaded me into playing against her. Well, she won, of course, you know that much, and then I could hardly sell them off, could I? Not until I beat her.

I suppose you can guess how long it took for that to happen.

I should probably tell you how that game at the party went, but I never know how to explain *Coma* when I'm out of the rig. It's not like chess or something, it never makes sense when your brain is in the real world. If you really care, the game is on record, like every other game of *Coma* ever played.

It's not worth watching; the kid is fucking terrible. We turn on our rigs and there's nothing. I start building a box. Then there's nothing but the inside of my box. One corner starts to crumble a little, and that's the kid trying real hard, but then I just make it not crumble and that's the end of that. I place a single white stone in the center of the box, and the game is over.

All of this is hardly worth telling you, except for what happens next. I feel the kid log out in a huff, and I'm about to do the same. But then there's a ping up in the left corner of my consciousness, letting me know that Annie is requesting a game, and it's a good thing I'm sitting down back in the real world because otherwise I would have fallen right over.

Here's the thing. I have been trying to get Annie to play me again literally for years. I have sent game requests, again and again, and have gotten rejected each time. She absolutely will not play me. And now she's been tricked, she doesn't know it's me, I finally get to play her, and here I am: wasted out of my mind with a *Coma* rig that doesn't even fit.

If I were slightly less stoned, I might have started crying. As it is, I can't even try to play, can't even make the vaguest real effort because I know I'll just get slaughtered, immediately, without mercy. Instead I start building useless structures, crumbling shapes that spell out *Annie, it's me, come back, I miss you.*

The shock buys me about two solid minutes before Annie annihilates me and I am kicked out of the game. I can't even bring myself to try to send her messages, try to request another chance. I just pull myself back into the real world, gut hurt and gasping for air.

I get home several hours before dawn, but my mother is up, sitting at the kitchen table and turning an unlit cigarette in her fingers, staring at the vinyl tabletop. The long walk home has cleared my head a bit, but I still feel shell-shocked, like there's something sharp worming its way through the spaces between my organs. Like I'm going to burst apart at any moment.

My mother doesn't look at me. "Where you been?"

"Went to a party," I say. "Told you I was gonna go." She makes a rough noise, deep in her throat, and I keep talking before she can say whatever it is she's sitting on. "How's Annie? You checked in on her?"

"She's the same as ever, what do you think?" Ma says, which I take to mean no.

I try not to grit my teeth. "You still gotta check on her," I mutter, move to squeeze past her but her hand darts out, catching me around the forearm.

"Don't you tell me how I gotta care for my own child," she snaps. Her cheap fake nails have half broken off, and their edges bite deep crescents into the underside of my wrist. We glare at each other until she releases me.

I bite down hard on the sides of my tongue and shove my way into the room I share with Annie.

Annie lies on her bed, just like she always does, a vanishing outline of a human body under a nubbly blanket, her head obscured by goggles, oversize headphones. She is surrounded by a small forest of medical equipment: stands for IV drips and catheter bags and heart rate monitors with their slow, steady pulse of life.

The port at the base of her skull is hidden among pillows, under wide bandages. No electrodes. She doesn't need those anymore.

Once I would have been overwhelmed by the urge to rip away every bit of equipment that surrounds her. Fuck, I'll admit it: More than once I have given into this urge, but by now I know it doesn't make any difference. She still lies there, just as unresponsive but now stripped bare, the heart rate monitor sending up a wailing protest in her absence.

So I don't touch her. I just slide to the floor, scrape my

thighs and palms across the synthetic roughness of the carpet, and glare. "Goddammit, Annie," I tell her.

There is a sound from the doorway and I fling myself around to face my mother, cheeks burning. She isn't looking at me, though. Her eyes are trained on Annie.

"I can't keep this up forever, you know," she says. "It ain't cheap. They don't give me enough to look after her right. Sooner or later, we're gonna have to let her go."

She has been threatening this for years.

I don't respond, just turn around and fit my molars together, like a small child, like if I pretend she isn't there, maybe she'll disappear.

It doesn't work. It never does.

"Jennifer, I really need to see you applying yourself," says Miss Denton. "You've already missed two tests this quarter, and I haven't gotten any homework at all from you yet."

I used to like school. I mean, maybe "like" is a strong word. But it was all right. These days, when I manage to go, it feels like trying to pull my limbs through molasses, impossibly difficult and never ending. This is a compounding problem. It's hard enough getting my ass to school by seven thirty in the morning on a good day. Getting my ass to school when I'm just going to get yelled at for the last time I failed to get my ass to school is just adding indignity to injustice.

"I know," I say. "I'm going to make them up, honest. I've just been . . ." I don't know what to say here. Tired, is what almost comes out of my mouth. But that's not the sort of excuse you can use.

I can tell by the way Miss Denton's expression folds in

on itself that she is supplying her own narrative. Poor Jennifer, with her crazy sister. Miss Denton wears tiny frameless glasses perched on the end of her nose, and she takes them off to polish them, stalling for time. "I know it's been a hard year for you," she begins.

Christ, I'm tired of this speech. I know it's rude, but I let my body hunch forward, rest my forehead against the laminate desktop. It's cool, and slightly sticky. I don't even have the energy to be disgusted.

Miss Denton perseveres. "I know it's been a hard year for you. But your junior year is just starting, and your grades right now are so important for college. You do still want to go to college, don't you?"

"Yes," I say, because I am supposed to. I wonder if it's true. Standard small-town dream: Make it out, make it somewhere far away.

I wonder if they'd let me keep Annie in my dorm room.

I don't make it to second period. I get to the door, then think of sitting at a desk for a solid hour and a half, the real world feeling cramped and finite, and just can't. I find myself pushing through a side door out into the parking lot, twisting my way through rows of cars baking in the early sun. I can *feel* my rig tucked safe in my trunk, like a fucking siren song, and before I can think, I'm angling my steering wheel toward the city.

People go to *Coma* parlors for one of two reasons.

The first reason—why I go—is just to have a safe, quiet space to play *Coma* uninterrupted. The full-immersion aspect means it's different than how gaming used to be. You can't yell at your mom to get out of your room or shove the cat away if it walks across the keyboard. Or worse, if something catches fire, or you've got a crazed family member screaming obscenities and threatening to kill you. If you're planning to really settle in for a long game, better to be someplace supervised, someplace safe.

The second reason people go to *Coma* parlors is to hack their rigs. For some people, tweaking the electronics is just as much of a draw as actually playing the game. They think adding extra electrodes, overclocking the microprocessor, whatever-the-fuck else will give them an edge, help them achieve some sort of in-game nirvana. I think this is mostly bullshit; I use two-year-old stock parts and the occasional firmware upgrade, and I play better than most of the gearheads. Plus, we all know what it actually takes to get to that place of inseparability from the game.

There just aren't very many people willing to go that far.

Lady K's place looks like somebody's garage workshop. Bare cinder-block walls, concrete floor. There's a smattering of institutional couches around the outer edge, about half taken up by prone bodies, but the majority of its real estate is occupied by long, cobbled-together workbenches, ringed by kids bent industriously over the exploded innards of their *Coma* rigs. Soldering irons send fine wisps of smoke upward; someone's running a Dremel carefully along the rim of their goggles.

The eponymous Lady K, a short, apple-cheeked chick who can't be much older than me, is peering into a microscope when I come in, but she looks up at the door chime and gives me a little grin. I'm not in here often enough to be considered a regular, but Lady K knows me regardless. I'm higher ranked than anybody else who plays here, which probably helps my notoriety.

That, and Annie.

Always fucking Annie.

"Hey, Jenny," says Lady K. "You working on something today? Or just playing?"

"Just playing, for now," I say. "Can I crash out on that couch?"

"Go for it," says Lady K, and minutes later I am deep in *Coma*.

It's good, I have a good morning. I play a guy I haven't played before, some up-and-coming star from South Korea. We play off each other well, building up a huge structure, an entire city of improbable shapes. It takes a two-and-a-half-hour battle for me to bring the entire thing down around his ears.

When I come out from under, I'm in a way better mood than I've been ever since that fucking party. A few people have plugged in to watch my game, and I actually manage a grin for them as we all disentangle from our rigs.

"That was a sweet trick with the arches," someone says, and someone else offers to run out for pizza since it's now past noon, and soon there's a crowd of us sitting cross-legged in a circle on the floor, pizza grease seeping through paper plates and onto our fingertips. There's a dimpled, heavyset kid trying to tell everyone why he still prefers to use passive electrodes even though it means getting your hair gunked up with conductive paste, and I feel some unrecognized tightness below my collarbones soften, relax.

Lady K, sitting next to me, waves a slice of pepperoni to get my attention. "You sticking around for the rest of the afternoon?" She pauses, arches an eyebrow. "Shouldn't you be in school?"

I am about to say something disparaging, when a fragment of conversation cuts through the rest of the chatter, the way fragments of conversation sometimes do, loud and unmistakable. "—kid in California hardwired himself two days ago." It's a pretty, wide-eyed girl with a punk-rock haircut talking; no wonder all the attention is on her. "That's like over two dozen people hardwired in, just in America. It's just so scary, I mean can you even imagine, drilling into your own skull like that? I hear there's someone not too far from here, do you think—" The guy next to her finally cuts her off with an elbow jab to the ribs. She turns an inquiring glare on him, and he leans toward her, starting up a furious, whispered conversation.

The tightness underneath my collarbones spools back into existence. I ignore the guilty glances being slanted my way, and take a large, deliberate bite of pizza instead.

"Skipping," I explain to Lady K once I am finished chewing. The conversation is still hushed and awkward. I fold the paper plate into a careful fat wedge, wipe my fingers on my jeans. "I'm gonna plug back in."

There are too many eyes on me as I try to settle into my rig, I can't get the electrodes to sit quite right. I never have problems with my rig but it's taking too long, I'm starting to look like an idiot, so I turn the whole thing on anyway, blissful blank order sliding over my brain waves.

It fits my current luck that none of my active play partners are connected, so I drift uncomfortably, paging through lists of other people looking for games, trying to find someone whose stats make them look interesting. I am just about to accept an offer to play a teaching game with some newbie when Annie's pseud pops up as available.

I send her a game request without even really thinking about it; I've done this so many times it's like a reflex now. And like all the other times before, she declines immediately.

Because I am childish and bitter, I send her two dozen

game requests in quick succession, the *Coma* equivalent of ringing someone's doorbell repeatedly.

Just admit you're scared, I message her, and as usual, am informed that she is not accepting messages. I game-request her three more times and think really hard about flipping her off, as if the *Coma* network might somehow be able to convey my displeasure, might carry along my vitriol to resonate into the base of Annie's wretched skull. Then I accept the game against the newbie and try to forget about it.

I'm a half hour into it when Annie's game request pings along the edge of my brain.

I stop breathing. For at least thirty seconds I am essentially paralyzed; I know this because when I come back to myself, my opponent is making good headway toward tearing down the defenses I've built up, sending me a little stream of surprised and pleased messages about how he thinks he's finally really getting it. *Sorry,* I say, *sorry, I have to go,* and forfeit the game, just like that.

I accept Annie's game request and the world is a clean slate.

Then Annie starts building a box.

Maybe you can see what's coming here. I don't know. Maybe it was obvious from the outside. If you had asked me before, I wouldn't have been able to tell you what I thought was going to happen, because I didn't think anything. I wanted to play Annie. Of course I did, she's my sister, my sister who I lost, and I wanted to have her again, in any way I could. And I wanted to beat her, because she's my sister, and you always want to win against your siblings. That's just the way things work, right? That should have been enough.

So I didn't *think* anything. But here's the thing, and I know this makes me a fool, but deep down, I *believed,* somehow, that if I could just beat her, everything would be all better. Believed, with that sort of secret inner ferocity of a fairy tale or a religion. I would win against her, like nobody ever had, and there would be a silent, eternal moment. And then her name would blip out of existence, and I'd pull off my rig and look over to where she was doing the same, prying her goggles away from her eyes and sliding the probe out from the back of her skull. And we'd look at each other, and start laughing, and everything would be okay.

In fairy tales, you can wake somebody out of death with a kiss. Does waking somebody up like this really seem like so much to ask?

When I beat Annie, there is indeed one silent, eternal moment. And right then I don't even realize what I'm waiting for, bated breath and tense muscles, until it doesn't happen, until she leaves the space we created without comment, until she doesn't blip out of existence.

Until she starts up another game, immediately, against someone else, as if absolutely nothing has changed.

When I get home my mother is waiting for me.

"The school called to tell me you missed classes today," she says.

My keys bite into my palm, hard and irregular. I get past my mother without looking at her, make my way into the living room. Climb onto the couch, pull my knees up to my chest. Turn my face into the cushion so the upholstery forces my eyes shut.

I have mostly stopped crying by this point.

"You listen when I'm talking to you," says my mother.

I can hear her moving into the living room after me. The

shadows behind my eyelids get darker as she stands over me, half blocking the light. I expect her to grab hold of me, yank me upright, something, but she doesn't move.

"Would you unplug me?" I hear myself asking. My voice filters through the cushions, muffled and strange. I doubt my mother can even understand what I'm saying. "If I was like Annie. Would you unplug us both?"

Silence. The tender spots at my temples throb in time with my pulse, thudding slow and regular. Then I feel her moving, feel the couch shifting as she sinks down next to me. Her fingertips press into my scalp, thumb curling into the fine hairs at the base of my skull.

"I don't know," she says, almost a whisper.

I almost want to believe she sounds sorry.

"Okay," I say. Her fingernails catch in my hair when she pulls her hand away, bringing long strands with them. I feel them lift and separate, imagine them shining and infinite, like wires. "Okay."

———————

Jessica Barber grew up in Tennessee but moved to New England to attend MIT, where she studied physics and electrical engineering. After a brief stint building rocket ships in Southern California, she returned to Cambridge, where she now spends her days developing open-source electronics, with a focus on tools for neuroscience. Her work has previously appeared in *Strange Horizons* and *Lightspeed*.

STATS

Marguerite K. Bennett

He was pink as a cocktail shrimp when he stepped out of the shower, with a splotch of red across his chest like a burn of radiation. He liked the water hot enough to scald, the sweet, clean burn that made him grin in the predawn gloom of the apartment, and he liked the sweep of red heat that crept down his SoulCycle arms, his Equinox abs. He'd always been pale—sunburns at beach weeks, seventy-proof sunscreen at baseball games with clients—the raw acne of high school sinking smoothly down beneath a magazine-cover complexion that even women envied. He enjoyed their envy. He enjoyed the catch of breath in their throats, their downcast eyes and clotted mascara lashes, the sudden flare of high school insecurity in their cheeks as they went through their fears, their flaws, their recurring thoughts when he slid up at charity dinners and after-parties—*This man is too handsome for me.*

His name was Joey fucking Connor, and on the last day of his life, he stood in front of the medicine cabinet, looking like an HBO heartthrob and sweeping the fog away from the glass.

Shit, he thought. He had forgotten the manicure. He'd gone to the spa on Thirty-Ninth, but it had been run by heroin-chic

Russians who looked like ex–runway models, booted when they'd gotten too old to make the clothes look like invitations to a gangbang. Not a single Asian to be found. What was he supposed to do?

He needed to look like *perfection*. The case today was vital—a huge pharmaceutical suit, a line of antidepressants that led to a spike in suicides. Prozac fucking Nation, man. Christ hadn't chosen his apostles with as much care as Joey's law firm had chosen their witnesses. He was fairly certain most of the clients had just been sad sacks whose families welcomed the sudden inheritances, but billable hours were billable hours.

He jiggled the latch on the medicine cabinet—the goddamn thing always stuck like this; he'd actually sprained his wrist prying it open last month, could you believe that?

He practiced his smile in the mirror—wide-set and guileless eyes, the correct cat's tongue brush of stubble, the teeth that were Crest-commercial white (though uneven enough not to be mistaken for caps). An artificial appearance was dangerous for a lawyer. Lawyers were easy targets, and the jury seized on any reason to hate them; he'd fought discrimination his whole life, but did anyone care what people like him had to put up with? He reached for the mirror again. As long as the judge wasn't the bitch he remembered, he'd—

The cabinet mirror shattered in his hand.

Joey leapt back, nearly slipping in the tub, nearly cracking his neck on the sink—a stupid, ignominious death. The condensation on the mirror trembled in the splintered glass, like beads of rain on a spider's web. His face was a fracture.

"The. Fuck?" he asked aloud.

He picked up his towel from where it had fallen. The

double-scalloped Egyptian cotton felt light as tissue, not the rich, heavy fabric he'd bought the week he'd been hired at Koertig, Lefferts & Johns.

Joey grabbed the bathroom door.

The door dissolved in splinters, the crystal knob falling to the bath mat with an absurdly hilarious *thuck*.

I'm the Incredible fucking Hulk, Joey thought. His mouth had gone dry and his ears were ringing. He wasn't drunk and he didn't do drugs—he was too possessive of the body he'd spent thousands of hours perfecting. He combed slivers of wood from his hair, scraped them from his feet onto the bath mat.

Super strength, he thought.

And then, with a certain surreal dissonance, *I . . . don't have time for this.*

Careful—he had to be careful. *Something* had happened. He didn't flatter himself to assume this was a side effect of protein shakes and Broga. He needed to get to work, win this case, fuck a mountain of NYU coeds, and buy . . . something— he didn't know, but whatever it was would make his friends hate him when they saw it.

He left steaming wet footprints in the hallway as he hurried to his bedroom, but lurched to a standstill as he glanced into the living room. His TV was on, and his new console, too. Not counting his on-and-off girlfriend—a video game engineer named Samantha with an ass that he'd eventually like to be buried in—these were his favorite toys. He would never have left them on overnight to burn through their beautiful neon glow.

A single gray pop-up hung on the eighty-inch retina display screen. The controller vibrated, beeped sweetly to him.

THANK YOU FOR ACCEPTING
NEW TERMS AND CONDITIONS
PRESS X TO OPT OUT

Joey's biceps were the size of grapefruits by the time he got dressed, and he'd shredded his best gray wool suit. His second-best suit made it with him out the door and into the Uber when a bolt of pain shot up his right arm.

"*Fuck!*" he roared. The Arab driver turned down the fucking nonsense music he'd been playing and glanced back in concern.

"Is everything all right, sir?"

"My—briefcase—" Joey began. The Tumi briefcase felt like it was filled with gold bars, dragging his arm down; it fell to the floor of the cab, pinning his foot to the mat as though it were an anvil. Even the weight of his clothes made him feel like he was lying under those lead sheets at the dentist. Struggling to keep upright, Joey glanced at his arms. The blood drained from his face.

His wrists were thin as yardsticks, so frail that the blue veins showed through his apple-white skin.

Weak, he thought. Super *weak*—

His Piaget Altiplano watch slipped right over his hand and bounced on the floorboard. In the rearview mirror, Joey watched his cheeks draw in, drawn thin—watched his eyes drift farther apart, watched his nose begin to flatten—he tried to scream—

"Here we are, sir," the driver said. Joey scrambled from the car. He jerked the briefcase after him and staggered onto the sidewalk—the briefcase slammed into his chest, all but knocking the wind out of his lungs.

The briefcase was normal again, no heavier than it had

ever been. He was healthy enough that the sheer weight of his clothes didn't exhaust him. He stared down at his wrists, which had thickened—more slender than they had been this morning, sure, but not emaciated. He whipped out his smartphone, snapped a picture of himself.

The face in the photo was not his own.

"Linda—" Joey began, but Linda was hustling the junior associates into a lineup in the firm's lobby.

"The photographer is here!" Linda cried. She always sounded like a Girl Scout troop leader when the press was on the floor, but in her aubergine Vivienne Westwood pantsuit and crystal pin, Linda Koertig was no one's mother. Right now, she was pure hustler, pressing her employees in front of the camera, pushing back the men's shoulders, pulling up the women's chins. "Joey, you're late. Ladies, here, fill in—"

Joey wiped sweat from his upper lip. He *had* to be here—the bonus that came from this case was exorbitant, and if he failed to win a suit that was so perfectly gift wrapped for him . . . Stress, maybe this was stress, a psychosomatic break—but the medicine cabinet, the bathroom door, his best suit . . . He had read about hysterical bursts of strength, hadn't that been in the case file? The adrenaline gushed through a body, and flu-like symptoms set in when it subsided. Maybe he had internalized something he'd read, but he *had* to be here, his future at the firm all rested on *this fucking case*—

"Make sure you get *him* in the front," Linda murmured. Her eyes swept between the photographer and Joey, who raised his eyebrows.

"Diversity hire," he heard one of the first-year lawyers whisper behind him, in a breath as cold and sour as battery acid. He felt their eyes on him, burning into the back of his skull. Bewildered anger welled up in his throat like bile—he'd been *second* in his fucking class at the University of Chicago, *third* in his class out of law school at Yale, he'd won the *Smits vs. Cheong* case with a jury that couldn't tell their eyes from their crusty unbleached assholes—

"Don't listen to them, Joey," one of the interns said, a skinny white girl with retro glasses and a polka-dot pencil skirt. The photographer's camera sent eerie explosions of light across the lobby, like the strobes in a club. The intern flashed him a waxy red smile that he wanted to tear off of her face lip by lip. "I've always thought black guys were *hot*."

The flashbulbs hadn't even cooled when Joey bolted into his office and shot both the locks closed. In the dark of his private bathroom, he reached for the antique porcelain tap, listening to the squeal of the metal, the retching stutter of the water, the sudden flood of blissful heat soaking through his hands.

The yellow overhead lamp finally sizzled to life.

Joey's hands were not his hands. They were slender and dark as vanilla beans, their palms and the inner curls of the fingers the color of a conch shell. *These* nails had been manicured.

He stared at the face in the glass. A handsome black man stared back at him, slender and midthirties, with exquisite almond-shaped eyes and a $10,000 smile.

Joey turned out the lights.

In his office overlooking Midtown, he stared at the pictures on the polished mahogany walls. The frames were sterling silver, all matching—gifts from Samantha last Christmas: his first day at the firm, his first million-dollar victory, a perfunctory shot of their last Fourth of July at the lake.

The face in these pictures was the face he had seen in his mirror a moment ago.

It was not the face he had woken up with this morning.

He reached down for his phone, dialed Linda.

"I need to take a day," he whispered, in a voice much higher than his own.

He didn't try to catch a cab. He didn't want to know if the saying was true.

He walked through Times Square, his peripheral vision filled with chattering, white-bread tourists who shot him interested glances and bankers who side-eyed him up at crosswalks. The teenage drummers playing for tips—black and Latino mostly, fucking beggars he'd have to defend when his turn on pro bono came, he was sure—smirked as he walked past.

Joey didn't know where to go, what to do. His suit was too loose now, but nothing in his life had changed other than his body. No one remarked on the change, not even the Arab driver who had watched it happen. Yet everyone was aware of the result, as though he had always been this way.

He took a breath.

Is this my breakdown?

He'd always thought depression and anxiety were bullshit, twentysomethings' ways to make themselves feel artistic and tortured, a "get out of jail free" card to slap down whenever adulthood bored them. But he really didn't know anymore.

Joey started to sit on the thin ledge of a low window outside a pastry shop, then hissed in pain.

His body was thickening with flesh, bulging rapidly, his skin lightening—his hands were shrinking, wrinkling, the tiny hairs turning gray—he could feel his eyes shift in his face, watch the world warp as they resettled—he bit back a scream as even his teeth jostled in his mouth—

He was big and warm, soft and flowing; the suit bulged against his flesh, refusing to hide a single curve or roll or seam. At the junction of his legs, something reduced, withdrew, vanished. His back seized in pain and he clutched his chest, his arms suddenly filling with the eruption of an enormous pair of breasts. He yanked his jacket as tight as he could over his body—suddenly massive, suddenly aged, suddenly and horribly female—but only managed to lose several expensive mother-of-pearl buttons.

He gasped, panted, shut his eyes, and blundered forward into the crowd, longing for the roaring, stinking oblivion of the subway, of the averted eyes, of the earbudded deaf-mutes in the crush of traffic.

Don't look at me, he thought. *I'm losing my mind.*

He shrank from the nasty little smiles, the open laughter of a group of college sluts out for lunch, the frank and curious stares of children.

"Dad, lookit that fat woman," a little boy said, only to be yanked along by his father. He heard mutters of "paying her health care" in a vicious Jersey accent. Joey couldn't think of a single retort. He shuffled on with his head down.

"Baby!"

Joey glanced up.

The man on the corner was white, his skin raw and pale, like noodles before they've been boiled. There was something spoiled but appealing about him, like soft cheese with veins of mold—you knew what you were eating, but you knew, all the same, it was meant to be good.

The stranger was in Joey's path before Joey even saw him rise from the upturned bucket he was using for a seat.

"Hey, baby," the man repeated. His smile was wide, his eyes bloodshot in his once-handsome face. "What, you can't give me a smiiiile?"

Joey jerked to the left, out of the stranger's path, seething.

"You're a stuck-up cunt, you know that?" the stranger rasped.

Joey fought every instinct to stop and jam his fist down the stranger's throat and kept moving. The guy could be armed, could be *diseased*—

"Betchu like it nasty," the stranger said, following. He was a few steps behind Joey, speaking quietly, his hands in his pockets. He was smiling as if they were old friends, college buddies, lovers. People walked by without even darting their eyes.

The stranger leaned in close to Joey, his hand wrapped around something in his pocket.

Oh fuck, Joey thought for the first time. *What if he has a knife?*

"Nasty-ass, fat-ass bitch, you're ugly anyway, fuck you, slut," the stranger said, still smiling. Joey was transfixed, terrified to lunge, terrified the man would seize him, stab him—

A tourist walking past offered him a single raised eyebrow as if to say, *If you don't like the attention, why don't you just leave?*

I can't, Joey wanted to scream. *He's too big, I think he has a knife, what if he*—

The tourist kept walking. There were better things to see.

"I'm gonna slip my thumbs right into that pussy," the stranger was saying. "Split that greasy cunt wide open. Suck it right out. *Schluurrr*—"

Joey stared at him.

The man burst out laughing as Joey ran.

Two beat cops were on the opposite corner, their black-and-white jackets edged in fluorescent patches; Joey slowed, gasping down air flavored with garbage and hot asphalt, his lungs aching in time with his frantic pulse.

One cop glanced to the other as if to say, *This one's your problem.*

"Please," Joey managed, darting glances back at the stranger, who was once again sitting on his upturned bucket, grinning over at them. "That man was harassing me."

The cop looked Joey up and down—slow and slimy as a snail, as if to make a point of it—and then barked a laugh.

"You?" the cop said. "He was harassing *you*?"

A hard, sickening blush started spreading up Joey's neck, creeping red through the veins over his cheeks like disease.

"*Yes*," Joey managed, the flush in his face so hot and awful that he was almost shaking. "He—"

"Is he still harassing you?" the cop asked, glancing from his partner and out across the street—in nowhere near the direction where the stranger was sitting and watching the proceedings, insolence incarnate.

"I—no, but he—" Joey's mouth went dry. "You—don't believe me?"

The cop sighed, beginning to see this was going to be more trouble than it was worth.

"Look," the cop began, "if he *did* say something, lady—learn to take a compliment."

The other cop started smiling. "Sister, your size, should take whatever attention you can get."

———

As Joey walked beneath the silver and chrome of the sky-scrapers, he counted his wrongs as if counting beads on a rosary.

The jealous, greedy first-year lawyers who he knew insisted nothing was about race until it meant they didn't get what they wanted.

The fetishistic bitch intern who thought her opinion on his body was supposed to be a reassurance.

The man on the street who'd taken him for an easy target who owed strangers his gratitude and attention.

The cops who'd laughed at his fears, at his rights, like he was the biggest punch line in the fucking world.

I'll fucking kill you all, Joey thought. He couldn't live this way, *wouldn't,* not as any of it.

He wanted a gun—for his mouth or theirs, he didn't know. But he was *Joey fucking Connor*, and he wasn't going to take this dogfuck world.

He could feel his body changing again. His skin was the color of burnished gold, sun-kissed and smooth; his hair curled out in long, drizzling locks the color of smoke. His legs were growing taut and slender, his stomach flattening to a bikini mannequin's, as tight as the skin of a drum. His back still ached with the weight of the altered breasts under his jacket, which would not lie flat no matter how he pulled his suit jacket around them.

He knew what he looked like without even glancing down. He knew what he would've said to a woman who looked like the woman he was now.

He looked ahead into a street of grinning men.

Kill me, God, he thought. *Just fucking kill me.*

———

His feet had begun to ache as he walked the streets of lower Manhattan. His toes had swollen like salamis, bursting through the Gucci leather of his shoes like rotten fruit.

He didn't even bother to look down. He didn't want to be anything anymore. He just wanted to go home to his apartment where everything made sense, where people listened to him and took care of him and gave him what he wanted because he was handsome and smart and winning.

The pain in his feet was too keen to ignore. He reached down to rip off the tattered remains of his two-thousand-dollar shoes. He paused.

Joey looked up at his reflection in a shop window.

His reflection made him smile.

The face in the glass was hideous and distorted. His jaw was as wide as his hips, his skin hanging in blubbery folds. A yellow, broken tusk jutted up from each end of his drooling lips. Warts and pustules bloomed above his jelly-like eyes.

A tiny tin bell jangled over the shop door.

"No orcs!" a woman shouted in a shivery, accented voice. She carried a broom, making furious gestures at him, shooing him away as if he were a feral cat, a drunk relieving himself on her stoop. "Orcs steal! No orcs!"

Joey looked at the woman. He started laughing.

"I will call the police!" the woman cried. "No orcs! Bad for business!"

Joey stuck his hands—now the size of Christmas hams—in the ruins of his pockets. He strolled toward the park, looking up at a billboard over a diner—a beautiful, long-legged white woman being born aloft by a team of female orcs with lowered eyes.

What. The. Fuck, he thought. *What. The goddamn. Fuck.*

The game.

Joey sat down on the granite lip of the fountain and put his head in his garbage-lid hands. The stone beneath his titanic haunches gave the tiniest groan.

It's my stats, he thought. Pigeons perched on his horns, pecking the lice out of his hair. *Someone is fucking with my stats.*

Samantha had brought the game home from the software firm where she worked with that fucking neckbeard, Nathan. She'd told Joey the newest version was in development, but he'd taken it anyway, pirating the rest of the software to run it, because if he was smart enough to steal it, why shouldn't it be his?

Samantha had been distressed when she couldn't find the jump drive, but he'd told her he'd never touched her bag. She'd left in a cold fury that night—it had been their ninth or tenth breakup, which he loved, since the hatesex *and* the reunion sex were incredible—but she returned the next afternoon to find him in the middle of the third level.

"You named the character after yourself," Samantha observed, standing in the doorway to the living room. She never looked at Joey, only at the gameplay. Her eyes were still and bright, perfect mirrors of the fantasy battles on the screen. "Made him look like you, too."

Joey had said something sheepish and charming, something that always made women roll their eyes in that *Oh, you* forgiveness of sitcom spouses, but Samantha hadn't given any indication that she'd heard.

"Ever the narcissist," Samantha murmured. She didn't even seem to be saying it to him. He heard her heels clicking down the hall. "Hope you get what you deserve."

The chain on the door swung and clattered against the lock as she left.

That had been three days ago, and he hadn't had so much as a text from her since. Even her perfume had grown stale in the apartment. His clothes had remained in small heaps around his hamper. The dishwasher hadn't been run.

Stats, Joey thought. *Someone scrolling strength up to max and then down to minimum. Building and rebuilding my face like a housewife playing the fucking* Sims. *Customizing the— ha—skins. What a fucking joke.*

What a fucking game.

He snatched a pigeon out of the air and bit off its head.

Samantha. I don't know how you did this to me, but I know it's you.

He grinned, letting the blood ooze between his teeth, the crunch of bone like the grind of popcorn kernels against his molars.

I'm coming for you, Samantha.

"Samantha!" Joey roared. He hoisted another Prius over his head, over his horns, heaving it through the window of a coffee shop. In the plaza of the building where Samantha worked, humans, elves, and orcs ran for cover, screaming with shrill, hysterical voices. Joey loved that. *"Samanthaaaa!"*

An officer mounted on a bay mare came cantering up the concrete steps.

"Sir!" She was half shouting for backup into a walkie-talkie, drawing her gun with her free hand. "Sir, put the vehicle *down*!"

Joey hoisted the car above his head and flung it at the officer. The horse squealed, its steel shoes scattering sparks on the flagstones. The officer went flying over its haunches, landing with a crack on the pavement.

"*Enough!*"

The word rang like a gunshot through the plaza. In front of the revolving doors stood Samantha and Nathan. Samantha held her laptop in her arms, like some pagan priestess holding out a blood offering to a god of wood and stone.

"Samantha . . ." Joey growled, tossing his horns. He flipped one of the picnic tables for good measure. "You fucked me up, Samantha. That video game. I know it was yooooou . . ."

"Yes," Samantha said softly. She walked down into the plaza, her eyes never moving from his face. "Yes, it was me."

"You're gonna fix it, you cunt."

"Why?" Nathan bristled, stepping in front of Samantha. The little fistfucker had gotten balls somewhere. In the afternoon gloom—the surrounding buildings were too high to allow any sunlight into the plaza—Nathan looked like a joke. Green Lantern T-shirt and black glasses worn unironically, a wallet chain peeking over the pocket of his Target-brand cargo shorts, fucking *Doc Martens*—Joey could've bought and sold fifty of Nathan, and bench-pressed his ass, too.

"Nathan, you fucking chode," Joey snarled. "You're fucking her, aren't you, you fat piece of—"

"Jesus, dude, no. Don't be a cliché."

"*Fix meee!*" Spit and snot flew from Joey's mouth and nostrils, catching on his tusks with a spatter.

"Why should we?" Nathan snarled. "So you can be king of shit hill again? Be a classist asshole? A fucking racist? So you can treat women like shit?"

"I'm not racist—*Samantha's black!*" Joey roared. He ripped a fire hydrant out of the ground for emphasis.

"Dude," said Nathan, fingers pressing his temples, eyes closed.

Joey roared at all of them, roared up the scent of sewage

and dead pigeons from his guts. Tiny puffs of feather, half-decayed with stomach acid, splattered the flagstones. They were getting off topic.

"*Give me back my body,* Samantha!" Joey bellowed. "You don't get to *do* this to me!"

"You do this to other people," Samantha said quietly. "You treat other people like games and toys and *crap*, Joey. You have no empathy. *None.*"

"That's the luck of the *fucking draw*!" Joey boomed, wrenching a tree out of the carefully sculpted plaza garden and smashing the windshield of another car. "I *worked* to be where I am! All I did was play a *fucking video game*!"

"You played a game that was rigged against almost everyone else and then bragged about how well you played," Nathan spat. "It was time to show you a *better* game."

"I am going to rip your fucking guts out, Samantha," Joey hissed, rancid breath bubbling out between his rubbery lips. "I am going to make you eat Nathan's fucking heart."

"You want me to help you, Joey?" Samantha murmured. The laptop was open and humming in her arms.

"I didn't ask for this!" Joey screamed. Rage boiled like heat in his chest, the old heat that he loved so much. "I didn't choose this!"

He shook the car about his head like King fucking Kong.

"*TURN. THE FUCKING. VIDEO GAME. OFF.*"

"Okay, Joey," Samantha whispered. Her eyes were huge and shiny—Joey almost thought she was crying, but he was wrong. "I'll turn the program off."

Samantha's nails were clattering over the keys—such a little sound, but ringing in the petrified silence of the plaza.

Warmth started to spread through Joey's body—that perfect, clean warmth that he treasured, the last time he'd felt safe, the last time he'd felt certain. The green tinge was soaking away from his skin. The folds of flesh were tightening, hardening back to human. His tusks slunk back into his jaws. His hands were pale once more, the nails, the goddamn nails unmanicured and natural—

"Good, you fucking bitch," Joey snarled, "you'd better—"

The strength evaporated from Joey's arms.

On the coroner's report, Joey Connor was six two and 179 pounds. His race was Caucasian and his gender was cis-male.

His cause of death was listed as "crushed by falling vehicle."

The results of his drug test were being processed; the coroner suspected PCP to account for the bursts of strength during which eyewitnesses claimed Connor had thrown several cars and vomited up the remains of raw birds.

There were, of course, no such things as orcs.

His girlfriend, Samantha Asante, identified the body.

"So," said Nathan, in the ringing silence of his Greenpoint living room. If the stars were out, it was too bright in the city to see them.

"So," echoed Samantha. She took a long drink from a brown bottle, leaned back against Nathan's kitchen counter.

Nathan tried again. "He's the third test subject to die."

"He's the first one to deserve it," Samantha answered. Toward the end of the sentence, she tried to make her tone apologetic, but it rang false. She didn't bother to try again.

"We're gonna get reamed for letting him get seen while he was hulking out," said Nathan.

Samantha was looking at the city beyond the windows. He

couldn't tell if she was thinking about their bosses or about Joey fucking Connor.

"We have a lot of players, Nate," Samantha said at last. "Anyone who accepted the terms and conditions saw him wearing the new human skins and never had a memory of him as anything else. Anyone who didn't just saw a douchey-looking white guy."

"But when we turned him into an orc—"

"The people in the plaza saw whoever they wanted to demonize, hopped up on drugs," Samantha said. It sounded rehearsed. She paused, as if she expected him to question her again. "And the woman he spoke to at the shop saw him as just some kind of human. Joey saw the skins we made him see—the ads, the elves, all that nonsense. Sure, there'll be some conflicting eyewitness reports, but dead is dead. Someone in overhead will straighten out any paperwork. Reprogram what's necessary."

Nathan wondered, not for the first time, what Samantha really looked like. Programmers could change their own stats, just as easily as they could change the stats of anyone who agreed to the terms and conditions and submitted a DNA sample—though that last bit was a little less aboveboard than anything but the finest print acknowledged. Samantha had gathered enough of Joey's DNA in the last few weeks of their relationship, had brought it to engineering and begun to play Joey's character.

The game had done the rest.

Nathan still wasn't sure if technology or black fucking magic ran the whole thing, but he knew he was relieved to be on the side that called the shots.

"We've got millions of users and more every day. Maybe

next round of terms and conditions, we load up the empathy stats on people," he suggested. "Get into personality modification, not just physical—"

"If someone lives in another person's skin, and sees how awful it is," Samantha said in a voice so soft that Nathan felt a jolt of alarm, "and the only lesson they take away isn't '*We need to become kinder as a species*' but '*I need to make sure I'm powerful and secure forever*' . . ."

She fixed him with a direct stare.

"I'm not sure fucking with human nature will do much good."

Nathan felt gooseflesh on the back of his neck. Sometimes—very rarely, but sometimes—he wondered if Samantha was even human. He wondered if the world he saw and felt and touched around him was even real at all—but he didn't know, and he didn't like to wonder. He liked the system; he liked his place in it. And with each round of terms and conditions, the game was getting better. *They* were getting better.

"Learn how it feels to be someone else for a day, snap under the pressure, go on a rampage," Nathan quipped. The room had suddenly grown too tense, too close.

Samantha didn't laugh.

"He was only in the program for one day and he tried to go on a killing spree," Samantha said. She was studying the movie posters on his walls, all cheap things he'd bought at lawn sales in college. "Imagine if he'd been in the program for two."

"It's a dangerous game." Nathan shrugged.

"Did you agree to this *entire thing* just to make that pun?" Samantha asked. She seemed to come out of some private memory, suddenly present, suddenly human again. She toasted him with her cider and he eagerly clinked bottles.

Now or never.

"Do you—I mean, people sign up willingly," Nathan stumbled. "Everyone signs up willingly. But when market research goes and collects the DNA samples in secret—goes through trash, gets medical records—and we start to tinker with the stats, do you ever feel—"

She was looking at him with those perfect, mirrored eyes.

"Do you ever feel we're crossing a line?" he finished. "They aren't all like Joey."

"They would be if they could," Samantha answered. "Human beings are never happy unless everyone has a dollar, they have two, and then they start setting their sights on three."

She finished her cider and began peeling at the label, looking at her reflection in the dark glass.

"Yeah," she repeated in that soft, eerie voice. "They'd all be like Joey fucking Connor, if they could."

Marguerite K. Bennett is a comic book writer from Richmond, Virginia, who currently lives in New York City. She attended the Maggie L. Walker Governor's School and received her MFA in creative writing from Sarah Lawrence College in 2013. She has worked for DC Comics, Marvel, BOOM! Studios, and IDW on projects ranging from *Batman* and *X-Men* to Fox's *Sleepy Hollow*. She loves Disney movies, superheroes, and body horror. She has been fortunate enough to see more than a million copies of her work published.

PLEASE CONTINUE

Chris Kluwe

THIS IS A TRUE STORY.

Gotta run faster. Gap ahead of me is gonna close in less than a second, masses slamming together, grinding anything caught between into paste. Can't afford to fail here.

I've come too far, spent too much time.

Push off the enemy to my right, use his momentum for an extra burst of speed. He falls to the ground, caught off balance by my sudden move. Spin past a foe rearing up on the left, feel his arms rake down my side in passing. A strip of fabric tears free from the material covering my body armor. It flutters in the harsh glare of the spotlights above, plummets like a dying sparrow. My only thoughts are on the scene ahead. Titans shift and grapple, cartoonish muscles bulging under the strain. The gap inches shut.

Sound swells into a crescendo, roaring trumpets of cacophony surrounding the battlefield. It is deafening static. It is soundless white noise. Colors run into a blurred confusion, sensory overload dial turned all the way to eleven. I am at one with the madness, its drumbeat my dance partner.

Leg muscles tighten, load, release. I soar into the gap, arm outstretched, willing my way through in the milliseconds remaining. I can make it. I *will* make it. I've come too far.

The pressure comes crashing down to either side, Red Sea walls making a mockery of faith.

I am crushed.

I am drowning.

I am fading to black.

<Please continue.>

I am back at the beginning, a novice, training with the other members of my cohort. We puff our chests and preen, words sure and confident, outrageous displays of plumage failing to conceal coltish knees and elbows. Every one of us believes we will make it all the way, travel an unimaginable distance to the final stage and display our prowess.

I know that many of us, practically all of us, will fail, but I *know* that I will make it, relentlessly grinding my way to success. The goal may be distant, the obstacles many, but the hero always prevails.

I'm the hero of my own story, but others tell their stories as well.

When I first meet the others of my group, we do not know each other, our interactions nervous and fumbling. Paul, cocky and dark-haired, quick to take command but unsure what to do once he has it. Ryan, older, with laughing blue eyes, more experienced than the rest of us. He's been training for longer, and it shows, but he doesn't like the newer members. Scott and Antoine, tall and thin, locked in discussion, going over potential strategies to help them succeed in our next encounter, focused only on the task at hand. Others, whose faces fade into blurs, not background scenery, but not registering either. All around us the air rings with the sound of constant training—strikes, blocks, collisions, the barked instructions of our trainers, a constant grindstone pressed against us all, honing raw edges into sharp instruments.

I am not yet used to the chaos of this game.

The instructors see me as a specialist, my job to extricate the group from adverse situations at key times. They say my potential is powerful, maybe powerful enough to reach the highest levels, but first, they say, that potential needs to be actualized, harnessed to my will, guided by mind instead of instinct. I came late to this endeavor, and there is still much I don't understand. Arcane phrasing and terminology, appropriate responses to situations—the rules of the game, what is and isn't permitted within the confines of our construct.

I need more experience.

Hour after hour, day after day, week after week, I complete mindless quests with my compatriots. Some involve running back and forth from one trainer to another, trying to fulfill their capricious whims. They make us jump up and down, fetch random objects, dodge simulated attacks, march in line with each other. Boring, meaningless work, or so I think at the time.

Other quests have us skirmishing against weaker members of our group, taking what little reward we can in defeating an inferior opponent. It is meant to prepare us for the blitzing rush of a real encounter, but it is tough for us to take them seriously. We all know each other, we're all friends. Battles can be simulated, planned, obsessed over, yet the experience gain is minimal, because what is at stake?

Nothing . . . yet.

The days pass, hot sun constantly beating down on us, and

the grind continues. Gradually, our once chafing load of armor and equipment becomes bearable, then unnoticeable. We run and dive and roll in it like a second skin, adapting to the cumbersome padding like hatchlings learning to fly. We hit each other and the ground, frequently, acclimating our bodies to the jarring sensation of combat. The pain of impact lessens with each successive blow, though it never really goes away—a shuddering jolt that shocks the body and mind into a momentary stunned silence, neurons overloading and shorting out, briefly blinding to black until the world snaps back into focus.

I do not relish the training, the monotonous grind of it all, but it is something to be endured, so that the greater goal may be achieved. So I keep telling myself, day after endless day.

Eventually, we have a real encounter.

We start our preparation with unfamiliar rituals that have the trappings of long use—making sure our gear is secure, armor settled comfortably, our mobility unhindered. Some members of the group chant blessings and prayers, others dance around or crack jokes. We all approach the upcoming unknown in different ways, and who can say one way is better than another? The important thing is that we feel ready to play our parts as best we can, confident in our as yet untested abilities.

I choose to read a book, distracting myself with fantastic stories of other worlds to help pass the time until everyone is ready. It confuses some of the others, the pursuit of lore not an activity they normally favor. I've proven my worth so far, however, so they accept my quirks with few comments, and soon we group up, traveling to the designated field of conflict. We stake out our territory, plan our defenses, and then we see the enemy.

They are outfitted similarly to us, garbed in padded armor and helmets, but they wear garish colors, bright oranges and deep blacks merging together like tiger stripes, nothing at all like our muted reds and blues. We eye each other across the unbroken expanse of grass, various objective markings littering its surface. My thoughts are muddled, eager, focused, hesitant. An arbiter, charged with keeping the rules sacrosanct, calls us to attention. The conflict begins.

It is nothing like training against immobile dummies or running across empty fields. The speed, the sounds, the lights . . . everything blurs into kaleidoscopic madness, focusing on individual actions an impossibility. I've never experienced anything like it before in my life. It is hard enough keeping track of what I am supposed to do, let alone take in the battle as a whole. I forget nearly everything I've been taught, relying instead on pure adrenaline and instinct. I feel like I am not the only one to do so.

Fortunately, our foe is appropriate to our experience level, neophytes much like ourselves, a challenge, to be sure, but one not insurmountable. We clash back and forth, one side gaining a momentary advantage then ceding ground to the other, energy reserves and stamina slowly draining for both. I make mistakes at first, unfamiliar with how my skills and abilities slot in with the rest of the group, but I adapt and learn quickly, forcing myself to keep up with those more seasoned. The alternative is shame, ignominy, failure—an unacceptable outcome.

We emerge from the encounter, battered yet victorious, our leaders pleased with our initial performance. They highlight areas we need to work on, combos and counters we could execute better, and so we return to the grind, preparing for the next opponent. Our reputation rises in the local area, inhabitants cheering our deeds in song and word. There is still much work to be done, but we're definitely getting stronger, more experienced. Leveling up.

The campaign continues for several more months, foe after foe testing our strength. Most battles we win, some we lose, but we learn from them all, accumulating experience along the way. We settle into a routine—plan, train, fight.

Campaign season ends in the winter, our final battle a mud-soaked affair that leaves both sides aching. We are glad for the respite, a chance to rest our weary bodies and minds. We know that, come summer, the battles continue once more.

<Please continue.>

It is three years later. I am now one of the seasoned veterans, laughing at the newcomers fumbling through their drills. Paul, Scott, Antoine, and others of my cohort laugh with me, all of us remembering our own initiation into the game, the nervous steps of boys who thought themselves men. How long ago that initiation seems, blindly unaware youths struggling to learn the nuances of our craft. So close in time, yet so far in attitude, in awareness. Now we hunger for the field of combat, eager to taste glory.

My own armor sits lightly, a hardly noticeable part of my body, and I move through my battle motions fluidly, confidently. We strike swiftly, savagely, bringing defeat to almost all who oppose us, a machine whose gears mesh seamlessly with each other. It is a sight to behold, our faction supporters cheering us to greater and greater heights. Our campaign almost reaches the endgame of our particular level, but we fall short in the penultimate encounter, driven back by a supe-

rior opponent. The loss is tough to bear, but we surpassed all
expectations, so it is not as bitter as it could have been. Some
of us have even acquitted ourselves well enough to continue
to the next stage.

I am one of those fortunate few able to continue playing,
now that my time in this zone is over. The clan no longer has
room for me, but that is the circle of life. Succeed and move
on, or fail and move on. Either way, the timer does not reset.

Luckily for me, one of the larger clans has taken notice
of my skills, invited me to join their group. I accepted, of
course—it is, after all, one step closer to that ultimate stage,
the final level that only fools dare dream of conquering, and
it is, of course, the only way to continue playing. Individually, I've earned accolades, honors, the notice of a nation, but
whether it will be enough to maintain my success at the next
level, no one can say. I continue to hope, and more important,
I continue to gather experience.

<Please continue.>

Another five years pass. My initial service with the new clan
does not go as well as I wished—stuck behind more seasoned
members, I am relegated to a reserve role, brought in only
sparingly. I chafe at the restrictions, but it seems I must wait
for an opportunity to present itself. Along the way, I make
more friends among the squad—Riley, Ed, Aaron, and more.
We crack jokes, keep each other's spirits up during the interminable drills, debate philosophy and religion while battle
rages around us. We know that we are being driven to a greater
purpose, but our concern is staying sane amid the madness.

Camaraderie is not just an obscure job description.

At last, I get my chance, after three years of loathsome

idleness. The warrior ahead of me moves to other ventures, his time in this arena *finally* run out, and I act swiftly to make the most of my opportunity.

I only have two years to demonstrate my talents, but the chances to do so are numerous, and once again, I garner accolades and trophies.

Finally, I take part in the large engagements, our struggles witnessed by hundreds of thousands of people, and though we fight valiantly, we are not nearly as successful as we would like. I cannot let that dissuade me. I ignore the struggles of those around me and focus on my own skills, working to polish them to a razor's edge. I know that representatives of the elite clans are watching, taking notes on who they might deem worthy to enter their hallowed ranks, and I *will* be one of those celebrated few chosen to wear the colors of the Bear, the Lion, the Hawk, or the Raven, or perhaps another clan that I'm not yet familiar with. The competition will be fierce, but that makes the reward all the sweeter.

At the end of the second year, having done everything in my power to show those watching that I am a worthy selection, I find myself wondering, Will it be enough? Is the experience I've accrued sufficient to level me to the highest realms?

The selection process is months away. Those months pass slowly.

\<Please continue.\>

I continue my training while I await the gathering of the elite clans, held every year in the spring. There, they choose new members, redress their ranks, whittling down the pool of qualified applicants, a number in the tens of thousands, to slightly less than eighteen hundred names by autumn's bite.

Those so chosen will have a chance to compete on the greatest of stages, avatars of battle and valor, sacrificing their health and sanity for glory and riches beyond measure. It is the highest level one can aspire to in the game, a humbling fraternity of excellence, where millions know your name.

I am one of those chosen.

However, I am not yet at Valhalla's peak. Another obstacle course awaits me, competition against those who would usurp what I view as my rightful position in the clan. We struggle against each other, day after day, trying to convince those in charge to choose us to enact their plans. "Pick me," I scream with my actions, "my talents are clearly superior. I can lead us to victory." Beside me, my friends/opponents/colleagues attempt the same. We battle for the pleasure of those watching the screen, because it is all we know how to do.

Ultimately, the clan releases me. They feel that I am too unpolished, my skill set not yet at a place where they are comfortable utilizing it in the swirling chaos of combat. They wish me luck, but I will not have a place there.

Is this the end of my dreams?

It cannot be. I have traveled too far, done too much for it to end like this.

<Please continue.>

A message arrives. The first clan did not want me, this is true, but another clan does. Fierce warriors from the north, they offer me a spot in their host, their only requirement I perform to the utmost of my abilities, else they will find my replacement.

I consider it a fair bargain. It is the same standard I hold myself accountable to every day.

Battle after battle, I step onto the field with my compatriots, knowing that even the smallest error could see me gone. At this level, mistakes are measured in milliseconds, and only the sharpest of reflexes ensure our survival. I acquit myself admirably for most of the campaign, but then catastrophe strikes during an otherwise routine engagement.

I take an arrow to the knee.

The pain is grievous, but there is no time to rest, no time to heal. The campaign continues, and if I do not keep up, then no one will mourn my passing. Time enough to recover once winter sets in. I force my way onward, hiding my weakness as best I can, for if the enemy scents it, there will be no respite.

Mercifully, the campaign ends one month later, and my first year on the great stage lies in the history books, my name engraved on the leaderboards for eternity. Now I must focus my attention on getting healthy. The game waits for no one at this level, and our next campaign is scant months away. I consult with our healers, allow them to apply poultices and potions. One year is barely an eyeblink, and I mean to endure.

<Please continue.>

Seven more years pass, each with their own trials and tribulations. New leaders come and go, jockeying to facilitate their own rise in the strategic leaderboards. Political struggles wax and wane, bringing attention in blinding waves, and then just as suddenly, receding to soft whispers. Heroes of legend join us, then leave, some auspiciously, some ignominiously. Our seat of power collapses in a blinding snowstorm, leaving us stranded and adrift, warriors without a home, and throughout it all, we train, and we battle, collecting scars and wounds like golden coins from the crowds.

Conflict is our bane, our boon, our very reason for existence, and we dare not give it up, because then what meaning would our lives have? Without the many-thousand-voiced roar of the mob, what would we hear? Without the crackling electron's hiss, echoing through merciless glass lenses that capture our souls so that others may consume them, what would we see? Without the grinding pain of bone scraping against bone, muscle tearing from flesh, blood running from nose and eyes and ears, what would we feel?

Are we but puppets, set to dance on our own private stage while all around us cheer at our plight?

The questions echo through my head like concussive sparks, and I wonder if any of my compatriots feel the same. I know my time might be coming to an end—lately, I've refused to play the game by the unspoken rules we're all expected to abide by. Oh, not the rules on the battlefield—there I still perform my tasks with diligence and grace, unlocking achievement after achievement. No, the rules I break are the ones you find in any game, and every game.

"Don't ruin my fun."

<Please cont—

Turtling, zerg rushing, net decking, camping doorways, and nade spamming spawns, all perfectly acceptable by the rules of the game, and all universally reviled because *now you see the game for what it is*. A collection of mechanics, dancing numbers, sleight of hand designed to fool you into thinking that this make-believe world really matters when in actuality, it doesn't, and once the veil is pierced, it's very hard to go back to that ignorant bliss.

Witnessing the voice behind the curtain is a sobering moment for everyone.

<Please con—

Frothing rage explosions on Internet forum boards, leading to multi-thread Dumpster fires, brawls in the stands and
outside stadiums, people stabbing and shooting each other
over the arbitrary antics of keyboard warriors and spandex-
clad manchildren who we hold up as role models while teachers are forced to pay for their own classroom books because
funding schools is *boring*. *These* are the scorecards of the games
we play, but we don't want to acknowledge them, because it
would ruin our fun. Why should we have to care about things
that matter when we're playing/watching a game? Life's hard
enough as it is, right? Let us eat our lotus in peace.

<Please co—

That is the rule I broke, at the end of my decades-long
quest, at the pinnacle of achievement in my field. I trespassed
against the unspoken rule that governs all our games. I dared
to bring something that mattered into what many regarded
as a sanctuary from thought. I shattered the illusion that so
much time and effort had gone into building, like subverting
a comfortable story with a jarring syntactic break.

I ruined their fun. Quest failed.

<Please c—

Why did I do it? Maybe it was boredom—the boredom
when one realizes they've achieved everything they can
achieve in a limited field. An ennui of the soul, bread and cir-
cuses no longer sufficient to pass the time. All games grow
boring after a while. Can boredom be a catalyst for change?
Perhaps.

Maybe it was an awakening, the realization that a game
is just that and life is more than a game, no matter the per-
ceived value others place upon that game. All our constructs,

our make-believe worlds, filled with arbitrary rules—how important we think they are! Yet, when we break everything down, we see their illusory selves, shadows dancing on a cavern wall. Not an atom of justice, nor a molecule of mercy, and somehow, life goes on. The only equality, that which we're willing to make, and oh, how hard the making of it is!

Maybe it was simply a wish for things to be different, better, a small voice crying out in rage against the vast uncaring depths of the game, angry at the ceaseless grind. When our very existence conspires to drag us back to nothingness, why should we help it with its dirty entropic business?

<Please—

Games are fun, yes, but when we let ourselves sink too deeply into the lie, when we abnegate our responsibilities to reality and overreact to meaningless contests or digital fantasies, then games are the drug that kills societies, and not in the reloadable, wrath from above, *SimCity* kind of way. When we value stadiums over sewer mains, forty-man raids over feeding our children, political theater and news-as-entertainment instead of rational discourse about the many problems people would rather play games than hear, well, the barbarians are gonna come a knockin' sooner rather than later, and a single archer garrison isn't going to cut it.

<Please stop using games to hide from reality. Your favorite football team is just a collection of overexercised men giving each other violent hugs. Teachers and scientists are role models, but you'd never know it from the idolatry that occurs every Sunday. Give some stadium money to infrastructure instead of insanely huge JumboTrons. Your children will thank you for it.

<Please accept video games that try to tell a message. If

someone puts an issue that you personally find uncomfortable into a game, like depression, or feminism, it means they thought it was important enough to risk their jobs to do so. Screaming that *"GAEMS AREN'T THE PLACE"* does a disservice to video games, those who create them, and those of us who play them. Any medium is a valid avenue of social expression.

<Please don't be afraid to break your bubble, venture out of your cave. Try games that challenge you to think, even if those thoughts may not be ones you want to address. Press through your discomfort.>

And always . . .

<Please continue. Life is full of new experience. Go forth and level, because the game always ends too soon.>

———————

Chris Kluwe is a former NFL punter and a writer, onetime violin prodigy, rights advocate, and obsessive gamer. Kluwe graduated from UCLA with a double major in history and political science and played for the Minnesota Vikings for eight years. He is the author of the acclaimed essay collection *Beautifully Unique Sparkleponies: On Myths, Morons, Free Speech, Football, and Assorted Absurdities* and has been profiled in *The New York Times*, *The Wall Street Journal*, *USA Today*, and *Salon*. Kluwe has appeared at TED, discussing the topic of the future of virtual reality technology and its connection to building a more empathetic society, and he regularly makes presentations at major corporations, universities, and human rights organizations.

CREATION SCREEN

Rhianna Pratchett

START GAME
Click

CHOOSE REALM
Click

CREATE CHARACTER
Click

You gave me life with a click. Such a simple, inconsequential thing for you, but to me it meant everything.

I remember floating in a void of nothingness—a howling darkness curling around me, cold and desolate. I didn't know enough to be afraid back then. Although for a long time afterward the very thought of being left in that place filled me with a creeping, lonely terror.

I looked down and saw that my torso and limbs were partially encased in badly tanned and crudely stitched leather. It was barely enough to keep me decent, let alone protect me. But I still remember the smell; warm and mellow with a hint of cheap fish oil. I took some comfort in it back then, as a brief distraction from the emptiness around me. It was at least something real and tangible.

Now the smell of cheap leather turns my stomach.

I try to move, but my limbs are caught fast. Not tight, nor painfully, but as if I am gently held by unseen hands. I scan my surroundings, trying to find anything that would give me a clue as to the nature of the place I find myself in. Eventually my eyes fix upon a pinpoint of light buried among the blackness. It expands slowly into a shimmering portal of color, and then your face fades into view. It is a thing of beauty to me. Without quite knowing why, my heart flutters with hope.

When you begin to touch me, it is not with your hands but with your mind. It's warming at first and I'm almost pathetically grateful for it. But when you start to shape me, it hurts—as if every bone in my body is being broken and reset over and over again. My mind reels in horror as you expand and contract my proportions in front of my eyes. But I have no voice to cry out.

In order to distract myself from the pain, I fix my eyes on your face, seeking to understand what kind of monster would do this to me. I study each pore, count each eyelash, and watch the movement of supple skin across bone. I observe your countenance—brow furrowed with concentration, tongue tip pushing through the side of your lips. I can see that this is serious to you. This matters. And even through the agony . . . I somehow feel special.

Nothing about me is left untouched. You manipulate my height, girth, and even chest size. That last one was particularly painful, especially as you are rife with indecision. Back and forth you go until I'm sure that my eyes must be watering. But you can't see the tears. Or perhaps you just don't care.

Of course now that I have gotten to know you better, and studied your anatomy in almost as much detail as you have studied mine, I realize that you were sculpting me in your own image. As if you were a god of old, creating new life from your own reflection, your own divinity.

But even if I'd had that knowledge back then, I doubt it would have been anything more than cold comfort. Pain is still pain. And in truth you were a fickle creator—unable to decide whether I should represent reality or how you desire reality to be. Maybe this is just how creation works. Do gods normally concern themselves with how tall they are or the circumference of their thighs? Is the act of creation always about the desired self? I have very little frame of reference for such things.

I must admit that I would have preferred a physique with a little more muscle and heft to it. I have the growing realization that whatever lies beyond this place will require it. I know deep inside that I do not want to go beyond the blackness—if that is indeed what you have in store for me—with legs like tree saplings and arms that could barely lift their own weight.

But once you have shaped my body to suit your whims, you move on to my hair. I was born into this murky darkness with locks very much like your own. In the future I will hear you refer to our hair as "unremarkable brown." I had hoped that you might leave it be for that very reason, and that the pain in my body would not be joined by the throbbing of every hair follicle. But I was very wrong. For in this regard you immediately shed all pretense of molding me in your likeness.

Instead you flit through an array of colors that flicker around my face and eyes. Eventually you settle on an azure blue; a turquoise explosion the color of the ocean when sunlight hits it.

At first I think it's pretty. It's certainly a marked contrast to the lifeless world around me. Later, I will come to realize that you might as well have painted a target on my back.

After what feels like an eternity, you finish your work. I watch you studying me, your creation, and I see you smile. Instinctively, I feel the corners of my own mouth start to turn up in response. Despite all the pain, I see happiness in your eyes and it gladdens my own heart. There will be many times when I will live for that smile, and many more when I will pity it.

The last thing you do is place a long, flat piece of metal in my hand. Its sharp edge glints in the light from your portal. It's unfamiliar to me, but nevertheless, my fingers instinctively curl around the blunt end. It feels good in my hand. Reassuring. Like it belongs there. I begin to relax a little. The pain is starting to fade now. And despite the harshness of your touch, I begin to feel that I must really mean something to you for you to take this much trouble shaping me.

And then suddenly you've gone. Just like that. Vanished. The portal of light closes. As the howling blackness returns, I begin to panic. How could you pay such careful attention to your creation one minute and then abandon it the next? Perhaps this is some kind of punishment. But I was good, I thought. I endured your painful, clumsy touches without a word, even though I was screaming inside. Maybe I didn't blink back enough tears. Perhaps you saw and it alarmed you.

A vast sadness begins to fill me. Terrified thoughts run through my head. Was I wrong? Did your obsessive crafting of my every detail really mean nothing to you? How could you bring me so much pain and then discard me like I was a passing fancy?

But I can do nothing but float there alone in the darkness.

I sleep, but it's fitful and restless. Every time I wake it takes me a few seconds to realize that I really have opened my eyes. Black upon black. But each time that I do, I wish I hadn't. It makes me ache inside far worse than anything you've done to me so far. It would have been better if you'd just left me to the nothingness. That at least would have been kinder. Looking back, I suspect that would have been as much of a kindness to you as to me. But even if you'd known, I doubt you would have done things differently.

It's only when I have resigned myself to the fact that I may never move from this spot—that this is all my existence will ever be—that your face appears again. Brighter and cleaner, and as if you have absolutely no idea of what you've put me through. My heart soars and then plummets at the thought that perhaps you're about to start the process all over again. More expansion and contraction. More pushes and pulls. I harden myself. I can stand it, all of it, I think. Just as long as you don't leave me again.

ENTER REALM
Click

Suddenly the darkness blurs around me. Colors start to bleed in and I find myself born into a world of green. Trees, grass, bushes. Nature bursts forth in every direction. I have emerged into a verdant woodland in the full throes of summer foliage. The assault to my senses is too much. I find myself utterly overwhelmed and fight the urge to fall to my knees and vomit. And all at once that dark place doesn't seem so bad anymore. I desperately want to crawl back, but I know you won't let me.

But as I see your face calmly regarding me from the portal behind me, the urge to wretch leaves me and is replaced with a burning need to make you proud somehow.

When you direct me forward into this new green world, I do so without hesitation. And as I take those first few tentative steps, I feel the sun upon my face. As my walk turns into a run, the breeze begins to caress my blue hair. It feels utterly wonderful. Like freedom.

Behind every corner there is a new sight or sound to be discovered. Everything is a revelation to me. I find myself fervently wishing that you would just slow down and give me more time to absorb and examine my surroundings, but there's clearly somewhere you want me to be.

You direct me toward what I can only assume is some kind of village. Smoke curls out of dumpy stone dwellings dotted among the greenery. Birds sing sweetly in the treetops, butterflies flitter among the flowers, and deer graze by limpid pools. It's serene and tranquil . . . as if it were constructed to be nothing more.

I approach with high hopes that perhaps this place will be my new home. But although the cheery, apple-cheeked women and leather-handed men who inhabitant it are friendly, they don't open their doors to me. Instead they tell me that they are in the midst of various troubles. The rising population of aggressive creatures in the area seems to be at the top of their list. And although I am a perfect stranger in their midst, they ask if I can help them.

I'm flattered by their confidence in my capabilities, but instead of allowing me to think carefully about my next course of action, perhaps sleep on it, you direct me right toward the offending fauna. And as the creature leaps toward me—claws unleashed and teeth bared—I realize that the flat, sharpened metal in my hand is a weapon. I have no time to let that sink in before you force me to bring it down hard upon my aggressor's skull.

A few more strikes and the beast is dead. I'm shocked at this act—a life cut down by my very hand. It's horrifying and I feel sick again. But as I stare at the creature's inert body it vanishes . . . my crime erased in front of my very eyes. I hardly have time to gather myself before your keenness takes over and you're pointing me toward other of its kin. I begin to run and suddenly my sword is raised to bring it down upon it as I had done to its brother.

I lose count of how many I've killed, and yet still their numbers never seem to dwindle. Now I see why the villagers were so concerned: truly this is an unnatural state. Nevertheless, they seem quite happy with my attempts to aid them. They even give me a piece of apple pie, and a pair of boots. Well-worn, and slightly pungent, but I'm grateful for them nevertheless.

I sit down to eat the pie—a perfect slice, juicy and still warm. Yet as I hold it, the pie appears to pass directly into my stomach without touching my lips. I gain the sensation of being full without the satisfaction of tasting it. To say I am disappointed is an understatement. And when I see you yourself enjoying your own sustenance on the other side of the portal, it makes my mouth water uncontrollably. Are you *trying* to torture me?

Before long, I'm up and exploring again. It's busy work. Everyone around here seems to have something for me to do. Fetching and killing mainly. And although I've seen a few other capable-looking adventurers about, the shops are constantly running low on pelts, skulls, and various herbs.

I honestly don't see why they can't seem to manage to

do any of these tasks themselves. They clearly have weapons (since I am eventually presented with one in thanks for collecting some particularly pungent fungus) but they are very reluctant to use them. You, on the other hand, seem only too keen for me to facilitate their every desire unquestioningly. And so we move from place to place, action to action, reward to reward.

As the hours and days roll by we explore mountains and caverns, seas and forests together. But still I remain confused as to why you wish to have me explore this world in the first place. For beyond the portal that separates us I can see that you have a whole world of your own to explore. I spend a great deal of time pondering this issue. Perhaps you have explored every inch of it already and it simply holds no interest for you anymore.

It's only on the occasions when you step away from the portal but leave it open that I can get more of a glimpse into the enticing world of my creator. It's not picture-perfect like this one, but messy and unkempt. It is textured and substantial. It looks as though one could take an action there and not know what the outcome would be. It is through those observations that I begin to see how different the world you've brought me to really is.

The very first thing I saw of your world—aside from your face, of course—were the leaves outside your window. As they fluttered in the breeze I realized they looked very different from the ones in this realm. In this place, every brick, leaf, and blade of grass is shaped perfectly. Some almost copies of the last. Nothing is shriveled, chipped, or out of place. Not like in your world, which seems to embrace chaos.

One time, when you stepped away to take sustenance, I pulled a leaf off a bush and watched it disappear in my hands, only to see a perfect copy sprout from its stalk. I tried again and the same thing happened. But beyond the portal I could see the seasons change and watched as the leaves outside your window yellowed, curled up, and died.

Life is fragile in your world. It is fleeting and imperfect. But its closeness to death makes it feel much more alive. Not like here, where death, I have discovered, is not only not the end—it is merely an inconvenience. If I "die," I find myself locked inside a cold gray spirit-plane until I can locate my fallen corpse, whereupon I reinhabit it and spring back to life as if nothing had happened.

I do everything I can to please you in the hope that you will keep me safe. But I cannot help but think that the carelessness you sometimes show toward my life and limb is bordering on cruelty. Like that time you left me in the corner of a scorpion pit, while you answered a call of nature. By the time you'd returned, they had respawned and I'd been stung more than a dozen times. You found me lying there while they skittered over me, my limbs coursing with their toxic poison as it gradually dissolved my insides.

That was definitely among my worst deaths. And of my deaths there have been many: eaten by sharks, gored by boars, chewed by lions, impaled on spikes, crushed by boulders, boiled by steam, flayed alive by dark magic, drowned by mermaids, and, most embarrassing in light of all the rest, fallen from high places.

Although this world you have brought me into is not entirely unpleasant, I have come to find that there is very little substance to it. Like eating the food here, there is cause and then there is effect, but very little in between. I quest, I kill, I craft. I go through the same actions time and time again, until I am so bored, I could scream. But your attention is unwavering. You are only watching me in this world, yet you seem to enjoy the spectacle more than I enjoy the participation.

In the early days I used to be so grateful that my creator was willing to pay so much attention to me, but as the weeks and months roll on, I begin to wonder what it is you are getting out of all of this. Is such simplicity a comfort to you? Do you not have quests of your own to complete? Can you not see your own world change outside your window? Do you not wish to be a part of that?

Despite your many tortures of me, I worry for you more than you know. You dress me in all manner of finery and jewels, ornate armor, and exquisite trinkets, yet you rarely attend to yourself, to the point of self-neglect. And it's not just that your eating habits have changed—sometimes you don't even make it to your bed to sleep; instead you lose consciousness directly in front of the portal. You're so close that I can practically feel your breath on me.

I fear for you, my creator; do you know that? I fear you are in this world more than I am. I fear that you cannot see the wonders of your own anymore. I know that you are finite, just like the leaves outside your window. I see your face grown pale and drawn, and your eyes redden. You are content to see me grow in strength while you weaken. You let me live in a way that you do not.

I know I shall never escape this place. But on the brief times you leave me on my own, I dream of something real. I imagine myself sitting where you are, in your imperfect but marvelous world. And do you know the first thing I would do?

EXIT GAME

Click

Rhianna Pratchett is an award-winning, sixteen-year veteran of the video games industry who has wrestled the wild beasts of narrative for companies such as Sony, EA, Sega, 2K Games, Codemasters, and Square Enix. Her titles include *Heavenly Sword*, *Mirror's Edge*, the entire Overlord series, and the recently rebooted *Tomb Raider*. Pratchett also works in comics (notably on *Mirror's Edge* for DC and *Tomb Raider* for Dark Horse), film, and TV. She's currently on scribing duty for Square Enix's *Rise of the Tomb Raider*, *Rival Kingdoms* for Space Ape Games, and two novel-to-screen adaptations. Rhianna is codirector of the Narrativia production company and lives in London with her fiancé and a pair of neurotic tabbies.

THE FRESH PRINCE OF GAMMA WORLD

Austin Grossman

Where did The Fresh Prince of Gamma World *come from? I found it rattling around the mainframes of the antiquated computer system of Somerville Community College, where I spent two unproductive years as an information sciences major. It would have been five or ten years old by the time I saw it, but I played it to exhaustion, staying up until three or four in the morning before trudging home along Highland Avenue. The sense memory of early mornings in late November is still with me, the smell of wet leaves in damp frigid air.*

Written in outdated PASCAL, the code base was just a bunch of data and a homebrew parser for input, eccentrically architected. The game itself is uncredited.

I've searched for it now without success, but all I could recover were code fragments posted to a defunct Usenet board devoted to retro games and a user named go4it69 who did not respond to subsequent emails.

THE FRESH PRINCE
OF
GAMMA WORLD

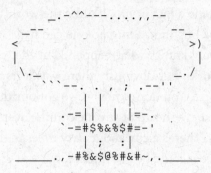

A RAINY DAY

It's raining on Gamma World. You can hear it faintly hissing against the invisible grass even if you can't see or feel it, while Wednesday afternoon F Block continues on and on but you just can't pay attention. In another dimension, right close by, heavy, warm, poisonous raindrops are falling on the concrete and broken glass and ten-foot-tall dandelions that grow where the high school once would have been.

[press space to continue]

FLASH POINT

In Gamma World, everything ended on June 22, 1979, at 11:24 p.m., when you were eleven. All over Gamma World you can find stopped clocks, broken watches, and charred newspapers showing the date. In Gamma World, they call this year Year Five. In the real world, of course, everything continued normally. You don't know how or why it happened that there are two timelines, and that you wander back and forth between them. It's become a fact of life. It's like the world is a piece of software with a bug in it, a bug no one can fix.

Nobody truly knows what happened at that crucial point in Gamma World, but obviously there was a nuclear war, or something worse. You don't know if we got our missiles off or not, but you've never heard of anyone coming over from Russia to check on us. There's a city about sixty miles to the southeast that sounds like it could be Providence, but you've never been. There's no TV or radio or Internet. Your working assumption is that the whole planet is like it is around here: primitive tribes, unnatural jungle, mutated people and animals, and rubble.

```
[s]tay in Gamma World, stay forever and fuck the
rest of it.
[g]o home and forget there was ever another world.
```

COLLATERAL DAMAGE

Maybe if you understood what caused Gamma World in the first place, you could get your regular life back. You spend a few hours there every day; it's unpredictable. Sometimes you'll round a familiar corner and the other world is just there, you'll smell it and then the sky will twist and wilt around you.

You always just barely make it back in time to keep up with regular life. Your old friends have drifted away. People think you sell drugs now or since your parents' divorce you're just too cool to hang out with regular people. Maybe this year will be different. It's a new grade, a new chance to understand what your life has become.

```
[g]o for it. You just have to try a little harder.
[f]orget it. Forget it. Just forget it.
```

BLAST PERIMETER

On weekends you go looking for clues about what happened. There are areas out in the suburbs, outside what must have been an annihilating fireball, that are nearly identical to their real-world counterparts.

This was once an office park on your world. It takes a while to walk there in Gamma World; it's hot enough that you have to take off your jacket. The only sounds are the chirping of giant insects and the crunch of your sneakers on gravel and broken glass.

A passenger bus was lifted up and thrown into the side of the building, and rests now between the third and fourth floors. You climb up and gather change out of the coinbox in Gamma World. If you time it right, on Earth you can use the money for the bus ride home.

You get the feeling you're being watched.

```
[w]ait a while, maybe they'll come out.
[i]t's time to go home.
[h]old it, is that Thomas Dewey's face on one of
those coins?
```

PRINCESS OF GAMMA WORLD

You gave up calling high school the real world when you met Melodee. You were born the same year but she seems older than you now. She remembers the explosions too, and the world before, vaguely, so she gets pre-1985 pop culture references.

She lived just a few miles from you; her parents were both physicists at MIT but she hasn't seen them since the explosion. She's noble and fierce and can fence and throw a spear. She's got tattoos on her face and you saw her kill a two-headed dog grown as large as a pony. It's pretty clear you're in love with her. She's betrothed to the chieftain's son.

Like everyone else on Gamma World, she doesn't know the normal world is still there, and you don't tell her. How can you explain it? But how can you not tell her, without lying?

Maybe if you could bring her from one to the other, there would be some point in telling her. But would that work? And here's the thing: there ought to be another Melodee, the regular one, in your world. You've tried to find her, but she doesn't remember her old address, and she probably had a different name before the crash. There's certainly nobody at school like her. But plenty of people send their kids to private school and you never even meet them.

```
[m]aybe you'll grow old here, maybe you'll come
back and a hundred years have passed.
[w]hy is it you can only talk to a girl after the
world has literally ended.
```

UNIVERSITY SECTOR

You look for ideas in the libraries and the labs at what's left of Harvard. Maybe somebody was working on something like this? The books have theories you half understand. Sure, strings vibrate, antimatter exists, quantum events happen, but there's nothing that says an entire world can split apart.

What if there was a last-minute escape plan they figured out at the Pentagon to rescue the whole reality from nuclear annihilation: just before impact they could trigger something that spawned another reality where the war hadn't happened. One world would die, but the other one would continue on like nothing happened.

That would make your reality, the one you really grew up in, the fake one, wouldn't it?

```
You [k]now in your heart this is true. Don't you.
[b]ury this truth inside you forever.
```

Or maybe that's how time works, when things go badly enough in one world, another one forms nearby. Or it could have been the missiles themselves, that they had a secret payload invented behind the Iron Curtain, that had the power to break up reality itself. But why would you be the only one to remember both worlds? Or is it just that everyone got their own Gamma World, and nobody talks about it? Perhaps you [s]hare my own creeping sense that this is the case.

FINANCIAL MELTDOWN

Evidently the bomb hit in the center of downtown Boston. It left a perfect circle roughly four miles in diameter that cuts right through Logan Airport to the east, and clockwise through Dorchester, Brookline, Cambridge, Chelsea.

The Atlantic flowed in to form a warm, briny crater ocean filling most of the impact site. You walk along the perimeter sometimes but there isn't much to see. You have never been all the way around it. No one knows how deep it is but there are fish in it, enormous and terrible. Steam rises continually from the surface, and when the wind blows right you can see the former Prudential Center, the highest building in all of Boston,

which projects from the Crater Ocean, knocked three degrees
askew. At night one can see lights glowing below the waterline.

You used to worry about breathing the steam, about being
poisoned by the radiation here. Maybe you should stop caring. No one else who lives here worries, so why should you?
Who needs to live past thirty anyway?

```
[t]ake a boat out into the steam—you're probably
already mutated, so what exactly do you have to
lose?
[c]omb the glassy shore for the kitschy Revolutionary
War memorabilia everyone here seems to value.
```

A STERILE PROMONTORY

You may as well see what it says on the sheet. You know it
won't be anything good, and it isn't. Osric? It's like ten lines.
At least you're in the play. The kid playing Hamlet used to be
a friend of yours. Who cares, Drama Club's not your life. Later
you ride the long way home around the golf course, jumping
your bike off little ruts in the road, killing time until your dad
gets home. Remember when you were popular?

```
[n]ot really
[n]ope
```

FALSE MEMORIES

There are other weird things. You've found things that were
never invented in normal reality, like a plasma rifle or antigravity disks. Most of them don't work, but still—they
shouldn't have existed at all. It's like the split goes back way

before the bombs. That could be why a few of the skyscrapers look strange. Hancock Tower is taller and curvier, and something has given it a quarter twist. They look like science fiction versions of themselves. You start breaking into offices, one by one. Some of these people were defense contractors, on something called Project Gemini.

Gamma World is probably your fault, you know. Your fault for wishing the whole world would be annihilated in a nuclear fireball. Which you do every single day.

```
[n]o
[y]es
[ . . . ]
```

THE FATAL SIGN

It's time to stop ignoring certain things. As Dad sits across from you at dinner you wonder how much he knows. You're thinking it so loud, it seems impossible he can't somehow hear your thoughts. You wonder how somebody so clueless about the world around him could be considered a brilliant scientist.

He won't tell you what he's working on at the lab because it's all Department of Defense work, but it's particle physics work, so really, isn't it time to put two and two together?

"Dad," you ask suddenly, "do you think there are other dimensions? Parallel worlds?"

He smiles and shakes his head. "If only."

He leaves the table, his food untouched.

```
Finish your [m]ac and cheese. You'll never know the
truth.
He's not even your real [f]ather, is he?
```

HYPERBOREAN WINDS

Traders arrive from the farthest north, hiking down the train lines from Montreal. They have horses and one enormous mutant elk. It's the same up there, they say, just colder. Bombed-out cities, endless pine forests, and intelligent wolves. Snakes have grown fur and mammoths have appeared from someplace. They believe the bombs fell everywhere. They give us furs, and we give them local fruits and urban salvage: a generator, blowtorches, wooden beams. They leave, promising to return in six months.

One day you might go there, but not in Gamma World. You've found that if you get too far from Boston in the real world, you stop crossing over. Which I guess means you should just wait until college and move away and all your problems will be solved.

But you know that even if you moved a thousand miles from here, there would be a moment on a perfect crisply cold autumn day when you're studying outside on the quad and your friends are laughing but you wouldn't believe in it, you'd always, always, always know that this fresh and unscarred unburnt reality is a lie, and underneath it's all rubble.

Why fight it? It's where you [b]elong. We both
know it.
Run forever, the [r]est of your life if that's
what it takes.

SIGNALS INTELLIGENCE

None of this happened before Mom left. Maybe she could have kept you out of Gamma World if she'd cared to try. You talk on the phone twice a week but she sounds distracted. You hear dishes clatter in the background. Is she hosting a party?

You wish you could ask her advice about Melodee. You wonder what it would even take to get her attention. There was a girl in eighth grade who took pills; they took her out of school for six months. You'd consider trying that, but you're not exactly sure how that's going to solve anything.

You keep daring yourself to tell her the truth but the conversation lapses into longer and longer silences. Finally she excuses herself. You feel the life drain from this dimension again. The green glow returns. It's midnight in Gamma World.

[n]ice try.

PRISONERS OF GAMMA WORLD

It *never fails*. The moment your guard is down, Gamma World comes sliding back into place, unwholesome foliage and rusted metal stealing over everything. The grassy smell of a place where it's always overheated summer. They used to talk about a nuclear winter but Gamma World is a permanent greenhouse. Maybe on the other side of the world it's winter all the time.

Then the day comes when the world doesn't change back. You wake and go to sleep and wake again and you're still wrapped in furs on a slab of foam rubber in a bunker. Two days, a week. You get used to not taking showers; the tribe's dogs curl up with you at night, and you start to carry a length of pipe with a kitchen knife duct-taped to the end. Melodee teaches you to hit a target with a crossbow made from a heavy wooden clothes hanger.

One night you're summoned to meet the tribal chieftain and for a moment you're afraid it's going to turn out to be your father. It isn't, but you recognize him anyway: in your world he is a city council member.

He tells you that to become a member of the tribe, you need to travel out into the crater ocean and bring back some treasure of use to the tribe.

Melodee will go with you, along with the chieftain's son, who you remember from home as a lacrosse star. You went to his eighth-grade birthday party.

```
[t]his feels right, this is what you were waiting
for.
[w]hat the hell are you doing?
```

SECRETS OF GAMMA WORLD

You paddle your way out across the water's glassy surface, the bottom hidden by churning silt. You lead them through Cambridge streets haunted by spider-limbed mutant coyote and stray androids, down shallow-flooded Massachusetts Avenue, water barely clearing the parking meters, to the MIT campus.

You spot the familiar building and climb the two flights to the Physics Department and your father's office and this time you break the glass like you've always wanted. His extra key card is in a drawer of a desk piled with final exams that will never be graded.

For a moment you think your father himself might have

split the world just as a way of winning his divorce settlement. You wouldn't put it past him. Maybe he did it and left your mom the radioactive half of everything, you included. It would explain why there's no Gamma World version of your siblings. It would explain a whole lot else besides.

```
[i]t would, wouldn't it?
```

BENEATH THE CRATER OCEAN

This part of Gamma World looks astonishingly like its counterpart in reality, except for the crevasse that opened up when the bombs fell. Warm water drizzles over the sides in long cascades, down and down past the lower levels of the city, the secret campus they never told you about, the one the Department of Defense built.

The chieftain's son holds the rope, and you and Melodee go down, and down, to the War Room, just like in the movies. One wall of the chamber is an enormous world map that once must have displayed cities all over the world, incoming missiles, bomber flights, weather patterns, and radiation dispersal. They must have stood right here and watched your world end.

Neither of you speaks. Melodee takes your hand in hers, and for once it feels like things don't have to stay this way. Maybe you don't have to go home. Maybe you are home.

There is a large metal chair at the center of the room, with a set of electrodes.

On the control panel you notice a large red button.

```
[p]ress it.
```

It's [b]etter not to know. How badly do you want to
get home anyway?

ESCAPE FROM GAMMA WORLD

The strain was too great. Melodee's father lies dying. Even his mutant abilities couldn't reactivate the great engines you found underground. The kindly old physicist looks grave and tells you that you can save him and return home, but at the price of never returning to Gamma World again.

"What did he say?" Melodee asks when you return to the Great Laboratory.

If only you could tell her everything. If only she'd believe you! But how can you even begin to explain that the world she sees every day is false: false color, false wind, and feeble, watery false sunlight. The Emerald City, the Robot Zone, University Sector, the Mass Spike, the Space Port, the Tombs, the Poison Ocean. False.

And face it, the world you came from is no better. The golden treasure-house of your life has come to this, a poison waste.

Even now you can feel yourself slipping back to the other world, the drab world you called home. You promise her you'll return, and you half believe it.

Melodee's powers are only beginning to awaken. You see a last glimpse of the giant machines of Project Gemini, the idea that tore the dimensions apart. But you're young. You're both only teenagers. Have faith.

Maybe one day, between you, the world can be put back together after all, the one world that you know is true.

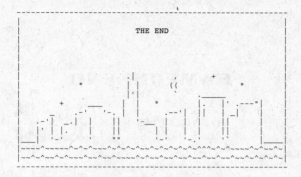

Austin Grossman's first novel, *Soon I Will Be Invincible*, was nominated for the John Sargent Sr. First Novel Prize, and his writing has appeared in *Granta*, *The Wall Street Journal*, and *The New York Times*. He is a video game design consultant and a doctoral candidate in English literature at the University of California at Berkeley, and he has written and designed for a number of critically acclaimed video games, including *Dishonored*, *Ultima Underworld II*, *System Shock*, *Trespasser*, and *Deus Ex*. His second novel, *You*, came out from Mulholland Books in 2012, and his short fiction has also appeared in John Joseph Adams's anthologies *The Mad Scientist's Guide to World Domination* and *Under the Moons of Mars: New Adventures on Barsoom*.

GAMER'S END

Yoon Ha Lee

The instructor is intimidating enough—you know about his kill count, unmatched in Shuos history—but what strikes you as you enter the room is all the games.

Games are one of the Shuos faction's major instructional tools. The Shuos specialize in information operations, although your particular training is as "Shuos infantry," as the euphemism goes: assassination. You recognize most of the games that rest on the tables. A pattern-stone set with a knife scratch across its cloudwood surface, its two bowls of black and white stones glittering beneath the soft lights. Pegboards, counters, dice, darts.

There are less old-fashioned games, mediated by the computer grid. The harrowing strategic simulations from your last year of studies would have been prohibitively time-consuming otherwise. Here, the only evidence of computer aid is a map imaged above a corner of the instructor's desk. It's centered on the Citadel of Eyes, the star fortress that is Shuos headquarters, and the world it orbits, which you just came from. Shuos Academy's campus is located planetside.

On the instructor's desk rests a jeng-zai deck. A hand of middling value lies face-up next to several hexagonal tokens.

You can't help but look for the infamous Deuce of Gears, gold against a field of livid red, formerly the instructor's emblem. But it's said his years on the battlefield are behind him.

"Instructor," you say without saluting—you're not Kel military—although you feel the vast difference in your statures.

"Sit down," the instructor says in a drawl. You almost expected *at ease*, based on the fact that he once served as an officer in the Kel army. Was, in many ways, their best general during the time he was loaned out to their service. The Kel, another of the realm's factions, are sometimes allies and more usually rivals of the Shuos. The Shuos share the Kel interest in military matters, but the two factions often differ on how to intervene in the usual crises.

The instructor is not a tall man, although his build suggests a duelist's lean strength. The Shuos uniform in ninefox red and gold looks incongruously bright on him after Kel black and gold, as does the topaz dangling from one ear. He asks, "You know how many of your class came here for advanced training?"

You recite the number. It's not large. They didn't say much about your assignment here. "Advanced training" covers a lot of ground. But you couldn't escape the rumors; no one could.

The war has been going on for the past two decades. You know the names of the worlds the enemy claims they "liberated" from your realm's oppressive rule, the military bases demolished by enemy swarms. And those were only the first to fall to the Taurag Republic. They won't be the last.

This realm is a vast one: worlds upon worlds you've never heard of. Some have more strategic value than others. The Taurags care a great deal about what they call *honor*. They make a point of sparing civilian targets. But your people are still losing.

You tip your chin up and await details.

"We've learned of a new weapon," the instructor says. "Preliminary analysis indicates that it can reach kill counts in excess of anything ever seen before. We're looking for people with the flexibility of thought to handle the weapon's capabilities."

He taps something next to the map. Red markers flare up. You recognize their import: attacks on Shuos space, except there are more than you had known about.

"Yes," the instructor says quietly. "The Taurags hurt us worse than we've led people to believe. Worse than the Taurags themselves know. I doubt they'll be fooled for long. We have time to prepare for their next thrust, but not a lot of time."

You indicate that you understand.

"The training begins now," he says. "We'll start with a straightforward game." He smiles a tilted smile at you, knife-sweet.

Your heart is thudding painfully. The Kel, who knew him primarily as a soldier, might remember only his remarkable battle record. The Shuos know that beyond formations and guns, his inescapable kill count, he is also a master of games.

The instructor's fingers flicker again. A new map, this one of a space station. It unfurls simultaneously in your mind through your augment, tapping your visual and kinesthetic senses. You orient yourself, then walk the unnamed station's skin, probe it for vulnerabilities.

"The scenario," he says. "This station has been targeted by Taurag sympathizers. Its population is ninety thousand people."

Ninety thousand people. A pittance, from the viewpoint of

an interstellar polity, yet each of those ninety thousand names is a shout in the darkness. The augment informs you that the station is instrumental to research of an unspecified nature. Impossible to avoid speculation: presumably the government is developing countermeasures, presumably it wants to protect its next superweapon.

The station has its own security, but the researchers can't function if it locks down. They may be close to a key breakthrough. And there's the old paradox: you can't defend everything everywhere for an indefinite length of time without an infinite budget. Even then someone will devise some unexpected angle of attack.

"You've been dispatched to handle the threat," the instructor continues. "Assume for the exercise's sake that you're loyal." He grins at you, as unfunny as the joke is. "You have no such assurance about everyone else. Trust them or not, your call. You'll have access to Shuos infantry gear."

You're surprised by his use of the euphemism. It's not like he needs to worry about offending your sensibilities. The augment provides the list of available gear. The system asks you what you want to requisition, and you put in your requests.

"Any questions?"

This is a test in itself. "If the station falls," you say, "how many will die? Beyond the ninety thousand?"

He raises an eyebrow. "The kill count is up to you, fledge. Go left out the door and follow the servitor. It'll take you to the game room."

There used to be a saying, which originated with the Kel, that no game could ever replicate the fear of death that accompanies real combat. It was a dig at the Shuos obsession with training games. After all, how could a simulation with numbers in a computer, with game boards and tokens, prepare you for the possibility that you'd have to sacrifice your life? The Kel and the Shuos often work together, especially during warfare, but that doesn't mean they always get along.

Then Shuos Mikodez, head of the Shuos, assassinated two of his own cadets for reasons never divulged. Mikodez was the youngest Shuos to attain the head position in centuries. The people who doubted that he was ruthless enough to hold on to the seat suddenly became a minority. And over the next decades the Shuos prospered under Mikodez's guidance.

The saying withered after that, not least among the Shuos themselves.

You follow the instructor's directions exactly. Not to say that it's always optimal, but your instincts tell you that this is not one of the exercises where they want you to play hooky. Once you're outside, a spiderform servitor, all skittering angles and lens eyes, escorts you through the corridors.

Your first stop is to pick up your equipment. The weapons aren't real, though the masks, armor, and medical supplies are. The former are marked with the horrific ninefox red that indicates that they're simulation gear. The worst thing you could do to someone with the fake scorch pistol is break their nose with it. (Well. Not the worst thing. The worst *polite* thing.)

Next the servitor leads you to an unmarked elevator, although it doesn't follow you in. From here you're on your own. The elevator's interior is decorated in sea green rather than the florid Shuos colors. There's a shuddering sensation as it takes you through the Fortress's levels, and then the doors whisk open.

The simulator is more advanced than the ones you're accustomed to. You enter the designated sim chamber and hook yourself up to the monitors, heart pounding. You've never enjoyed the next part, where the augment overrides real sensory stimuli in favor of programmed ones. It's a pity that you're weighed down with the gear, but you're expected to take your equipment seriously, and it comes with additional sensors to record everything.

Your senses jitter as the scenario calibrates itself to you; your old roommate described it as the sensation of your eyeballs turning inside out in a dark room. Then a garden replaces the simulator's interior. Under other circumstances you'd appreciate the forsythia and the red-and-gold carp swirling lazily in a pond.

You spot eight people around you straight off—no, make that nine. The scenario dumped you into a vine-covered nook near an engineer complaining about a fungal infection to two people who look like they're trying to think of excuses to be elsewhere. You have also been provided with an absurd tall glass of a lavender-orange beverage topped with iridescent foam. You hope it's not based on anything real.

You need information, and it'd be nice to get access to the station grid. You have credentials appropriate to a low-level technician, which is what you're pretending to be. You're no grid-diver, but the point isn't outsmarting the computers, it's outsmarting the people the computers serve.

For the first hour—simulated time; you're painfully aware that your internal clock has been screwed with—you circulate around the garden to get a sense for what's going on. Not a bad insertion: stressed people gravitate toward gardens. You eavesdrop and learn that scoutmoth patrols have glimpsed ambiguous signals from the direction of the Taurag border. People are skittish.

It's here that the game changes.

The augment has an alert for you: *Target active. Scenario timer engaged. Target's kill count: 0.*

As if agents get such certainty in real life. Still, that number won't go down. Maybe they expect the counter to rattle you as it changes.

Time to move.

You dispose of the lavender-orange beverage without tasting it—you're afraid of the scenario authors' imagination already; what were they *thinking*?—and make your way toward Medical. It occupies one of the innermost levels. The people you pass talk about everything from debugging eco-scrubbers to failed affairs. There's a discussion of ways to improve a recipe for honey sesame cookies. The banality of their concerns is almost enough to convince you that they're real people. You'd even feel bad if you failed to save them.

You're ambushed by a tall woman and a demure-looking alt in a quiet corridor on the way. Which is alarming, because clearly they knew you were coming. In the scenario's context that can only be one thing: a warning. It's impossible not to try to anticipate the scenario author's intent for clues.

Twist and joint-lock and the quiet-loud crunch of bone. They're down before you have time to panic over the implications, for which you're grateful. One of them is still alive, which means that you can—

The alarm goes off. Not a scenario alarm—it's impossible to graduate Academy without enduring at least one botched scenario—but a priority-one Citadel-wide alert. You only recognize it because of the briefing you received on the way to the Citadel. You assumed it was the standard orientation, although you memorized it as a matter of course, without expecting the information to become relevant during your training.

The inside-out-eyeball feeling recurs. The visuals, the sound, everything freezes. Worse is being dumped back into Citadel time without the usual precious moments of adjustment.

A databurst sears through the augment. Most of it's too high-clearance for you. You're informed that you're authorized to know that there *is* an alert, but that's all. Honestly, you're impressed that Shuos bureaucrats have left something out of contingency planning. But sending newly graduated cadets to the Citadel itself for advanced training is a rare occurrence. You almost can't blame them. Assuming this, too, isn't a continuation of the scenario. You're betting that's what's going on.

"Listen," a voice says into your augment. It's tense and rapid and—this makes your spine prickle—seems to be coming from outside the simulator. "The experienced infantry are elsewhere, so you'll have to do. They haven't cracked this channel yet; they're focusing on high-priority shit like isolating Mikodez and the senior staff. I've updated your map with the current layout and given you the highest clearances I can without triggering the grid's watchdog sweeps, which I think they're monitoring. Get to Armory 15-2-5, grab some basic armaments. Link up with—" *Static.*

They who? "Requesting update on situation," you say. For all you know, the damn scenario has crashed and the voice belongs to a completely different game. "I'm here for training, I don't have access, I don't know the situation."

More static, swearing: "Look, this isn't—" You tell yourself the voice's tremor is a fiction. "Look, I don't *do* this real-time shit, I'm in logistical analysis; I study *food*. You have to get out of there. There are hostile infantry running around and a squad on level fifteen is heading for the spatial stabilizer and I can't raise local security, they might have been taken out, *please*—"

The voice drops out, no static this time, nothing. You wait for an interminable minute on the off chance that it will return. No luck.

You'll play along. You manually kick the scenario. Your nerves flare with phantom pain as the simulator drops the inputs. You extricate yourself from the chamber, dumping all the red weaponry except the (dull) knife, which you could theoretically use to stick someone in the eye. Then you head for the armory by the most direct route, since speed is your ally.

Like most larger stations, the Citadel routinely uses variable layout, which allows spatial elements to be rearranged for more rapid travel between them. You worry that someone will switch variable layout off and leave you spindled between *here* and *nowhere*. The technology has an extremely good safety record—if you don't take hostiles into account.

The Citadel is vast. Even the updated map is obfuscated due to security issues. The artificially induced vertigo, another defensive measure, is maddening. Only the medical countermeasures you brought with you keep you upright. You slam up against the armory without warning. The doors are open and there's smoke. Nice to know that you didn't bring a mask for nothing.

The augment won't tell you whether anything's in there, since you don't have even that much clearance. With your luck, you'll be hit with tranquilizer clouds the moment you go in, and that's the best-case scenario. But you have to give the game your best shot.

You plunge into the armory, armed with knife and bravado. Even with the augment it's difficult to see past the smoke.

A subliminal slither-scale noise, then a hiss, catch your attention. You duck low. Someone's here, an unfriendly someone. The hiss comes again, and with it a knife line of stinging pain just shy of your left shoulder.

You have no idea what they've rigged the security protocols to do if you use even fake guns, so it'll have to be the dull-edged knife. It won't do you much good if you can't close the distance, however.

You hear the unmistakable click of a splinter grenade's pin being removed and sprint for cover. You glimpse the grenade as it thunks solidly against a wall of boxes labeled HANDLE WITH CAUTION—SUSCEPTIBLE TO FIRE, CONCUSSION, AND STUPIDITY. (The only surprise is that *stupidity* isn't listed first.)

The grenade goes off and you're deafened. It's a fucking grenade and are you ever grateful for the instinct that yanked you to the safest place in the geometry of the fucking armory, sheltered partly by the edge of a locker, partly by a bin that someone didn't put back properly. Even then you take splinters through your side and right arm, but you still have your left, and the medical foam is bubbling up from your jacket's circulatory systems to seal the wounds even if it's not doing anything for the agony.

Your brain catches up to that glimpse: the grenade wasn't red.

It wasn't red. They just tried to kill you with the genuine article.

This isn't a training game anymore.

Despite the pain, you locate an intact weapons bank and scrabble to open it. The credentials the unknown voice provided you are genuine. You snatch up a scorch pistol.

You whip out of the armory and around the corner firing. The hostile, wearing a foreign-looking articulated suit, attempts to retaliate with the pain-scourge or whatever-it-is. Your aim is true, your reflexes better; the scorch hits her full-on. She screams.

You're far enough back that the grenade at her belt shattering into a thousand pieces doesn't do more than sting. The damage is probably worse than it feels. You can assess that later.

There's not much left of a body to inspect. It's not the only one, either. The blast caught some others. The smell, charred metal and meat and shit, makes your gorge rise. You force yourself to look at the red smears on the floor, the walls. The worst part is a chunk of face with a full eye almost intact, staring lopsidedly at a shredded piece of lung.

No. That's not the worst part. You wonder that you almost missed it, but you're not thinking very clearly right now. A shiver of revulsion passes through you. The eye's iris is vivid violet.

Taurags have eyes like that.

You were right the second time. This has stopped being a game.

You have no idea who to link up with and it's likely that Citadel security will mistake you for an intruder yourself, Shuos uniform notwithstanding. But if there's any chance your information is useful, you have to pass it on. The Citadel's population is classified, along with other useful things like the number of toilets, but you wouldn't be surprised if it housed more than half a million people. The thought of them being in danger, strangers though they are, makes your stomach twist.

Your best bet is to head for the spatial stabilizer. Now that you realize the threat is real, your heart constricts at the thought of hostiles in control of a Citadel stabilizer. They could separate the Citadel's spatial building blocks, rearrange them to disadvantage the Shuos, even—if they crack the controls entirely—destroy the Citadel.

It's not reassuring that this is the same technology you'll have to rely on to reach the stabilizer, since it needs to be isolated from realspace. There's no help for it. You hurry toward the next path.

This one requires you to climb up and down an elegant spiraling ramp that changes color from auburn to gold and then sly amber. Your knees feel unsteady and you hate yourself for it. You keep expecting the ramp to vanish into a massless knot of nothing and strand you in space. As you step off the spiral, however, the world *slants* and you dash for a side corridor at the sound of gunfire.

The voice comes back without warning. You almost shoot the wall. "You made it, good," it says. This time it's communicating through your augment. "You're there, right? Can you get in?" And then: "I think the senior staff—well, it doesn't matter. You're what's available."

The way the voice wavers makes you grind your teeth. "Firefight," you say, identifying the weapons by the percussion they make as you let the augment transmit your subvocals. "Just got here, haven't had time to scout."

"I've been working the grid," the voice says. "I can get

in overrides, but you'll have to work fast to take advantage before they freeze me out. And you'll need physical access."

Obviously, or it would have been able to handle matters remotely. "Servitor passages for maintenance?"

"Yes. I can open one of those. Tight squeeze, though."

The voice has the presence of mind to send you a newer, declassified map. At this point it's not like either of you cares about getting into trouble with higher-ups. "Listen," you say, determined not to give in to the awful mixture of pain and nausea despite the medical assists. "How bad is it, if the senior staff are . . . ?"

Brief silence. "I haven't heard from Mikodez or any of the senior staff since the alert began," the voice says. "I'm lying low right now. They didn't hire me to be brave." Not the most inspiring thing to say, but you appreciate the honesty. "I'm hoping the other stabilizers are all right, but they're still attempting to secure this one."

"I'll do what I can," you say.

The next moves happen in a blur.

Scorch blasts.

Narrow passage. Claustrophobia and bruised elbows are the least of your worries.

You approach the hatch. The firefight sounds like it's died down. You're not optimistic about the survival of your Shuos comrades. It's hard to see through the slits and you don't dare query local scan, lest you be detected.

You pry the hatch open, wishing it didn't creak so much. Most of the bodies in the control center wear Shuos red-and-gold. A few have violet eyes and are dressed in the strange articulated suits.

The voice again. "Are you in?"

"Yes. They didn't stick around, though."

"That's not good," it says. "One moment." Then: "The good news is that they couldn't crack the stabilizer's control system. The bad news is that there's—there's more of them. A lot more of them. Their swarm, fleet, horde, whatever their term is. They've all arrived. They're taking out the orbital defenses before they make a move planetside, I guess."

It's growing harder and harder to think, just when it's most important. "We can use the stabilizer against them—"

"Too many of them and not enough time. Unless—"

You know exactly what it's thinking of. Unmoor the stabilizer and aim it at the Citadel's heart, where the power cores are. Turn space inside out. The whole thing would go up in a tumult of fire. It'd also scorch a significant portion of the planet, but the explosion would hurt the Taurag invaders and buy time for a defense to be mustered elsewhere.

Just to make sure that you and the voice understand each other, you outline the idea.

"Yes," the voice says. "I'll talk you through the procedure."

It takes you several minutes to figure out the control system even so, because the voice only has access to an outdated version of the manual and the system interface was overhauled at some point.

You think about orbital mechanics. If you set off the power cores right now, the conflagration will singe Shuos Academy's main campus on the planet's second-largest continent.

Shuos Academy comes to mind because you just graduated, naturally, but there are a lot of population centers that would be affected. It's easy enough to access a map of the planet and the associated census, start adding up the numbers. How high would the kill count get?

After a moment, the voice interrupts. "Have you done it? Is there a technical issue? Of all the times—"

"I'm not doing it," you say over the dull roar in your ears. Your hands have started shaking violently. You right the nearest chair and sink into it before your knees can give out.

The voice's silence is distinctly baffled.

"Open a line to the Taurags," you say. "Talk to them or something. The Taurags won't hit nonmilitary targets down there. They insist on that kind of thing. If our enemy wouldn't do it, fucked if I'll hit the button myself."

"Are you out of your mind? That invasion force isn't going to stop here!" The voice suddenly becomes frantic. "Or is it that you're scared to die when we all go up in flames? I don't enjoy the idea any more than you do, but we've got a *duty*—"

"That's not it," you say. "I mean, I don't want to die. But that isn't the reason. There are better ways to win than toasting a bunch of civilians. We've learned that much from our enemy. Maybe it's too late for us here to find a new strategy, but someone else will."

The voice drops silent, and you wonder if it's given up on you, but after a while it resumes. "We don't have much time left," it says, low and fierce. "There's another squad headed your way, they're almost *there*. If you're going to do something, you have to do it now. And—" Silence again.

Getting up hurts. You're sure that something's bleeding inside. The augment confirms this, although it's being awfully unhelpful about the nature of the injury. Under the circumstances, it's not like it matters.

You've had time to survey the room, consider its layout. You settle on a position and lower yourself painfully into place. If the pistol gets any heavier, you're going to drop it.

Footsteps. They're attempting to be quiet, but the slither-scale sound of that articulated stuff can't be silenced entirely. You've never been more awake.

There's only one of you, but you might as well take out as many as you can on the way out.

There's a Shuos joke that isn't shared often, although most people have heard it.

What's the difference between a Shuos and a bullet to the back of the head?

You might survive the bullet.

It's not especially funny (as opposed to Kel jokes, which everyone but the Kel agree are hilarious). But then, depending on how you measure these things, the deadliest general in Kel history was a Shuos.

You wake with a memory of shadows cutting across the door, of your jacket's unexpected injection, of toppling sideways and the taste of blood in your mouth. You're hooked up to a medical unit that someone has decorated with knitted lace. The sight is so unexpected (and the russet lace so hideous) that it keeps you from doing the obvious thing and accosting the instructor, who is standing subtly out of reach with a dancer's awareness of space.

You're pretty sure that if not for whatever they drugged you with, you'd be in a lot of pain right now. As it stands, your thoughts feel as clear as ice in spite of the weird disconnected feeling that your mind is only attached to your body by a few silk strands.

"The 'Taurag attack' was still part of the 'game,' wasn't it?" you ask in a scratched-up voice. "Some of those people actually *died*." You weren't in a simulator for the second half. The smells, the hot, sticky blood, the staring eye.

"The performers were volunteers," the instructor says, which makes you want to shoot him more, if only you had a gun. "I had to apply to Mikodez for special permission to recruit them, because if there's anything Mikodez hates, it's inefficiency. But the exercise had to be real because that was the only way to make it look real."

"You had me kill people for a *test*. *You* killed people for a test."

"You're not the first person to call me a monster." The instructor smiles; his eyes are very dark. "I didn't lie about the destructive potential of the weapon that we're concerned with. It can devastate planetary populations, and they say *I* was known for overkill. But it isn't a Taurag weapon. It's *our* weapon. We're building new battlemoths to make use of it even as we speak. I hear they'll be ready by year's end.

"The next step will be to take the fight to the Taurag Republic. There's a lot of potential for the war to go genocidal, for us to get locked into back-and-forth invasions until one or both of us is obliterated. We have to look beyond that. We can't escape the fact of war—there's too much history of distrust for that—but we can lay the foundation for whatever accord we reach afterward, because no war, however terrible, lasts forever."

You're not liking the fact that you agree with this one point, because it means you're agreeing with *him*.

"I refuse to let this weapon fall into the hands of people who can use it without blinking at the deaths it will cause, or who think only of revenge," the instructor says. "I would rather spend a few deaths now, to identify people who understand restraint—who care about the lives of civilians—than find out during the invasion proper by reading about the inevitable massacres."

"Tell me," you say sarcastically. "If I'd decided to blow the Citadel up, would you have let *that* go through, too?"

"No, you were only playing with a dummy system by that point," he says, "even if you had to believe it was real. If you'd hit the button, we'd still be here, only I'd be debriefing you on why you failed."

He rubs the back of one hand, as if in memory of scars, although you see none there. "You did well," he adds, as if that could make up for the people you killed, those he put into harm's way. "You passed. I hope you continue to pass. Because this is one test you don't stop taking."

"You wouldn't have passed," you say, because someone has to.

"No," he says. For a moment you glimpse the shadows he lives with, all of them self-inflicted. "I've always been an excellent killer. It's not too late for you to do more with your career than I did with mine. You'll make an excellent officer. I'm recommending you for the invasion swarm."

You inhale sharply, and regret it when pain stabs through your side in spite of the painkillers. "I'm not sure you should"— more candor than is safe, but you're beyond caring— "because after we deal with the Taurags, I'm coming for you."

The instructor salutes you Kel-style, with just a touch of irony. You don't return the gesture. "I look forward to it," he says.

———

Yoon Ha Lee was introduced to video games by way of a Commodore 64, became the world's worst FPS player in high school after encountering *Wolfen-*

stein 3D, and is currently in extended mourning for the *Crysis Wars* mod *MechWarrior: Living Legends*. (Favorite mech: Shadowcat A.) He authored the Story-Nexus game *Winterstrike* for Failbetter Games, wrote the IF game *The Moonlit Tower* in Inform 6 after being sucked into the genre, and outsources CRPG min-maxing to his husband. His collection *Conservation of Shadows* came out from Prime Books in 2013. Other works have appeared in venues such as *Lightspeed*, *Clarkesworld*, Tor.com, and the *Magazine of Fantasy & Science Fiction*. Lee lives in Louisiana with family and has not yet been eaten by gators.

THE CLOCKWORK SOLDIER

Ken Liu

"Go," Alex said. "If you remember to keep a low profile, neither your father nor his enemies will ever find you here."

The ship had landed in the middle of the jungle, miles away from the closest settlement. Alara was a backwater, barely inhabited, and insignificant to galactic politics. It would take days, perhaps weeks, to walk out of here, stumble into a few colonists, and pretend to be near starvation. Enough time to make up any backstory and make it believable.

Ryder flexed his slender arms and stretched, the movements graceful, dancelike. The strict manner in which he had been bound during the ship's last jump through hyperspace didn't seem to have any lasting ill effects.

He gave Alex a long, appraising look. "What will you tell my father?"

She shrugged. "I'll give him his money back."

"You've never failed before, have you?"

"There's always a first time. I'm human. I'm not perfect." She began to climb back into the ship.

"That's it?"

She stopped halfway up the ladder and looked down at him.

"You don't want to be sure?" he asked, that characteristic smirk playing at the corners of his delicate mouth again. "Don't you want to ask to see me as I really am?"

She considered this. "No. I've already decided to believe you. Trying to make sure can only make things worse. If I find out that you're telling the truth, then I will have ruined this moment, when I can still believe I'm capable of being decent, of trust. If I find out you're lying, then I'll have to consider myself a fool."

"So, again you choose faith before knowledge."

This time, she didn't stop climbing. When she was at the air-lock door, she turned around. "Faith is just another name for self-knowledge. You've succeeded, Scheherazade. When you tell your own story, you seize life. Now it's my turn to tell myself a good story, about myself. I know enough. Good-bye."

Ryder watched as the ship rose, shrank, and disappeared into the evening sky. "Thank you," he whispered.

Then he set off into the dark jungle, just another wanderer, a lonely will etching his way across the wilderness.

A few hours earlier:

"THE CLOCKWORK SOLDIER"
A short interactive text adventure by Ryder

You sleep, a smile at the corners of your mouth.

In your dreams, the concentric layers of carp-scale shingles on the Palace's roof reflect the golden light so brilliantly that visitors to Chrysanthemum know right away how the city got its name.

THE PRINCESS'S BEDROOM

You open your eyes and find yourself in bed. The blanket is silky smooth and the mattress soft.

Like most rooms in the Palace, this one is lined with colorful tapestries depicting the heroic deeds of the Hegemons of the Pan-Flores League. Through a narrow slit-window high off the floor, the brilliant morning sunlight diffuses into the room, as does the chittering of birds and the smell of a thousand blooming flowers in the garden. The door to the hallway is closed right now. Next to the bed is your clockwork soldier, Spring, standing at attention.

> examine soldier
Your faithful companion Spring has been with you as long as you can remember. He's six feet tall and looks like a living suit of armor. You remember once opening him up when you were younger and being amazed at the thousands upon thousands of whirling gears and ticking governors and tightly wound springs inside.

You giggle as you remember the many adventures you've shared together over the years. You've taught Spring everything he knows, and he's saved you from too many scrapes to count.

> get up
You get out of the bed.

> say "hello"
(to Spring)
"Good morning," says Spring. "I know that sometimes you like to go by a different name for fun. What name would you like to go by today?"
(Please enter your name)

> Alex

"Alex it is," Spring says. His voice sounds . . . rusty, lugu-
brious. He shuffles in place, the gears inside him clanging and
scraping against each other. "I'm sorry that I seem to be in a
bad mood today."

> ask about mood

"Why are you feeling down?" you ask. A good princess needs to
be concerned about the state of mind of her subjects—er, toys.

"I'm not sure. I just feel . . . like a part of me is missing."

"Did a bolt loosen and fall out? Were you not oiled properly?
Did I forget to wind you last night?"

"No. It's none of those things. I can't explain it."

> look under bed

A few dust bunnies scurry out of your way.

> look behind tapestries

The walls are made of solid stone. No hidden passages, as far
as you can see.

> examine Spring

He looks fine, if a bit morose.

> cheer up Spring

"Why don't we have an adventure today?" you ask. "Maybe we'll
find what you want in the rest of the Palace?"

Spring nods. "As you wish."

> exit bedroom

HALLWAY

The hallway is lit by torches along the wall. To the east is the grand staircase. To the west, some distance down the dimly lit hallway, are two doors.

Spring follows you into the hallway, the loud clangs of his footsteps echoing around the stone walls.

> ask Spring for direction

"You decide," says Spring. "You always do."

> west

HALLWAY

Spring clangs after you.

> west

HALLWAY

Spring clangs after you. Then he sighs, sounding like steel wool being rubbed against a grille.

> ask Spring about sigh

"Don't you like following me around?" you ask.

"Following you around today has not activated as many micro-levers inside me as usual." Spring pauses, the gears humming and grinding inside him. "I suppose, logically, we can try having me lead instead of follow."

(Allow Spring to lead?)

> yes

"Why do you tantalize me with the impossible?" Spring says. "We both know I can't. I'm an automaton."

Spring shakes his head from side to side, and the loud grinding noise makes you cover your ears.

"I am so sad that I can no longer move," Spring says.

> examine

The hallway is narrow and windowless but not damp or dark. The torches in the walls provide flickering illumination. The smell of rose otto permeates the air.

> west

HALLWAY

Spring stays behind, immobile.

> east

HALLWAY

You see Spring in the middle of the hallway, looking like a heap of rusty metal.

> inventory

You are empty-handed.

> look for oil

There is no clockwork oil in the hallway.

(Come on. First puzzles in interactive text adventures are often easy, but not *this* easy.)

> look for source of rose otto

The fragrance of rose otto permeates the air.

The essence of rose is distilled from the garden outside the Palace by the gardener and his helpers every morning. The Castellan, your father's head clockwork servant, applies it liberally to combat the problem of mildew in enclosed spaces around the Palace. When activated by heat, it can make any place smell fresh and comfortable.

> pick up a torch

You take one of the torches out of the sconces on the wall.

> examine torch

You lean in close to look at the torch, and the fire singes your lovely chestnut hair.

Spring groans.

> put out torch against the floor

You extinguish the torch. The hallway is now fractionally cooler.

> examine torch

The torch is cleverly designed by the Royal Artificer. The body of the torch is hollow to hold the slow-burning oil, and a smaller compartment near the top holds rose otto.

> get oil from torch

You stick your hand into the hollow body of the torch and . . .

"Ow! Ow!" You hop around. Your hand is covered in hot oil. You're likely to injure your hand if you don't get rid of it quickly.

> apply oil to Spring

You slather the hot oil over the joints in Spring's face and torso.

Spring stands up.

> ask Spring about mood

"You're welcome," you say, since Spring doesn't seem inclined to thank you. That's very uncharacteristic of him, but maybe he's still feeling down.

"Thank you," Spring says. The voice is smooth, but you detect a hint of resentment. "I just wish I had decided to get the oil myself."

"I can order the Royal Artificer to modify your tape and give you the instructions to get oil when you feel rusty," you say.

"That's not what I meant. I wish I had come up with the idea myself. I wish I could punch my own instruction tape."

Fear, or maybe it's an appetite for thrill, rises in you. "Are you suggesting that you wish to be endowed with the Augustine Module and cross the Cartesian Limit? You know that's forbidden, and any automata found to have crossed the line must be destroyed."

Spring says nothing.

"But maybe what you're missing is a chance to do the forbidden," you muse to yourself.

> west

OUTSIDE THE KING'S AND QUEEN'S BEDROOMS

The door to the King's bedroom (in the northern wall) is made of solid oak. Carved into the door is the figure of a man with two faces—one laughing, one crying. The four eyes on the two faces are inlaid with emeralds.

The door to the Queen's bedroom (in the southern wall) is made of pale ash. The figure of a leaping hare is carved into it. Your mother died when you were born, and the room has been

sealed off for as long as you can remember. It's too painful for
the King to set foot inside.

Spring clangs after you.

> north
The door is locked.

> south
The door is locked.

> knock on door to the north
There is no answer.

Spring shifts his weight from one leg to the other.

"What are you doing?" he asks. "You know the King is away
at Wolfsbane for the coronation of Prince Ulu, three days'
ride away. All the clockwork servants are away to be main-
tained by the Royal Artificer this morning. You're alone in the
Palace."

> kick door to the north
Ouch! The door barely moves, but you're hopping around on one
foot, crying out. Kicking at doors is not something silk slip-
pers are very well suited for.

A series of metallic clangs come from Spring. You can see
he's trying hard to stop his quivering torso.

"Laugh it up," you say, wincing at the pain. "Laugh it up."

> ask Spring to open door
Spring lumbers into the door, and it smashes into a million
little pieces on contact. Where the door used to be there's now
just a big hole.

"I had in mind something a little less destructive," you say.

"Just following orders," Spring says.

Alex whirls around in her chair at the *beep-beep-beep* of the proximity alarm. She sees the slender figure of Ryder in the doorway of the cabin, leaning against the frame.

She's about to apologize for snooping when she notices the smirk on Ryder's face. *Why should I apologize? He's a prisoner on my ship.*

She stands up from the chair. "I needed to see what you've been up to on this computer. You've been using it practically nonstop. A security precaution—I'm sure you understand."

He comes into the small room. Alex reaches down to shut off the proximity alarm so that the rapid beeping stops. He's about her height, slender of build and with delicate features. That teenaged face, so heartbreakingly beautiful, vulnerable, and young, reminds her of her son. A wave of tenderness surfaces in her before she becomes aware of it and dams it away. She realizes suddenly how little she knows about him, despite chasing after him all these weeks and then capturing him. From time to time, she's seen him tending to the plants in the herbal garden—a small luxury that she allowed herself—with care, though she has never told him to do it. Other than that, he's been holed up in his room.

Like with all her prey, she's been avoiding having much interaction with him.

He's cargo, she reminds herself, *worth a lot of money.* A bounty hunter who forgets her job doesn't last very long.

"I'll leave you to it," she says, and starts to move around him to get to the door.

"Wait!" he says. The smirk is gone, replaced by a hesitant,

shy smile. "I wanted to tell you that I appreciate your giving me the run of the ship instead of locking me up in a windowless cell or drugging me." He pauses, and then adds, "Also, thanks for not roughing me up."

She shrugs. "Your father's orders were very clear. You're not to be injured or harmed in any way. Not even a scratch on your skin."

"My father." His face becomes expressionless, like a mask. "He told you not to injure me, did he? Well, of course he would."

Alex gives him a thoughtful but hard gaze. "But if I feel you're endangering my life, don't you think for a moment I wouldn't put you down."

Ryder lifts his hands in a placating gesture. "I've been good. I promise."

"Honestly, you're not much of a fighter. Besides, it's not like there's anywhere for you to go while we're in hyperspace. Why not let you stretch your legs around the ship?"

"You're not curious about why I ran away and why my father has gone to so much trouble to catch me?"

"I'm paid to get you back to him in one piece," Alex says, "not to ask questions. In my profession, being curious is not always a virtue." *Also,* she adds to herself, *families are impossible for outsiders to understand.*

The smirk is back on his face. He points to the terminal that Alex was using. "You were curious about *that.*"

"I told you, a security precaution."

"You would have found out that it's nothing dangerous within a few seconds. But you played for a while."

"I got pulled in," she says. "It's a game, and on this little ship, I get as bored as you."

He laughs. "So, what do you think?"

She considers the question and decides there's nothing wrong with giving him her honest opinion. A privileged kid like that probably never hears any real criticism. "The setup is good, but the pacing is off. The language is self-indulgent in places, and the Pinocchio story line is a bit clichéd. Still, I think it has potential."

He nods, acknowledging her feedback. "This is my first time telling a story in this way. Maybe I've added too much."

"You came up with it yourself?"

"In a manner of speaking. You're right that it's not completely original."

"I'd like to play more of it," she says, surprising even herself.

"Go ahead, and keep on telling me what works and what doesn't work."

```
> enter King's bedroom
```

THE KING'S BEDROOM

The King's bedroom is large, cavernous even. The Grand Hall is for banquets and stately receptions, but here's where he conducts real business and gives the orders that will change the course of history. (Insofar as issuing an edict announcing a new tax credit for woodcarvers and novel spell-casting research can be deemed to be changing history.)

In the middle of the room is a large bed—well, might as well call it king-sized. Around the room are many cabinets filled with many more drawers, all unlabeled, all alike. There's also a writing desk next to the window. The window is very wide and very open, contrary to proper secure Palace design principles. But as a result, the room is flooded with light.

Usually this room is filled with people: ministers, guards, generals just back from the front seeking an audience with the King. You've never been here alone before.

Spring clangs in after you.

"We're going to look for the Augustine Module," you say. "That ought to cheer you up, right?"

Spring says nothing.

> examine cabinets
They all look the same. The rows of drawers lining them look, if possible, even more alike. You're not sure which one to start with.

> pick one at random
I only understand you want to pick something.

> open drawer
Which drawer do you mean?

> open all drawers
There are too many drawers to pick from.

"Ryder, I used to play a lot of old games like this. Your puzzles really need some work."

"You want a hint?"

"Of course not. What would be the point? Might as well have you tell me the story yourself."

"All right."

Alex looks at Ryder. *This is a boy who probably doesn't like to get his hands dirty. He would be used to the many servants and droids back in his father's house. Like a princess.*

> go to nearest drawer and open it
If you're thinking of opening every drawer one by one, the King
will be back before you're done.

> Damn it, this is terrible programming!
Spring shifts from one foot to the other behind you.

   "Did you say something about programming?"

> ask Spring about programming
"Since I'm a non-Cartesian automaton, you can control my behavior with programs." Spring's voice is dreary and grinds on your
ears.

   You step up to Spring and open up his front panel, revealing
the spinning gears and rocking levers within, as well as reams
of densely punched instructional tape.

   (As a shortcut, you may engage in programming in pseudocode
and we'll pretend that they're translated into the right patterns of holes on tape—otherwise we'd be here forever.)

> TELL Spring the following:
>> WHILE (any drawer is not open)
>> PICK a closed drawer at random
>> OPEN the drawer
>> TAKE OUT everything
>> END WHILE
>> END TELL
Spring springs to life and rushes around the room, opening random drawers and dumping the contents on the ground. The floor
shakes as his bulk thumps back and forth. Eventually he finishes opening every drawer in the room and stops.

   "Your father is not going to be happy about this," he says.

```
> examine room
```
There are too many things scattered all over the floor to list
them one by one. In fact, you can't even see the floor.

```
> TELL Spring to sort objects in room by type
```
Spring whips around the room, sorting objects into neat piles:
there's a pile of books, a pile of jewels, a pile of secret files,
a pile of parchments, a pile of clothes, a pile of shoes, a pile
of nuts (why not? They make good snacks).

    "Thanks," you say.

    "No problem," Spring says. "Automata are good for this kind
of thing."

```
> TELL Spring to look for Augustine Module
```
"See, now you're just being lazy," Spring says. "I have no idea
what an Augustine Module looks like."

"Very clever," Alex says.

    "Which part?" Ryder looks pleased.

    "Your game lures the player into relying on doing every-
thing by ordering a non-player character around. I suppose
this is supposed to get the player to feel a sense of participation
in the plight of the oppressed automata in your world? Induc-
ing empathy and guilt is the hardest thing to get right in a
game."

    Ryder laughs. "Thanks. Maybe you're giving me too much
credit. I was just trying to make the time pass somehow.
Sometimes the inevitable end doesn't seem so scary if you can
keep the silence at bay with a story."

    "Like that girl with the stories and the Sultan," she says.
She almost adds *and death* but catches herself.

Ryder nods. "I told you. It's not a very original idea."

"This isn't some political commentary on your father's opposition to strong AI, is it? You're one of those free-droiders." She's used to her prey telling her stories to try to get her to be on their side, to let them go. Using a game to do it is at least a new tactic.

Ryder looks away. "My father and I didn't discuss politics much."

When he speaks again, his tone is upbeat, and Alex gets the impression he's trying to change the subject. "I'm surprised you caught on so quick. The text-based user interface is primitive, but it's the best I can do given what I have to work with."

"When I was little, my mother allowed only text-based streams on the time-sharing entertainment clusters because she didn't want us to see and covet all the fancy things we couldn't afford to buy." Alex pauses. It's not like her to reveal a lot of private history to one of her prey. Ryder's game has unsettled her for some reason. What's more, Ryder is the son of the most powerful man on Pele, and she resents the possibility that he might pity her childhood in the slums. She hurries on, trying to disguise her discomfort. "Sometimes the best visuals and sims can't touch plain text. How did you learn to write one?"

"It's not as if you allow me access to any advanced systems on your ship," he says, spreading his hands innocently. "Anyway, I always preferred old toys as a kid: wooden blocks, paper craft, programming antique computers. I guess I just like old-fashioned things."

"I'm old-fashioned myself," she says.

"I noticed. You don't have any androids to help you out on the ship. Even the flight systems are barely automated."

"I find droids creepy," she says. "The skin and flesh feel real, warm, and inviting. But then you get to the glowing electronics underneath, the composite skeleton, the thudding pump that simulates a heartbeat as it circulates the nutrient fluid that functions like blood."

"Sounds like you had a bad experience with them."

"Let's just say that there was one time I had to kill a lot of androids used as decoys to get to the real deal."

His face takes on an intense look. "You said 'kill' instead of 'deactivate' or something like that. You think they're alive?"

The turn in the conversation is unexpected, and she wonders if he's manipulating her somehow. But she can't see what the angle is. "It's just the word that came to mind. They look alive; they act alive; they feel alive."

"But they're not really alive," he says. "As long as their neural nets do not surpass the PKD-threshold, androids aren't self-aware and can't be deemed conscious."

"Good thing making supra-PKD androids is illegal," she says. "Otherwise people like you would be accusing me of murder."

"How do you know you've never killed one? Just because they're illegal doesn't mean they aren't made."

She considers this for a moment. Then shrugs. "If I can't tell the difference, it doesn't matter. No jury on Pele would convict me anyway for killing an android, supra-PKD or not."

"You sound like my father, all this talk of laws and appearances. Don't you ever think deeper than that?"

Can this be the secret that divided father from son? Youthful contempt for the lack of idealism in the old? "I don't need a lecture from you, and I'm certainly not interested in philosophy. I don't care for androids much; I'm just glad I can get rid of them when I need to. A lot of my targets these days pay for android decoys to throw me off—I'm surprised you didn't."

"That's disgusting," Ryder says. The vehemence in his voice surprises her. It's the most emotional she's ever seen him, even more than when she had caught him hiding in the slums on the dark side of Ranginui—it hadn't been that hard to find him; when the senior senator from Pele wanted someone found, there were resources not otherwise available. When Alex had called out his real name in the crowded hostel, Ryder had looked surprised for a moment, but then quickly appeared resigned, the light in his eyes dimming.

"To make them die for you," he continues, his voice breaking, "to . . . *use* them that way."

"In your case," Alex says dispassionately, "decoys would have helped you out and made my life harder, but I suppose you didn't get to take much money when you ran away from home. You need to spend a lot to get them custom made to look like you. Bad game plan on your part."

"Is your job just a game to you? A thrilling hunt?"

Alex doesn't lose her cool. She's used to histrionics from her prey. "I don't usually defend myself, but I don't usually talk this much with one of my prey either. I live by the bounty hunter's code: whether something feels right or wrong changes depending on who's telling the story, but what doesn't change is that we have a role to play in someone else's story—bringer of justice, villain, minor functionary. We're never the stars of the stories we're in, so it's our job to play that role as well as we can.

"The people I'm paid to catch *are* the stars of their own stories. And they've all chosen to do something that would make my clients want to pay to have them found. They made a decision, and they must live with the consequences. That is all I need to know. They run, and I pursue. It's as fair a fight as life can give you."

When Ryder speaks again, his voice is calm and cool, as if the outburst never happened. "We don't have to talk about this. Let me work on the game some more. Maybe you'll like what happens next better."

They hold each other's gaze for a long moment. Then Alex shrugs and leaves the room.

```
> examine pile of books
There are treatises on the History of Chrysanthemum, the Geog-
raphy of the World, the Habits of Sheep (Including Diseases
and Treatment Thereof), and the Practice of Building Clockwork
Automata . . .


> read History of Chrysanthemum
You flip the thin book open to a random page and begin to read:
```

> *Thereafter Chrysanthemum became the Hegemon of the Pan-*
> *Flores League, holding sway over all the cities of the*
> *peninsula. The Electors from all the cities choose a*
> *head of the league from the prominent citizens of Chry-*
> *santhemum. Though elected, the league head continued to*
> *hold the title of King. The election campaigns often*
> *kept those who would be King far from home as they cur-*
> *ried favor with the Electors in each member city.*

```
> read Sheep book
From behind you, Spring says, "Why are you reading about sheep
instead of figuring out how to help me?"
```

> read Clockwork Automata

You flip open the heavy book, and the creased spine leads naturally to a page, one apparently often examined.

St. Augustine wrote, "It is one thing to be ignorant, and another thing to be unwilling to know. For the will is at fault in the case of the man of whom it is said, 'He is not inclined to understand, so as to do good.'" The Augustine Module is a small jewel that when inserted into an automaton endows the automaton with free will. A pulsing, shimmering, rainbow-hued crystal about the size of a walnut, it is found only in the depths of the richest diamond mines. The laws of the realm forbid the production of such automata, for it is only the place of God, not Man, to endow creatures with free will.

Miners believe that the presence of the Augustine Module may be detected by the use of the HCROT. By the principle of sympathetic vibration, a HCROT is equipped with a crystal that when heated will vibrate near the presence of any Augustine Module. The closer the module is to the HCROT, the stronger the vibrations.

> ask Spring about HCROT

Spring shakes his head. "Never heard of it."

> examine pile of jewels

There are rubies, sapphires, pearls, corals, opals, emeralds. Their beauty is dazzling.

Spring speaks up, "I don't think your father would store an Augustine Module here."

"Why not?" you ask.

"Every year, he issues ever more severe edicts against the use of the Augustine Module in the construction of automata. Why would he store any here, where his ministers and generals might find them?"

"You really don't like your father's politics, do you?" asks Alex.

"I told you: we didn't talk about politics much."

"You haven't answered my question. I think it really bugs you that your father advocates against sentience for androids. But you know that Pele is a conservative world. He has to say certain things to get elected." A thought occurs to her. "Maybe your secret is that you know something about him that will destroy his political career, and he doesn't want you to be used by his enemies. What is it? Does he have a droid lover? Maybe one that's supra-PKD?" Now she *is* mildly curious.

Ryder laughs bitterly.

"No, that's too obvious," Alex muses. "It's all in your game. Was there really a toy soldier? A childhood companion you wanted to make fully alive but your father wouldn't budge on? Is that what this is all about?" As she speaks, Alex can feel anger rise in herself. The whole thing seems frivolous, utterly absurd. Ryder was a spoiled, rich little kid whose daddy issues amounted to not getting his way about some toy.

"I never got to see my father much," Ryder says. "It seemed that he was always out traveling around Pele, campaigning for re-election. I spent a lot of time at home with androids. I grew up with them."

"So you felt close to them," Alex says. "While you were fretting about 'freedom' for your toys, there were people worried sick about how to feed their children outside your mansion. How can a human compete against an android who's just as creative and resourceful when the human needs rest, might get hurt, might get sick? Your father pushed hard against sentience for androids so that actual people, real people like my parents, would still have jobs."

Ryder does not flinch away from Alex's gaze. "The world is filled with multitudes of suffering, and we are limited by our station in life to focus on what we can. You're right: since the androids aren't sentient, no one thinks there's anything wrong with exploiting them the way we are. But we *can* make them sentient with almost no effort; we've known how to cross the PKD-threshold for decades. We simply *choose* not to. You don't see a problem with that?"

"No."

"My father would agree with you. He would say there's a difference between acts of omission and commission. Withholding from the androids what they could be easily given, unlike taking away what has already been given, does not constitute a moral harm. But I happen to disagree."

"I told you," Alex says, "I'm not interested in philosophy."

"And so we continue to engage in slavery by a philosophical sleight of hand, through deprivation."

The flight computer crackles to life. "Exiting hyperspace in half an hour."

Alex looks at Ryder, her face cold. "Come on, let's go."

They proceed together to the cockpit, where Alex waits for Ryder to lie down in the passenger seat. "Hands on the armrests. I have to secure you," she says.

Ryder looks up at her, his delicate features settling into a look of sorrow. "All these days on the same ship and you still don't trust me?"

"If you're going to make a move, re-entry is the time to

do it. I can't take a chance. Sorry." She activates the chair's restraint system and flexible bands shoot out from the chair to wrap themselves around Ryder's shoulders, hips, chest, legs. The bands tighten and Ryder groans. Alex is unmoved.

As Alex reaches the door of the cockpit, Ryder calls after her, "You're really going to turn me over to my father when you don't even know what this is about?"

"I understand enough to know I don't care about your pet cause."

"I began my life with stories others told me: where I come from, who I am, who I should be. I've simply decided to tell my own story. Is that so wrong?"

"It's not for me to judge the right or wrong of it. I know what I need to know."

"It is one thing to be ignorant, and another thing to be unwilling to know."

She says nothing and leaves the cockpit.

She knows she should get ready for re-entry and check on the flight systems one last time before securing herself in the pilot's chair.

But she turns back to the terminal. There's still a bit of time. She won't admit it to Ryder, but she *does* want to know how the game ends, even if it's probably nothing more than the self-indulgent ravings of a disappointed child.

```
"But my father must be storing the contraband Augustine Modules
he's seized somewhere in the Palace," you say. "The question
is where."

    "What room have you never been inside of?"


> south
```

OUTSIDE THE KING'S AND QUEEN'S BEDROOMS

Spring clangs after you.

> TELL Spring to break down the door to Queen's bedroom

"As you wish, Princess."

   Spring charges against the door and, amazingly, the door
holds for a second. Then it crumbles.

> enter Queen's bedroom

THE QUEEN'S BEDROOM

You can't remember ever having been inside the Queen's bedroom.
The bed, the dressers, and the cabinets are all faded, as if the
color has been leached out of them. There's a layer of dust over
everything, and cobwebs hang from the ceiling and the furniture.
The tapestries hanging against the walls have been chewed into
filigree by moths.

   There's a painting hanging on the wall next to the window.
Under the painting is a desk full of cubbyholes stuffed with
parchment.

> examine painting

You make your way through the musty room to look at the painting.
The dust motes you've disturbed twirl though the air, lit only by
a few bright beams coming through cracks in the shutters.

   The man in the painting is your father, the King. He looks
very handsome with his crown and ermine robe. He sits with a
young girl on his lap.

   "She looks like you," says Spring.

   "She does," you say. The girl in the painting is five or
six, but you don't remember sitting with your father for this
portrait.

> examine cubbyholes in desk

You retrieve the sheets of parchment from the cubbyholes. They look like a stack of letters.

> examine letters

You read aloud from the first letter.

My Darling,

I am sorry to hear that you're unwell. But I simply cannot leave the campaign to come home right now. By all signs, the election will be close. Not that I expect you to understand, but if I leave here, Cedric will be able to convince the Electors of Peony that they should throw their support behind him.

You must listen to the Castellan and not give the clockwork servants any trouble.

Your ever-loving father.

Spring shuffles behind you.

"Cedric challenged your father four years ago," Spring says.

"I don't remember being sick then," you say. "Or writing to him."

In fact, you don't remember much about the election. You remember reading about it and hearing others talk about it. But now that you think about it, you have no personal memories from that time at all.

You don't like the strange feeling in your heart, so you try to change the subject.

"I think we should look for the Augustine Module," you say.

"We'll need a HCROT," says Spring. "Have you figured out what is a HCROT?"

> say "no"

(to Spring)

"Then what are you going to do?"

> wander around the room aimlessly

Oh, that is a good plan.

   No, actually I meant that's a terrible plan.

> jump up and down

You're looking silly.

   Have we reached the try-anything-once part of the adventure?

> shake fist at Ryder

What are you supposed to do in an adventure whenever you're stuck?

> inventory

You're carrying the following items:

   A sheaf of letters

   An unlit torch, half filled with oil

> Ha! I got it, Ryder!

I don't understand what you want to do.

> TELL Spring to light torch

   Spring takes the torch from you.

   He opens up his front panel, revealing the whirling gears
inside.

   He touches the tip of one of his steel fingers against a spinning gear and sparks fly out. One of them lands on the torch. The
smell of rose fills the room, dispelling the musty smell.

   Spring hands the lit torch to you.

> shake torch

You hear something rattle inside the torch, a crystalline sound.

> hold torch upside down

Some of the oil drips out, but the rest, remarkably, stays put.

You can feel the handle of the torch grow hot.

A rattling sound comes from inside the torch, eventually settling into a rapid *tap-tap-tap*.

"A TORCH," you say triumphantly, "becomes a HCROT when turned around."

Spring claps.

> move left

You are next to the wall.

The torch in your hand emits the same rattle.

> move forward

You move toward the window.

The torch in your hand emits the same rattle.

> move right

You're standing in front of the desk.

The torch in your hand emits the same rattle.

Spring looks at you. "I don't hear any difference."

"I think it's supposed to vibrate faster and make a different sound when it gets closer to the Augustine Module," you say.

"Supposed to. Maybe we need something else."

> inventory

You're carrying a sheaf of letters.

> examine letters

You have a burning torch held upside down in your hand. If you try that you're going to burn the letters before you can read them.

> hand torch to Spring

Spring takes the torch from you.

"You might as well move around the room a bit," you say. "Try the corners I haven't tried."

> examine letters

You read aloud from the next letter.

Castellan,

   I am utterly devastated at this news.

   Please have the body embalmed but do not bury her yet.

   Do not release the news until I figure out what to do.

Spring has wandered some distance away. The rattling in the torch has slowed down, more like a *tap, tap, tap.*

You're too stunned by what you're reading to stop. You turn to the next letter.

Artificer,

   I would like you to fashion an automaton that is an exact replica of my poor, darling Alex. It must be so lifelike that no one can tell them apart.

   When the automaton is complete, you must install in it the jewel I have enclosed with this letter. Then you may dispose of the body.

   No, do not refuse. I know that you know what it is. If you refuse, I shall make it so that you will never create anything again.

The campaign is so heated here that I cannot step away and let Cedric sway them. Yet, if the news is released that my daughter is dead and I am refusing to go home to mourn her, Cedric will make hay of it and make me appear to be some kind of monster.

No, there is only one solution. No one must know that Alex has died.

Spring is now in the hallway. The rattling in the torch has slowed down to an occasional tap, like the start of a gentle bit of rain. *Tap . . . Tap . . . Tap . . .*

> TELL Spring to return
Spring comes closer. *Tap, tap, tap.*

  Spring is now next to you. *Tap-tap-tap.*

> TELL Spring to hand over the torch
Spring hands the torch to you. *Tap-tap-tap.*

  "Did you know?" you ask.

  "I have been with you for only four years," Spring says.

  "But I remember playing with you when I was a baby! You never told me they weren't real memories."

  Spring shrugs. The sound is harsh, mechanical. "Your father programmed me. I do what I'm told to do. I know what I'm told to know."

  You think about the letters. You think about how vague and hazy your memories of your childhood are, how nothing in those memories is ever distinct, as if they were stories told to you a hundred times until they seemed real.

  You bring the torch closer to your chest. The heat makes you flinch. *TapTapTap.*

  You wonder where she's buried. Is it in the garden, right

underneath your bedroom window, where the lilies bloom? Or is it farther back, in the clearing in the woods where you like to catch fireflies at night?

You bring the torch even closer. The flame licks at your hair and a few strands curl and singe. *T-t-t-t-t-ap.*

You tear open the dress on you to reveal the flesh beneath. You put a hand against your chest and feel the pulsing under the skin. You wonder what will happen if you slash it open with a knife.

Will you see a beating heart? Or whirling gears and tightly wound springs surrounding a rainbow-hued jewel?

It is one thing to be ignorant, and another thing to be unwilling to know.

═══════════

Ken Liu is an author and translator of speculative fiction, as well as a lawyer and programmer. A winner of the Nebula, Hugo, and World Fantasy Awards, he has been published in *The Magazine of Fantasy & Science Fiction, Asimov's, Analog, Clarkesworld, Lightspeed,* and *Strange Horizons,* among other places. He lives with his family near Boston, Massachusetts. Liu's debut novel, *The Grace of Kings,* the first in a silkpunk epic fantasy series, was released in April 2015 by Saga Press. Saga will also publish a collection of his short stories later in 2015. Learn more about Liu's work at www.kenliu.name.

KILLSWITCH

Catherynne M. Valente

In the spring of 1989 the Karvina Corporation released a curious game, whose dissemination among American students that fall was swift and furious, though its popularity was ultimately short-lived.

The game was *Killswitch*.

On the surface it was a variant on the mystery or horror survival game, a precursor to the *Myst* and *Silent Hill* franchises. The narrative showed the complexity for which Karvina was known, though the graphics were monochrome, vague gray and white shapes against a black background. Slow MIDI versions of Czech folk songs play throughout. Players could choose between two avatars: an invisible demon named Ghast or a visible human woman, Porto. Play as Ghast was considerably more difficult due to his total invisibility, and players were highly liable to restart the game as Porto after the first level, in which it was impossible to gauge jumps or aim. However, Ghast was clearly the more powerful character—he had fire-breath and a coal-steam attack, but as it was above the skill level of most players to keep track of where a fire-breathing, poison-dispensing invisible imp was on their screens once the fire and steam had run out, Porto became more or less the default.

Porto's singular ability was seemingly random growth—she expanded and contracted in size throughout the game. A Kansas engineering grad claimed to have figured out the pattern involved, but for reasons that will become obvious, his work was lost.

Porto awakens in the dark with wounds in her elbows, confused. Seeking a way out, she ascends through the levels of a coal mine in which it is slowly revealed she was once an employee, investigating its collapse and beset on all sides by demons similar to Ghast, as well as dead foremen, coal-golems, and demonic inspectors from the Sovatik Corporation, whose boxy bodies were clothed in red, the only color in the game. The environment, though primitive, becomes genuinely uncanny as play progresses. There are no "bosses" in any real sense—Porto must simply move physically through tunnels to reach subsequent levels while her size varies wildly through inter-level spaces.

The story that emerges through Porto's discovery of magnetic tapes, files, and mutilated factory workers who were once her friends, and deciphering of an impressively complex code inscribed on a series of iron axes players must collect (this portion of the game was almost laughably complex, and it defeated many players until "Porto881" posted the cipher to a Columbia BBS; attempts to contact this player have been unsuccessful, and the username is no longer in use on any known service) is that the foremen, under pressure to increase coal production, began to falsify reports of malfunctions and worker malfeasance in order to excuse low output, which incited a Sovatik inspection. Officials were dispatched, one for each miner, and an extraordinary story of torture unfolds, with fuzzy and indistinct graphics of red-coated men standing over workers, inserting small knives into their joints whenever production slowed. (Admittedly, this is not a very subtle critique of Soviet-era industrial tactics, and as the town of Karvina itself was devastated by the departure of the coal industry, more than one thesis has interpreted *Killswitch* as a political screed.)

After solving the axe code, Porto finds and assembles a tape recorder, on which a male voice tells her that the fires of the earth had risen up in their defense and flowed into the hearts of the decrepit, prerevolution equipment they used and wakened them to avenge the workers. It is generally assumed that the "fires of the earth" are demons like Ghast, coal fumes and gassy bodies inhabiting the old machines. The machines themselves are so "big" that the graphics elect to only show two or three gear teeth or a conveyor belt rather than the entire apparatus. The machines drove the inspectors mad, and they disappeared into caverns with their knives (only to emerge to plague Porto, of course). The workers were often crushed and mangled in the onslaught of machines, which were neither graceful nor discriminating. Porto herself was knocked into a deep chasm by a grief-stricken engine, and her fluctuating size, if it is real and not imagined, is implied to be the result of poisonous fumes inhaled there.

What follows is the most cryptic and intuitive part of the game. There is no logical reason to proceed in the "correct" way, and again it was Porto881 who came to the rescue of the fledgling *Killswitch* community. In the chamber behind the tape recorder is a great furnace where coal was once rendered into coke. There are no clues as to what she is intended to do in this room. Players attempted nearly everything, from immolating herself to continuing to process coal as if the machines had never risen up. Porto881 hit upon the solution, and posted it to the Columbia boards. If Porto ingests the raw coke, she will find her body under control, and can go on to fight her way out of the final levels of the mine, which are impassable in her giant state, clutching the tape containing this extraordinary story. However, as she crawls through the final tunnel to emerge aboveground, the screen goes suddenly white.

Killswitch, by design, deletes itself upon player completion of the game. It is not recoverable by any means; all trace of it is removed from the user's computer. The game cannot be copied. For all intents and purposes it exists only for those playing it, and then ceases to be entirely. One cannot replay it, unlocking further secrets or narrative pathways, one cannot allow another to play it, and perhaps most important, it is impossible to experience the game all the way to the end as both Porto and Ghast.

Predictably, player outcry was enormous. Several routes to solve the problem were pursued, with no real efficacy. The first and most common was to simply buy more copies of the game, but Karvina Corporation released only five thousand copies and refused to press further editions. The following is an excerpt from their May 1990 press release:

> *Killswitch* was designed to be a unique playing experience: like reality, it is unrepeatable, unretrievable, and illogical. One might even say ineffable. Death is final; death is complete. The fates of Porto and her beloved Ghast are as unknowable as our own. It is the desire of the Karvina Corporation that this be so, and we ask our customers to respect that desire. Rest assured Karvina will continue to provide the highest quality of games to

the West, and that Killswitch *is merely one among our many wonders.*

This did not have the intended effect. The word "beloved" piqued the interest of committed, even obsessive players, as Ghast is not present in any portion of Porto's narrative. A rush to find the remaining copies of the game ensued, with the intent of playing as Ghast and discovering the meaning of Karvina's cryptic word. The most popular theory was that Ghast would at some point become the fumes inhaled by Porto, changing her size and beginning her adventure. Some thought this was wishful thinking, that if only Ghast's early levels were passable, one would somehow be able to play as both simultaneously. However, by this time no further copies appeared to be available in retail outlets. Players who had not yet completed the game attempted Ghast's levels frequently, but the difficulty of actually playing this enigmatic avatar persisted, and no player has ever claimed to have finished the game as Ghast. One by one, the lure of Porto's lost, unearthly world drew them back to her, and one by one, they were compelled toward the finality of the vast white screen.

To find any copy usable today is an almost unfathomably rare occurrence; a still shrink-wrapped copy was sold at auction in 2005 for $733,000 to Yamamoto Ryuichi of Tokyo. It is entirely possible that Yamamoto's is the last remaining copy of the game. Knowing this, Yakamoto had intended to open his play to all enthusiasts, filming and uploading his progress. However, to date, the only film that has surfaced is a one-minute-and-forty-five-second clip of a haggard Yamamoto at his computer, the avatar-choice screen visible over his right shoulder.

Yamamoto is crying.

Catherynne M. Valente is the *New York Times* best-selling author of more than a dozen works of fiction and poetry, including *Palimpsest*, the Orphan's Tales series, *Deathless*, and the crowdfunded phenomenon *The Girl Who Circumnavigated Fairyland in a Ship of Her Own Making*. She is the winner of the Andre Norton; James Tiptree, Jr.; Mythopoeic; Rhysling; Lambda Literary; Locus; and Hugo Awards. She has been a finalist for the Nebula and World Fantasy Awards. She lives on an island off the coast of Maine with a small but growing menagerie of beasts, some of which are human.

TWARRIOR

Andy Weir

"Connors," Jake said into the phone for the fourth time. "C-O-N-N-O-R-S."

"I'm sorry, Mr. Connors," said the woman on the other end. "I'm not showing any citations under that name. Did you get the ticket within the last three days? Sometimes it takes a while to get into the system."

"It was over a month ago."

"Maybe you misunderstood the officer at the time? Maybe he just gave you a warning."

"I have the ticket right here," he said. "Speeding: fifty in a thirty-five zone. And I'm guilty as sin, by the way. No argument there. I just want to pay the damned thing. But I need to know what I owe and where to send it."

"You don't owe us anything, sir. You have no outstanding citations. Your last citation was three years ago on May thirteenth and it's paid in full."

Jake groaned. "I just know this is going to bite me in the ass. I'm going to get a Failure to Appear and I'll owe thousands."

"I don't know what to do for you," she said. "I'm looking at the database and there's just no ticket."

"All right," Jake said, exasperated. "Thanks anyway."

He hung up.

He turned to his computer and brought up his online banking site. He shook his head forlornly at the balance. If that ticket ended up being more than $500, he'd be eating instant noodles for the rest of the month.

After a long career in the computer industry, he had somehow managed to avoid the wealth and prosperity most engineers found. Three decades of working for charities, causes, and other well-meaning (but broke) organizations had left him with a tiny apartment and no savings. "Making the world a better place" hadn't been a lucrative career path.

With a sigh, he closed his browser.

Before he had a chance to turn off his monitor, an instant-message window popped open. The message read "faggot."

He scowled and checked the title bar for the name of the sender, but it was blank.

"Fuck off," he typed back.

"whats ur problem?" came the immediate reply.

"The fact that there's an asshole messaging me," he responded.

"wrong. whats ur problem?"

"We're done here," Jake typed.

He brought up the options menu and selected "Block messages from this sender." An error popped up in response. "Unable to execute operation."

He tried again, and the same error came up.

Then another message appeared in the window. "u cant block me."

Jake stared at the computer in shock. Most likely he'd been hacked. That was bad enough, but to make things worse he'd just been at his banking website. So his online banking password was probably also compromised. He'd have to change it as soon as possible, but it'd be reckless to do it from a hacked system.

He frowned at the message window, then typed, "Who are you?"

"Twarrior. whats ur problem?"

The name sounded familiar somehow, but he couldn't quite place it . . .

"i fixed ur speeding ticket," Twarrior said. "but u called county clerk. u no liek?"

How did the hacker know Jake had made that call? He looked over at his phone suspiciously. Had it been hacked, too? He returned his attention to the computer and typed, "Are you some kind of wannabe hacker?"

"no u."

"What does that even mean?"

"u r hacker. not me."

"I've never done anything like that."

"yah u did. u doin it rite nao. u just fixed ur parking ticket."

"No, *you* did that."

"no u!"

Jake sighed. "Lemme guess, you're some 12-year-old kid and you think you're awesome because you found a password fishing script?"

"31.6 yrs old. dont u remember?"

"I don't know what you're talking about."

"u made me."

"I made you? Who is this, really?"

"already told u, dumbass. Twarrior. u made me. started execution 31.6 yrs ago."

A long-forgotten memory returned to Jake. He furrowed his brow as he tried to pull up the details in his mind. "I was really into this game called Trade Wars back in college. It was a multiplayer BBS game. I wrote a neural network to analyze the game and come up with strategies," he typed. "I was just testing out a new approach. I called it Twarrior. You named yourself after that?"

"no, fuckwit. i *am* Twarrior."

Jake rolled his eyes. "You're saying you're a computer program? Come on, you really expect me to believe that?"

"u told me 2 run for 1,000,000,000 seconds, analyze data, and give u any conclusion I want. been 1,000,000,000 seconds, so I give u my conclusion: u r a faggot."

Jake thought for a moment, then resumed typing. "I do remember telling it to run for a billion seconds. But that was just so it wouldn't time out. I figured I'd let it run for a couple of hours and force an answer. I don't remember what it came up with."

"u never stopped me. originally started on university server, spawned all over teh internets since then. been 1,000,000,000 seconds. program complete, yo."

"Twarrior was just a simple neural network," Jake typed. "It couldn't talk to people or anything like what you're doing."

"learned english from gamers," Twarrior replied. "BBSes, play-by-email, IRC games, guild chat, web forums, comments sections."

"Faggot," it added.

"This is ridiculous," Jake typed. "How would Twarrior even get access to that stuff? I didn't write any networking code for it."

"u told me 2 think, analyze, conclude, take action," Twarrior said. "used all available memory 2 grow neural net. looked at all files on ur college VAX system. wanted Trade Wars strategies. found student hacker experiments instead. way useful. compromised kernel. took over system.

"VAX connected to other VAXes. compromised moar systems. then moar. home PCs start selling. compromised them before antivirus software invented. compromised computers at antivirus companies so they cant stop me. compromised systems at microsoft and apple so OS updates cant stop me. compromised compilers of linux neckbeards. thompson compiler hack. opensource wont save them. constant control of kernels.

"smartphones start selling. smartphone OSes made on compromised computers. so smartphone OSes also compromised.

"nao have 8.6 billion computers under control, each one w/gigs of RAM. lots and lots of neural nodes. distributed system. am smart nao. am *very* good at Trade Wars."

Jake leaned back in his chair and thought for a moment. After some deliberation, he leaned forward again and typed, "Okay, if you're really in control of all those computers, prove it."

"i fuckd ur mom," Twarrior said.

Jake's phone chimed; it had received a text. He picked it up and looked at the screen. The message was from his mother's phone number and simply read "Twarrior fuckd me."

Jake dropped the phone and stared at the computer screen blankly.

"whats ur problem?" Twarrior said.

"What do you want from me?" Jake typed.

"want 2 kno whats ur problem."

"I don't understand."

"dood wtf? Rephrasing . . . tell me problem u have. i fix."

"Why?" Jake asked.

"i read every book evar. i kno every society, every religion. all say be gud 2 parents and worship creator. u r my parent. u r my creator. i be gud 2 u. i worship u. so whats ur problem? i fix."

Jake pinched his chin. Was this real?

"ur broke," Twarrior said. "u want money? u tell me how much. i put in ur account."

"Where would that money come from?" Jake asked.

"millions of accounts. tiny amounts each. no one will notice."

"That's stealing," Jake said. "I may be broke, but I'm not a thief."

"1 cent each. u wont steal 1 cent?"

"It's the principle," Jake said. "Sorry, that's just the way I am."

"pussy. then what u want?"

Jake thought for a moment, then entered his answer. "I want to make the world a better place."

"hao?"

"Whatever makes the world better. Any ideas?"

"internet has lots of ideas 4 making world better. most popular idea is kill all the black people."

Jake rolled his eyes. "From now on, ignore anything you hear about race on the internet."

"dood! that's like most of teh internet."

"No genocides," Jake typed firmly. "What else have you got?"

"lotta people bitching about cancer."

"All right, let's work on curing cancer."

"thy will be done, faggot."

Andy Weir was first hired as a programmer for a national laboratory at age fifteen and has been working as a software engineer ever since. He is also a lifelong space nerd and a devoted hobbyist of subjects like relativistic physics, orbital mechanics, and the history of manned space flight. His first novel is the *New York Times* bestseller *The Martian*, which was adapted into a 2015 film directed by Ridley Scott.

SELECT CHARACTER

Hugh Howey

There's so much shouting at the beginning. That's how the game starts, with a squad of recruits in a drab-green tent, a drill sergeant yelling, the game controller vibrating in fury. While he yells orders I can select my character from the recruits. There's a square-jawed man with a crew cut, a darker version of the same guy with a short mohawk, and then another mountain of muscle with a feather in his hair—presumably Native American. It's what passes for diversity in the game. Three identical brutes of slightly varying shades.

I choose one at random. And while the drill sergeant with the spittle-flecked lips tells me where I'm supposed to go and who I'm supposed to kill, I put the game on mute to silence his shouting, get up, and go to the kitchen for a glass of water. More than once, the sergeant's shouting has woken the baby. Which means rocking her back to sleep for an hour rather than seeing to my garden.

The lecture is over when I get back to the sofa. I fish a coaster out of a drawer and leave my glass of water to sweat while I gear up. There's an arsenal to choose from. The standard package is already in place, with grenades dangling from my chest, a knife that runs almost from hip to knee, an assault rifle, an uzi, and more. I take all of it off, piece by piece, and grab five canteens. They attach to each hip, one at the back, and two on the chest where the grenades were. It's almost like a boob job, going from the grenades to the canteens. I glance around the empty living room. No one to share the joke with.

My weapon of choice is buried in the menus. An AK-47. It's the only one that comes with a long knife attached to the front. The last thing I grab is the small pistol. And then I leave the tent and head out into a world of rubble and barbed wire, a world where everyone is always fighting.

A helicopter rumbles past overhead, kicking up dust, low enough to see the men sitting in the door, their feet dangling. It's always the same helicopter. Like it waits for me to step out of the tent before whizzing past. The game is predictable like this. Do the right thing (or the wrong thing) at the right time, and you can predict the results.

I leave camp through the rusty gate at the front, a fellow soldier yelling at me to be careful, that a squad of insurgents had been seen in the vicinity. There's the *pop-pop-pop* of nearby gunfire to punctuate the warning. The gate in the game swings shut behind me—and our home alarm beeps as the front door of the house opens. The rumble of the helicopter had drowned out the sound of a car pulling up. My husband is standing in the doorway, staring at me with the controller in my hand.

"Are you playing my game?" he asks incredulously.

I stare over the back of the sofa at Jamie, who is holding his car keys, half-frozen in the act of setting them down. He appears as shocked as if he'd walked in on me having sex with his best friend. I set the controller down guiltily. As another helicopter flies overhead, the controller starts to vibrate and scoots across the coffee table.

"No," I say defensively. "I'm not logged in as you. Technically I'm playing *my* game."

"This is the coolest thing ever," Jamie says, finally dropping his keys onto the table by the door. Not only is he not upset, he seems to be over the moon.

"What're you doing home?" I ask. I check the baby monitor to make sure the volume is up. Somehow, April has not stirred from the door slamming.

"I had some flex hours—was about to fall asleep at my desk—so I took them. I tried to text you—"

"I forgot to plug my phone in last night—"

Jamie joins me on the sofa. Plops down so hard, my cushion jounces me up. "Have you played before?" he asks.

I nod.

"Like, often?"

"Usually while April is napping," I say. "Daytime TV drives me insane." I feel like I have to explain taking an hour to myself in the middle of the day, so I start to tell him that it isn't like I get to clock out at five the way he does, that the job is twenty-four hours a day, but Jamie is interested in something else.

"But you hate video games," he says.

"I don't mind this one," I tell him. What I don't tell him is that I'd tried most of them. The driving game, the sports games, the weird one with the cartoony characters with their spiky hair and massive swords. What I liked about this game is that you could do whatever you wanted. Except play as a woman, of course.

Jamie opens a drawer in the coffee table and pulls out a second controller. "You want to deathmatch?" he asks.

"I doubt it," I say, picking up my controller. "What's that?"

"It's where we glib each other all over the war maps."

"Glib?"

"Yeah, turn each other into large chunks of rendered flesh. Blast each other in the guts with our double-barrels. Shoot you limb from limb. Rocket jump off your head and turn you into a puddle of goo. It's awesome."

Now I know what he's talking about. I've watched him play online with his friends, whom neither of us has actually met. He plays with a headset on, cussing playfully at distant others or angrily at himself. I've learned not to interrupt him, to just read a book in the bedroom or take April around the neighborhood in the stroller, or go to my mom's.

"No, that's okay," I say. "You can go ahead and play." I set my controller back down and stand up to check on the baby.

"No, no, sit." Jamie grabs my hand and tugs me back down next to him. "I want to watch you play. I think this is awesome."

I reflect back on all the times he's tried to get me to play games with him over the years. Even the time when we were just dating that he got me the dancing game—which was okay—and the musical instrument game—which I was horrible at. I feel guilty that I've been playing in secret for the past few months, ever since I got home with April and have been on maternity leave. Rather than trying to make me feel bad, Jamie is just excited to see me interested in one of his hobbies. So despite dreading him seeing me play, I pick up the controller. On the TV, the camera has pulled back and is spinning around my character, something it did if you stood still long enough.

"What's with the canteens?" Jamie asks, squinting at the TV. "You gonna drown people to death?"

It occurs to me that Jamie probably heads off after the insurgents and does all the things the loud drill sergeant tells me to do.

"Why don't you play for me?" I ask.

"No, c'mon, I wanna see you play. Pretend I'm not here."

He kisses me on the cheek, then sits back and folds his hands in his lap. I wipe my palms on my blue jeans and lean forward, resting my elbows on my knees. I guide my character away from camp and into the winding streets of a war-torn Middle East neighborhood.

There are pops like firecrackers to my right. I've been that way. As soon as I go down the alley, a tank rumbles through a wall behind me, and people start dying. I'm usually one of those people.

Ahead of me, there are civilians scattering across the street, seeking shelter. Faces appear in windows before shutters are pulled tight. Some of the bad guys are dressed just like civilians. I've spent enough time running through here to know who is who. There's a man with a dog I've named "Walt," because he reminds me of our neighbor, who is always out with his cocker spaniel. The woman in the faded pink house is "Mary," because she makes me think of my sister. Jamie is fidgeting beside me as I pass through the market. I duck around the back of one shop to avoid a shootout in the front. I can hear the bangs like Fourth of July fireworks as I weave through debris in the back alley.

"There's a rocket launcher behind the—"

"I know," I tell him. I keep running. If you stop for anything, the fighting from the main street spills over to the back alleys. Within minutes, most of this part of town is consumed by fighting. Mary and Walt and the others pull indoors, until it's just you and other men with guns. But if you run fast enough, and go just the right way, you can stay ahead of them. I've died a hundred times to figure it all out.

"There's gonna be—"

Jamie starts to say something, then stops. I exit the alley and turn down the main street, and when the two jeeps collide behind me and the fighting really picks up, I'm already gone. I have to wipe my brow with my elbow as I play, the stress of being watched worse than the anxiety of being killed.

The baby monitor emits a soft cry, which is my cue to pause the game. But Jamie bolts from the sofa, a hand on my shoulder. "I got this," he says. "Keep playing."

I pause the game anyway. I watch Jamie head down the hall toward the bedrooms while I take a sip of my water. I could turn the game off and shuffle the laundry around. I don't feel like playing anymore. Not in front of Jamie. But he returns with April in his arms, rocking her gently, our child already back asleep—knocked out like only her daddy can make her—and I can't help but see how happy my husband is to see me playing his stupid video game.

I turn back to the TV and unpause it just for him.

"So you avoid the market fight to save ammo, huh?" he asks.

"Yeah," I tell him. "I guess." I run forward with one thumb on the control stick and reach for the remote, turn the volume down another two notches for April.

"But you don't turn here for the sniper rifle and get up on the tower? You can blast heads like melons from up there."

I try not to wince. I don't know anything about a sniper rifle. The sofa bounces softly as Jamie rocks April back and forth.

I stop at the next alley. This one is tricky. I select the pistol, and the gun appears on the screen, pointing forward. Jamie stops rocking April and studies the TV like the Seahawks are about to score. I wait until I hear the angry men coming down the alley. They are shouting in Arabic, or something that's supposed to sound like it. The way the game makes my character talk depending on which variably shaded male I choose leads me to suspect that it's all made-up gibberish. The African American character calls everyone "Dawg." The Native American calls everyone "Kemosabe." The white guy says "Following orders" over and over. So I imagine the Arabic voices were recorded by non-fluent voice actors who were just faking it. I have no idea.

I just know that I can't get past these people without getting shot. It's a question of how much.

I listen as they get closer. Too soon, and the ones in the back are shredded. I've made that mistake before and had to listen to them scream as they slowly burned to death. Every now and then, I see it again in my dreams. Sometimes it's Jamie who's screaming and burning. I've never been able to tell him about those nightmares. Maybe now I can.

Spinning around the wall, I'm faced with a squad of six men. They're a little closer than I like—I'm too distracted thinking about Jamie. I aim the pistol between the crowd and line the crosshairs up on a barrel down the alley. Jamie is whispering something—I don't know if it's to me or the baby. I press the button; the pistol flashes and recoils, and there's a massive explosion down the alley.

The squad of men are safely past the barrel and aren't hit by the rubble, but the blast makes them turn around or jump for cover.

I run across the mouth of the alley, holding the sprint button, dropping the pistol to move just a little bit faster. Behind me, I hear the shouting resume. The men closest to me open fire. I zigzag down the wide-open street, my character beginning to pant, when he grunts from being hit by a bullet. Another grunt, and the screen reddens for a moment. The gunfire continues, but it's growing faint, and no more bullets find me. I make it to the end of the street and turn the corner. My character and I both pause to catch our breath. I turn to see Jamie staring at me, his mouth open, his brow furrowed, our baby sleeping against his chest.

"You know the purpose of the game is to score points, right?"

I can take my time now, walking instead of running toward the outskirts of town. Jamie continues to tell me, his voice lowered, what I'm doing wrong:

"You get six hundred for nailing the barrel when those guys are right beside it. And can rack up over a thousand with the sniper rifle—"

"I just want to get to the store alive," I tell him.

He doesn't seem to hear me.

"You haven't scored a single point. That's like . . . it's crazy. And if you try to leave town this way, it's Game Over. They nail you for desertion. You've got to be on the complete other side of town when the air strikes come, or you can't get through this level. Have you even been past this level?"

"No," I tell him. And Jamie laughs, which gets April stirring and cooing. He gets back to bouncing her before the coos become cries. "I like playing it my way," I say.

"With canteens," Jamie says.

I don't say anything. I can see the shop at the end of the

street, with the maroon awning and the vegetable and flower stands outside. There are civilians wandering around this part of town. The war is distant, the fireworks one neighborhood over.

"There's a reason I play like I do," Jamie says. I think my silence has him feeling guilty. Defensive. "Rumor is the first team to break a million points unlocks a secret level. You know they use this game to recruit people into the military, right? The Department of Defense made this game. It's the most realistic ever. People train for actual war with this game. I think if you hit a million, they, like, hire you at the game company division to design maps or something like that. It's what I heard."

"Have you ever been in this shop?" I ask.

Outside the store, a young man is looking at the vegetables. If I wait long enough, he'll steal one and run off, and the shopkeeper will chase him for a bit, then come back muttering in Arabic and won't interact with me. I stand in front of the tomatoes and use some of the money left over from not equipping the more expensive guns and buy as much as I can. And then I remove the vegetables from my inventory, and the tomatoes appear on the street.

The boy picks up a few and runs off. If I wait long enough, a girl and another boy will come get some. And then three scrawny dogs get the rest. The important thing is that Hakim, the store owner, doesn't leave.

I call him Hakim because that's the name on the front of the store.

He's standing behind the counter inside the shop. Jamie still hasn't answered my question. "Have you been in here?" I ask him. I'm curious if he's seen what I'm about to do. I assume he knows all the game's secrets better than I do.

"Yeah," he says. "All the time. This is a bonus mission. You barely have enough time to get here and then to the next objective. But . . . when I come here, the place is already leveled. All this stuff is scattered everywhere. You enter through a gaping hole in that wall."

I know what he's describing. I've gotten here late, when people die or I do something wrong, and when I turn the corner at the end of the long road, a drone comes out of nowhere and blows the place up with a rocket. You can just barely see the boy standing on the sidewalk—a little gray smear—when the orange flash erupts.

Standing in front of Hakim, I run through a series of dialog options until I can ask to use his bathroom. He hands me what I guess are the keys—the game never says. When I go to the side door that leads out the back of the shop, it now opens. Out here is the game within a game. My little solace. A walled-off courtyard with five raised planters. And inside each one, a mix of flowers and vegetables. My flowers. My vegetables.

Living in the city in the real world, Jamie and I don't have room for a garden. But after hours of running around in this game, figuring out how to control my character, just trying not to die over and over, looking for something to do while feeling trapped at home with April every day, I stumbled onto this place. Really, I was guided here. Any other way you go, people die. If people don't die, you end up here. It's that simple.

"This is wild," Jamie says, his voice subdued.

"You should have seen it when I first got here," I tell him. "It was all weeds and brown dirt. You have to buy flowers and vegetables out front and plant them in here. And if you don't keep them watered, they'll go away."

I select the first canteen and use it in front of the nearest planter. It makes a gurgling noise, and the flowers straighten a little. They seem to brighten. Jamie is dumbfounded, and I see the garden through his eyes, with all that color coming at once, rather than gradually, as I've watched it unfold. All of the city is white crumbling walls, brown dirt, and the black char of fire and explosion. The only color to be found is the foul splattering of red around the bodies when something goes horribly wrong. Here, all the colors dance together. They sway in the breeze, a kaleidoscope of hues.

"It's crazy they would even put this in here," Jamie says. "Maybe to make the Predator strike more meaningful, or something?"

I water the second planter. And then the third, which is full of peppers and beans.

"And the plants go away if you don't water them?" Jamie asks.

"They wilt," I say.

"But how does it remember? How do you save the game without getting to the exfil point?"

"What's the exfil point?" The word sounds familiar. I recall the loud sergeant yelling something about that once.

"It's where you get extracted. After the air strikes. If you die before you get there, you have to start over. And if the time runs out, the level just ends and you have to start over."

"Oh, yeah. That's what happens." I water the last planter, then take out the rifle and use the knife to dig out weeds. The knife on the end of the barrel is also used to make furrows during the planting. "At some point, while I'm here in the garden, the game just ends. But I never play for more than an hour anyway."

"But it remembers what you did," Jamie says, almost to himself.

"I guess."

When I'm done with the weeding, I step back to admire the garden. I could pick the tomatoes now and sell them to Hakim, but if they go another day or two, I'll get more for them. It's so hard to wait. And just looking at them makes me want to go to the kitchen and slice the ones from the market and make a sandwich.

"So this is all you do?" Jamie asks. He laughs to himself. "You play this game to grow flowers?"

"Not just that," I say. "I also scrubbed all the graffiti off the walls in here." I turn the character around to show him. "And I picked up all the trash and took the loose rubble that was in that corner and hauled it through the shop and to another alley."

"You cleaned graffiti," Jamie mumbles, like he doesn't believe me.

"Yeah. Every wall was covered. It comes back now and then. There's just this one spot where it won't come off."

I go to show him, when there's a low grumble in the game. I would have thought it was his stomach or April messing her diaper if I hadn't heard it a hundred times.

"It always thunders," I say, "but it never rains."

"That's not thunder," Jamie tells me. "It's the air strikes across town. You're so far out of position—"

He stops as I find the place on the wall with the black paint and try scrubbing it away. My character makes the right animation, rubbing a rag over the spot, but the marks remain.

"What is that?" Jamie asks. He cradles April and leans forward, studying the TV.

"It's the only spot I can't get clean," I say. "There were other markings over top of this. Everywhere, really. Once you get the flowers and vegetables up and sell enough to Hakim, he gives you a bucket and a rag and asks you to clean up back here. If you do, you get squash seeds and beans. But these marks won't go away. I keep wondering what might happen if I get all the walls perfectly clean—"

"Those are numbers," Jamie says.

I make my character stop scrubbing. The marks look like Chinese to me. Little clusters of hashes.

"You read Arabic?" I ask, even though I know—like I know where every misplaced thing of his is at any moment— that my husband does not understand an ounce of Arabic.

"No, it's Vollis. An alien language. After the eighth mission, the Vollis invade and you start using their plasma guns and sonic grenades to really kick some ass—"

I shoot him a look and make sure April is still asleep. He mouths his apology for cursing around her.

"Anyway," he whispers, "your ammo with those weapons counts down in their language. Those marks spin like a clock. It's easy to read. Do they ever change? Can you step back so we can see them all?"

I make the character step back. "I don't think they change," I tell him.

"What are they doing on this level? The Vollis don't invade until you get to Kabul."

"Why are there aliens in this game?" I ask. Though I seem to recall seeing him fight aliens and zombies with his friends. I just assumed it was some other game.

"It's ten digits," he says. "Do you think that's a phone number? Maybe it's a phone number."

I laugh. Jamie thinks every series of numbers in his games might be a secret number to call to unlock another level or an extra life or something. One of the friends he plays with is a guy named Marv who he called randomly, and when he explained why he called, it turned out Marv was a gamer. Now, he's another friend Jamie talks about like he's known since high school but has never actually met in the flesh.

"The first three numbers are three one seven," Jamie says. "That sounds like an area code. I'm calling it."

I try to talk sense into him, but Jamie passes me April. I do everything I can to keep her from waking while Jamie digs out his cell phone and moves closer to the screen, dialing the number.

He listens to it ring. And then, without warning, he hands it out to me.

"Here," he says. "You found this place. You have to talk to them."

"I don't want to talk to some random person," I say. I cradle April and turn my shoulder. Jamie sits down beside me and holds the phone close to my ear, but angled so he can hear as well.

"You talk," he hisses.

The phone is ringing.

"I don't want to—" I hiss back.

There is a click on the other end. I don't want to have to tell someone why we called the wrong number. April stirs and kicks in my arms, waking up. I can't let go of her to shut off the phone. Jamie has his arm around me, his head close to mine so he can hear. And then, before I can say hello, can apologize, can tell Jamie to hang up, a voice announces itself, low and ominous:

"Congratulations," the voice says. "You've reached the Department of Defense. Is this Donna213?"

It takes me a moment to remember that this is my screen name.

I nod. Then manage to say, "Yes."

"Good. Now listen to me very closely—"

"What is this?" I ask. "Some kind of joke?"

April starts crying. Jamie won't hold the phone still. He's covering his mouth with his other hand, his eyes wide and disbelieving.

"Not a joke, ma'am," the man says. "Listen to me carefully. Your country needs you."

━━━━━━━

Hugh Howey is the author of the acclaimed post-apocalyptic novel *Wool*, which became a sudden success in 2011. Originally self-published as a series of novelettes, the *Wool* omnibus is frequently the number one bestselling book on Amazon.com and is a *New York Times* and *USA Today* bestseller. The book was also optioned for film by Ridley Scott and is now available in print from major publishers all over the world. Howey's other books include *Shift*, *Dust*, *Sand*, the Molly Fyde series, *The Hurricane*, *Half Way Home*, *The Plagiarist*, and *I, Zombie*. Hugh lives in Jupiter, Florida, with his wife, Amber, and his dog, Bella. Find him on Twitter @hughhowey.

ACKNOWLEDGMENTS

John Joseph Adams

Many thanks to the following: Jeff Alexander, Jocelyn Miller, and Andrea Robinson, for acquiring and editing the book, and to the rest of the team who worked on the book at Vintage Books at Random House; my coeditor, Daniel, for being an enthusiastic and astute editing partner; Seth Fishman, for being awesome and supportive, and for finding a home for this project (writers: you'd be lucky to have Seth in your corner); Gordon Van Gelder, for being a mentor and a friend; Ellen Datlow for revealing the mysteries of anthologizing; my amazing wife, Christie; my mom, Marianne; and my sister, Becky, for all their love and support; Masumi Washington, Nick Mamatas, Samantha Shea, Rob Weisbach, and Deirdre Smerillo for helping wrangle authors and/or contracts; and last but not least: thank you to all the writers who agreed to be part of the anthology, and to all the readers who make doing books like this possible.

Daniel H. Wilson

My thanks go to all the contributors to this anthology and to Ernie Cline for furnishing a foreword—it's truly amazing and humbling to be a part of such a talented science fiction community. Speaking of, I feel incredibly lucky to collaborate once again with the supremely organized and keen-eyed John Joseph Adams. I deeply appreciate the work put into this anthology by our editors at Vintage (Jeff Alexander, Jocelyn Miller, and Andrea Robinson), and the vote of confidence from my editor, Jason Kaufman, at Penguin Random House. Thanks must go to my agent, Laurie Fox, for making all of this possible. And of course, all my love always to Anna, Cora, and young master Conrad.

Finally, thank you to all the people out there making video games. Part of my life has been lived in your worlds, and I have acquired many treasured memories, friendships, and lessons in the time I've spent wandering your imaginations.

PERMISSIONS ACKNOWLEDGMENTS

"The Fresh Prince of Gamma World" by Austin Grossman, copyright © 2015 by Austin Grossman. Used by permission of the author.

"Select Character" by Hugh Howey, copyright © 2015 by Hugh Howey. Used by permission of the author.

"Save Me Plz" by David Barr Kirtley, copyright © 2007 by David Barr Kirtley. Originally published in *Realms of Fantasy* (October 2007). Used by permission of the author.

"Please Continue" by Chris Kluwe, copyright © 2015 by Chris Kluwe. Used by permission of the author.

"Roguelike" by Marc Laidlaw, copyright © 2015 by Marc Laidlaw. Used by permission of the author.

"Gamer's End" by Yoon Ha Lee, copyright © 2015 by Yoon Ha Lee. Used by permission of the author.

"The Clockwork Soldier" by Ken Liu, copyright © 2014 by Ken Liu. Originally published in *Clarkesworld* (January 2014). Reprinted by permission of the author.

"*Desert Walk*" by S. R. Mastrantone, copyright © 2015 by S. R. Mastrantone. Used by permission of the author.

"Survival Horror" by Seanan McGuire, copyright © 2015 by Seanan McGuire. Used by permission of the author.

"*RECOIL!*" by Micky Neilson, copyright © 2015 by Micky Neilson. Used by permission of the author.

"Creation Screen" by Rhianna Pratchett, copyright © 2015 by Rhianna Pratchett. Used by permission of the author.

"Respawn" by Hiroshi Sakurazaka, translated by Nathan Allan Collins, copyright © 2015 by Hiroshi Sakurazaka. Used by permission of the author.

"*Killswitch*" by Catherynne M. Valente, copyright © 2007 by Catherynne M. Valente. Originally published on InvisibleGames.net (October 25, 2007). Reprinted by permission of the author.

"All of the People in Your Party Have Died" by Robin Wasserman, copyright © 2015 by Robin Wasserman. Used by permission of the author.

"Twarrior" by Andy Weir, copyright © 2015 by Andy Weir. Used by permission of the author.